MONICA LA PORTA

PAX IN THE
LAND OF WOMEN

BOOK TWO OF THE GINECEAN CHRONICLES

To my husband, Roberto. Always.

TABLE OF CONTENTS

CHAPTER 1

"I don't have all day to wait." Pax spoke with no superior tone while absentmindedly playing with the family ring on her finger, the double crown design appearing and disappearing as she rolled it. She didn't realize her words could be misinterpreted. In her mind, she was stating a fact. She just didn't have the whole day to wait for her luggage to arrive to Sundial.

"I'm truly sorry for the inconvenience, Mistress." The servant girl, a young maid wearing the customary dark dress that covered her from head to toes, was sweating profusely.

"I need a bath. Traveling by shared car is disgusting." Again, Pax was merely saying what she thought. Floria, the Layan's chauffer and bodyguard, had been unavailable to drive her around the country.

"I'm sure it is," the girl conceded.

"I'll call you if I need anything. Thanks, for now." Pax closed the door on the girl and threw an annoyed look at the bedroom. *Her* bedroom for the rest of the summer. She wanted to talk to her friend, Lexi, but her cell phone was traveling with her bags in the opposite direction of the farm. An honest mistake, the servant girl had told her. Pax hadn't cared to listen to the reason why the mistake was honest. Her only concern was about her cell phone and the fact she hadn't memorized Lexi's new number. Pax resigned herself to endure the whole day without talking to her twin, which is what they called each other when they weren't arguing about something, and tossed her clothes on the bed on her way to the bathroom. The shower didn't have the steamer function and the sauna looked old. The day hadn't started under the best of omens.

"Towel?" Pax asked from the shower booth, facing with irritated eyes a column without the air-dry command button. "Towel!" She repeated twice before remembering she had dismissed the servant

1

girl, whose name she hadn't thought to ask. "Great," she mumbled under her breath while reaching for her discarded clothes on the floor. The shirt clung to her wet skin, and the tight pants got stuck on her legs. The day wasn't improving. Several swearwords that would have made her two proper and famous mothers cringe flew out of her mouth, and she fastened the belt with a satisfied smile.

"Excuse me?" She peeked around the door. "Anyone here?" Pax was starting to reevaluate the nuisance of having a full staff of helpers 24/7 at her service back home. The lack of privacy she and Lexi had been complaining about nonstop now seemed the lesser evil. She ventured from one end to the other of the deserted hallway. She was on the second floor of the main building, wondering if she should have paid attention during the short walk from the entrance to the dormitories. Upon her arrival, the servant girl had informed her about the accident regarding her luggage, and that had been the cherry on top. Pax, who had been tired already from the long, sleepless night spent traveling in a filthy car, had seen red.

She idly looked outside one of the windows that faced lush gardens two floors down. She still didn't have a clue of where she could find the servant girl and the towels. Pax sighed when she had to decide to go left or right at the end of the hallway. *Right*, she thought. *Always turn right when you don't know the geography of a place. Easier to retrace your steps that way.* Lexi's words. They had been camping together every summer since first grade. Pax and Lexi had shared the most incredible adventures for the last twelve years and that advice had come in handy on many of their nighttime wanderings. But not this year. Pax was looking for reasons to be unhappy. The idea of spending the summer before going to college doing charity work wasn't hers. It was her mothers' plan.

"*It's going to be good for our image to show how we, as a family, support our electors,*" Maurice had proclaimed with her white smile, while Anna, her factotum, memorized notes.

"*And, it's going to be a formative summer for you.*" Claudine had expressed a whole concept in a few words.

"*The Priestess even said she'll drop by for a visit while you are there. She's taking an interest in your mother's career,*" Anna added to seal the deal.

Pax knew better. The whole purpose of sending her to Sundial for summer camp was that it was conveniently located in the middle of nothing and would separate her from Lexi. If the experience proved to be formative for her and good publicity for her mothers' career, even better. She had to repress a smile. If they only knew.

Pax kept wandering around aimlessly. She stuck to the always-turning-right philosophy and went up and down flights of stairs, barely noticing she was changing floors. Pax was engrossed in her plans about the hundreds of different ways she was going to make her dear mothers pay. A smile came across her face as she envisioned a breakfast ruined by pouring salt in her mother Claudine's favorite coffee. *Yes, I'll do that,* she thought. She was still unsure of what to reserve for her mother Maurice, but she had two full months to come up with something memorable. Pax didn't know how long she had been walking, but she started to realize she wasn't in the main wing of the building anymore. She couldn't remember when she had last peeked outside. The hallway ahead of her was dark, barely lit by few light sconces, and there wasn't a single opening to the outside world. When she walked too close to the brick wall and brushed it with her hand, she found it cold and wet. Faint noises were coming from around the corner at the end of the long hallway. She let out a sigh of relief.

"Anyone there?" Pax called. She advanced, hoping to find if not the servant girl—that would have been asking too much—at least someone who could help her. She didn't like the idea of walking back by herself. A scream stopped her in mid-step. She froze just before the corner. Several women were shouting at once, and the startling noise of clanking metal filled the air. Pax debated for the briefest moment if it was better to run away from there and try to find her way back to her room by herself.

"Keep him down!" a hoarse voice commanded and a cry echoed soon after a sharp thud.

Someone was in pain. Pax reacted without thinking and walked toward a scene she wasn't prepared to see. "What are you doing?" she screamed, horrified. Two women, farm guards from the uniforms they were wearing, stared back at her, frozen in the act of lowering their fists on a worker. The servant girl she had been looking for was holding a long chain that ended at the man's neck.

"Who are you?" one of the guards asked, still keeping the worker down in a pool of his own blood.

"Mistress! What are you doing here?" The servant girl turned around and stared at Pax in anguish. "This is not the place for someone of your status." The chain rattled on the floor when the servant girl moved.

Pax shivered at the sound.

"Mistress?"

The second guard looked up at Pax and after a few seconds, her eyes focused on her features. "Mistress Layan, I am Caren, the chief-in-command here, and my colleague is my second, Lauren. What an honor to have you staying at Sundial."

"Mistress, you shouldn't be here. This area is dangerous." Lauren had relaxed her hold on the bruised head. The worker wasn't putting up any resistance now.

"What are you doing to this man?" Pax asked, trying to hide the shock rocking her body. The violence they had used on the worker was unconceivable in her world.

"This *man* incited rebellion." Caren said the word 'man' with disgust and gave the unconscious body a shove.

Pax almost yelled. She bit her lip, hard. She knew better than to show her distress over the man's conditions. "Stop hurting him," she said, almost in a whisper.

"This is standard procedure. I assure you he'd have worse treatment in other places." Caren hadn't noticed the look in Pax's eyes.

"I told you to stop, now." She was angry and her voice was low and cold. Finally, the three women seemed to notice her.

The girl snapped at attention with worried eyes. "We are displeasing the mistress. Maybe you want to take the worker elsewhere?" she said with the most polite tone.

The two guards looked at each other with knowing eyes and started moving the body.

"I'm coming with you." Pax didn't let them say anything back. She followed the parade, closing the ranks, her chin up and a look of defiance on her face, daring them to try to command her back to her room. They were smarter than that.

"I'll have the tour of the facility now," she said in a tone that told them how inferior they were. Despite all the theatrics she was pulling, Pax was on the verge of throwing up. She put a hand on the wall to steady her trembling legs and waited a few seconds for the black dots to disappear from her sight. Once her vision was fully restored, she wished it hadn't. She couldn't remove her eyes from the body being held like a sack of garbage. She had never witnessed violence in any form, and the drops of blood trailing on the floor were making her lightheaded. She wanted to ask if the man was still alive, but she knew the question would have sounded improper.

"Do you have a good infirmary facility?" Pax asked instead.

"Oh, yes, on the second floor, at the end of the right wing." The servant girl pointed at the general direction and then added with a proud smile, "The one and only of the whole Desertica region."

Pax wondered what happened to anybody who needed help and wasn't lucky enough to live close by. It had taken the whole night to reach this place, lost in the middle of a desert that stretched for hundreds of miles.

"Sundial is the biggest farm around here, and we have the best specimens. This man, for example, is one strong worker. He's still alive only because of that," Lauren answered Pax and then added, "Although if he keeps asking for better treatment for the rest of the herd, he's not going to reach his thirties."

"You'll see how clean their cells are and how well they are fed," the girl said, tentatively smiling at Pax, who regarded her with nothing more than a glance.

She was intent in not showing her discomfort at the sight of the chambers aligned along the wall like dark gaps. At regular intervals, the moldy brick walls opened on bottomless pits void of any source of light. It looked almost as if they sucked the warmth from the surroundings, spitting out despair, the moans and the whispers coming from the cells giving body to the image. She brushed one of the metal bars and a pale finger touched her hand. She jumped back, but managed to silence her mouth before the guards could see her reaction. The servant girl, though, was staring at her with a strange expression on her face.

"Maybe the senator would like to take a tour herself?" Caren asked with a mellifluous tone.

Pax hated the way people used her to get to her mothers. "I'll ask her about it as soon as I call home." Years of practicing her public persona were paying off.

The two guards and the servant girl smiled back, visibly relaxing. They didn't know Pax yet.

"Let's drop this one in his cell and we'll walk you around," Caren said, while gesturing her second in command to lay the worker on the floor. She reached inside her shirt and showed Pax a bunch of keys dangling from a long, metallic chain.

"We're old-fashioned here. We took example from the Tarin accident. They're becoming smarter, these workers. We don't let them near any electronic devices. Nobody has escaped Sundial under my command. This farm is the safest place for a woman to work." Caren was positively beaming.

Lauren and the servant girl were smiling at Pax, waiting for her reaction.

"I'm glad to hear that." Although Pax had studied the Tarin accident at school, she didn't remember the details regarding the famous insurrection that had caused the death of several guards. Learning hadn't been high in her list of priorities. Nevertheless, she managed to sound as if she did remember. It was enough. The three women were already savoring the senator's visit as a done deal. Pax could only look at the two black eyes and the bloodied face.

Caren and Lauren pushed the worker inside his cell without noticing he had regained consciousness. They didn't beat him again, and that was fine with Pax.

"Follow us, Mistress Layan. I'm sure you'll have a lot to report to your mothers tonight." Caren used the same greasy tone she had used before.

"I'm sure I will." Pax's lips involuntarily turned up when she saw that the worker reached for the small bed and sat in the dark. The dark eyes never left the hold on hers.

"The gardens or the recreational facility?" Caren's voice snapped Pax out of the spell.

"The gardens," she answered, walking ahead of the guards. She couldn't help but notice that another two eyes were focused on her. The servant girl's. "What's your name again?" Pax asked her. She didn't mean to sound rude, but the girl's attitude was unnerving her.

"Celeste."

"And how old are you, Celeste?" Pax was openly assessing the servant girl.

"Almost eighteen."

"You look younger." Pax felt something stirring inside at the thought of commanding a girl one year younger than she was. The mixed emotion aggravated her mood. "I need towels in my bathroom." She didn't know why she was getting angry with the servant girl and felt ashamed of the way she was acting. Her mothers had raised her to be a good person. Instead, she was acting like a spoiled child. Lexi would have given her a severe scolding if she were there.

"I apologize, Mistress. I was going to the laundry room when I was called to help... with the *situation*." Celeste lowered her eyes and turned around.

Pax didn't have time to thank the girl before the two guards whisked her away. She made an effort to memorize the route they were taking. The two guards talked incessantly while they went up two floors and ended on a large landing.

"This way to the grounds is faster. From this side of the building, we don't have to descend another story of stairs. When Sundial was built, it was decided it should follow the natural slope of the terrain." Caren walked so fast that Pax almost couldn't keep up with her. They wanted to be sure to pack as much as they could in their tour before she reported back home.

"I bet that not even in Ginecea you'll find a better kept botanical garden." Lauren offered some food for thought. "We have the largest number of hybrid orchids in the whole state. Our botanist created a new variety last year and we're waiting for the official recognition." She opened a door that led to a brighter hallway.

"It should happen any day now. Maybe you'll be here for the celebration." Caren slowed down before a series of windows and indicated an elegant structure made of opaque glass. "That way is the nursery. We can't go inside now, but if you are interested, we could obtain a special permission for you."

"It won't be necessary. I don't have a green thumb and I wouldn't know the difference between a sprout and a blossom, anyway," Pax answered calmly, but realized the guards weren't pleased with her reaction. "I can be more useful helping somewhere else; I'm good at keeping things organized," she said, as if that would explain her lack of interest in the baby orchids sleeping in the dark, hot greenery.

"Of course." Caren seemed to read Pax's words for what they were, an excuse, but moved along. "This way to the main garden and the butterfly pavilion; the lavender plants are in full bloom." She raised one eyebrow in a silent question.

"Maybe tomorrow," Pax answered and then didn't say anything else for several steps, glad the two women didn't find the need to fill the silence. She was going to have a long conversation with her mothers about what she thought of being forced into petty politics. So deep in pitying herself, she didn't notice they were already outside, strolling along a shallow creek. A few elderly workers were tending the lawn, and one of them raised his tired head to look at her. Pax felt uncomfortable and broke eye contact right away.

"*If you look right when you should look left, problems don't disappear. They are just out of sight.*" Lexi's words echoed in her mind. Once more, Pax cursed the unknown person who had sent her luggage somewhere else.

"They are still useful to tend the lawn." Lauren misunderstood Pax's reaction.

"We don't let them go to waste in some retirement facility, if we can help it," Caren explained with the same pride she showed every time she talked of her management.

Pax tried to hide the shiver at hearing the word *retirement*. It was the way of the new government to utilize old, unsavory names and put a sweeter coat on them, or change them altogether. Lexi once had gone for hours in a tirade against the use of retirement centers and how older workers were left there to die of negligence and, as she heard somewhere, starvation—although she had whispered the last statement. It wasn't a coincidence that soon after Pax had confronted her mothers with a long list of questions regarding the morality of their actions, they had started looking at Lexi with different eyes.

"Good of you," Pax commented with a practiced smile. Now, Lexi's words made perfect sense. *Why get rid of a worker when he could be used until his very last breath?* It was indeed a waste, as Caren had just said. She soon lost all interest in the tour, while Caren and Lauren explained in detail every single flower the botanical garden produced and even what it didn't and why.

"And we are now at the center of the recreational facility." Lauren smiled at Pax, who hadn't noticed that they had already left the outdoors.

They were now inside a cavernous space. A big pool sat in the middle of the room, casting a peaceful shade of light blue on the ceiling. Pax experienced some peace for the first time since she had left home. She loved swimming. Aside from talking with Lexi, it was the activity she liked the most.

"You can use the facility any time you want. We've lifted the time restrictions for you," Caren said, expecting Pax to be pleased.

"Thank you." She was indeed pleased. Sometimes being a famous daughter paid off. She was truly grateful for this gift. Water was expensive so far out in the desert, and the costs of maintaining such an oasis must have been exorbitant. No wonder they preferred to keep the slaves working as long as they could.

Later in the afternoon, when she was back in her room, Pax thought of what she was really going to say to her mothers. She was still angry at them, and her luggage was only halfway to its destination. A long swim alone in the placid waters of the pool had partially improved her mood, but she was still unsettled by what she had seen. Two black eyes were burning holes in the back of her mind, and she couldn't drive off the memory of the body being dragged around. *They were men,* Maurice would have said with delicate shrug. Still, the last thing she saw before drifting to sleep was the image of one of those men. And those eyes.

CHAPTER 2

"Mistress, dinner is ready. If you would do us the honor of accompanying us," Celeste's voice came muffled through the wall. Pax swung open the door, facing a startled servant girl.

Somehow, the deference the young girl showed put Pax in the wrong state of mind again. "Of course," she said, trying to check her temper. It wasn't that Pax wasn't used to being treated differently from the other girls she knew; she was plenty used to that. Pax had come to terms with the fact that being the daughter of two powerful women meant not having a private life a long time ago. It was something else.

"I hope you like our fare. I'm sure you are used to—" Celeste started, but Pax stopped her right away.

"I'm sure your food is excellent." Pax wanted to scream at the servant girl that she couldn't possibly know anything about her, let alone the quality of the food she ingested every day. Years of studying etiquette prevailed, and she plastered another fake smile on her face.

"The cook will be overly pleased by your presence." Celeste relaxed her shoulders and led her down another hallway.

This one was dark, but not oppressing. Pax thought idly that the farm was infested with hallways and that orienting oneself through them was a nightmare. By a strange association of ideas, the sudden desire of asking about the prisoner came to her mind, but she closed her mouth before she could utter the words. He was only a man, after all.

"The place of honor has been reserved for you, obviously." Celeste opened a heavy door and festive light spilled into the hallway.

"*Obviously,*" Pax repeated under her breath. She was going to cover her gaffe when she saw the dining room. The expression in her staring eyes gave away her surprise.

"I apologize; we don't have enough personnel to use maids to serve in the dining hall as well." Caren greeted her inside and showed her the seat at the head of the big table.

"I—" Pax didn't know what to say in response. A man wearing black gloves poured some water for her, and she backed against the solid wood of the chair.

"Don't worry. They are instructed to avoid any physical contact." Caren put a sympathetic hand on Pax's arm.

She shivered. "It's not that." Pax was going to say she had never been served by a man, not once in her life. But she realized her words were going to be misunderstood again. For some reason, she didn't want that. But she also couldn't say that she didn't like the sight of the shackles circling the thin arms under the gloves.

"We've taught our workers how to be discreet," Lauren added, sitting on the chair next to Caren's. Both laughed, followed by the other women already at the table.

Pax didn't. She could read through the lines. She had never thought, until now, how the word *worker* was another euphemism recently come into vogue. Pure breeds didn't like to sully their mouths with the word *slave*.

A few minutes of tedious presentations and greetings kept Pax from lashing out inappropriately. She forgot the names the same moment they were graciously presented, but smiled throughout the process. The act was becoming increasingly difficult to maintain. She hoped Caren was going to tell her exactly how she was going to volunteer at the farm. The sooner she started, the sooner she was back with Lexi.

"No, I haven't had time to call my moms, yet," she responded to someone's inquiry. She noticed the slight disappointment in the blond woman's face. Pax complimented the flavor of the stew she hadn't touched, not even with the fork dangling from her hand. The woman smiled a perplexed smile and left her alone.

"A special treat for our guest." Caren snapped her fingers rather loudly and two men opened the French door at the other side of the room. Three men dressed in black were waiting outside.

The fork Pax was playing with landed on the ceramic plate, spilling meat juices on the immaculate tablecloth. The blond woman patted her arm to reassure her that there was no problem at all. Pax looked at her and then realized she had said she was sorry out loud.

One of the men came to her side to offer her first choice of the petite pastries he was balancing carefully on a tray. Pax didn't want to raise her eyes to his face, but the hand holding the tray was shaking, and bruises hideously stained the olive skin. Pax followed the cruel pattern of blues and purples until they disappeared under the sleeve only to reappear at the neck. Suddenly, she was staring at two black eyes—the same two black eyes she couldn't seem to be able to forget—and she felt like she was freefalling. Someone tugged her elbow and broke the spell. Pax looked away, but for the briefest moment, her eyes lingered again on the bruised face and couldn't help to whisper a second time, "I'm sorry."

"Did the slave do something improper, mistress?" Lauren was looking at her from across the table.

Pax couldn't help but think the word 'slave' was indeed crass and that she didn't like Lauren one bit.

Caren immediately yanked the chain around the man's neck.

"No, no!" Pax heard her voice coming out of her mouth before she could control its tone. *It was only a man.* A few seconds of awkward silence filled the room. Pax was aware of all the faces staring at her, but only one made her feel uncomfortable. His.

Sleeping that night proved impossible. Pax tossed and turned for hours. The mattress was the exact combination of firm and soft. The sheets were smooth as silk on her skin. The pillows were scented with lavender. Furthermore, temperatures in the Desertica region tended to vary greatly between day and night, and with the window left open, the room was refreshingly cool. The silence was pleasantly interrupted by distant noises coming from the fields surrounding Sundial. Still, her eyes refused to close because every time she tried, two dark eyes invaded her vision. Then the memory of the bruised skin and the trembling hand would come to haunt her.

Next, the features of a face so swollen she couldn't even imagine how it normally looked would make her stomach squeeze.

A gentle knock on the door found her wide-awake and on the verge of fainting.

"Mistress? Your baggage is here. I thought you would want to know—" Celeste was already inside.

Pax made a mental note to remember to lock the door. "What time is it, Celeste?" She didn't bother to sound pleasant.

"I can come back later," the girl said while retrieving her steps.

"Nonsense. You're already here." Pax stood up with a yawn and went to sit by the desk. "You think it's too early to have some breakfast?"

"It's actually too late, but *you* can eat whenever you want. I'll ask the cook to prepare something right away." Celeste was out before Pax could tell her what she usually ate for breakfast.

"I still don't know what time it is," Pax yelled to the hallway. She looked around, wondering if maybe the best course of action would be to sleep the day away. She could hear her mothers' voices scolding her already. Finally, her eyes focused on the only thing that was going to make her bear her summer sentence. The sight of her sports bag by her bed made her smile immediately. She spilled the contents of the bag on the bed and regarded her cell phone as a long-lost friend. "Of course," she said to the display that showed all the missed calls. Lexi had called thirteen times. Bless her heart.

"How dare you give me the silent treatment? It's you who left me here." Lexi's voice resonated in Pax's room as loud and irritated as if she was there.

"Good to hear you too, Lexi." Pax couldn't help but laugh.

"You couldn't call me earlier?" Lexi was probably facing her vanity mirror preparing for some event her mothers had planned for her.

Pax thought for a second that, for once, she wouldn't have minded participating in some boring parade. It was a horrific realization. "As a matter of fact, I couldn't. My luggage took a detour. And, just for the record, I didn't leave anybody. I was forced out here."

"I don't know if I want to believe you. Anyway, I miss you too much." Lexi's anger never lasted long. She was another public child and used to keeping her personal outbursts in check. Her mothers, Mia and Paola Corellis, were respectively the Ginecean Prime Minister and a highly influential lawyer. Lexi and Pax were constantly under the scrutiny of the tabloids.

"Same here." Pax loudly yawned again.

"Worked too much yesterday?" Lexi was teasing her.

"Like a slave." She automatically repeated a joke she had heard all her life, and as soon as she said it, she remembered what she had thought about Lauren the night before. While Lexi laughed at it, she felt dirty by having said it and changed subject. "So, news?" she asked, while pawing through the contents of the sports bag scattered on the bed.

"Same old, same old." Lexi's voice held a hint of sadness that, lately, was becoming part of her.

"Did your mothers find out?" Pax knew she had to ask, but really didn't want to.

"No! Heavens forbid. I wouldn't be talking to you now, if they did." Lexi managed a half-hearted chuckle.

"How is she?" Pax and Lexi rarely mentioned Aria's name, the fathered girl who worked for the Corellis. They were worried, and for good reason, that their conversations weren't always private.

"Fine, she's fine. Stronger than me, as usual." Lexi sighed.

"She's used to that. She knows the social rules and her place in this world." Pax felt her stomach squeeze again.

"I hate it. I hate all of it. Who decides the rules?" Lexi vented out with the usual tirade.

Pax couldn't find anything else to add to that. Her stomach had reached the size of a walnut and was still shrinking. She made the mistake to close her eyes for a moment.

"What happened?"

"Nothing."

"You gasped." Lexi knew Pax too well to let it slip by.

"It's nothing, really." But the black eyes were still haunting the room.

"Mistress? Your breakfast is ready." Celeste ended Pax's conversation with Lexi at just the right moment.

"Thanks, Celeste," Pax said, meaning it this time. She gladly saluted a reluctant Lexi and followed her maid outside the room. She clutched her cell phone tight, though.

"Your schedule is also ready. Caren hopes that you'll like it. Otherwise, she'll change it."

"No changes for me." Pax needed to let them know that she didn't like the special treatment. Mostly because they had to understand it wasn't in her power to influence her mothers' political decisions. Sometimes people tended to forget she could barely vote. And they also didn't know she wasn't going to follow her mother's career. If she could help it.

It turned out she had slept through the best part of her first morning of volunteering at the farm. Her breakfast, according to the time of the day, ended up being an early lunch. Pax had dreaded entering in the dining room, but her meal was already on the table and she was left alone to consume it. She was glad for the lack of human company, of any gender.

"Since you showed an interest in the recreational facility yesterday, you will start there." Lauren greeted her with a pat on her shoulders, interrupting her inner peace.

Pax hadn't heard her come in, and she didn't like to be surprised, but smiled, nonetheless. "Perfect. I'm ready." She wasn't hungry anymore, and she didn't want to linger. She intensely disliked any form of chitchat with anyone who wasn't Lexi. Once inside the cavernous room, the blue waters of the pool had the desired effect of calming her. She thought that the strange pressure on her chest was becoming a constant side effect of this summer camp.

"You'll check the conditions of the facility and note on this log if anything needs to be done. This is the direct line with the maintenance crew." Lauren, who had insisted on accompanying her to the recreational facility to explain her job, showed her a telephone hanging from the wall. A ledge, or a shelf, was clearly missing.

"Are there any men working here?" Pax asked and tried to keep her voice neutral.

"Not during your schedule. We saw your distress in their presence and decided to assign you a rotation that would help in that sense," Lauren said in a tone that Pax was sure was meant to be gentle.

She experienced a strange juxtaposition of feelings. Relief, but also something else. Disappointment.

"Every two or three hours you can take a break. Lunch is—" Lauren checked on her watch. "—actually in half an hour."

"Thanks, I think I'll skip lunch."

"Dinner is at eight o'clock every night."

"Eight? Isn't that late?"

"Desertica region schedule. You might've noticed that it's too hot during the summer to eat any earlier. You'll get used to it. Or, you can always ring for snacks to be delivered here."

"I'll be fine."

"Do you have any other questions?"

"None I can think of."

"That's all, then. If you don't mind, I've something else to attend to," Lauren finished, saluted, and stormed off.

Pax didn't mind at all. She had been parked there, in that huge room, where she could do almost no damage, she was sure. But she couldn't do any good, either. She should have felt angry, or at least annoyed, by the lack of trust showed. In reality, she knew all too well they were bearing her presence only to please her mothers. She was utterly useless.

"Lexi?" She reached for the phone as soon as Lauren disappeared behind the door.

"You think I've nothing else to do than wait anxiously to hear from you?" Lexi's welcome back. Always a rare treat. Her rude outbursts were the reason why they had become friends in the first place.

"*I* have nothing else to do," Pax admitted.

"Interesting job, I assume." Sarcasm really became Lexi, when she was at her best.

"They think I might be able to manage to stay in one place without disrupting anything."

"Well, can you?"

"Maybe. I'm not sure. Today at least." Pax was all for being honest lately.

"I touched her hand…" Lexi's abrupt change of topic made Pax jump in her seat.

"Lexi! Someone could have seen you and reported to your mothers. If they know—" Pax regretted immediately her words.

"Don't worry. I'm not stupid. I wouldn't put her in danger. I—" Lexi's voice softened. "—couldn't live if they sent her away from me."

"Oh, Lexi." Pax's voice softened, too.

"I know. So many girls out there, and I had to fall in love with the only one I can't have."

"How did it feel?" Pax felt a strange tingle at posing the question.

"My heart exploded. My lungs stopped pumping air. She looked at me and I wanted to hug her forever." Lexi still sounded breathless.

"But you didn't, right?" Pax looked anxiously left and right as if someone could intercept their conversation.

"I didn't."

"Be careful, please. If not for you, do it for her."

"You don't have to remind me of that."

"Sorry, I didn't mean it that way." Pax didn't know what else to say. Thankfully, Lexi helped her by changing topic. After few minutes of idle chat, they hung up. Pax hadn't noticed that during her phone call a crew of men had entered the room, accompanied by a guard.

"I apologize. We were told we could use this time." The guard shot her a nervous glance.

Pax looked at her and then at the clock on the wall. Finally, she realized what the woman was trying to say without being rude. She wasn't supposed to be there during lunchtime. Lauren had explained how they had designed her schedule to minimize any contact with the men. A plan that could only work if she followed the schedule. Then again, both Caren and Lauren had completely misunderstood her *discomfort*.

"I'm finishing my log. If you don't mind my presence, I'll stay." Pax phrased her intentions in a way that the guard could feel at ease.

"Of course." The guard led the men to a corner to work on a wall.

Pax hadn't noticed before, but the facility was being remodeled and they were building what looked like a new room. Not that Pax understood anything about interior design, but the building seemed fine the way it was. She attempted to busy herself with filling the log, a task that was far from being finished.

Her eyes kept traveling from the blank form sitting on her knees to the dark corner where the men were hauling bricks. Once or twice, the guard caught her looking, and Pax immediately returned to the log. Two hours later, the wall had reached a noticeable height, but the pen dangling from her fingers hadn't produced a single intelligible note. On the other hand, lots of circles embellished the page that wasn't blank anymore. Pax's disappointment was finally tangible when she realized that no set of black eyes was going to stare back at her from the corner. The shift ended and the guard left with a nod of the head. Pax responded in kind. She decided it was time to take her break. Not that she had done anything to deserve it, but she was sure nobody was going to complain even if she took the whole summer as a break.

She stripped to her underwear and dove into the blue water without a single splash. On the bottom of the pool, everything was silent. Pax sat on the tiled floor, moving her hands slowly. She stayed there until her lungs could take it no more. Her eyes broke the surface and she knew it right away. He was there, watching her. She spun around in a vortex of water until she found him standing by the door. He was alone. No guards restraining him.

"Thank you." He brought his right hand to his heart, bowed his head, and left.

Pax was simply too overwhelmed to even think to have a reaction. Any reaction. And then was glad for it. She would have done something that would have attracted unwanted attention. Pax realized she was instinctively trying to protect him. Maybe she should have been shocked. But then again, feelings weren't available at the moment. He had thanked her. For what? He had come to talk to her. He had risked another beating to thank her. It didn't make any sense.

Pax's first reaction, when she finally had one, was to flip open her cell phone to call Lexi. At the first ring, she thought better of it.

But Lexi called her back right away. "In the mood for prank calls now?"

"I punched your code number by mistake." Pax couldn't remember the last time she had lied to Lexi. Had she ever lied to Lexi? Maybe not.

"Something happened." Lexi knew every nuance of Pax's voice.

"You sound like Claudine." *It's hot in here.*

"No, you're upset."

"And *you* are worse than Claudine." Pax knew she was treading dangerous waters with Lexi.

"What is it?"

"I just saw someone." Pax had to give her something.

"Is this another guest at Sundial?" Lexi was relaxing.

Good, Pax thought. "*Guest* is not the right word," she admitted between her teeth. It felt wrong. *She felt wrong.*

"So, this someone works or lives there at the farm." Lexi was satisfied by the angle the conversation was taking.

"Definitely. I must go now. I've got to demonstrate I'm not here just to waste our supporters' money." Pax imitated Maurice's voice.

"*You* really sound like her." Lexi laughed.

"Thankfully, it was Claudine who gave me the DNA," Pax repeated what she said anytime someone claimed that she had her mother Maurice's character. "Although, I love them both very much."

"Amen," Lexi finished. "Mother's secretary is having a conniption. I have to go to wear that darn dress. The Summer Ball can't go on without me, it seems. But, we'll talk later," she added with a menacing tone.

CHAPTER 3

Pax was surprised she had forgotten about the Summer Ball. To think that a chance to miss it had been the only redeeming quality of spending the whole summer at the farm. Pax hated the parade of hypocrites and self-righteous plaguing the annual charity ball that was hosted by the president at her residence in Ginecea City. Her mothers knew it and every year had dreaded her reaction, until they had decided to send her far away from Lexi for two long months. It wasn't a coincidence Pax had arrived at Sundial two days before the ball. Maurice knew how to take advantage of every little opportunity. Both Maurice and Claudine were worried that Lexi and Pax would start something serious now that they were going to college together. And they didn't like Lexi's revolutionary ideas. With Maurice running the campaign for president, they couldn't afford loose cannons in their midst, especially around their perfect, beautiful, smart daughter, so well loved by the public.

Little did they know that Pax and Lexi were just friends. Very good friends. They used to joke that they were twins, mythological figures in a society where mothers needed a special license from the Priestess to conceive a second daughter. They often finished each other's sentences. But they had never been physically attracted to one another. It was true, though, that they couldn't go one day without talking. Pax was confident their friendship was going to survive their long summer of separation, unless Lexi did something stupid and dangerous. Pax couldn't understand what was happening to her friend, but she respected her feelings. It would have been much easier if Lexi had fallen in love with a nice, suitable girl. But things normally didn't go as planned. Or at least that was what Lexi used to say.

Dinner arrived and found Pax still trying, not so hard, to write something on the log. At five past eight, she decided that everything was in perfect order and that she couldn't delay eating. She waited another five minutes without knowing exactly why, and then she finally ambled toward the dining hall. The room was already full of tired women and several men serving them. Pax shivered slightly at the sight, but took her seat without arousing attention by her reaction. Obviously, everybody noticed her arrival. She suffered graciously, or so she hoped, the onslaught of greetings and questions about her first day of working at the farm. *Working.* She wanted to laugh.

"No, I haven't called my mothers, yet." Both the question and the answer sounded like déjà-vu. She hadn't thought, not even once, to call home. On the other hand, her mothers hadn't tried to reach her. There were no missed calls from the house number. She wondered why. Maybe something had happened. No, she would have been notified immediately. Then why hadn't Maurice and Claudine called her? Pax felt hurt. Not even two days out of their sight and they had already forgotten their precious daughter. Pax knew she was being childish, but couldn't help it. And at eight o'clock at night, it was still hot and her clothes—which had dried on her skin after the swim—were now soaking wet again. *Why is the air-conditioning not working?*

"Your mother's secretary left a message for you. She said to call her back as soon as you could," Caren announced, interrupting Pax's train of thought.

"Pax, please unlock the receiving calls. I've been trying to reach you for the last forty-eight hours." Anna was tired, but her voice was contained as usual.

Pax had called back right away, leaving her meal untouched on the plate. "Sorry—" She was feeling a little bit guilty. She had disabled all the incoming calls with the only exception of Lexi's as soon as she had gotten the cell phone back. She had done it out of habit. Her cell phone was a glorified walkie-talkie she used to communicate with her friend. Pretty much an expensive private line. She had also removed the clock, since she didn't like to acknowledge the passing of time.

"I wanted to let you know that your mothers had to fly overnight to Samara. I didn't want you to be worried."

Pax couldn't help but notice the way Anna said the last sentence. She felt suddenly guiltier. "Samara?"

"They went to show support to the population. They were able to raise money for the earthquake relief fund and it was the right thing to go there," Anna explained.

Samara was a heavily populated city in the Mountainous region that had been struck by a disastrous earthquake just two days before Pax had left for the summer camp.

"Of course," she muttered. Her mothers were genuinely driven to help any cause if it was in their power to do so. She loved that in them. They didn't do it for the show. Although it had helped their careers a great deal.

"They're fine. Don't worry. I'm flying there to take care of them as soon as I'm done with the press release," Anna continued with a different tone. A hint of happiness and satisfaction emerged from her voice. Barely there, but present enough to be detected.

"A press release?" Pax asked because she knew Anna wanted her to ask it.

"Maurice got the final endorsement!" Anna couldn't contain her joy.

"This is great! More than great! Excellent!" Pax was jumping up and down. It was momentous. She thanked Anna for being so considerate and reaching her before she would hear the news from the media. It had been extremely nice of her, considering how much work she had and the load that was going to burden her from now on.

"Lexi! I have to tell you something! Where are you?" Pax had done the first thing that had come to her mind: call Lexi to tell her that her mom was officially running for president. In the excitement, she had forgotten her friend was probably busy dancing around at the ball. Her stomach grumbled noisily and she remembered her dinner was waiting for her, now cold and probably tasteless.

"Everybody is in the video room. I can stay with you, if you'd like some company." A woman, one of Caren's crew, was finishing her meal when she had come back to the dining room.

What's your name? Mary. No, Marta. Marion? "Oh no, don't worry. It's nice of you… but you don't have to stay for me. I'm tired and I'll go to bed right away. Thanks a lot, though." Pax really wanted to be alone.

The woman—she had a Marion's face, Pax had finally decided— finished her meal clearly relieved of not having to keep her company, and then, after a few nice words, was out of the room.

"Thank Heavens," Pax murmured, happy to have the place all to herself.

"I don't like their company, either." His voice resonated from outside the door that led to the service room.

Pax stared at the dark shadow while the cold piece of vegetable she was eating got stuck somewhere in her throat.

"But they're mean to me. What's your reason?" he asked, emerging slowly into the light. His face, if possible, was even more swollen than before, sporting new hematomas and split lips.

Pax thought, while choking, that even the act of talking had to be unbearable. She saw how the skin stretched on the yellow-purple-black spots on his face and she felt pain herself.

"I see. You aren't going to talk to me." His voice had a bitter tone and Pax felt it as a stinging slap. He stepped back, turning his body away from her.

"Wait!" Pax raised her voice.

He stopped and spun around.

"Wait," she whispered, looking for something else to say.

"I'm waiting. Care to add something else to the command?" He shot her a glance. Was he smiling? Although his facial features were hidden by the bruises, his eyes gleamed with amusement.

"I'm not commanding you to do anything," she felt compelled to explain.

"I'm pleased to hear that, since I have no intention of following your orders," he said.

"But—" *You have to!*

"It's not in my nature." He dismissed her unspoken words with a shrug. "Do you like your dinner?" he asked, as if they were exchanging pleasantries.

Pax felt she was either dreaming or hallucinating.

"Do you?" he repeated his question as if he really wanted to hear her answer.

"It's cold." Pax couldn't believe it was really happening. "I've never talked to a man before," she blurted out. And then she blushed and didn't even know why.

"I thought so," he said. "Are you worried they can see you talking to me?" He didn't add, *without ordering me around.*

"Yes." Pax felt bad at admitting it.

"Don't worry, your reputation is safe. I have friends looking out for me. They're going to warn me in time if the women are coming," he said when he saw her puzzled expression. "Do you like it here, Pax?"

"No." She couldn't muster more than one-word sentences. And how did he know her name? There was also the way it had sounded on his mouth. *Pax. What an unusual name*, everybody always said when they first heard it. She had never known what to think about it, other than the fact that it had been her Grandmother Rosie's whim. But now, for a brief moment, it had sounded… right.

"Did your mothers give you permission to talk?" Again that tone. He was making fun of her.

"And your name is?" she asked, piqued by his remark. She realized as soon as she asked it that a more appropriate question would have been how he knew her name.

He didn't let her talk. "And there I thought you were never going to ask," he said, but despite his tone, he looked surprised. Then he shrugged his shoulders and scoffed at her, "Or maybe you got confused. My number's too long to remember anyway. I can show it to you, if you want." He went to uncover his left arm.

Pax raised one hand and stopped him. "I asked your name, not your number." She was hurt by his words. The situation was potentially very dangerous for her. If anybody strolled by and took in the whole scene, a scandal was the least of her problems. Then she realized for him it was even worse. Her stomach left its place to relocate near her throat.

"You're a little scary thing. I am sure your nails can cut glass." Now he was definitely laughing.

Pax was completely disoriented by the absurdity of what was happening. "Do you have a name?" she insisted, incensed by his words.

"My friends call me Prince," he said, and this time his voice was humble.

Pax was taken aback by this. "Prince?" she had to repeat it out loud. It was such a nice joke. Memories of bedtime stories about valiant princesses fighting villains came to her mind. She had never heard of a prince; she didn't even know that word existed.

"I was told I have blue blood in my veins." He sounded defensive.

"Prince."

"Okay, stop repeating my name. If you can't show some respect for my blood line, don't say anything." Despite his words, Prince looked on the verge of laughing.

Pax idly thought for a second of how easy it was to decipher his mood by the look in his eyes. *Imagine when his face heals and I can see his features when he talks. What in Heavens am I thinking?*

"Bye, now," he said and left her with her cold dinner.

A few seconds later, two women came to join her for some dessert. Pax gulped down whatever was on her plate and stormed out of the room with the excuse of a terrible headache. She went to sleep with several unasked questions.

The new day started with the realization she had to find a way to sleep well at night or she wasn't going to survive the summer. That was exactly what Pax thought between one weird dream and the next: death by sleep deprivation. She had set the alarm clock on her cell phone, enabled incoming calls from Anna and her mothers, and tried to reach them several times. She felt strange and uneasy and wanted to be hugged, although she knew she was too old for that. She wanted to talk to someone, but she wasn't sure that even Lexi could understand what was happening to her.

She had engaged in a conversation with a slave. *A man.* They were mean creatures. Brutal beings. Evil, some said. Women couldn't trust them. But he hadn't looked mean or evil. He had only looked badly beaten.

Prince.

She knew his name. How unreal was that? And the name was Prince. She had to talk to Lexi. But what was she going to say? *I enjoyed very much exchanging pleasantries with a man, a man, working here at the farm? And, by the way, his name is Prince?* If earlier she had wondered about it, now, after further examination, Pax had no doubt whatsoever it was too much even for Lexi. Oh, and if only her mothers came to know about her forbidden moment of madness… Maybe they were going to lock her up somewhere. Anna would see personally to that. Discreetly, without fanfare, a simple press release would explain how heartbroken Maurice was that her only daughter suffered from an incurable disease. That could clean her path toward the presidency, Pax thought darkly. She was being unfair. Anna was a good person. And her mothers loved her. They would probably ship her to Grandma Rosie, Maurice's mother, her only living grandmother, who lived at the end of civilization anyway and didn't like company. Yes, that was definitely more likely.

She went through breakfast as if she weren't there and continued the day in the same fashion. Celeste avoided her, and the other women probably thought she believed herself to be too good to acknowledge their company. Any other time, Pax would have made amends, but this time, she barely understood she was being churlish. Her mind was wired on looking for him. Prince. She feared and hoped to see him appearing from behind a corner in the dining room or strolling toward her in the recreational facility. He didn't. Still, she waited. And waited. Until it was night again and her log was as empty as it had been the day before.

The day after, Pax was late on purpose for breakfast, lunch, and dinner. She didn't dare to admit it, but she wanted to see if changing her schedule could help her see him again. She figured he was relatively free to move about only when the surveillance was at a minimum. And the surveillance was at the minimum only when the women's presence was scarce. It didn't work. Pax entertained herself with several questions regarding how he could move freely at all, when he spent most of his time chained up somewhere. Or how he knew her name. And why she wanted to see his face again.

She spent another tedious day of volunteering in the cavernous room in such fashion and realized she had to do something. Anything to change this situation that was driving her crazy. The log hadn't received any special attention, but every corner of the recreational facility was examined by a very scrupulous Pax. She took a good look at the room that was being built and tried to imagine what it was for with its white tiles, shower stalls, a built-in table, and a small rectangular window that didn't open to the outside. The most peculiar detail about the place was the two rows of refrigerators lying against one of the walls; there were at least eight of them, still wrapped in plastic. She finally decided to write a note stating she wasn't being helpful there since the facility was in excellent condition. Maybe she could have lent a hand where the workers were, to facilitate the guards' jobs. Yes, that was a better use of her time and resources.

"I'm not sure that we can find something really suitable for you there. Not among the workers. Definitely not." Caren's answer was immediate.

Pax had knocked on the chief-in-command's door as soon as she had finished her solitary dinner. If Caren had been surprised to see her, she didn't show it. Lauren and another three women were there, sitting at a round table. One of them she recognized. It was the polite Marion from a few nights earlier. Pax had interrupted a game of cards. She was about to apologize when Marion put her cards down with an interested look on her face and spoke. "I need help in the nursery, since the official acknowledgment finally came through. I'm sure that our honored guest would appreciate it if we celebrate the new hybrid orchid while she's working here at the farm."

Pax could recognize a politician when she saw one, and Marion was brilliant. It suited Pax's plans well, though, and she smiled back. "I'll tell my mothers right away. Claudine loves orchids." She complimented herself on her cleverness. She had hinted that her mothers could be interested in participating in the celebration, without committing them to anything.

"I thought you weren't interested in the nursery," Lauren said while Marion shot her a menacing glance.

Caren coughed something down her throat.

"You'll love it. And we can probably dispense with the usual analysis. Don't you think, Caren?" Marion intervened before Lauren could say anything else.

"I'm sure Mistress Layan has never been in contact with any of the species normally carrying parasites that attack the orchids," Caren said, looking directly at Lauren. The second in command lowered her eyes on the table.

Pax shifted her eyes from one woman to the other trying to capture a glimpse of the silent conversation that was clearly taking place. "I haven't traveled recently," she said, hoping it was what she was expected to say.

"Just perfect," Marion beamed.

"It's settled then. If you want, you can start tomorrow morning." Caren seemed glad to have pleased the honorable guest and impatient to start the game again.

"Nine o'clock. Please, be punctual," Marion added softly while picking up her cards. The botanist and the chief-in-command exchanged one brief look. The women were already dealing a new hand.

"Absolutely. See you tomorrow." Pax understood she wasn't wanted anymore and left with a lingering feeling she had just done them a huge favor and not the other way around. She smiled nonetheless. She was now out of the recreational center and closer to the fields where the workers were.

CHAPTER 4

The smile didn't last long. Pax was closer to the fields, but only geographically. In any other sense, she was as far away as possible from the workers. The hybrids were so fragile and precious that Marion allowed very few of the other women inside, and only after scrupulous scrutiny. No man could enter the sacred place under any circumstance.

"Who knows what they carry," the botanist said with a grimace, almost whispering the word "they." As if merely saying the pronoun out loud was going to contaminate and wither her babies.

Pax realized then she had been granted a special permission. She should have been thankful and even flattered by it, but the comprehension that she was now where they had wanted her in the first place kept nagging at the back of her mind. She was once again a pawn in a game she didn't have any interest in playing.

It had taken just a few minutes to assess the hole she had dug for herself. The place was hot, humid, and slightly claustrophobic, even for its considerable size. After only a few hours of volunteering, she started to wonder how she could get out of it.

"Pax, could you move that vase so the orchid is not under the direct light?"

Marion was a nice and maternal woman, and Pax greatly appreciated those traits combined with her being such a good diplomat, but still couldn't achieve the impossible.

She really didn't care about planting, plowing, weeding, seeding, or whatever one was supposed to do in the near proximity of greenery of any sort, kind, or shape.

"Don't you think that this orchid is a lovely shade of purple?" Marion had gone on and on about the intricacies of leaves and petals.

Pax soon developed a strategy to deal, in a polite way, with the stream of constant blabbering about the beauty of the botanical world. She nodded the first time and alternated nods and bland, positive comments from then on.

"Hmm," Pax added a non-committal sound to the nodding to create variety.

"Do you want to send a picture to your mother Claudine to show her the hybrid?" Marion had changed strategy as well. She had already asked if she had heard from her mothers.

Marion was really good. Pax almost smiled.

"Which one do you think is best?" Pax was not to be outdone.

"I'd say the pale pink one against a dark drop." Marion had given serious thought to the idea. "I think I have a black cloth we can use, somewhere." She went to a chest hidden under one of the tables laden with pots and vases. "I thought I saw it here—" She moved around the nursery, leaving opened drawers in her wake, but she didn't find what was looking for. "Do you mind waiting while I go to my room to fetch another piece of fabric for the picture?" She already had a foot outside the nursery.

"Not at all," Pax said to the closing hatch. She opened her shirt and wished she had worn shorts, or even a skirt, instead of the heavy pants that were weighing down her legs. *I'm going to take root here.* The idea made her smile. The shushing sound of the pneumatic door announced that Marion was coming back.

"That was fast," Pax said without looking at the entry.

"And I thought you missed me." Prince's voice resonated in the room.

It shook Pax, and her hands automatically went to close her shirt. "No, but you're late." She didn't know why she had answered that way. It wasn't as if she was counting time. Three days to be exact. And several hours. And was she happy to see him? Or angry that he hadn't come looking for her earlier? And what if Marion found him there? And why was she even thinking those sorts of thoughts?

"Force majeure." He waved his hand in the air.

Pax noticed new bruises on his arm. His face was getting better, though. The skin was less swollen, although it wasn't possible to see any more of his features. "They hit you again?" she asked, her voice trembling slightly.

Prince's eyes locked on hers and didn't let her go. "I was in the wrong place," was all he said.

"I'm sorry." Pax moved toward him.

"Don't," Prince said, with a voice so low Pax wasn't sure he had talked at all.

She stopped anyway.

"Don't pity me," he said slightly louder. His voice was cold and mean.

Pax felt the air in her lungs leaving in one single motion. *That must be what it feels like to receive a punch in the stomach,* she found herself thinking.

"Never," he added, and the temperature in the hot nursery dropped several degrees.

"I didn't." Pax was surprised she could still articulate a sentence. Her legs moved back several steps until she touched the bench behind her. "You shouldn't be here."

"I know." And he left. Again.

Pax sat on the floor, resting her back on the leg of the bench. She was utterly confused and even nauseous. *He was a man.* Why didn't she associate that simple concept with the obvious reaction of screaming, running away, calling for help, and so on? She should report his activities for what they were: potentially criminal and probably aimed to hurt her. He knew her name. He knew *who* she was. Maybe he wanted to take some revenge, and she was the ideal candidate.

"Pax? Where are you?"

She hadn't heard Marion coming back. "I'm here. Just a sec. I spilled something." Pax emerged, taking care to smear her hands with dirt.

"My wife is using the drop I was looking for, but this one is dark enough." Marion showed her a piece of murky-green fabric. Pax made a scene of cleaning her hands on her legs and gave the cloth a thorough look.

"Let's shoot some pictures to send to my mom." She hoped Marion hadn't realized she needed a support to stand up. The realization the other woman had almost caught her sent thrills up her spine. It was part fear, part euphoria. Her heart was thumping loudly and rapidly in her chest and her voice sounded strained by a marathon. On top of everything else, there was the terror that the guards would catch Prince out of his cell. The detailed image of the first time she had seen him popped violently before her eyes: the blood and the shape of his body resting on the floor; the complete absence of any movement; the chest that hadn't moved at all.

"What a lovely sight," Marion said, looking at the arrangement she had made with the pink hybrid orchid and the dark green backdrop.

Pax breathed slowly to avoid throwing up on it. "Dramatic," she suggested.

* * *

"Are you having any fun?" her mom Claudine asked later that night when Pax called.

"Did you like the picture I sent you?" Pax tried to evade Claudine's sixth sense.

"Very much. How are you?" Claudine was the kind of mother who could read minds if she were so inclined.

Pax should have known better. "Fine. The kids are nice to me." She tried the old joke. She had said it the first day of kindergarten and used it ever since.

"Which means something's bothering you. What is it?" Claudine was like Lexi. She never released her prey until she was satisfied with it.

"I'm tired. I sleep poorly. I miss Lexi." Pax wasn't saying anything that wasn't one hundred percent true.

"Hmmm."

"I'm not in love with Lexi," Pax said with a sigh. Every conversation regarding her friend ended with the same statement, accompanied by a variety of facial expressions. She turned off the light, closed her eyes, and slowly massaged the arch of her nose.

"No, but she isn't good for you, anyway." Claudine was typing something on her laptop.

Pax could hear her long nails tapping rhythmically on the keys. Her mom could multitask like nobody else. "I want to be like you when I'm big."

"I see. We're using the whole repertoire tonight. Should I be worried?" Claudine had stopped typing.

"Of course not. I'm just being sentimental, that's all." Pax felt a stinging tear roll down her cheek. She wanted to be able to talk to her. Really talk to her. *Mom, I can't stop thinking about Prince. And I'm scared. And thrilled. And horrified. Or… I should be horrified.*

"Pax?" Claudine could detect a whole conversation out of a pregnant silence.

"Mom?" Pax hated when she couldn't stop crying. She hated even more when she had to fake that everything was peachy.

"Pax? It's your other mother. The one you like the least. How are you, sweetheart?" Maurice had hijacked the conversation.

Pax could hear Claudine complaining over the phone. "Hi, Maurice! Have you saved orphans and resurrected innocents?" She found that being funny was easier with her mother Maurice.

"Both. Three times already, and I still have a few hours until midnight. Have you spread mayhem in the last two days?" Maurice couldn't multitask and was less perceptive than Claudine, but she was funny.

Pax loved that about Maurice. With her, she could lower her defenses. "Yes. And I'm fine, as I already said. No need to smother me with the assault of your combined affection." But she was strangely glad for it.

"We're going to stay in Samara longer than planned." Maurice hesitated a moment before continuing, "But if you need us, we'll come back right away."

"Mothers! I am fine!" She paused a moment to compose herself. "At the end of the summer, I'll be out of the house, anyway. College, remember? Don't you think I might be able to manage a few days without you?"

"It's us who can't manage without you." Maurice's voice was so soft, and her words completely unexpected.

Pax looked at the ceiling and moved the cell phone away from her for a second. It wouldn't do to sob after her declaration of independence. "I love you, too," she managed to say with a pang of guilt. Maurice wasn't the cuddly mother. Pax rarely felt the need to reassure her mother she loved her. Instead, she normally showered Claudine with hugs and kisses.

"Sweetie, we're going to be unreachable for several days. Anna's coming with us to bring help to an isolated community nestled up in the mountains." Claudine's voice resonated in the distance.

"I'm so proud of you two." Pax thought that the word "proud" wasn't enough to describe what she felt for them.

"We're proud of you, too," Claudine said and then hastily added, probably to lighten the moment, "By the way, Grandma Rosie sends kisses and hugs."

"When did you hear from Grandma?" Pax realized it had been months since the last time they had mentioned the elusive Rosie. It was funny she had recently thought about her, as her jailer, nonetheless.

"I called to give her the news," Maurice answered, but her voice was covered by a loud noise.

"What is that?" Pax asked, trying to understand what was happening.

"Nothing. Some workers are unloading boxes of first-aid kits on the floor," Claudine yelled to be heard.

"We've to go now. I wish we could talk longer. We'll call you as soon as possible. Love you, pumpkin." Claudine's usual good-bye.

Pax smiled. She was a woman, but her mom still called her pumpkin. "Love you, moms," she yelled back.

"We love you, honey." Maurice ended the call with a kiss.

Pax kept her eyes on the blank ceiling long after the communication clicked to silence. When the cell phone chirped again, announcing Lexi's call, she didn't take it. It was the first time she hadn't accepted a call from her friend. Her eyes were swollen and her throat felt dry, even though she hadn't talked much. She hugged the pillow, longing for human contact.

"Bad timing?" Prince was standing at the door, his silhouette dark against the illuminated hallway.

Pax froze in her bed. She hadn't heard the door opening.

"I can come back another time." His words and his gentle tone clashed with the reality of his action. Prince closed the door behind him and slid closer to the bed. The pale light coming from the window cast a long shadow of his body against the wall.

Pax started shaking.

"But maybe I can rest here for a few minutes, since you are so kind." He sat down on the bed. The mattress sank under his weight. His hand landed a few inches from hers.

Pax's breathing became erratic. The warmth emanating from his skin contrasted with the cold that was gripping her body.

"You are always such good company." He seemed to laugh, but something was wrong with him.

He doesn't sound so smart, Pax thought in the midst of a frightening moment of lucidity.

"If you don't say something back, I'll touch you to see if you're alive." Again his teasing lacked sharpness. "Okay, I'm doing it now."

Pax jumped away even before Prince could attempt to put his threat in action.

"I'm relieved. I was worried you weren't whole in the head. You still have that stare, though…" He was going to say something else, but a low grunt escaped from his mouth instead. A long silence followed the sound, and then an even lower growl as his body sank on the bed.

"What—" Pax couldn't finish the sentence. Prince's hand was covering her mouth. When her heart slowed down enough and she was able to listen to any other sound that didn't come from her, she realized someone was knocking on her door.

"Don't give me away." Prince was speaking in her ear. His breath was hot, but his tone was icy.

"Mistress?"

"Yes, Celeste?" Prince had removed his hand, but Pax felt her lips stinging. She looked at the door and panic showed in her eyes. He mouthed, "It's locked," and then, "Breathe and relax." Pax didn't think she could feel relaxed ever again. When did he lock the door?

"Hmmm… we have a situation." Judging from the tone in her voice, Celeste was on pins and needles.

"What kind of situation?" Pax asked with a tone she hoped sounded sleepy and annoyed.

"Nothing serious, but you better stay inside your room." Celeste was clearly looking for the right words. "And keep your door locked."

"Why?" Pax couldn't release Celeste without pestering her. She would have suspected something was wrong.

"A worker escaped. But everything is under control." Celeste was now speaking very fast. It was clear she wanted to end the conversation as soon as possible.

Pax was overly glad for that. "I hope so," she added for good measure.

"Good night, Mistress." Celeste's steps echoed in the silent hallway as she moved away from Pax's door.

"What happened?" Pax turned toward the bulk on her bed, frustrated with having to talk to a shadow. She reached for the switch.

"Don't turn on the light." Prince moved slowly.

"I'm not used to being commanded. It's not in my nature, either." Funny moment to remember she had a tongue.

"Oh, I'm sure," he said without sarcasm.

"Now tell me why I shouldn't turn on the light." Pax was surprised her first question wasn't why she shouldn't scream for help. Maybe the adrenaline surge was replacing her brain cells with pudding. If she let enough air in her lungs, she could still muster a good shout, though. Instead, Pax used what was left of her brain to command her hand to turn on the switch. She would have indeed screamed if Prince hadn't promptly shut her mouth again.

"This is why," Prince said with a sad and painful smile.

Pax couldn't understand how he could move, or even talk, without fainting. What could be seen of Prince's skin was matted in blood and dark bruises. "Why?" She couldn't really find the words to ask how anyone could inflict that kind of physical pain upon another human being. She was horrified.

"It's okay. It isn't any worse than other times. I just need to rest." Prince didn't wait for her permission. He lay down, his head close to her. "They never go too far. They need me too much to kill me right away," he murmured.

"What do you mean?"

"I'm their best semental."

"You're a semental?" Pax asked, surprised by that fact.

"I'm telling you: their strongest specimen. I was told by a professional."

"But aren't sementals normally kept somewhere else?" No good pure breed talked about that, but everybody knew of several semen factories scattered around the country. And as far as she knew, Sundial wasn't one of them. Her mothers would have never sent her to a semen factory.

"I don't know about other places. I'm here." He shrugged ever so slightly, wincing in the process.

Pax winced in sympathy. "I don't know what to do," she said, astonished she felt the urge to caress his head, but didn't dare move one single muscle.

"Nothing. Just let me be." His voice was a whisper of warm air against her skin.

Pax's hand hovered for a moment; then she put it back on her lap and closed her eyes. She waited until his breathing relaxed and then moved ever so slowly on the bed to put some space between them. She wanted to ask why he had been punished this time. How he had escaped? What would happen to him when they found him? Because they were going to find him. Of that, Pax was sure.

Pax slept a few minutes at a time. The position, sitting against the wall, wasn't conducive to relaxation. Every single squeak in the hallway woke her up immediately. Prince's movements provoked the same reaction. All combined, it was more than enough to discourage her from achieving any form of sleep. But the fact that in her room, on her bed, so close to her, there was a man, was the reason that won over every other. A man was lying on her bed. A man named Prince. They were alone in her bedroom. She was aware she was infringing a taboo profoundly ingrained in the society she lived. She shouldn't be able to do so. She should feel soiled. She should feel anything but what she was feeling. She should be puking in disgust at the idea of touching him while he was sleeping. But the idea visited her mind. She did her best to cast it away as an unwelcome and dirty thought. But it came back. Several times. And she didn't feel soiled, not even once.

CHAPTER 5

When morning came, Pax was surprised she had been able to close her eyes even for a mere sixty seconds. Exhaustion had overridden her body, leaving her brain no choice on the topic. Whatever it was, she was glad for it. She kept her eyes closed for a few minutes more, but she knew he was still there. Prince's body was now a familiar shape, changing the shadows on her bed.

"I probably should thank you," he said.

"*You think*?" She almost laughed; then reality dawned on her and her lips straightened in a hard line.

"Thank you, Pax." Prince opened his eyes. "Don't worry. I'm leaving. I won't cause any trouble for you."

"It's too late now. I'm already in trouble. The sun is up." Pax's head tilted toward the window. "I can't let them find you here, in my room," she added more for herself than anybody else.

"I understand your concern." His voice was tight and guarded.

"Do you?" Pax couldn't help to retort. "Stay here until I come back." She rotated her finger to let him know he had to turn around. She donned the first shirt and pants she found and left the room without looking back at him.

"Mistress Pax! I was just coming to wake you up."

Pax was taken aback to see the maid's worried face hovering outside her room as soon as she stepped out of it. Had she been waiting there for Pax to wake up?

"New procedure?" Pax asked, closing the door firmly behind her. She hoped Celeste hadn't had time to look inside. She turned around, locked the door, and put the key away, trusting the maid wasn't observant and didn't consider she had never done it before.

"No, no. It's not a new procedure. I was just walking around."

"Well, is there anything you should tell me?" Pax couldn't let her persona down. She had to press her advantage.

"No, but I can walk you to the dining room, if you'd like some company." The girl was torturing her nails.

"Okay, that's enough. What's going on here?" Pax stopped and faced Celeste.

"Nothing at all."

"I'm going to call my mothers." Pax hated to use her position, but the rest of the universe expected her to. It was almost funny she was extorting information she already knew everything about, first hand.

"The worker is still at large." The maid sighed, resigned.

"Who?" Pax hoped to sound convincing in her acting.

"The troublemaker. The one you saw."

"It's just *one* man. I am sure Caren knows how to deal with this kind of problem." Pax dismissed the whole notion as if it were a minor bump on her busy schedule. "I don't need company to eat breakfast. I'm sure you have better things to do."

"Actually, yes."

Did Celeste mean it? Pax should have felt offended, but instead she was almost proud of her. She didn't let the servant girl see her lips curving up for the briefest second.

Pax reached her destination without interruptions. She noticed that apart from Celeste, she hadn't seen anybody around. The dining room was completely empty. Pax decided to eat fast and immediately go back to her room. The whole situation was becoming eerier by the second. She was going to stash some bread in her pockets to feed Prince, when Marion appeared at the door.

"Are you done?" she asked Pax with a big smile that didn't hide the dark circles under her eyes.

"Almost." Pax wasn't fooled by the accidental dropping by when nobody else was out and about. First Celeste, now Marion; they were escorting her from one place to the other.

"I need another coffee. I didn't sleep well last night and I need to wake up." Marion sat down at the table.

Pax ate the piece of bread meant for Prince and then drank another cup of coffee. The day promised to be long.

It proved to be longer still. Pax was never left alone for more than five minutes, and she never had a chance to sneak back to her room. Marion was considerate enough to order sandwiches for lunch, so they could keep cataloguing the bulbs with no hurry. She listened the whole day to Marion, dreading the moment when someone was going to call the nursery with the news that they were out of danger. The phone rang five times and each time, Pax stopped breathing and waited for Marion to announce triumphantly they had found him. She kept thinking of all the possible scenarios. They weren't going to look for him in her room, not right away, at least. But he could have done something stupid. Like deciding to go somewhere else.

The nursery was hotter than the day before, and the humidity had grown exponentially. Pax's shirt was soon soaked with sweat, but when she mentioned the need for a bath, Marion let her use her private shower stall inside the nursery. A change of clothes was also provided. She could only thank Marion for being so kind to her. Under the rain of cold water, Pax felt the urge to laugh hysterically. She took her time to calm down before going back in.

Marion occupied the remaining time before dinner with all sorts of menial tasks. After cataloguing the bulbs, they moved the sprouts around more than was necessary and cleaned the tables as if a surgeon needed them to operate. Pax was aching to go back to her room and check on Prince, but Marion expressed the desire to take a walk before eating. The direction toward Pax's room was as good as any other to stretch her legs. Pax felt that, all of a sudden, she was too hungry to bother changing for dinner.

The dining room was full. The women were chatting and laughing, but an undercurrent of fear was charging the air. They were all acting on Pax's behalf. Or better said, on Pax's mothers' behalf. They needed political support to keep the government funds coming their way. Putting the future president's daughter in danger wouldn't speak well of them. She smiled reassuringly and some of the faces relaxed under the masks.

It was a chilling affair, dinner. Pax attuned her senses to capture even the slightest allusion to what was happening. Of one thing she was certain. Prince was still free. Caren was too tense, and Lauren caressed her hands once or twice when she thought nobody was looking. Marion chattered the whole time without saying anything at all. Celeste was all *mistress this* and *mistress that*, annoying Pax more than ever. Finally, the cake was brought and Pax politely excused herself, admitting she had eaten enough for three people and wished to retire. Caren and Lauren exchanged looks, but they couldn't find a way to escort her to her room without explaining why she needed such protection. Pax saw the frustration on their faces and slipped away before they could muster a plausible reason to follow her.

She ran to her room and tried several times to center the key inside the lock. She cursed the lack of electronic keys at the farm. Consequentially, she also cursed the Tarin rebellion that had made that lack of modern electronics a necessity to keep the workers in check. Her hands were trembling and she kept looking right and left. Any time soon, someone could appear around the corner, offering to help her with the key. Finally, the door opened and she closed it rather loudly behind her. The room was dark, and she stumbled to find the switch. Her fear became reality before her eyes. The room was empty. Her bed was neatly made. She sank on the mattress and covered her face with her hands.

"Are you always so gloomy?" He came out of the bathroom she hadn't thought to check.

Pax was so worried he had left that she had simply accepted it at the first proof of it. "You're here," she said and felt stupid and happy. She also felt incredibly relieved and happy. And definitely stupid again. He was only wearing his pants.

"You told me to stay put."

"You said you didn't follow orders—" Pax closed her eyes in frustration; she couldn't look at him. "—forget it. I've had enough of this game." She lay down, releasing her arms on the bed. The presence of his body nearby was too tangible.

"You were worried for me." Prince's voice was surprised.

Pax refused to raise her head to look at him. She also refused to say anything back.

"And you aren't denying it." He crossed the space from the bathroom to the bed and sat down. He remained silent for several long minutes. "You're not going to cry *man*." He sounded dumbfounded by that realization.

"I'm also feeding you." Pax sat upright and emptied the contents of her pockets on the coverlet.

"How did you manage?" Prince was already reaching for a morsel.

"Faking a huge appetite and taking advantage of the fact I was in a room full of women devoted to putting on a good show for me. Nobody looked at me the whole dinner." Pax was staring at Prince, trying to decipher his thoughts. Did men think in a different way? She realized she didn't know much about men, apart from what she had been instructed since she was a little girl. *Never get close to them.*

"What's so funny?" Prince asked with his mouth full.

"The irony of this situation," she stated. "Put something on."

"I'm not going to catch a cold."

"Please." Pax blushed and hoped he hadn't seen her.

"Since you ask so kindly." Prince seemed oblivious to her embarrassment. He slowly reached between the bed and the wall. "Where's it?" Lowering his arm farther down, he cursed under his breath. "Where the…" His hand reemerged with his shirt clutched in his fingers and he donned it, wincing.

"Thank you," she murmured.

Prince raised his head at her words and looked at her. Pax didn't breathe. He went to the bathroom where he turned on the water and came back a moment later.

"Now what?" he asked, leaning against the wall.

"*Now what*, what?" Pax repeated, raising her eyebrow.

"It seems we have to share the bed again," Prince said with a matter-of-fact shrug of his shoulders.

Pax noticed the expression on his face when he did so. He was in a lot of pain. She felt the irrational urge to massage his arms to ease his ache. "You should sleep on the floor," she blurted out.

"As the good slave I am." His words were pure venom.

Pax gasped at how painful they were to hear. Not so long ago, she had joked about the subject. "Am *I* treating you like a slave?" She was hurt that he was hurt. It was difficult for her to understand how this was happening, but what Prince thought meant a great deal to her. How that could possibly be was beyond her. *You are just a man*, Pax thought for a second, and she gasped again. This time she had felt soiled, dirty, and unworthy.

"No. You aren't," Prince admitted after a moment. He was having some sort of private conversation as well.

"I can sleep on the floor. You don't look well." Pax took one of the pillows and slid on the carpet.

"We can share the bed. It's big enough to avoid each other." Prince took the pillow from her hands and put it back on the bed.

The bed isn't big enough, Pax thought, but she had hoped to sleep on it. She didn't want to examine why her heart seemed so pleased with his words.

No sleep was accomplished whatsoever. Not on Pax's side, at least. She wondered, during the long night, how long one's mind could go without regular rest until it turned to mush. Hers felt almost there. Maybe she would wake up and find she had dreamed the whole thing. She could imagine Doc Cassandra's serene words when she would recount her nightmare.

"*How's your relationship with Maurice nowadays?*" her therapist would ask from her antique desk. Maurice's dominant attitude toward the people in her life was a recurrent topic in their sessions. More than once Pax had thought, and sometimes even commented out loud, that maybe Maurice was the one needing therapy. *But you must love the people who gave birth to you, no matter what.* That was her mantra when she was mad at her mother.

When the moon was high in the night sky, Pax finally came to wonder what would be the good doctor's reaction at her confession. Not that she was ever going to tell anybody what she was thinking.

"*You see, I spent two nights in bed with a man. Yes, a man.*" Shocked silence. Pax was somehow satisfied to be the one making the therapist speechless. She pondered for a while if it was worth also explaining she was effectively harboring him. That would have sent the doctor to a therapist. It seemed fitting.

"*I'm pretty sure I also... liked it.*" Pax would blush at that. She must retain some decency after all, even in a projection of something that would never happen. Her moms would be notified, probably. The patient confidentiality was overruled by the discovery of criminal traits or even the slightest suggestion of perversion. She gave another thorough look at Prince's chest moving slowly and sighed. It didn't feel wrong. She had tried to muster the mandatory feeling of uneasiness to no avail. Maybe she really did need therapy. No, she really couldn't talk to anybody she knew who loved her. Which left only one solution.

"Are you sleeping?" Pax murmured ever so softly. If he was, her words wouldn't have woken him.

"No."

He didn't move at all. Pax let out a deep breath. She didn't even know what she wanted from him. "How do you feel... being here with *me*?" Her words came out strained and probably meant for bats, or other night creatures with extremely good hearing. The very long and awkward silence that followed reinforced her assumption.

"I shouldn't be here." He had heard.

"I already know that." Pax strangled the pillow she was hugging. It was better to continue her fantasy-session with her therapist. Even in her imagination, Doctor Cassandra was more useful than having this stupid conversation with Prince.

"But I want to be," he finished and then sat with his back against the wall, mirroring her position, but for the choked pillow. His hands were peacefully resting on his lap.

"You want to." Pax would have taken in stride almost any answer he would have given, but not that one. Not in one million years. Because it was exactly what she wanted to hear from him.

"I do." Prince was now studying her face.

Pax strangled her pillow with a vice grip that left her own arms aching.

"Do you?" he asked, never lowering his eyes from hers.

She found that she couldn't answer. She tried to. "Do I what?" Pax never played dumb. She truly was at the moment.

"I'm not going to spell it out for you." Prince was getting annoyed.

"I shouldn't," she confessed.

"So, you do, but feel wrong," he summarized with evident satisfaction.

"Is it the same for you?" Pax thought she didn't feel wrong at all. She had to shut her mouth before she said it out loud.

"Yes. I don't know why I react the way I do with you." Prince's eyes were now the only thing Pax saw. "I should hate *you*." His statement cut the connection between them abruptly.

She took in his whole body and saw, once again, the bruises and the swollen face. She felt guilty, even though she had never laid a hand on anybody.

"Not for this." Prince gestured to his body as if he had read her thoughts. "This is nothing."

Pax didn't want to hear his reasons to hate her then. She was sure he had plenty, but it wasn't her fault the world was as it was. She hadn't made it so.

We are equally culpable. Lexi's voice had the bad habit of popping in Pax's mind when she least needed it. The reasoning behind the statement was that everybody needed to stand up against the wrongs that were committed every day.

"You know why I'm still alive?" Prince asked in a way that meant only the beginning of an ugly confrontation.

Pax hadn't really envisioned a night of heated discussions when she had asked him if he was awake.

"Do you know why they, *you*—" He corrected the pronoun to include her personally. "—bother to give me food and water every day? Even though I'm such a nuisance?" He scooted on the bed until he was mere inches away from her. "*Do you?*" His voice had risen dangerously.

"No, I don't know." Pax hurried to answer, hoping that he would lower his tone. She didn't dare ask for it.

"I'm the best semental in the whole county," he said, looking straight at her. He was waiting for her reaction. When none came, he gave it another try. "My semen is the best you can find on the market. The best maids come from men like me." He looked satisfied by the shocked expression on her face this time. "I thought so. I knew you were too good a family girl to be troubled with this kind of information," he snorted. "You women need your slaves to do all the things you don't want to. But we aren't good enough to be in your royal presence, so you use the best of us to give you watered-down slaves. *Our daughters*."

Pax knew better than to interrupt his tirade.

"I bet my life on it that you have plenty of fathered girls at your service, and I wouldn't be surprised if you don't even remember their names." He shot her a glance that left her chilled to the bones.

In the midst of that conversation, her mind went to Lexi and her forbidden love. Pax wanted to say a lot of things, but her tongue got stuck inside her mouth. "I—"

"You think that since you haven't used me, yet, you are excused?" Prince surprised Pax, reading through her as if she was made of glass.

"No, I know I can't be excused." She moved her hand on the bed until she brushed his. "I never thought of using you." She didn't add that she had never consciously thought of using any man in her life, either. She had never been cruel to any of her helpers, and she did remember most of their names. Lexi's words came to her mind again, loud and clear.

"I'm not feeling well," Prince said and brought both his arms around his stomach.

For a split second, Pax was glad for the change of topic. Prince's groans erased that thought from her mind right away. "What is it?"

"I don't know. My stomach hurts so much." Prince was now doubling over the bed, rocking his body.

"You need help." Pax realized how impossible it was to get any help for him the moment the words escaped her mouth.

Prince screamed once and then went limp.

"Oh my... oh my..." Pax automatically reached for his pulse. "Think... think," she repeated while pacing through the room. She stopped twice to touch him, to be reassured that he was still alive. *I must find help.*

Pax left the room and her reasoning behind. She acted more than thought. She went with her instincts without slowing down to ask herself what she was doing. The hallway was dimly lit and she ran, hoping to find the infirmary before someone would see her. Her legs found the way, directing her through that maze of turns and bifurcations. When she found the door she was looking for, the idea that it had been all in vain hit her. The lights in the infirmary were lit. Muffled voices came from inside. Pax rested against the wall, not knowing what to do. She couldn't go back. She had to help Prince.

"I knew they were going to retaliate. But poisoning the meat?"

Pax made out Caren's voice.

"What did you expect?" Lauren's.

"It means they think we have him," Caren reasoned.

"It also means that since we don't have him, he could be anywhere. Even outside this farm." Lauren sounded resigned to the idea. "Let's hope the desert is going to bury him under tons and tons of sand."

"That would be convenient." Caren's voice was low, but the finality in her tone was icily clear.

"Not a word to anybody outside the farm. Not a single whisper about this little situation must reach the Priestess. Do you understand?" Caren spoke deliberately slow.

"That's not possible! You know I must report to Ginecea about the insurrection and the food poisoning. It's not just about the workers; several women were involved—" a fourth voice said. A woman with a crisp, northern accent.

"Linda, you won't report a thing until I say so," Caren hissed.

"We can't risk our enterprise by being discovered. Even you should know better than that," Lauren said in a milder tone. "And the Priestess would be displeased that we aren't to be trusted with her principal—"

"With our stock," Caren abruptly finished for Lauren.

"I told you from the beginning that hiding the Priestess' semen bank here at Sundial was a horrible idea. And look at us now," Linda said.

"Don't say it out loud! Have you gone insane?" Caren's voice had a hint of panic.

"We must keep everything under control. We can't lose our cool," Marion said hastily and then added, "Not now that we have the chance to show our hybrid to a senator. Maybe even the future president. Imagine the good publicity for our farm. We need all the help we can get."

"What we need is to hide in plain sight with the help of Marion here." Caren's voice managed to be almost soothing.

"Exactly," Marion said.

"We can't blow this opportunity," Lauren added.

"If the daughter reports anything, *anything*, back home, we are screwed." Marion pursued the thought, raising her voice.

"Caren, you have to deal with this." The botanist was serious. She frightened Pax.

"I don't think—" Linda couldn't finish the sentence.

"Linda, don't be difficult. You know there isn't any other option." Caren was lowering her voice. Pax strained her ears.

"No, I guess not," Linda said. "But first we have to deal with the food poisoning."

"How bad is it, doctor?" Caren asked.

"Since almost everybody who ate the meat has been throwing up for hours, it's safe to say that the problem will be under control before dawn," Linda answered. "I expect to be called once or twice more, but by now, those who would have shown symptoms already have."

"I think that it's better to go check on our guest. Let's hope she isn't lying senseless on the bathroom floor." Lauren's voice came dangerously close to the door.

Pax had one second to decide what to do.

"What the—" Lauren was almost knocked over by Pax, who ran in and threw up all over her. Marion, Caren, and the unknown woman, came immediately to help Pax up. Lauren scooted over and let the others take care of the guest while she went to remove her clothes. "I was just thinking of you," she murmured under her breath.

"My stomach is killing me," Pax moaned with tears in her eyes.

"We had some problem with the food," Caren said.

"Make it stop! I can't stand to throw up anymore." Pax was now sweating. Fear was helping her a great deal in faking symptoms.

A woman wearing white scrubs approached her. "I'll give you something. I'm Doctor Linda," she said, opening a drawer.

"I also fainted back in my room. Before throwing up," Pax remembered to say.

"Hm. It kicked you hard." Doctor Linda seemed to think about it for a few seconds. "You don't seem so fragile." She moved to a glass cabinet and picked up a box.

Pax wasn't sure if she had to say something else. She couldn't realistically fake what she didn't have much longer.

"Are you allergic to any medication?" the doctor asked, still frowning at some thought she was following.

"I don't know." Pax knew it was the wrong answer the moment it left her mouth.

"You don't know if you are allergic to anything?" Now Linda was looking directly at her in disbelief.

"Anna keeps the records." Pax's face was pasted with an unhealthy sheen.

"And who's Anna?" Linda asked.

"My mother Maurice's personal secretary." Anna was actually more a factotum for the whole family, but her official job description was the one Pax had just offered. "I can call her right away, if you think it's important," she added wickedly, showing them her cell phone.

"There's no need to disturb the senator's secretary over this. I heard she's busy bringing relief funds to the victims in Samara." Caren was shooting menacing glances at the doctor, who in turn was starting to look sweaty herself.

"I think we can manage with something for the pain and a high spectrum antibiotic. I'll just give you a lower dosage, just in case." Linda turned around to sort the prescription.

"Maybe you can lie down on a cot until the pain is bearable," Lauren offered. She had donned a green gown.

"I can stay with you, if you need anything," Marion chimed in.

"If you don't mind, I prefer to be close to my bathroom. I feel more comfortable that way." Pax smiled thankfully, remembering to show some residual pain on her face.

"Yes, it's understandable." Marion squeezed Pax's arm in a gesture meant to convey her sympathy.

"Thanks," Pax murmured while making a show of breathing in and out.

"Okay, here it is. Gulp these down. Have some water." Linda handed her a glass and two pills. Pax ingested the pills, one at the time, and then drank from the glass.

"Now, you should be okay through the rest of the night, but if you aren't feeling better in a few hours, I want you to call me and I'll send more medication." The doctor wrote her telephone number on a piece of paper, folded it in half, and gave it to her.

"Thank you so much." Pax accepted it and made to leave.

"Wait, I'll walk you to your room." Caren was at her side before Pax could say anything at all.

During the long walk, Pax managed to look in enough pain and discomfort not to talk, but fit enough to be allowed back in her room.

Caren was troubled by her own thoughts to try any unilateral conversation. "Should I send for Celeste to clean your room?" she asked once before Pax's door.

"No, there's no need to wake up my maid. I managed to reach the sink in time. I just need to let some air in." Pax centered the key inside the lock at the first try. Keeping her body between the open door and the room, she thanked Caren again. "I'm sorry for Lauren's clothes," she added, before closing the door behind her. She waited to hear Caren's steps grow distant and then spat the pills on her hand.

"Are you awake?" Pax asked the shadows in the room. Prince was in the bathroom, as much she could assume from the light showing through the doorframe. "Prince?" She softly pushed the wooden panel and found him heaving on the toilet. Although the scene wasn't happy, she felt better already. "Good," she commented after he finished.

"Good?" He could barely talk.

"Your body is purging itself," she explained while reaching over with a wet towel to refresh his face. She hadn't thought twice about what she was doing, and he let her do it.

"Purging what?" Prince's eyes were shining bright. He was slowly coming back.

"Nothing serious. Food poisoning." The irony wasn't lost on Pax, who started laughing.

"It's not hilarious that you tried to kill me."

"It's actually very funny. Your friends gave you food poisoning. You weren't supposed to eat the women's food." Pax moved his hand that was stopping hers and kept cleaning his face. "I didn't eat the meat because I saved it for you. Nothing like protein to make you feel stronger, or so I was told." She brushed his face with her fingers.

He shuddered.

"Sorry," she whispered. Something got stuck in her throat. The swelling on his face was still there, and she really wished now to see his face clean and healthy. "Here, have some chewed medicine. It's the best kind." Pax tried her best to dry the two pills with a cloth and then brought them to his lips.

"Well, thank you," he replied with sarcasm. But he opened his mouth, accepting the gift from her. "Disgusting."

"I had to vomit on someone to get them. Show some gratitude." Pax reached for a glass on the sink. She was going to help him with the water as well, but he put a hand on hers.

"I'm grateful."

Pax looked at him with disbelief written on her face, but he was being dead serious. He then guided her hand holding the glass toward his mouth and drank from it. Pax found the gesture too intimate to bear. An awkward silence followed. Prince seemed at a loss for words as well. She stood up straight to put some distance between their bodies. It was of no avail. They could have been separated by concrete walls and she could still feel him.

"I'm afraid of you," she finally said.

"I can hardly do you any harm." Prince looked at himself and then at her. He went to embrace the toilet once again.

"No, I don't think you want to. But you will." Pax leaned against the sink to find some connection with a reality she wasn't sure she could accept. "You're not safe here anymore." She continued her train of thought without filling him in. "We need to sleep, if even just half an hour." She left the bathroom and went to the bed.

A loud bang on the door evaporated the last remnants of a particularly scary nightmare Pax was having. Prince's presence by her side made her wish to jump back in the nightmare.

"Mistress? Are you okay? Please answer me!" Celeste was yelling outside the door. She was going to barge in as soon as Pax would open the door.

"Close yourself in the bathroom. Now!" Pax half pushed, half pulled, and partly kicked Prince until he was semiconscious on the bathroom floor.

"Celeste! Why in the Heavens do you need to make such a ruckus?" Pax opened just enough of the door to show herself.

"Mistress Pax, you look... you look—" Celeste's eyes were so wide, Pax worried she could see more than she wanted to show.

"I threw up the whole night," she said rather icily.

"Oh, you were resting."

"Yes, emphasis on the past tense. I *was* resting, before you decided it was time to wake me up." Pax couldn't help but yawn in her face.

"I came here to help." Celeste lowered her eyes.

"Help with what?"

"I was told to come and clean your room and see if you needed any medical attention."

"I'm feeling better. Regarding my room, I intend to sleep for another two days. If you don't mind, of course." Pax really fought the urge of being nicer to the girl, but she needed her out of the way as fast as possible.

Celeste turned around with her head still lowered, but added at the last moment, "If you need anything, *anything at all*, please think of me."

Pax closed the door with a big sigh of relief.

"You can't pull it off much longer. You know that, right?" Prince was looking at her from the bathroom. He was wide-awake.

He looked more awake than she felt, at any rate. "I'm not that rude, normally." She felt the urge to excuse her behavior.

"I know," he simply replied with a nod.

Pax felt happiness radiating through her body like a web of positive thoughts. She shook her head. "I think I've successfully avoided volunteering today." She sat down on the chair facing the desk. She didn't have time to enjoy her small victory, though. The voice she wanted to hear the least boomed through the door.

"Mistress Layan?" Lauren only knocked once.

"Something's wrong," Prince said.

"Mistress, open the door. I will be in and out in a second." Lauren was forcing the handle.

Pax could hear approaching steps and hushed voices getting closer. Lauren wasn't alone. She looked at the window facing the garden. Prince walked to it and opened the windowpane.

"I'll manage. Close it behind me," he said and climbed over the ledge. Pax looked at him disappear to who knows where and shut the window the same moment the door sprung open. She managed to look as if she was coming out of the bathroom.

"I apologize, but you weren't answering." Lauren wasn't sorry. Celeste was there, along with two guards Pax hadn't met.

"I was busy." Pax gave Celeste a reproachful look.

The maid shrugged her shoulders, but remained silent.

"After last night we were worried for you," Lauren stated while taking in the whole room. She moved to the bathroom.

Pax sat at the desk to hide her nervousness. She had to lay her hands on the table to steady them. She gave them her best haughty look and started playing with her cell phone. She flipped it open several times, hoping that the sharp sound unnerved the women. Finally, she couldn't remain silent anymore. "My stomach ache isn't worth this amount of trouble. You shouldn't fret so much over me."

"You are fine then, mistress?" one of the two guards asked nervously.

"I think the air in the room smells rather stale." Lauren went to open the bathroom window and looked outside thoroughly. "Such a nice day, isn't it?"

"I have no idea." Pax was sweating now. She stepped closer to the window next to her. Celeste beat her to it.

"Let me help you, mistress." She opened the window, and as Lauren had just done, checked the fineness of the day. Lauren exchanged glances with Celeste and finally moved outside the room.

"I see that you're faring better. We'll leave you to rest some more." Lauren called the other women with a nod of her head.

Pax let out all the air in her lungs, locked the door, and rushed to the window. She didn't even wait to be sure nobody had lingered outside the room. Prince was nowhere to be seen. She looked down and her head swooned with vertigo. She hadn't realized how far the drop was from there.

"A little help here." Prince's voice came from the right corner.

She leaned out enough to still be safely inside the room and looked down again. He was there, dangling precariously from a jutted water drain located under the ledge.

"Now, if it isn't too much to ask."

Prince's hands were sliding down. Pax grabbed one of his hands, but the situation went from desperate to dramatic. She wasn't strong enough to haul him up.

"No!" She dug her heels in the floor and pulled until her hands became slippery. She was losing him and the fall would kill him for sure. She managed one last effort and almost doubled over the windowsill. Prince's weight risked bringing them both down.

"Let me go," he said.

Pax stared in horror while she envisioned his body on the ground below: motionless and bloody. She screamed and pulled until the pain was too much to bear. Her eyes went blank and she sank on the floor with a thud.

"You are heavier than I thought," Pax said, staring at Prince's face hovering over hers.

"You've thought about my weight?" Prince didn't seem to feel the need to move any time soon.

"Get. Off. Me" She could barely breathe; he was crushing her.

"Why? Can't you take a little bit of roughhousing?" Prince said, but decided to turn around on his back. He raised his head and rested on his bent arm so that he could keep looking at her. "You're soft."

"And you're not." Pax was inhaling and some color had found its way back to her cheeks. "You're different from me," she stated without a hint of sarcasm. She was actually intrigued by what she had just accidentally discovered.

"What did you expect? I'm not a woman."

"Thanks for explaining that."

"I'm not," he repeated softer.

"I don't know how you are… built," Pax confessed in a whisper.

What really stung her was that he clearly knew about women a great deal more than she did about men. She didn't want to know how he did. It pained her.

"Just a few differences, here and there," he said and then sat and helped her sit up as well. "They thought I was keeping you hostage."

She took his hand gingerly. "Celeste saw you."

"Yes. Your maid saw me and didn't say anything."

"Why?" Pax was getting increasingly worried.

"And how would I know?" Prince shot an accusatory glance back at her.

"I thought—" *You two knew each other…*

"I've to leave."

"Care to share your insight on this decision?" Pax was going through a roller coaster of different emotions. On top of that, her brain once in a while sent her signals. Like right now. *It's better if you leave.*

"There're going to be repercussions," Prince said, one hand on the doorknob.

"Hey, wait a minute. What do you think you're doing?" Pax was behind him in a second.

"I'm endangering lots of people. There're men who've been covering for me. They'll be the first to be punished." Prince wasn't looking at her.

She moved around, forcing him to face her. "They've managed to slip poison in the dinner meat. It seems to me that they can manage just fine."

"I'll endanger you." He sagged on the floor.

"I know you are going to harm me. I already told you. But not in the way you think." Pax had softened her words at the end. She reached out her hand to touch his face and sighed.

"I don't want anything to happen to you." Prince lowered his voice to a volume barely audible.

"I hoped so," she whispered back.

She saw him opening his mouth to say something, but a loud noise drowned out his words.

CHAPTER 6

One moment, Pax was talking to Prince, and the next, she was trying to locate the source of the sudden commotion. She realized soon enough the fire alarm had gone off. Panic rapidly swelling in her chest, she listened as the metallic sound of the hatches going down to secure the various sections of the farm became louder. An acrid smell was invading the air. Something was burning. Tongues of orange fire licked the open windows and spread inside the room. Pax's eyes started burning and painful tears obscured her sight. The air in her lungs felt poisonous. The temperature was climbing. Without saying a word, Prince threw her inside the shower stall and soaked both of them with cold water. Pax felt momentarily better.

"We're going to be trapped. We have to get out now." Prince put a wet towel on her face and locked her elbow in a vise grip. They moved through the room in a haze of colors and sounds.

Pax screamed under the makeshift mask and Prince said something she didn't hear. She froze for a second. Her lungs couldn't pump air and the temperature was already too high. He cradled her in his arms and ran away from the room. The hallway was getting smaller as more and more sections were sealed before their eyes. Pax pushed her face against his chest and found peace for a moment. Right at the center of a burning inferno, she experienced peace. *Peace,* of all feelings, as never before.

Prince eventually let her down to open a door that was stuck. He pried it open only to find that the flames had already engulfed the space. There were several other doors to try, but it was like playing a guessing game with no air left to breathe. Another hatch went down right behind them. Only three doors left to open and find a way out. If there were any.

Pax felt sluggish and heavy. Every step was harder than the one before. She stumbled against one of the doors and it burnt her skin.

The pain woke her up immediately. "Not this one," she yelled over the fire alarm blast. The door she was looking at was changing color. She could see the fire leaping under the metal.

"Stay close to me." Prince tentatively reached for the door closer to him. He didn't have to touch it. He moved to the last one, pulling Pax with him. "It will be okay," he said to her.

Pax reached for his hand and carefully bandaged it with the wet towel. He locked eyes with her for the briefest moment and then pulled down the handle and went inside. It was barely possible to see what was left of the furniture. The room was engulfed in orange and red. The smoke had a bitter aftertaste. Pax saw Prince looking around, and driven by desperation, she did the same. She thought she saw something blue lurking in the background and indicated the spot to him. She squinted through tears and a solid wall of gas now permeating everything. There was definitely something blue cutting through the monotony of reds. Prince nodded at her, then removed the towel from his hand and covered Pax's nose and mouth with it before she could say anything. He ran through the room and pushed Pax in front of a hole in the wall that had probably been a window a few moments before.

"Jump after me." And he disappeared into the blue.

Pax didn't think at all. The heat was eating the fabric of her clothes already. She followed him without looking down. A blank void and a whooshing sound surrounded her confused senses. After a moment of pure fear that stretched in time so long she thought it was never going to end, Pax landed in his arms.

"You're light," Prince commented as if finishing their earlier conversation.

Pax felt him shiver and hugged him closer.

"I need to sit down a second," he said and gently put her on the grass.

Pax looked up and started shivering herself. The windows on the second floor were gone. The whole side of the building was turning black. They were sitting on a small hill that almost reached the second story. Pax stared ahead of her, trying to locate her room. When her eyes focused on the burning walls facing the end of the slope, she gasped in realization.

"No, we wouldn't have survived the fall from there," Prince commented as if he had heard her thoughts. "The adrenaline rush is winding down, I'm afraid." He was talking to her, but his eyes were staring at the sky.

Pax thought of doing the same, but her senses were tingling madly. She looked around to decide what to do next. "We're close to the recreational facility."

Prince didn't seem to register her words.

"We have to go somewhere else." Pax was already standing up, but Prince wasn't moving. His eyes, although open, weren't really looking at anything in particular.

"Everybody is going to take shelter at the swimming pool. We can't remain here. Someone is going to see you." She pulled on his arms to wake him up. The first two tries didn't produce any reaction. Finally, Pax slapped him and cringed when her open palm hit his marred skin.

"Ouch!" He finally came back from wherever he had been.

"Follow me." Pax could already hear voices coming from the northern end of the building, where the recreational building connected the gardens to the main body of the farm. Her legs started moving faster.

"Where are we going?" Prince was now running with her.

"The nursery is the only hope we have." Pax was counting on Marion trying to save her precious orchids and activate the emergency procedures that would maintain the safety of the plants. She was also counting on Marion having already left the nursery.

If Prince had any doubts about her statement, he didn't say anything. "This way is shorter." He led her through a copse of cypresses and a section of the garden that was under maintenance.

The glass ceiling of the nursery appeared above the trees and she finally inhaled some air. Pax hadn't realized she stopped breathing. As they approached the building, she strained her ears to capture any noise coming from it. She was hoping to hear the sound of the emergency generator coming to life, but other than the flames bursting through the dried grass, nothing else was audible.

"We're going to be entombed in a glass inferno if we go inside. It was a good idea, but we need to find somewhere else to go." He was already scanning the receding green of the garden, but the places they could escape through were being eaten by the flames at an impressive speed. "You must go to the pool," Prince finally stated.

"We can't go there." She looked at him with imploring eyes.

"We aren't. You are."

"No, I'm not leaving you here."

"Yes, you are." Prince hauled her on his shoulders as if she were a bag and made to run away.

"Wait!" Pax hit him in the back with her fists. "Stop! I am telling you to stop!" She kept hitting him, but Prince wasn't bent on listening to her pleas. "Listen." She finally had his attention for a brief moment. The hum of the generator resonated through their labored breaths.

Prince put her down and turned around.

"The nursery's aeration and water systems are on." Pax massaged her chest where it had been slammed against Prince's shoulders. They walked back silently as the lights inside the nursery lit up in a pale yellow glow. "I'll go inside. Walk around and wait for me to open the back door." She squeezed his hand and went for the main entrance.

"Marion? Marion, are you okay?" Pax opened the glass door and looked for the person who had just activated the generator. At first, she didn't see anybody. The blast of dying trees coming from outside was even louder than the machines working inside the nursery. She focused on any sound that didn't belong to either of them. She was about to call out to Prince when a feeble moan drew her attention to a spot behind a column. She ran toward it, worried that someone was hurt.

"Pax! Thank Heavens, you're safe." Marion was sitting on the ground, cuddling a small terracotta vase as if it were a child. She looked at it and the realization of what she was doing hit her. She stood up uncertainly and put the vase on the bench behind her. "I saved them." She turned around, showing with a gesture of her hands what she was talking about.

"Is someone else with you?" Pax, now reassured that Marion wasn't injured, had to be sure they were alone.

"I came here to save them." Marion's voice had a dreamlike tone. Pax wasn't sure the woman was talking to her, although she had acknowledged her presence. "I had to decide," Marion continued.

A conflagration exploded outside. The glass walls rattled, showing orange and red clouds moving fast. For a moment, everything inside the nursery was tinted a bloody shade. Marion gasped and whispered something Pax couldn't hear.

"The farm needs my orchids to obtain funds." Marion was now looking straight at Pax, and she shivered despite the heat. "I did the right thing. My babies are our front..." The woman lowered her head and started crying.

Pax turned her back to the woman and ran toward the private bathroom at the end of the big room. She reached for the door and Prince almost fell on her.

"What took you so long?" he asked, gasping for air.

"The botanist lost it completely," Pax answered.

Prince looked at her and then grimaced in pain. "Help me clean this wound." He removed his shirt to show her what he was talking about.

Pax gasped at the cut on his back. "How—"

"I don't know how or when it happened." He went to the mirror and turned around to look at it.

"Is it painful?" Pax couldn't see exactly how big the wound was. Blood covered his back in dark stripes that were drying fast.

"It's not deep; I just can't reach it by myself."

"Here—it's going to be easier to clean under the shower." She directed him toward the shower stall. "There must be some water left. I'll look for the first aid kit." Pax moved in the cramped space of the bathroom, trying to avoid touching Prince. "Here it is." She held the white box in triumph only to be disappointed when she discovered most of the basic items were missing. "No gauze. No disinfectant. Just bandages."

"It's okay. Direct some water on the wound. That should be enough to remove the dirt. At least it's not going to get infected."

Prince let Pax close to him in the shower. She reached over him to turn on the faucet. She was so conscious of his body next to hers that every movement took forever. She was so embarrassed that, even in a situation like this, she couldn't think straight.

"I think we should hurry," he suggested with a gentle voice. One of his hands came to rest on her arm. The gesture was meant to reassure, but Pax lost control of the showerhead at his touch. A vicious jet of water hit his wound. Prince screamed in pain while doubling over her. They both ended on the wet floor.

"Pax! Oh my Heavens! What is he doing to you?"

Pax raised her head and saw Marion staring at her. She was covered in watered-down blood, helplessly sprawled under a half-naked man. Pax realized a second too late what the scene looked like.

"Help! I need help, immediately," Marion screamed in the emergency phone, while aiming a broom at Prince.

Pax was terrified by the implications of that situation. She opened her mouth to try to explain, but Prince beat her to it.

"Don't move any closer or I'll kill her." Prince's voice didn't waver while he circled Pax's throat with his arm. Then he whispered in her ear, "Make a scene. This is the only way out for you."

Pax struggled to free herself, to explain what was going on, but Prince restrained her mouth with his hand. She made the scene he wanted. Rage overwhelmed her and she started crying. Marion became more frantic, watching Pax being hurt by the worker.

"Don't do anything stupid." Marion lowered the broom, but didn't step back.

"Let me go, and she'll be safe," Prince announced his terms with studied coldness. At the same time, he caressed Pax's skin with one finger. "Don't say anything. They aren't going to believe you, anyway," he whispered while she was sobbing in despair.

"Release her and you're free to go," Marion said after a brief exchange with someone on the phone.

Pax wanted to say that it was a trap, but he bent his head to brush her skin. Then he was gone and she was being hugged by a trembling Marion. The back door slammed and the heat wave scorched her.

"Oh, sweetie, you're safe now. He can't do anything else to you. It's done. Everything is fine now." Marion was cradling Pax in her arms the same way she had cradled the vase.

Pax listened to what Marion was saying and felt sick.

"He won't get far. Caren is already on her way. They'll kill him. Don't worry. He won't be able to touch you again. I promise."

Marion was caressing her face in a maternal gesture. Pax's stomach lurched one more time and then she let it go, unable to bear the sound of Marion's voice any more. Two distinct gunshots echoed inside the dome.

CHAPTER 7

"Mistress, can I bring you some water?" Celeste had been fussing over Pax for hours.

"No, thanks. I'm not hungry. I'm not thirsty. I'm not cold. I'm not warm. I'm not tired." *I don't feel a thing.* Pax didn't say it, but anybody owning two neurons could see that easily. Several hours earlier, she had walked to the recreational facility in a state of daze, escorted by overly concerned guards who had kept asking if she was okay. The feeling of being trapped in a nightmare was still there. The aching in her heart was growing stronger. The presence of so many women, scared and wounded, made everything worse; the constant crying coming from the makeshift O.R., hastily erected in the backroom for the ones who couldn't be transported to the infirmary, was an assault to her fragile nerves.

"Is there anything else, *anything at all,* I can do for you?" Celeste patiently repeated one more time.

Something in the girl's tone and expression finally got Pax's attention; she raised her eyes to face her maid and then remembered how Celeste had covered for Prince in her room. She almost said it out loud, but the uproar in the cavernous room was such that nobody would have heard her, anyway. Pax realized who the one lacking grey matter in the brain was. "*Anything?*" she asked with her heart torn between hope and dread.

For a moment everything went still. Pax had the awful feeling that she had misjudged the girl's meaning. When the answer didn't come, she turned toward the wall to hide the flood of tears that threatened to fall.

Then, when she couldn't repress them any longer, a finger gently tapped on her shoulder, coaxing her to turn around.

"Anything." Celeste looked directly in her eyes when she answered.

"I need to know." Pax held her breath, still unable to trust Celeste with a spelled-out question.

"He's still alive. They took him to the infirmary."

The whole afternoon, Celeste had been going in and out of the recreational building; now Pax knew where she had been. She exhaled, her heart thumping wildly, her voice barely making it out of her lips. "He's alive." She thought for a moment, wanting to ask why Prince was being taken care of at the infirmary. It didn't seem right he had been accorded such privilege, but a woman strolled by them and lingered one moment too long for Pax to voice the question. And then, she was too relieved to hear he was being taken care of, anyway.

Celeste waited for the woman to move away and nodded at Pax. "They're waiting for your mothers to arrive. They want to make an example out of him." Her voice betrayed deeper emotions.

"Why?"

"Kidnapping, rape, and attempted murder of the future president's daughter. He couldn't be in any more trouble if he had killed you." Celeste poured her some tea; in the midst of such chaos, she had found time to collect what she needed to brew hot tea.

Pax accepted, looking at the tray, balanced on a rickety stool, with its cups and saucers, wondering at the whole situation and how the most normal things could become surreal. "He didn't do any of those things. And he would've never raped me." She didn't know how that certainty was engraved in her mind, but she knew it. "Nobody asked *me* what happened."

"And they are not going to. Caren is too scared your mothers are going to raise hell as soon as they see you. She doesn't know how to handle the situation. How to handle you. Mistress, you're supposedly in shock, and no doctor is going to visit you unless it's your family physician, authorized by your parents."

"They're going to execute him without a trial?" Pax was shocked and terrified.

"He's not a woman. Marion's testimony of how he was tearing you apart is more than enough. You were trying to escape and he was keeping you down. You were screaming and crying to be freed.

Your torn clothes were bathed in blood. He doesn't have a say." Celeste steadied Pax's hand.

"He never had…" The tea was spilling out of the cup and on her lap. Pax barely noticed; she nervously started tapping her family ring against the cup. She stood up, raising her voice, "Let's go find Linda. I'll ask the doctor to check me."

Celeste put a firm hand on her knee. "Once they realize you weren't touched, they'll rejoice at the news that Marion stopped the animal before he could brutalize you. Caren will be happy for you, and happier for her. Your *friend* is going to be killed anyway," the maid whispered and shook her head gently.

Pax sat down again. Several faces turned around to see what was going on. She saw sympathetic, stretched smiles on those faces and hated them. "I need to see him."

"Mistress, you look worse. Maybe I should accompany you to the infirmary." Celeste's voice had an authentic note of worry. She helped Pax to her feet and then carefully led her out of the room. Their slow procession was followed by dozens of eyes. The other women pitied her fate. She wanted to scream the truth.

"I heard he has been shot up with sedatives," Celeste explained as soon as they were out in the hallway.

Pax followed the girl outside of the recreational facility and toward the main building, barely noticing the destruction she was walking through. The air was breathable again, but the smell was pungent and made her eyes water. They stepped over debris that once had been the second floor bedrooms, now lying scattered across the ground. The gardens were now part of the hallway in several points. The night was eerily illuminated by lingering flames.

"The fire devastated the farm in a matter of minutes," Celeste said while her eyes wandered through the ruins.

Pax felt she should have been more sympathetic toward the tragedy that had just destroyed the community, but her heart could muster very little for them.

"Fortunately, the food poisoning kept most of the women working inside around the only place in the farm that was minimally touched by the flames: the sick bay across from the infirmary."

"How lucky for them." Pax forced the words out of her mouth. Not because she wished the women living and working there any harm; she was actually relieved to hear that, but her thoughts were somewhere else. "What about the men?" she asked after a long pause. "How many casualties among them?"

"I don't know," Celeste admitted with a sigh.

"Is anybody going to help them?"

"No."

Pax was suddenly aware of the fact that a few days before, she wouldn't have asked those questions. Knowing that men had died would have saddened her, but she wouldn't have thought twice about their fate.

"Here we are. Mistress, I have to ask you to be careful." Celeste regarded Pax with a long stare that wasn't deferential at all.

"I won't put you in danger," Pax responded in kind.

"No, you misunderstand me. I'm not worried for myself. It's you who has to be careful. Whatever you say, think twice before you do it." Celeste was a different person. She didn't even look so young anymore.

"Who are you really?" Pax asked.

Celeste opened the infirmary door without answering.

"Doctor Linda? Mistress Layan needs something to relax. She's still very agitated." The maid, who now even looked taller, strolled toward the center of the infirmary where the doctor and several nurses were taking care of patients.

"To be expected in her—" The doctor inserted a long pregnant pause. "—situation. Come here, Pax. I'll give you something to help your nerves." Linda gestured to follow her to a cubicle enclosed by a makeshift tent. "Every bed is taken, both here and in the sick bay. I can still give you some privacy, though, if you don't mind the crude accommodation."

"It's more than fine to me." Pax scanned the room to see where they were keeping Prince.

"Don't worry. You won't see him. I would never put you in a position where you have to confront your tormentor." Linda had seen her eyes wandering and drew her conclusions.

"Thanks, Doctor. The mistress is already too distraught as it is." Celeste gently led Pax inside the cubicle and closed the tent around them. "Play the victim; otherwise his sacrifice will be in vain." Celeste took her hand and squeezed it until it hurt.

"Why are you doing this?" Pax asked, while caressing her hand.

"I have *my* reasons." The girl stopped talking when the tent opened.

"This is a sedative. You probably need to sleep. This should be enough to make you sleep through the rest of the night. So when your moms are here tomorrow, you will feel much better." The doctor was smiling at her. Pax put the pill on her tongue and then brought the glass of water to her lips.

"Good, in a few minutes, you'll start feeling relaxed. It's better if you lie down here so I can check on you once in a while." Linda took Pax's vitals and then let her down on the gurney inside the cubicle. "Again, I'm sorry we don't have anything better to offer you now. Celeste, if you don't have anything else to do, I could use some help here."

"My main obligations are toward Mistress Layan. I can stay as long as she stays."

Pax was left alone in the sterilized coldness of the cubicle and she wondered if maybe gulping down the sedative wasn't such a bad idea. She eventually spat it out. She closed her eyes in case the doctor or one of the nurses came to check if she was already asleep. She could hear Celeste's voice coming from somewhere in the room, but her words drowned in a sea of humming noises. Several minutes passed, punctuated by the soft crying coming from the other tented cubicles.

"Celeste, it doesn't help me to be here if I can't see him," Pax snarled low as soon as the maid came back to check on her.

"He isn't here at the moment. Linda is removing the bullets from him. I can't do anything while they're closed inside the O.R."

"What bullets?" Pax was already halfway through the cubicle when Celeste forcefully pulled her back on the gurney. "You told me he had been sedated."

"That's all I knew. It seems that he gave them hell before the sedative put him down. He was trying to reach the wall. Outside the wall, there is a system of caves where he could have escaped for good. They couldn't let him. Caren gave the order to shoot him."

"Did they hurt him badly?" Pax was imagining Prince being hunted like an animal. *He was only a man*, Maurice would have said in any other situation. But Pax hoped her mom wouldn't justify such measures. For some reason it was important to her that her mothers weren't like these women at the farm. Or so many other women in the world.

"I don't know. I will tell you as soon as the doctor comes out of the O.R."

"I need to know your reasons." Pax wasn't one to question gifts when they were freely given, but now nothing seemed right. She had been questioning herself as well.

"Same reason you have." Celeste said it as if she were throwing a gauntlet.

Pax realized it had taken a huge leap of faith for the girl to help her and Prince. In doing so, Celeste had put herself on the line worse than Pax. She was a senator's daughter, after all. Celeste was just a fathered woman. "I owe you an apology—"

"How is the situation here?" Caren's voice echoed in the room outside the tent.

"I'm done with the fugitive. He was only grazed by two bullets. We were lucky the sedative started working before a third one found a vital organ. He'll be up and about in no time. Tomorrow you'll have him ready for the show," Linda answered from a far corner.

"I heard that Mistress Layan came here."

"Yes, she was very tense and needed to relax. She's sleeping now. Celeste?" Linda's voice grew louder as she came closer to the cubicle. Pax closed her eyes immediately.

"I'm here with her. She's sound asleep." Celeste moved the tent aside to let them know she had heard the conversation. She lowered her voice so that the other two women would follow her example.

"Did she say anything to you?" Caren asked Celeste, who had closed the tent behind her. Pax strained her ears to follow the conversation. Thankfully, the women weren't minding the volume of their voices.

"Not a lot."

"Let's hope that executing the bastard is going to placate the senator. I had a terrifying conversation with her a few minutes ago. Our farm could be closed after this disaster. First, the slaves try to poison us, then set the place on fire, and finally, a fugitive attacks her daughter. Our only card is to have this dealt with without any publicity. We can't afford an official investigation, or a public hearing. " Caren was seriously concerned and kept raising her voice.

"We don't want another Tarin, for sure." Linda sounded shaken.

"Heavens, no! I don't want to consider the extent of destruction the Priestess would ask for to cover up her involvement with our farm. We don't have a tenth of the resources they had in Tarin. And everybody knows what happened there. If the truth of what we do here comes out, we don't have a chance. That damned slave must be our scapegoat." Caren's voice was crazy with worry.

Pax heard the woman's words and felt a fury building inside her, even though she didn't have a clue of what Caren was talking about.

"*And* we also don't want anyone meddling with the way *things* are run here," Linda added.

Pax shivered at the doctor's tone of voice.

"Let's hope that giving the Layans what they want is going to stop further questions about our farm. Again, we really don't want another Tarin." Lauren's voice had joined from a distance.

"Is he presentable?" Lauren asked.

"He'll be. There are old scars on his hands and neck that can't be covered, but for the rest of the body, clothes will suffice. His face is still a mess. I applied some salve to reduce the swelling." Linda's voice was all over the place.

"Good enough. He has to look fit and in perfect health. The Layans must think of him as a savage who wanted to kill their daughter, not a scared, beaten pup in need of care," Caren spoke again and her words chilled Pax to the core.

She realized nobody in that room cared if Prince had wanted to rape her or not. Marion's tale had given them the perfect opportunity to cover whatever the fire threatened to expose. *What is really going on here?*

"Don't worry; the senator will be angry enough to forget how liberal she pretends to be." Lauren came close to the tent.

"Mistress is sleeping." Pax saw Celeste's shadow hovering before the curtain.

"How strong was the sedative you gave her?" Lauren pushed Celeste inside the cubicle.

Pax tried to relax her muscles and slowed her breathing.

"Strong enough to make her sleep several hours. Why?" The doctor came inside the tent.

"You are going to wake her up. I think it's better if you leave," Celeste said.

"I think it would be better if she were unconscious until tomorrow. A stronger dose is what she needs." Lauren ignored Celeste. She came even closer to touch Pax's face. "Yes, disorientation from anesthesia and a little bit of physical pain when she wakes up, and she's going to support whatever we say." Then she added, talking to Celeste, "Never forget your place in this world."

"Marion could have found them a few minutes later—" Caren said with a sigh.

Pax almost gasped; Caren was actually complaining that Prince hadn't had enough time to do her any harm.

"How can you even think something like that? The poor girl was being held captive by a man, for Heavens' sake. I can't even imagine what kind of horror she lived through, even if for a few minutes," Linda said. "Although, having dealt with this worker... I must say I'd never thought him capable of what you say he did." She paused for a moment. "Really hard to believe—"

"Did I or didn't I tell you over and over again that they're nothing more than animals? And you still doubt?" Lauren interjected.

Pax was starting to be terrified by the way things were settling.

"Anyway, you aren't touching her to corroborate your story. There is no need to fabricate proof." The doctor put one hand on Pax's shoulder.

"We need the senator and her lovely wife to be completely taken by their daughter's tragedy. We can't afford to have them poking around. They weren't supposed to visit now, of all times." Caren got in the discussion.

"Marion's words will suffice. Celeste, pull that chair out and sit by her."

"Linda, you're being stupid," Caren said.

"Yes, Doctor, you should reconsider your position," Lauren added.

Pax heard the curtain being moved and steps moving away from the tent.

"Celeste, whatever happens, do not move from her side." The doctor's words came after a long moment of silence.

"I won't," Celeste answered and then, after a few seconds, whispered in Pax's ear, "You can open your eyes now."

"Do you know what happens here?" Pax asked right away in the lowest voice she could manage. Her heart was racing as if she were running.

"I do," Celeste answered.

Pax begged Celeste to tell her several times, but the girl wouldn't budge. A commotion of loud voices interrupted their conversation. The maid went to check, leaving Pax alone with her thoughts.

"What is it now?" Linda asked, worried.

"There're three women trapped under what remains of the stables," someone answered.

"I'm coming." The doctor's hurried steps echoed outside the infirmary.

"Celeste, see if I can come out of here. I want to see him," Pax hissed under her breath at the maid's shadow outside the tent. She swung off the uncomfortable, makeshift bed ready to sneak in the operating room.

"What are you doing here?" Celeste's voice was upset.

Pax immediately lay back on the gurney.

"Move away and let me finish this," Lauren said.

"What—" Celeste yelled.

Pax felt it before Celeste could finish her sentence. The shock of being punctured by a needle made her open her eyes wide and sit straight up. A cold liquid percolated inside her veins.

"Did I wake you up, Mistress? Oh, I'm so sorry. Don't worry though, you're going to sleep better than ever in a few minutes." Lauren was looking down at Pax with a cold gleam in her eyes.

75

"Her mothers are going to destroy you for this," Celeste hissed from the corner and went to caress Pax's hand.

Lauren struck the girl with full force. Celeste screamed and Lauren hit her again. "I told you to remember your place. Now shut up before I have to silence you for good."

"You're making a huge mistake." Pax was shaking uncontrollably. "I'll tell my moms." Her eyes were tearing and her voice sounded far away from her mouth.

"The beauty of the anesthesia I just used on you is that you won't remember what happened right before I injected you. You'll just remember you took the sedative the doctor gave you." Lauren spoke calmly while Celeste was crying and Pax's head was spinning.

Reality went black and soundless in a matter of seconds. The darkest night engulfed Pax's mind.

CHAPTER 8

"Pax! Honey!"

Pax woke at Claudine's cooing words. Her mother's voice was a feeble sound, trying to emerge from a sea of noise. Loud explosions echoed inside her head. "What's…?" The question never left her mouth.

"I'm going to kill the bastard who did this to you with my bare hands." Maurice was pacing around the bed.

In her daughter's eyes, she looked more like a tiger than a woman.

"We thought she was safe here. We would have never, ever, left her in your hands—" Claudine's voice choked and she couldn't finish.

"Is she in pain? Are you, sweetie? Where is the doctor?" Maurice was almost yelling.

Somewhere outside the room, sirens and screams were fighting for supremacy for which one was the loudest.

"The generator building exploded. She was called there to see to the wounded, but she is coming as soon as possible." Caren was standing by a corner, trying her best to be out of Maurice's way. She was also nervously shooting glances at the window.

"Moms?" Pax croaked and found talking rather painful. She gingerly touched her face and winced.

"Pax! Look at me, pumpkin." Claudine was now crying.

Pax wasn't sure her mother was the only one crying beside her bed. She could hear others crying, but they sounded far away.

"Don't scare her." Maurice put a hand on her wife's shoulder to calm her down. She had lowered her voice, but Pax had heard her, and now, she was scared.

"You're right, but I can't bear to see what—" Again, Claudine couldn't finish the sentence.

Pax stirred against her mother's gentle touch. Pain accompanied every movement.

"Pax? Can you hear me?" Maurice's hands joined Claudine's on their daughter. They both caressed her as they had when she was younger.

"Moms?" Pax felt disoriented. Maybe she was still sleeping, but her mothers were real, and so was the pain, growing in intensity. And there was a terrifying noise that didn't belong to the room.

"Please speak to us, love," Claudine asked softly while kissing Pax's hands.

"I feel dizzy," Pax said.

"Maybe she needs to rest some more?" Caren proposed.

"Is that what the doctor prescribed?" Maurice asked with a snarl. Caren didn't even try to answer.

"How could you put our daughter in the same room with her attacker?" Claudine was crying again, although she was holding back her sobs. Maurice touched her slightly on the shoulder.

"Don't you have separate facilities for the men?" Maurice turned to look directly at Caren. "Don't you have a penitentiary infirmary where you keep your wounded criminals?" Her tone was frosty, but the hand caressing Pax was shaking.

"We don't have that kind of money. And he was sedated," Caren answered, carefully measuring her words.

"But he's considered dangerous!" Claudine was outraged by her words. "Were you looking for this to happen?" Despite the outside noise, Claudine's words hung in the air with frightful clarity.

Pax witnessed the whole conversation in a haze; her eyes felt heavy, and sounds offended her ears. She looked at the women staring at each other. Her mothers were focused on finding someone to blame, and Caren was there. Pax was curious about Caren's answer to Claudine's accusation. Meanwhile, Doctor Linda had entered the room. Claudine and Maurice turned around to meet her.

"Nice meeting you, Senator, Milady." The doctor came closer to shake hands with the Layans. When she saw Pax, she gasped. "What happened to her?" she asked Caren.

"While the room was unguarded, the slave attacked her again," Caren informed Linda.

Pax felt the pain in her body flare up. The skin on her face stretched as she tried to say something.

"But how?" Linda was immediately silenced by a simple glance from a nervous chief-in-command.

"Yes, how exactly did that happen?" Maurice asked.

"As I told you, he wasn't as sedated as we thought," Caren answered and then turned toward Linda. "Celeste is missing, along with the worker."

The news had the effect of a cold shower on Pax. She couldn't believe what Caren was saying. She wanted to scream that it was a lie, but everybody talked at the same time. Pax's words went unheard, drowned under an onslaught of recriminations. Claudine caressed her daughter's hand and asked everybody to shut up.

"Pumpkin, I'm here. Mom's here," Claudine whispered in Pax's ear while cradling her.

"Go outside to talk about what happened. Don't you see that it's distressing her?" Maurice scolded Caren as she regained some composure.

"I'm sorry. It wasn't my intention." She didn't leave the safety of her corner, though.

"Baby, don't be afraid. We're here now." Claudine kept stroking Pax's hand to calm her trembling.

"Who fixed the cuts on her face?" Linda had enough of the bickering and went to assess the situation of her patient. She checked the bandages covering Pax's face and cursed softly. She removed one of them and went to pick up the disinfectant bottle. Pax cringed and moaned. It was enough for the two distressed mothers to start ranting again.

"Lauren found her like that. She brought her in this room, gave her the first aid, and then left to pursue the fugitive." Caren provided the information promptly. She wasn't paying attention to the Layans anymore. She was focused on the view from the window and looked rather worried. Claudine and Maurice looked incensed by her apparent lack of interest in Pax's predicament.

"Lucky for her that Lauren was around," the doctor commented deadpan.

"Is anything broken?" Claudine clutched Maurice's hands, bracing for the answer.

"No, fortunately not. It looks worse than it is. I'm going to rub some cream on her skin. That will take care of the swelling." The doctor disinfected a cut on Pax's right cheek and then left again. She came back a few moments later and spread a minty ointment on Pax's face. The relief was immediate. Pax moaned softly and closed her eyes.

"Your eyelids are swollen," the doctor said as an afterthought.

"Is there anything strange in that?" Claudine asked.

"She was beaten," Caren turned around to answer.

"Can I do something else for you?" Doctor Linda looked straight at Pax.

"I don't know; my head is killing me," Pax answered slowly.

The noise level in the room was becoming unbearable.

"You shouldn't be so sluggish," the doctor said.

"Lauren gave her a painkiller." Caren incinerated the doctor with a look, but then a loud crash resonated outside the room and she turned to the window.

"Or more likely three," Linda commented under her breath.

"Is it normal that she is still so... sleepy?" Maurice asked, leaning closer to the doctor.

"I'm sure it's pretty normal, given the circumstances." Linda didn't elaborate her statement.

"My head is splitting in half," Pax complained again.

"Do something! Don't you see she's suffering?" Maurice commanded the doctor. She had never been able to cope with Pax's pain. Normally, Claudine took care of that rather efficiently.

"I think is better if she doesn't take anything right now," Linda said, earning Caren's interest.

"Is there something you are not saying?" Claudine asked, raising her voice enough to let them know they better have a good answer.

"She was already treated with strong painkillers during the night. I don't want to risk an o—" Linda didn't finish the sentence. She looked at Caren, who had made a sound between choking and coughing. "—A reaction of any kind." Linda hurried to say. "She'll feel better soon," she added, before answering her beeping cell phone.

"News from the generator building?" Caren asked as soon as Linda closed the phone.

"Yes. Unfortunately, I have to leave again. There's a woman trapped under a fallen archway. I'll have to amputate both of her legs to save her. Caren, I need you to come with me." Linda wiped some sweat from her forehead, gave the Layans a few recommendations for Pax and then left.

"I'll be back as soon as possible," Caren said, looking rather uncomfortable, and followed the doctor outside.

"*Mothers*, when did you arrive?" Pax tried to use the mocking tone that made both Maurice and Claudine equally annoyed. She didn't want them to be so scared for her. The effect she was looking for was effectively killed by the sound of her voice. Too slow and barely understandable.

"Not soon enough, *dear daughter*." Maurice understood what Pax was up to and tried to answer in kind.

Claudine turned around to hide another sob. Pax thought it would have been nice to feel carefree and happy again. She managed to open her eyes completely and saw they were finally alone.

"Moms, none of what they said to you is true." She made an effort to enunciate every word.

Her mothers reacted immediately. "What do you mean?" Maurice stood up. When she was agitated, she couldn't sit down.

"You have to promise to believe what I'm going to say. And that you're not going to be mad at me."

"You know we believe you, sweetie. And why should we be angry at you? You didn't do anything to deserve this!" Claudine patiently stroked her daughter's hand.

"Of course. You can say anything to us. You know that." Maurice sat down again to show her unconditional support. "So, what is it, honey?" She had lowered her voice to a sweet whisper, as if she was speaking to a little child. Maurice subdued was almost scary. It didn't help that the outside world seemed as if it would collapse at any moment.

Pax gathered the necessary courage to tell her mothers what had happened, and she intended to tell them the whole truth. She opened her mouth to start what was going to be a very long and complicated tale, when a contrite-looking Marion burst into the room.

"Oh dear child, I don't know how to tell you this—"

The botanist realized Pax wasn't alone and briefly introduced herself to Maurice and Claudine. The Layans weren't grateful for the interruption, and that froze her tongue.

"What is it, Marion?" Pax asked gently, hoping that whatever the problem was, the woman, if treated politely, would leave soon.

"A tragedy," Marion's finally said, after a moment of awkward silence.

Her words had the effect of waking Pax completely. Her head cleared suddenly, and she sat straight against the headboard. Even her eyes felt less swollen. Claudine fussed about her sudden movements, but Pax couldn't hear her mother talking. She only had one thought piercing through her mind like a hot dagger. "He—"

"Yes, the worker attacked another woman." Marion nodded and went to lay a hand on her leg in a maternal gesture of comfort.

Pax shuddered at the touch and looked at Marion, utterly confused by her words.

"Pax, the man who attacked you… he killed Celeste." The woman let it out between sobs she couldn't control.

Pax started screaming that it wasn't true. Three women hovered around the bed to assist her. "No! You're lying!" she cried, trying to get up. Two firm hands pushed her down on the mattress. She barely heard someone telling her to calm down.

"I know, I know. It's impossible to believe that our dear, sweet Celeste is dead. I know." Marion's voice was offensive. The incessant wailing coming from somewhere outside covered their voices and was offensive.

"No, it can't be. He hasn't killed her." Pax was now angry, and every caress she received from Marion was as painful as a slap on her face. She cringed and tried to pull away from her touch. Claudine and Maurice kept talking in turns about the necessity to lie down and relax. She ignored them.

"Caren and Lauren will bring him to justice, you'll see. Celeste will be avenged," the botanist said with a conviction that bordered on hysteria.

"I'll call immediately for reinforcements." Maurice's face was a mask. Pax knew that expression her mother was wearing would hide her emotions. She was set on solving the situation. "The sooner this criminal is brought to justice, the sooner we can leave this place."

"Mom will help," Claudine told Pax with a gentle nudge.

"Don't worry, pumpkin. You won't be forced to stay here any longer than necessary." Maurice accompanied her words with a hand on her daughter's shoulder.

"No, you don't understand. Listen to me. It's not what you think. Please!" Pax was so anxious to make her mothers understand that she was now shaking from head to toe.

"Did you have to come and break the news like that?" Claudine yelled toward the other woman, while Maurice went outside to speak on the phone.

Pax was yelling so loudly she was drowning out all other sounds.

"I had to tell her," Marion said, fighting to be heard but not daring to raise her voice against Claudine.

"No, you should have waited and asked us if it was the right thing to do." Claudine was practically screaming on top of Pax's voice.

"Mom! Stop talking and listen to me."

Claudine turned around to look at her daughter as Maurice came back inside. Marion was staring at the three of them, unsure of what the wisest thing to do was.

"Help! We need help now!" Pax's pleas were interrupted abruptly by someone shouting from outside. Marion went to lean out of the window and have a look at what was happening.

"We need hands!" someone yelled.

Marion nodded in acknowledgment.

"The recreational center is collapsing; we need help to move the debris before it's too late!" The voice was now louder. Marion turned inside to look at Maurice.

"We have to do something. There are a lot of women in there." Marion's voice broke.

"I called for help. It'll be here in less than an hour." Maurice came closer to the window and answered directly to the woman outside.

"We don't have an hour! Please, hurry! Please—" A loud crash covered the woman's words.

"The south wall of the recreational center has just fallen," Marion said.

Maurice leaned over the windowsill and gasped.

"They need help now." Marion looked at Maurice and Claudine and then bolted out.

"I can't stay here without doing anything." Maurice followed Marion with an apologetic look at her daughter.

"Mom, please don't leave. I need to talk to you," Pax cried.

She saw Maurice disappearing behind the door and turned her eyes on Claudine. Her mother was fighting the impulse to stay. A few seconds later, a second crash echoed inside the room. This one was louder than the first. Screaming and crying followed immediately. Claudine looked outside and her eyes widened in horror.

"Mom, you must stay. It's important," Pax said, but her mother was already walking toward the door. "Mom, please, just five minutes. I promise it won't take longer, and then you can go."

"Honey, we can talk later. I'm sure that whatever it is, it can wait. I'm sorry, but I must see what I can do for them." Claudine looked one more time at Pax and then ran outside.

Pax didn't know what to do other than collapsing on the bed and letting out all the tears left in her eyes. She couldn't move without someone else's help, and her head was swaying as if she were riding waves. She wished she could pass out. Time didn't fly while she was conscious. She felt powerless. Nobody appeared at the threshold of her room to bring good news, bad news, or any news at all. Only the terrible sounds from outside kept her company. Finally, she summoned enough strength to raise her body from the bed. She tried to lower her legs on the floor and found that she was still dizzy.

She waited a few minutes until the alignment of floor and walls was right again. Then she pushed down and tested her lower body. Pax reached for the wall with her hands and steadied herself. Several tentative steps later, she was able to take a glance at the scene outside the window. It was still day, she realized, disconcerted that probably only a mere half an hour had passed since her mothers had left her. There were dark clouds covering the blue sky. The stench of burnt rubble was full of chemicals. Her nose became painfully aware of that. Once her brain realized it, her lungs refused to inhale any of it. She fought for air for several seconds; then she stopped arguing with her body and an eerie silence wrapped her thoughts.

"Breathe, damn it." Two strong hands were shaking her. "Breathe."

"Prince?" A steady stream of oxygen brought back her obstructed vision. Two dark eyes were staring unblinkingly at hers. "It's you." A surge of happiness possessed her and the feeling proved too heavy for her body to bear. She staggered in his arms and he carefully supported her. A shiver shook through her at the thought that his presence could easily be a figment of her imagination. She leaned against his chest and breathed him in to make sure he was real. "You're here." Her hand found his heart and she cried and laughed at the same time.

"Are you well?" Prince asked. He raised her chin with one gentle finger and winced.

"I'm not that ugly," she said, trying to smile for him.

"You look like me," he answered.

Pax felt the inexplicable urge to laugh again, but then she saw him. "Don't look at me that way." She didn't want him to be worried.

"Is there anything—" he started to say, but she caressed his hand with slightly shaking fingers and gestured him to look outside.

"Yes, there is. Run away as fast as you can. You shouldn't have come."

"I couldn't leave without seeing you one last time." Prince's words had a finality that left Pax breathless. "I simply couldn't," he repeated when she shook her head.

She wanted to say so many things her head hurt. "They're saying you killed Celeste. You really must disappear."

"I didn't kill Celeste!"

"I know you didn't. They are framing you to hide something from my mothers." Pax looked at him, and she saw the relief in his face at hearing her words. "Go!" she yelled, panic swelling in her chest when Claudine's familiar voice echoed from the hallway.

Prince's head snapped toward the hallway and then he ran toward the window. Someone from outside saw his silhouette standing in her room and started screaming.

Pax looked around to see if there was any way out for him, but he was trapped. "Prince?" she called his name and for the second time she wished she could say so much more to him.

"Sooner or later it was bound to happen," he said. His voice much calmer now, almost unnaturally calm, when he walked back to her. "But there is something I must do—"

Prince lowered his head until his mouth was a breath away from hers. He heard the steps coming closer, but didn't hurry his movements. He simply hovered there, as if nothing else mattered. Pax's heart stopped beating and she waited for him. Prince closed the gap between them and let his lips brush hers. A subtle pressure from his part and Pax's lips opened to receive him. For a moment, she breathed from his mouth. A second later, all hell broke loose.

"Pax!" Claudine screamed, and she lunged from across the room. "I won't let you finish what you started. Move away from her!" She attacked Prince before Pax could say anything. "I will protect my daughter with my life, if I have to. Do you understand me?" She started pummeling him with fists and kicks.

Prince, at first, didn't defend himself. "It's not what you think. I'd never lay a hand on her," he said several times while Claudine was yelling at him. Finally, when her fist hit his chest for the tenth time, he reacted automatically. Pax saw him standing in all his height to strike back.

"Stop!" she cried.

Prince froze with his fist hovering over Claudine's face.

"Stop," she repeated, while trying to put her body between Prince and her mother. She looked back at Prince and the expression on his face made her shiver. He looked as if she had hit him hard.

"I'm no assassin. I'd never hurt anybody." Prince's arms fell down his side.

"I never doubted it," Pax whispered to him, but not soft enough that her mother couldn't catch the exchange between the two.

"What is going on here?" Claudine's voice betrayed her confusion. "I am asking you what is going on! Pax, please, tell me why you are talking to that man?" She looked at her daughter for answers and shivered.

Pax opened her mouth to answer her mother, but dark spots filled her vision and, right on cue, her legs buckled under her. Prince scooped up Pax gently and put her back on the bed.

"I'm fine," Pax answered Prince, who was still cradling her against his chest. She reveled in his warmth for a few seconds before remembering her mother was in the room. She turned around and saw her staring back. "Mom—" She was cut short by the look on her mother's face. For a moment, she saw herself with her mother's eyes, leaning against a man, not a bit afraid of being in his arms. Even worse, she didn't seem disgusted by his touch.

"Move. Away. From. Her," Claudine commanded as soon as her voice came back.

Prince executed her order immediately. But Pax didn't run toward her right away as she ought to. Instead, she remained on the bed, beside him. He towered over her in a protective manner.

"Pax, what's happening?" Claudine's voice was a tormented shrill.

"What I have been trying to tell you all along," Pax said.

"And what is it?" Angry tears were running down Claudine's face.

"Prince didn't do anything to me." Pax was surprised that her voice had become steadier.

Claudine gasped, "Are you defending a *man*? And why are you calling this... slave by his name?"

"He doesn't need to be defended." Pax knew she was cutting her mother's heart into a thousand pieces. She felt her own heart bleeding at the pain she was inflicting to one of the people she loved the most, but she couldn't help adding, "He's innocent."

"Pax, have you gone insane? This man has killed your maid." Claudine looked at her daughter, but she never acknowledged Prince's presence beside her.

Pax moved her head from side to side, negating the accusation. "He's the victim here," she answered before Prince would say something for himself.

"Sweetie, you are suffering from severe shock. You were brutally attacked," Claudine said.

Pax wanted to cry in frustration. She knew her mother simply couldn't see the truth. She would have believed any farfetched explanation. Anything but what her eyes were showing her.

"*This* slave left you for dead. He—" Claudine couldn't say the words. "You are traumatized. But we've already called your doctor, and whatever happened to you... Cassandra is going to heal you. Caren told us that they found you covered in blood, but everything can be fixed. *Everything.* You don't have to feel this way because he harmed you. You'll forget he even touched you." She came close to Pax and reached for her hands.

Pax gently warded her off. "He's never touched me without my consent," she said with a tone that left no doubt.

Claudine let out a breath of relief. Pax watched as millions of thoughts passed through her mother's mind. *This animal hasn't abused my daughter, my precious, gifted daughter.* Then she saw the exact moment when Claudine understood the meaning of her words. Her mother stiffened, disgusted by the thought. *The slave hasn't touched her without her consent.*

"What did you let him *do* to you?" Claudine became pale and sat down on a chair.

"I... nothing!" Pax hastily answered. She felt embarrassed at the mere thought she was having that conversation with her mother. The look on Claudine's face was more eloquent than a thousand words. Pax's stomach contracted, leaving her with a sour taste in her mouth.

"Nothing happened," Prince answered before Claudine could ask again.

"Don't you dare talk to me!" Claudine turned to face only her daughter. A pure breed never talked directly to a worker. Names changed, but a worker was still a slave. "Pax, is it true?"

"I give you my word—" Prince put a hand on Pax's shoulders, but Claudine yanked her from him with a rage that left even Pax speechless.

"Your word is worth nothing. Don't you ever touch her again," Claudine spat out, forgetting she was addressing the man, while furiously hugging her daughter.

"Mom, please listen to me. He could've beaten us and left us injured, or worse. But he hasn't." She tried to reason with her, but at the same time, she wanted Prince free and miles away from that room. "Prince, leave and don't turn back." She looked at him, hoping he could see in her eyes how much she wanted him alive and well.

"I can't leave you like this," he said.

"Please, do it for me." Pax wanted to run into his arms more than anything else, but Claudine was holding her so tight that even talking was a struggle.

"It's already too late," Prince said and Pax looked at him, wondering what he meant. Then the noise of loud steps became impossible to ignore.

"Help! I need help!" Claudine started screaming, never releasing Pax, who was now straining to reach for Prince.

"There is nothing you can do." Prince wasn't even trying to escape. He just had eyes for her.

"Claudine!" Maurice burst inside the room followed by Caren, Lauren, and several other women. Caren aimed her gun at Prince. Pax realized Caren was waiting for him to move, giving her the reason she needed to kill him right there and then.

Prince looked at Pax one last time, "We never had a chance in this world." And he moved ever so slowly toward her.

Caren smiled and raised her gun, centered on his heart, and moved her finger to press the trigger. Prince closed his eyes and looked at peace with the universe. Pax screamed and escaped Claudine's tight embrace. Maurice, who was staring at the scene from the door, saw Pax putting herself on the receiving end of the bullet and screamed even louder than her daughter. Without thinking, Maurice pushed Caren's hand away. The gun fired. Chaos descended in the room.

"Why did you stop me?" Caren yelled at Maurice, who was now looking aghast and utterly speechless.

Pax was firmly embraced in Prince's arms and she was talking to him in a soothing voice. Claudine was crying desperately, asking Pax to move aside.

"I won't move," Pax answered without even turning her head to confront the rest of the room.

"Don't do this," Prince whispered.

Maurice looked at him and then at her daughter again.

"No, I won't let them kill you for something you never did." Pax hugged him closer. She hated that her voice shook and that her arms were trembling. And she hated more than anything else the disbelief showing on her mothers' faces. Soon, they would understand what she had in mind.

"Pax!" Claudine reached out to touch Pax. She moved back, taking Prince with her. Maurice walked toward Claudine and took her hand. Claudine shook her head at the silent question on Maurice's mouth. Then she simply sagged on the bed behind her.

"Pax, please calm down, breathe, and think of what you are doing," Maurice finally said, slowly enunciating every word. Claudine let out a sob and then covered her face.

"Mistress, I promise he'll have a trial if you move aside and let us take charge of him." Caren spoke and the room fell instantly silent.

Lauren gaped at her with a puzzled look, without lowering the gun she was still aiming at Prince.

"Pax, pumpkin, listen to her. I'll personally supervise the process," Maurice added, with an uncertain voice.

Pax had to lower her eyes. "Mom—" She wanted to be reassured she could trust her mother's words, but couldn't finish the sentence. She was shocked by the realization that when it came to Prince's life, she didn't trust anybody. Not even her mothers, whom she worshipped.

"Yes, the slave will be fairly judged." Lauren seized the moment and nodded at Caren. Then she slowly lowered her arm and reached for something in her back pocket. She went for Pax with what should have been a reassuring smile and walked around Prince to get hold of him with the handcuffs dangling from her hand.

Pax didn't let her touch him. She heard herself emitting a sound close to a low snarl and moved to shield Prince from Lauren. "Don't even think about it," she said to Lauren and then looked around to face everybody.

"Pax, I know you are confused, but try to be reasonable. It's for the best." Maurice was already moving toward the unstable trio. "The only chance this worker has to remain alive is to have a trial. There is no other way around it. You must understand that you are further compromising his situation." She was one step away from her daughter and had one hand outstretched toward her arm.

"She's right," Prince whispered in Pax's ears.

She shook her head.

"You were worth it." He brushed her neck and suddenly stepped back, putting distance between their bodies. He was immediately flanked by Lauren and Caren.

"No!" Pax screamed. In the blink of an eye, Maurice was holding her by the arm, and Lauren had taken one of Prince's hands behind his back to secure it. A silvery sparkle in Lauren's hand caught her attention, and then she saw Caren had raised her gun again at the very last moment.

"Nooooooo!" Pax jerked out of her mother's hold and hit Lauren with all her strength, causing the woman to lose her balance. The sound of a metallic object falling on the floor clanged loudly. Before anybody else could do anything, Pax retrieved a small, but sharp, knife and pointed it at Lauren. "Why do you want him dead so badly?" She made a tremendous effort to speak and be understood. It was of vital importance to her that her mothers would see with their own eyes that things weren't exactly how they looked at first glance. "See? He would've never reached any trial." If she'd had any doubt before, now she knew. Lauren was going to provoke Prince, giving Caren a legitimate excuse to shoot him. In the following chaos, nobody would have doubted the chief-in-command had acted promptly to save Pax's life. And it would have worked if she hadn't seen the knife.

Pax shivered, and suddenly, her legs weren't cooperating. Prince had been close to being killed before her eyes. Thoughts that she could have turned around a second later stormed her mind. The light in the room could have been dimmer and she could have missed the sparkle of the blade. Her mother could have held her in place. Any number of different actions would have ended with his death as result.

"I can't trust you anymore," she said to her mothers. The pain she was inflicting on them was nothing compared to the horror of being sure they would have seen to Prince's death, anyway.

Claudine gasped and Maurice's eyes filled with tears. "Don't do anything you'll regret." Maurice's voice was broken.

"I won't," Pax answered back.

A sense of calm descended on her and gave her the strength to keep talking. "We're leaving now. Don't follow us. If you do, you'll have to shoot me first." She took a long breath, hating herself for using her mothers' unconditional love that way. She started walking toward the door.

"Are you sure you want to do this?" Prince asked.

"Yes."

She didn't slow down, but at the very last moment, before leaving the room, she stopped and turned around. "Never forget I love you." She didn't wait for her mothers to say anything back.

CHAPTER 9

"What do you think happened to Celeste?" Pax asked from her makeshift bed on the ground.

"From what you told me, I think she was silenced because she threatened to talk to your mothers." Prince shrugged his shoulders while trying to revive the small fire he had managed to produce out of dry weeds and anemic pieces of wood.

Pax nodded; she had meant to ask something else entirely, but she wasn't sure she was ready to know what had happened to the girl. "I was mean to her." She couldn't help but feel guilty about Celeste.

Prince looked at her, understanding donned his tired face, and he turned toward the fire again. The night was cold and the terrain highly uncomfortable. They had walked for several hours, leaving the farm, and life as they knew it, firmly behind them. Pax had stumbled one time too many and Prince had decided to stop where they were and rest—exhausted and hungry, but free. Since everybody was looking for them in the caves, Prince had decided to risk it and stay out in the desert. He had told her there were a few oases scattered along the endless expanse of sand, but they hadn't found one yet. Only bushes spread along the dunes, ghostly, silvery skeletons hiding scurrying rodents.

Pax noticed the care Prince took to contain the small fire and the way he kept looking over his shoulders. "You're worried someone is going to see us," she said, and then when he didn't deny it, she added, "Put it out."

"You're too cold."

"I'll be fine." Pax moved closer to him.

"I think you're in shock." Prince made her lean against him and caressed her arms slowly.

"I'll be fine," Pax repeated softly. She felt some peace in Prince's warmth, and for a few minutes, she was contented to look lazily at the flames. But it didn't last. The thought of Celeste reemerged, and she felt awful again. Pax straightened up and turned to face Prince. "I wish I had acted differently." She hugged her legs and closed her body in a tight ball, resting her chin on top of her knees. Images of Celeste, lying dead somewhere, filled her mind. All of a sudden, she felt chilled, and although she tried, she couldn't stop trembling.

"Come here." Prince enclosed her in his arms and stroked her.

"It's nothing."

"I can hear your teeth rattling. I'll gather some more wood for the fire." He went scanning the dark surroundings.

Pax put her hands over the fire, but the chill was seeping to her bones. *Maybe I'm in shock. I shouldn't feel so cold. Is it supposed to be freezing at night in the desert? I don't know... Where are you?* She tried to remember how far away the circle of desert shrubs they had passed earlier was. She couldn't see Prince and a sense of despair possessed her. "Don't leave me alone, please." She hadn't meant to say it out loud, but he heard her and was by her side in a moment.

"What do you need?" he asked, hovering over the fire.

"Nothing. Stay here with me for a while, please." She was fighting the urge to cry and losing the battle.

"Sure." Prince scooped Pax up and cradled her on his lap, covering her like a blanket.

"What now?" Pax asked after a long silence.

"I don't know. I've never been free before," Prince answered. His hand traveled slowly from her shoulder to her face, coming to rest on her head, his fingers slowly unraveling a lock of tangled hair. "I've been commanded all my life." When he was done, he ran his hand through it and then placed the long lock over her shoulder and uncovered her ear. He bent and his lips briefly touched her skin. His breath was warm and sent shivers from her ear to the tip of her toes.

Pax felt a strange mix of happiness, satisfaction, and something else that started in her stomach and wreaked havoc through her body. Her past experiences couldn't explain what was happening to her. She could remember several occasions when a girl she had liked had awoken similar emotions. But comparing those ghosts of feelings with the sensations Prince's touch was creating was like comparing an excellent meal with the mere act of eating to prevent starvation.

"I hate that they beat you because of me." Prince raised her chin, applying the smallest amount of pressure on her skin.

Pax felt self-conscious of her bruises. "I hate them for much more than that." She looked at him and realized the light of the fire was illuminating his face. Not a marred palette of swollen blue and purple anymore, but a face with distinct features, emerging from the sea of scars and bruises. His eyes had always fascinated her, since the first time she had seen him. Now, she could see that he had a straight nose, despite the abuse his face had taken over the years. He also had a full mouth, and he seemed younger than what she had originally thought. His face wasn't near healed, but Pax found herself looking at him in utter fascination.

"Why did you save me?" Prince asked suddenly and Pax blinked.

"What do you mean?"

"You should've listened to your mothers."

"And you would be dead," Pax retorted.

"Yes."

Prince's tone revealed it was exactly the outcome he had expected. The realization was painful. Pax was used to thinking that her life was precious. She couldn't have imagined it wasn't the same for everybody. She couldn't bear he had been treated like an object. "I couldn't just let them kill you." She touched his face, tracing the line of his nose and then his lips. On principle, she would have never excused the use of violence against any other human being. But she had really meant to say she couldn't imagine a scenario where he wasn't alive. She just couldn't contemplate the idea.

"I owe you my life." Prince removed her hand and put it in his. His voice was very low, but the meaning was loud and clear.

Pax shivered under his gaze. She knew the strength it must have taken for him to say something like that. She felt a stab of pain in her heart. "You don't owe me anything. You'll never owe anything to anybody else in your life. Never again." She came closer until his breath was brushing her lips. She felt a magnetic attraction impossible to ignore. The first time he had kissed her, she was too confused and worried to have any presence of spirit to reflect on what was happening. And then her mother had caught them. But now...

"I've been dreaming of being alone with you." Prince was watching her in a way that made it hard not to look away.

Pax wanted to hide her ruined face, but he was keeping her still with his hand. "I don't want you to see me like this." She didn't like to sound silly, but the words had escaped her mouth before she could stop.

"You are the only woman I have ever wanted to be with." He closed the infinitesimal gap left between their lips and kissed her. At first, it was nothing more than a simple caress on her swollen mouth.

"Oh, Prince," Pax murmured softly when he pressed his hands on her back to bring her whole body closer to him.

"You're so different from the others—" Prince stopped in mid-sentence, and then, when Pax stiffened in his arms, he hastily added, "I didn't mean it that way. You don't compare to any other human being. You are simply Pax. And I want you."

"Don't—" Pax started to speak, but Prince laid a finger on her mouth to silence her and then leaned closer.

"It's true," Prince confessed in her ear, and Pax shivered against him. He moved back to look at her again and smiled. Then he removed his shirt and carefully spread it on the ground beside her. He kneeled back before her and ever so slowly, without breaking eye contact, he started lowering her on the shirt. He stopped when Pax put a hand down to steady herself.

"I'm scared." Pax blushed at her admission. She couldn't help but stare at his naked skin. She wanted to touch him, but at the same time, she felt small and too exposed under his gaze. She wasn't completely sure she understood what was going to happen, but at the same time, she didn't want to stop him from showing her.

"I don't want you to be. I'd never force you to do anything you don't want to." Prince's eyes became distant while he helped her back up.

"Like you were," Pax couldn't help saying, and she regretted it immediately when she saw the hurt and the shame on his face.

"Like I was," he replied and started moving back to put some distance between them, but she reached out a hand and gently touched his chest.

"I trust you." Pax could barely move, and she was terrified. She breathed slowly and lay back down on the shirt. She stared at him a few seconds without saying anything. Her heart was running wild, and her stomach was in knots.

"You're so beautiful." Prince was looking at her as if he could see beyond the beaten skin.

Pax felt herself choke on pure air. "Join me," she said with barely a whisper. She looked at him, hoping to find he was as breathless as she was and was rewarded with his unfocused gaze.

"I've never wanted anything so much in my life." Prince went down on his elbow and touched her lips again. "And I shouldn't." He kept his body at an angle. "You know I'm different from you." He looked at her as if waiting for her to say something, but she didn't know what he wanted to hear. "You know that, right?" The last sentence was a heartfelt question.

"I suppose so." She frowned. She had never thought about that particular question. She had never had any real contact with men in her life. All her maids were fathered, but they were still women. How different could he be from her? "You're taller than any girl I've been with." She blushed again. "I'm sorry." She shouldn't have mentioned her past girlfriends to him. It didn't seem right. She didn't really want to know all the lovers he had taken.

Prince smiled at her apology. "It's okay; I'm taller than most men as well."

"You also have facial hair."

"That I do." Prince took one of her hands and guided her to touch his chest.

Pax didn't say anything back. She was rather fascinated by his bare skin glistening in the red light of the fire. *Your chest is flat*, she thought. She had noticed that earlier on from the way his shirts clung to his chest—the workers' wardrobe was quite revealing in its utilitarian way. Still, she almost gasped when her fingers made contact with his body and she had the first tangible proof he wasn't any of the girls she had made out with before. She knew he wasn't soft, as she was. She had experienced that when they had landed on the ground after escaping the fire. But she hadn't expected him to feel so different to the touch.

Prince stood still, allowing her to study him. Pax reached out with her other hand and pressed it on his heart. "It beats louder than mine," she said, surprised.

Reflexively, Prince mimed her act, laying his hand on her to feel her heartbeat. This time, she couldn't suppress the cry that escaped her mouth. She hadn't anticipated the burn from his touch or to feel her heart skip a beat.

"I didn't mean to scare you," Prince said and removed his hand.

"I like it." Pax took his hand in hers and brought it back to her chest. She saw the way his mouth slowly relaxed in a small smile and she smiled back at him, pressing his hand over her heart to let him feel what he did to her. Prince tentatively opened his fingers under hers and slowly moved his hand over her shirt to caress her. Pax saw his eyes light up in delight when her heart started acting out. "I like it," she repeated, worried he was going to stop, her voice coming out labored. Her heart was taking residence in her throat, while both his hands were now traveling the length of her body, up and down in a hypnotic motion. The temperature went from cold to too warm in a matter of seconds.

"I want to see your skin." Prince's voice was choked; his movements had become frantic, still gentle, but hurried, as if the fever she was feeling was consuming his body as well. Then, he stopped.

Pax opened her eyes, vaguely remembering she had closed them at some point, looked up at his serious face, and nodded at him. "Yes." She reached for the hem of her shirt and started pulling it up.

"Let me do it." Prince replaced her hands with his and slowly finished what she had started. Pax stood there before his eyes, wearing only her bra and adding a deep blush to her already colored face. "I've never undressed a woman before." He caressed her collarbone and moved down to the hollow space between her small breasts. They both shivered at the same time. "Thank you." Prince kissed her softly.

Pax couldn't believe she was allowing him what she had never allowed any of her girlfriends. He went to unhook her bra, his fingers light as feathers on her back, and she gasped at the sensation he had provoked. She felt the cold air of the night skimming her skin with hundreds of needles, but at the same time, his fingers left a trail of flames flickering and burning where he touched. "I've never been undressed before."

Prince stood rigid for a moment and she had the sinking feeling she had said the wrong thing. When she was going to say she was sorry, he nestled his head atop her heart and softly kissed her breast. "Thank you," he murmured, covering her in kisses. He gently rested longer on her nipples. "Thank you," he repeated after a while.

Pax felt at ease, and when Prince's hand traveled down to open the first button on her pants, she simply looked at him to remember the moment forever. She had never felt so alive. So desired. She wondered for a brief moment how she had come to be in this position. She had been raised in a strict family. All her dalliances, even if, at the time, they had seemed extremely outré, they were nothing more than youthful experimentation. "I don't know what to do," she said, looking directly at him.

"My sweet little Pax." Prince's eyes became liquid. He kissed her lips gently and then took her face in his hands. "I never thought I'd ever feel so... happy." He kissed her again.

"I'm happy, too—" Pax said when he paused for a second.

"I know; I can feel it." Prince was now propped on an elbow, still caressing her slowly, his movements charged with a different tension and his expression showing a hint of darkness that wasn't there a mere moment before. "I'm terrified I'm going to ruin this."

"You can't ruin what we have," Pax said with great certainty.

"But I could," he sighed.

"How?" Pax sat back up, took his hand, and kissed it.

"You could be repulsed by me," Prince said, an edge to his voice, his hand stilling in hers.

"I'd never be repulsed by you." Pax was worried by the turn the conversation was taking. She wanted him closer, and it seemed to her that, at the moment, they weren't close enough. She murmured so, surprised by her own words.

"Even when I was beaten within an inch of my life, I've never felt as scared as I do now. I want you *closer,* too, but you don't know what I'm talking about." Prince gently, but resolutely, opened her fingers to free his hand from her hold.

Pax felt as if he had slapped her. The pain she saw etched in his eyes fueled her own physical ache. "What do you mean?" Her fears worsened tenfold by his silence. She rose on her elbows and held herself tight in a vain attempt to ban the cold seeping into her, freezing her. She wanted him to hug her, but the rigidity in his posture prevented her from pleading. "Is it because I'm a woman?" she asked with a mere thread of voice. She didn't want to know. And to make her feel even worse, he wasn't looking at her.

"I can't," he said and closed his hands in two fists.

"You can't because I'm a woman." She blindly searched the ground with her hands until she found her shirt and her bra, then slowly rose to her feet. "I understand." She wasn't going to let him see her tears.

"No, you don't understand—"

"Explain it to me." She hugged herself, crossing her arms around her body and wishing they were his.

"It has nothing to do with the fact that you're a woman. It is because you're... *you.* And I couldn't stand your rejection, when you realize how different we are." He finally looked at her.

"Then tell me!"

"I don't think this is the right moment..."

"Why not?" Pax waited for his words to come, but Prince lowered his head and didn't finish the sentence. Her eyes smarted. "I'm tired, and I'm not in the mood for riddles." She was feeling even colder now with her shirt on.

"I'm sorry." He stood up and tentatively put an arm around her waist.

Not as much as I am. Pax thought for a second to refuse him, but the longing for his closeness won. She melted against his chest. She turned her head, though, so that her tears weren't falling on his skin. Prince moved his arms up and embraced her in a tender hug. She hoped he had changed his mind. Instead, he slowly leaned his head until it rested on her shoulder, and they stayed like that until it became awkward.

"I think we should rest a few hours before leaving." Pax was the first one to break the silence. She also broke the embrace and went to sit by the small fire. She wanted to scream at him. To make him explain why she wasn't good enough, but it hurt so much, and she simply couldn't face the truth.

"Yes." Prince went to sit on the opposite side of the fire and eliminated the flames by scattering the coal around.

Pax saw him looking at her, but she didn't dare move. They didn't exchange a word the whole time. Then, when she finally lay down to try to sleep, he returned and arranged himself around her body, enclosing her in his arms. He safely nested her head against his chest, but never uttered a sound. Pax couldn't help but silently cry. Eventually, a combination of self-pity, fatigue, and several other sentiments she didn't have a name for won over her exhausted body, and she slowly fell asleep. She was constantly aware of his body against hers, even in her dreams. Every time she moved, she felt Prince rearranging his body to match hers. Every time a lament escaped her swollen lips, she felt him kissing her head softly.

Pax woke to a new day under a steady shower of water and the smell of wet cinders. She had slept through the rain, thanks to the sheltering body carefully protecting her from nature.

"You're soaking wet," she murmured while touching his hair, a dark shade of brown now and plastered against his face.

"How are you?" Prince opened his eyes slowly.

"Better." And she meant it, although her bruises weren't the only cause of her pain. The desire of being closer to him was still there; it hadn't lessened. But the new day had brought the realization they were together and alone.

"Regarding last night…" Prince started.

Pax, her breath caught in her throat, patiently waited for him to say something else, again. The same scene from the night before unfolding before her eyes in a torturous déjà vu. She looked at him and attempted a smile, hoping it was enough to make him find the words.

His lips curved up in response and he sighed while shaking his head. After a few seconds of silence, Prince bent to brush her lips with a soft kiss. When he finally opened his mouth to talk, she put a finger on it and shushed him.

"The ground is shaking." Pax suddenly moved away from his arms.

Prince looked around, surprised by her statement. He shot her a puzzled glance, and then his eyes widened in response. The sand was vibrating in undulating waves. A low rumble accompanied the ripples altering the landscape ever so lightly.

"What is it?" she asked while scanning the horizon for an answer. Prince was staring ahead of them, his eyes focused on what seemed a dark cloud, approaching quickly. She was going to ask a second time, when he stood up, bringing her with him with a firm grip on her arm.

"Stay behind me," he commanded without giving further explanations. He didn't have to.

"Who are they?" Pax asked as soon as the cloud came close enough to reveal what it was made of.

"*Fringe citizens*," Prince answered grimly.

Pax didn't say anything. Something in the scene unveiling before her eyes asked for silence.

"I won't let them hurt you," he said and squeezed the arm he was still holding.

She looked at him, nodded, and then faced the herd of horses galloping toward them.

"Don't move." Prince firmly pushed her behind him.

She peeked from under his arm and waited for something to happen. Time seemed to freeze while the dust slowly, but inexorably, engulfed them, until breathing became nothing more than a coughing fit. The horses came dangerously closer. Not that it was possible to discern anything when there was as much sand in the air as there was on the ground. But their smell permeated much of the plane, and the sound of their beating hooves was deafening. One or two horses turned around Pax and Prince.

Prince was whipped by one of the mare's tails, but he kept his ground and didn't let Pax move. She was strangely fascinated by the scene, until another horse seemed to charge them and she realized she should have been terrified.

"What—" yelled a man riding a black stallion that had almost knocked Pax over. He brought his horse to a precipitous halt, and then swore loudly when he took in Pax's presence behind Prince. In the distance, semi-hidden by the cloud of dust, there were other riders winding their way through the dunes.

"Let us go. We didn't see you. You didn't see us," Prince said with a voice that was preternaturally calm.

Pax shivered. She could have survived the stampede of horses. But a pack of men?

"No, can't do." The man, athletic and in his early fifties, dismounted and tried to get around Prince.

Prince moved as well, preventing him from doing so, but it was a futile exercise since the man had already seen there was someone else behind him. It was soon clear to Pax he wasn't expecting to find a woman.

The man's eyes froze on her and his expression changed for the briefest moment. "*This* is quite interesting."

Pax saw him smiling a cold smile, his teeth white against his sunburned face, and shivered.

Meanwhile, a group of men had arrived and flanked Pax and Prince on either side. They were young, around Prince's age, and looked eager to take a break from their duty. Pax stopped breathing.

"Give her to me." The older man acknowledged the others, and almost at the same time, he reached for the gun resting inside his holster. "Get out of the way, before something happens."

"Don't come close to her." Prince's voice came out icy while he slowly moved aside in a vain attempt to shield her from view.

"You got it all wrong, child," the man said, slightly turning toward his crew and then taking a good look at Pax from the side. The men agreed loudly.

"And who are you?" the man asked Pax.

"She's nobody. Just a maid I kidnapped from the farm," Prince answered before she could say anything.

"And why would you do something so… stupid?" the man asked, now staring at Prince. Something in his tone betrayed an odd feeling. Disappointment?

"Revenge," Prince answered with a deadpan tone.

Pax cast a glance toward the man to see his reaction.

"Hmm. Amusing." The man looked everything but amused by Prince's answer.

Pax would have sworn the man looked disgusted. But she didn't have time to think about it, as he turned around toward the cheering men and added, "You'll tell us your story tonight at the bonfire."

Before Prince could say anything back, another two men arrived, and a few seconds later, another three joined the group.

"Lucas, what did you get this time?" one of them, a young man with a heavily scarred face, asked from a distance.

"Not our usual catch." Raising his voice, the older man answered the newcomer, but kept his eyes on Prince.

"How many do we have?"

"Two…"

"Is that a woman?"

"Yes, Horace, *that* is a woman." Lucas didn't sound happy about confirming it.

Pax felt panic swelling in her chest when she saw Prince looking around for a way out and then looked back at her with pain in his eyes.

"Guys, we've company, and also entertainment for the ones who have a taste for this sort of thing." The man called Horace sneered, indicating Pax with his gun.

"Stop it!" Lucas silenced him.

"I wouldn't even think about it, if I were you," Prince snarled at the new arrival at the same time.

Pax shivered at the way the other men looked at her and then at Prince. She knew he shouldn't have defended her so blatantly, twice in a matter of minutes, not if he wanted the other men to believe that she didn't mean anything to him. Pax noticed how Lucas was observing them silently.

"And who are *you*?" Horace asked, circling around with his mount and taking care to raise some more dust in his wake.

"I'm a fugitive." Prince raised his chin defiantly.

"That's it? And do you think we should be impressed?"

The men laughed.

"We're all fugitives!" Horace said with a derisive tone meant to elicit the others' laughs.

"Enough already." Lucas' voice had the effect to sober the more raucous outbursts, but the murmuring continued.

Pax heard the men animatedly arguing about her fate.

"Maybe we can leave the woman here and go back home," someone suggested.

"No, we can't. You know the Priest's rules. Now, let's stop wasting time. I want to get back before we're caught out here." Lucas remounted his black stallion and made a sign for the others that Pax didn't understand immediately. After a few seconds, his intentions were made clear. A horse was brought forth and he turned around to face Prince squarely in the eyes. "Don't try anything stupid or you'll regret it. Understood?"

Several men raised their guns to drive Lucas' point home. Pax looked around and fought the urge to cry. "We don't have a choice."

"No, we don't..." Prince's voice sounded hollow. "I've never ridden a horse before," he then confessed in a low whisper that unfortunately wasn't low enough. A few insults came his way. Pax squeezed his arm back.

"You've five hours until our destination to learn the basics," Horace said, finding his own words rather amusing. The other men thought so, too.

Prince took a good look at the recalcitrant beast and stepped forward. He pulled Pax with him, keeping her shielded from the others' eyes. "I took a lesson or two," Pax spoke very softly to him when he put a hesitant hand on the mare. Prince nodded without turning his head. "Be firm," she suggested and he promptly steadied his hand. "Now put one foot on the stirrup, grab the saddle, and push yourself up." She moved closer to the horse to calm the animal with a few soothing words.

Prince followed her clues, and after one botched attempt, he managed to straddle the horse. The men cheered his success with mock praises and a handful of offensive comments about his manhood, but at least they didn't try to irritate his mount.

"Help me on, please." Pax raised her hand and he took it after centering his body on the saddle. "Now simply follow him. Soon, it will become second nature for you. I promise." Pax adjusted her body on the saddle right behind him and slid her arms around his waist.

"Good, hold tight and don't slow us." Lucas gave Prince and Pax a last pointed look and then turned around to face the others, who were preparing to leave.

"What about the rest of the herd?" one of them asked.

"I'm afraid we have to let them go. We'll have to do with the horses we already corralled," Lucas answered.

"But, Lucas! If it weren't for those horses, we would've never rode this far—"

"It must be a sign then. We were meant to find these two today."

Horace, angrily commanding his brown mount, came closer to Pax and Prince and yelled at them. "It's all your fault, but if it were up to me—"

"Horace, I suggest you keep your temper under control. Our job is to find stranded souls, not horses," Lucas answered the young man.

"Yes, but we have nothing and it's not every day that a herd of wild horses—"

"A man's life is still more valuable." Lucas raised his voice several notches and silenced the man. "*You*, never stray. Don't make me come after you," he said to Prince in a lower tone, and then he launched his horse into a gallop.

Pax patiently guided Prince during the five hours that it took to navigate through the dunes to reach the men's destination. After a first moment of hesitation, Prince followed her directions to the letter and he managed to learn the basics and a little more in the process.

"I know where these men are taking us," Prince said once he had relaxed enough to feel comfortable riding the horse and having a conversation at the same time.

"Do you?" Pax asked, hearing the undertones in his voice. A mix of fear and excitement.

"At the farm, the workers like to tell stories at night. One of my favorites is about the City of Men. A mythical city, hidden in the desert, governed by men and inhabited by men only. Not all the versions of the tale coincide, but the majority of them concur on the bit about the male sovereign. I dreamed of this place for countless nights."

"I hope for you that you're right," Pax said without thinking.

"I fear I might be." Prince leaned back and Pax hugged him closer, squeezing her arms around his waist.

"I'm going to be okay," Pax murmured to his back, trying to hide the tremor in her voice.

"There're other tales about the City of Men." Prince paused for a moment and Pax slid her open palms over his chest to find his heart. "They say the workers are free to take their revenge on the women."

Pax had already come to the same conclusion. Even without knowing anything about the City of Men, she found it easy to believe that, after so many centuries of being enslaved, men would want to inflict the same treatment on women, given the opportunity.

"I'd never harm another human being." Prince looked around and then brought Pax's hand to his mouth and kissed it softly.

"I know."

"We'll run away the first chance we get." Prince was thinking out loud and Pax could feel his heart beating faster. She had nothing to contribute to that and kept silent.

"You two, ride along with me." Lucas, whom Pax had noticed had been looking at them the entire time, didn't wait for them to move. He brought his mount close to theirs and never let them ride alone from then on. Once or twice, he tried to engage Prince in a conversation about Sundial and how he had managed to escape while kidnapping a maid. Prince gave short answers, mostly yes and no, and revealed nothing about them.

Pax buried her head against Prince and let the horse's gait lull her into dozing on and off. She didn't care that her affectionate conduct betrayed Prince's lies about her abduction. His own behavior had been in contrast with his words, anyway. The only thing she could think of was that this was possibly the last time she could touch Prince, and she didn't want to let go of him until the very last moment.

CHAPTER 10

They arrived late in the afternoon, after having eaten dust for hours while riding under a relentless sun. Chewing on the sand, Pax regretted miserably the rain of the morning, but kept her unhappiness to herself, although her mood spilled inevitably in her thoughts.

"You must hate me," Pax stated once Lucas finally moved ahead to talk to one of the younger men. Prince turned around, his eyes were wide and his mouth froze in an unspoken question. "*This*, the City of Men, is your dream come true," Pax said, trying to find the right words. Prince waited patiently for her to finish the concept. "You're finally free to live the life you want, and you're thinking about running away from it to keep me safe."

"First of all, I would never hate you. And second, I didn't know you before, otherwise I would've dreamed of you." Prince turned to face forward and pressed her hand to his mouth for a quick kiss before Lucas came back.

Pax didn't say anything else because the older man was already riding his horse flush with theirs. She made sure Lucas wasn't looking in her direction and ran her fingers up and down Prince's chest to tell him without words how much she had liked his answer.

"We're almost home," Lucas broke the silence abruptly.

Pax raised her head from Prince's back to look at the older man. Lucas wasn't talking to them.

"We've found two strays," he murmured something else Pax didn't catch and then closed his cell phone. Lucas regarded Pax with a look of either annoyance or concern, but then something caught his attention and he moved ahead.

"Pax?" Prince put a hand on hers and applied some pressure.

"Yes?"

"Look." Prince's voice was low, but Pax heard the choked tone and craned her head outside to see what was shaking him.

"Oh..." was what she managed to say at first. "It looks... unreal." She slightly moved on the saddle to take a better look at the scenery. Nested between two canyons there was an amazing structure. Depending on the angle, it could look like a natural formation of sandy planes and casually placed boulders. All it took was a turn sideways to see that nothing was casual.

"Even after hearing about it so often, I can hardly believe my eyes," Prince said.

"I've never seen anything like it," she commented, taking in the sandy-colored city coming to view before her eyes. She kept moving her head this way and that.

"It's different from anything I've ever seen, too." He nodded in agreement and then added as an afterthought, "Not that I've seen a lot."

"I..." Pax felt a pang of pain at his words.

"It's okay." Prince dismissed her apologies waving his hand in the air. "It's bigger than I thought."

"How do you think they hide the city? Apart from the fact that if you blink your eyes you can miss it altogether. I mean, it's still a big secret to keep from Ginecea."

"I have no idea. I guess that it's impossible to see from the air, and no woman in her right mind would venture here in the middle of nowhere," he said, lowering his voice.

Pax took a brief look at the rest of the convoy and felt uneasy. Their captors were slowing down, and Lucas seemed agitated about something. After his questioning, apart from riding side by side with them, the man had otherwise ignored Prince and Pax, and everybody else had, thankfully, followed his example. The pain from the harsh ride, the hunger, and the thirst were bad enough by themselves. They had been left to their thoughts and their growing discomfort for several hours. And Pax couldn't have asked for anything better, given the circumstances, although, there was something bugging her at the back of her mind now that they had reached their destination.

"It isn't good they allowed me to see this place, is it?" she asked in a low whisper before Lucas moved back to their side.

"You don't know that," Prince answered.

Pax detected the doubt in his voice, but decided not to press the subject.

"She'll stay here," Lucas shouted from where he was, and then when he saw their puzzled faces, he pointed at what looked like the outskirts of the city. A few low houses dotted the stretch of desert in a circular pattern. At the center there was a gazebo.

"I won't leave her alone." Prince waited for Lucas to ride back before talking.

Pax heard the fear in his voice and hugged him tighter.

"You really don't have a choice. But I can make it easier for you," the man answered Prince, pointing the gun at Pax's head. "Off you go now," he said to her, completely ignoring Prince.

Pax dismounted before Prince could say anything.

"I'll be fine," she said to him while Lucas forcefully escorted her toward the small hamlet, his hand grabbing her at the shoulder with more strength than necessary. The long ride had left Pax's body tired, and every step was heavy and painful.

"Give her something to do," Lucas yelled to someone who wasn't in sight and then let her go with a push that unbalanced her shaky legs.

Prince had dismounted as well and was at her side in no time, preventing Pax from landing on the sand. "You can't—" he started to say, but was immediately stopped by a gunshot fired a few inches from Pax's foot.

"Before something unpleasant happens, shut your mouth and get back on the horse," Lucas said.

"Go, please," Pax begged him with a thread of voice.

"Listen to her," Lucas said, looking at his men, who were monitoring the scene from their mounts. Some of them manifested their opinions about the utility of women in general.

"I don't want to leave you here." Prince was still looking for a way to turn the tables, but several guns were now lazily taking aim at her head. "I'll find a way to come back to you," he finally said.

He brushed her forearm with his fingers, but took care not to be seen by their audience.

"I trust you," Pax said and started walking toward the first house with an open door. She didn't want Prince to see her tears and didn't want to compromise his already weak position. She put one foot in front of the other until she stood before a sandy-colored building. She didn't turn around, even though her heart ached to see him one more time.

"Come inside, so I can shut the dust out." A woman in her forties unceremoniously pulled her in and closed the heavy hutch with a series of metallic noises.

"Much better, don't you think?" She smiled, satisfied, after having checked the locks.

Pax didn't have anything to say to that remark and so said nothing. Although, had she been in possession of all her mental faculties, she would have probably answered that it didn't seem better at all. But she was surprised to see a woman there.

"Are you thirsty?" the woman asked, walking briskly through a well-lit room. She was thin and small and probably looked younger than she was.

Pax nodded slowly and followed her to a nook at the other end of what looked like a living room. In the circular space there were couches, small tables, lots of plants hanging from the ceiling, and at the center there was a small pool, probably collecting rainwater.

"I can fix something for you, if you are hungry." The woman showed Pax a stool nested under a table hung to the ceiling with two ropes and delimiting the nook from the rest of the big space. She went to a cupboard to retrieve a bowl she filled with a thick, dark soup from a pot sitting on the stove, then leaned under the table to retrieve a wet jug and poured some clear water in a glass. "Do you eat meat?" she asked from behind the floating table.

Pax nodded again.

"Okay, you must stop that. It's getting rather annoying. Talk to me or go hungry. You decide." She showed Pax the bowl with what looked and smelled like stew and the glass with the water.

"I'm starving, and I eat meat. I don't even remember when the last time I drank anything was." Pax looked straight at the woman without cowering.

"They didn't cut your tongue then. Very well."

Pax thanked her and started eating.

"You look... different." The woman was still standing by the other side of the table, rocking back and forth on the balls of her feet and watching Pax with a curious glance. "Who are you?" she asked abruptly.

"A maid from Sundial," Pax repeated Prince's lie. She didn't lower her gaze under the woman's stare. Pax felt hot and cold at the same time.

"The farm?"

"Yes, the farm." She put down the empty bowl, but kept hold of it.

"No, I don't think so. Even covered in sand, disheveled appearance and all, you look everything but a maid. But it's better if you stick to that." The woman gently took the bowl from Pax's hands, went to the stove, and brought it back full.

Pax looked down at the dirty stains she was leaving on the table and tried to wipe her hands on her dusty clothes and wondered what she looked like. "Thanks," she said again. The first helping of stew had barely undermined the aching pain in her stomach. She gulped down the glass of water and was even more grateful when it was refilled with hot tea.

"Why are you here?" the woman asked, looking at Pax intently.

"I was kidnapped by a man." Pax shivered guiltily at the mere idea of incriminating Prince of something he would have never done.

"Work on it. It doesn't sound believable yet; it's the way you say it." The woman seemed honestly concerned about Pax's lack of lying skills.

Pax, now sated, started wondering at the only question worth asking at the moment. "Why are you giving me shelter?"

"What's your name?" the woman replied.

"Pax," she answered automatically.

"Unusual name, that is. It can't be fake." The woman seemed really intrigued by it, and Pax immediately regretted not having thought longer before answering.

"What's yours?" Pax wasn't interested in knowing the woman's name, but she needed answers and she had to start somewhere.

"Cordelia. I help keep little women like you alive. That's what I do. And that's why I'm giving you shelter. And because Lucas asked me."

"How did you end up here?" Pax couldn't help but wonder.

"I was born here. My parents ran this place before me," Cordelia said matter-of-factly.

"I don't understand. Why were you born here? You're a woman."

"My parents had me here. They loved this place." She went to open a drawer.

"Your mothers came here?" Pax asked, wondering how plausible it was for two women in their right mind to decide to have a baby in the middle of the desert.

"My mother and my *father* came here," Cordelia corrected Pax with a smirk.

"Your mother and your father… raised you here," Pax repeated what the woman had just said to test how it felt. Even in her mouth, the words sounded impossible. But the woman wasn't laughing at her joke.

"Yes, they built this place, the Sanctuary, my mother called it, for me to grow up free and safe." Cordelia had stopped looking at Pax. She seemed lost in her memories. "Once… not so long ago, the other houses were inhabited. But, now it's only this one—"

Pax wasn't interested in listening to desert stories. "What am I doing here?" She didn't feel at ease enough to waste time in idle conversation and resorted to changing the subject.

"Lucas saved your life by sending you here," Cordelia said, snapping out of her reveries.

Pax found the woman's way to answer with seemingly off-topic replies was wearing down her nerves. "It sure doesn't seem so—" She couldn't help but snort at the idea that the man who had threatened to shoot her had done anything to help *her*, a woman.

"But, why?" she asked, just to keep Cordelia talking. Maybe, eventually, the woman was going to say something useful.

"Why? Because he knows your "kidnapper" can't protect you in the City of Men. And the Sanctuary is off limits for the men under the Priest's orders. So you are safe here."

"Who's the Priest?" Pax asked.

"He's the man who founded the City of Men," Cordelia explained.

Pax heard the affectionate tone in the woman's words, and once again wondered about what it meant. "But why would Lucas care about my wellbeing?" She came back to the main question.

"He's a decent human being and would never hurt a woman, that's why!"

Pax was taken aback by the woman's vehemence.

"Lucas is a smart man, and I'm sure he's read through your lies. He's speedily removed you from the other thugs' hands. You should be thankful to him, instead of questioning his method. These are dangerous times to be a woman here." Cordelia took Pax's plate and ran it under the water faucet in a sink jutting from the wall.

Pax saw how Cordelia used the water with great parsimony. "Right. Because any other time would be just peachy to be a woman in a place full of men." A cold shiver ran down her spine.

"It wasn't always like this in the City of Men." Cordelia's eyes went wide and she turned around to busy herself with something.

Pax didn't ask anything else.

"When the other girls come home—"

"Are there other women living here?"

"Yes, three of them. As I was saying, when they come back home, I suggest you keep to yourself. The less you say, the less attention you're going to attract, which, in your case, is going to be paramount if you want to keep up the charade of the kidnapped maid. Now go have a bath before the shower is taken." Cordelia walked past a door opening to a little washroom and waited until Pax went inside. "Fresh towels are on the rack." She closed the door. "Water is rationed; the tank is filled every other day, so don't waste it." Her voice came muffled through the wall.

Pax looked in the mirror and didn't recognize her face; caked dirt covered her skin and spikes of brown sand had replaced her hair; even her eyes seemed of a different color. Her own mothers couldn't have recognized her. She sat on the floor, incapable of deciding if she wanted to cry her eyes out, or if she wanted to do as suggested and clean the dust and the dirt from her pores. She finally opted for crying under a faltering trickle of lukewarm water. She would have lingered and purified her thoughts as well, but, remembering Cordelia's words, once her skin came back to its original color, she reluctantly turned off the shower. She didn't want to go outside and face whatever was waiting for her on the other side of that door. The decision was taken from her with a loud knock on the wooden frame.

"There're three people who need the shower. Come out!" a voice that didn't belong to Cordelia bellowed from the outside world. "I hope for your sake that you didn't use all the water!"

Pax wrapped a big towel around her wet body, picked up her clothes in a heap and left the room. She stopped at the door to face three irate girls.

"Move out of the way!" one of them said and went straight to the shower without bothering to close the door for privacy. The other two went inside, leaving Pax completely puzzled about the whole situation.

"Don't stare at us!" a blond girl demanded, while in the process of cleaning her teeth. The first one finished the shower in record time, and the second was already taking her place in the stall. Nobody thought even for a second to strip behind the screen supposedly there for that reason. Pax couldn't help but be surprised by their behavior.

"You'll get used to it." Cordelia had brought new towels for the girls. "Try to blend in. I'm saying this for your sake. Don't make unnecessary enemies looking so prim." She had lowered her voice at the last moment.

"I heard about you at the camp," the blond girl said.

"I though women weren't allowed inside the City of Men," Pax shot back without thinking.

"*You* are not allowed," the blonde answered in a tone Pax didn't like.

"Yet," Cordelia rectified the statement and then admonished the girl. "Cara, try to be nice to her."

"So, you came with the dark one?" Cara asked while drying her body.

"He looks yummy. Beaten and scrawny, but yummy," the shortest of the three added.

"Tai, when did you have time to take a look at him?" Cara asked, surprised by the information.

"When they were escorting him to the bonfire for an audience with the Priest," Tai said and then added, "I was with her." She pointed at the third girl who had remained silent and was looking at Pax with great interest. "I was helping carry medicines and other stuff, so she didn't have to go back and forth."

Pax wanted to ask lots of questions, but at the moment, it wasn't wise to sound too interested in anything.

"Sonia, how is the Priest doing?" Cordelia went to the kitchen nook and poured some water from a big clay jug into the kettle, then lit a match, opened a drawer under the stove and ignited a small-contained fire.

"Not better than yesterday. I don't think he's going to survive the summer. Too hot during the day and too cold at night. We're trying to better weather proof his room, but this climate is too extreme to be contained with mere insulation." Sonia walked to the floating table, waiting for the tea.

"Are you here to stay?" Sonia finally spoke to Pax.

"I don't understand your question." Pax moved to the table and asked Cordelia if she could help with something.

"You didn't ask for *sanctuary*." Cara seemed to realize something that was escaping Pax's comprehension altogether.

"She's a maid, and she was kidnapped by the man Tai saw," Cordelia supplied tersely and handed the kettle to Tai who carefully transferred the water from the kettle to a teapot that looked as if it had seen better days.

"Are you leaving any time soon?" Tai released a handful of dried leaves into the teapot, waited a few moments, then sieved the tea with a cloth and poured the tea for everybody. Meanwhile, Cara had buttered some dark bread.

Pax's eyes went from one face to the other, silently asking for an explanation.

"You are free to leave anytime." Cordelia gave Pax a hard stare.

"But you said that Lucas—" She realized that she was talking too much.

"Lucas is not going to chase you in the middle of the desert," Sonia said with her mouth full of bread.

"No, he's probably not going to." Cara and Tai agreed before raising their cups.

"But I thought I was a prisoner."

"What are you blabbering about? We are all here because we want to be." Sonia gently pushed a steaming cup toward Pax.

"You're women! Why do you want to stay here?" she asked for the second time a question that didn't seem to have a decent answer.

"Why do *you* want to live anywhere else?" Cara put her empty cup on the table with more strength than necessary.

Pax felt the ripple of anger passing through the objects until it reached her hand. She instinctively stepped back.

"As a fathered woman, you should know what she's saying." Cordelia gave her a pointed look.

"Why would *we* like to go on being some other woman's slave?" Sonia refilled her cup and then did the same for Cara.

"Do you think that since we are fathered we can't try at least to decide who to serve?" Tai's voice was soft, but cut Pax's heart deeper than the others' words. And then the meaning of what they were saying finally hit home.

"I think everybody should be free to live their life the way they want." Pax thought of Prince and the way he had been treated all his life. She thought of Celeste and the way she had treated her. Her eyes clouded with tears.

Nobody said anything, but a common decision regarding the new guest was taken by the four women in the room. Pax felt the change in atmosphere as if it was tangible.

"Listen, girl, unless you have any intention to betray us, you are welcome here," Cordelia said and three heads nodded at the same time.

"Don't worry; I've too much to lose," Pax answered; then she looked around and added, "And I'm not going anywhere." It hadn't taken long to make up her mind. In the split second she had realized she could go back to her perfect world and her perfect mothers, she had also come to the conclusion she wanted to stay where Prince was.

CHAPTER 11

"Is the bread ready?" Sonia asked for the third time in less than an hour.

"No, it's not." Pax didn't bother to check inside the cupboard where she had put the dough to rise. It was too early.

"Is anything else ready I can eat?" Sonia went to open several drawers in the kitchen cabinets.

"If you stop pestering me, I'll fix a sandwich for you."

"You know I don't want sandwiches when I'm hungry."

"Which means that you're not hungry." Pax had been reciting from the same script for the last two weeks, to the point that she had already started working on the sandwich. Not that she didn't agree with Sonia. The bread, if that dark lump of coarse flour could be called such, hardened almost immediately after baked and wasn't easy to chew. On the other hand, the dried meat was exactly that and the cheese something to forget altogether. Still, it was sustenance for the body.

She had been offered the position of cook and she had accepted. Baking was something she had once, a long time ago, it seemed, enjoyed. And she still did, apart from the fact that preparing meals at the Sanctuary was a constant challenge. At the Layan mansion, Louise, the cook, normally prepared all the ingredients on the table for her to use, anything she wanted and more than she needed, and often already measured. Here, everything was rationed and there weren't many ingredients available. Cordelia had lent Pax a recipe book her mother had written over the course of several decades. More a journal about the harshness of life in the desert than a culinary text, the battered pile of papers kept together by two ribbons was full of notes on how to use certain ingredients to substitute others that were impossible to find. Pax, thankful for the help, had started experimenting from it and filled her days with lots of cooking.

Anything that would make the time go by was more than welcome. Pax had asked for permission to be allowed admittance into the city, but she had been refused five times already. Meanwhile, she hadn't seen Prince for fourteen days, several hours, and a number of minutes. She longed to feel the dark gaze of his eyes on her face and the warmth of his hands on her skin.

"Do you miss *him*?" Sonia accepted the plate from Pax with a silent thanks.

She didn't answer. Instead, she decided it was time to check if the yeast was working its magic.

"I'm not judging you. Unless he's violent or abusive, I don't think there's anything wrong in fancying a man," Sonia continued.

Pax thought about the girl's choice of words. She had already noticed a few old marks on Sonia's arms and legs. It was impossible not to, when nobody seemed to need any privacy at all around the house. But she'd never asked what had happened to her. There was only one rule in the house, and Pax had committed to it wholeheartedly from the start. She hadn't said anything about her *kidnapping*, and she hadn't asked anything personal about anybody else.

"Just make sure he feels the same way you do." Sonia took the sandwich from the plate and went to sit on one of the couches facing the rainwater pool. Pax followed her and sat on the opposite couch. "A spell of dry weather." Sonia was contemplating the empty pool and then looked up at the circular opening on the ceiling that allowed the rain to fill in the shallow space. "I felt that way for a long time before I let the others help me." She wasn't eating.

Pax looked at her and blinked her eyes.

"Dry. I lost a baby… a year ago," Sonia continued her soliloquy.

"I'm sorry." Pax fought the urge to ask several questions. First of all, how Sonia had gotten pregnant—because she must have gone to the Temple, but from what she knew, Sonia was already living at the Sanctuary a year or two ago—and then how she had lost the baby? Pax resigned herself to expressing her sympathy without barging into the girl's privacy.

"And the worst of it is that, being a nurse, I knew what was happening, but I couldn't save her."

Pax felt her stomach contract at Sonia's words.

"I owe my life to Lucas, you know?"

"How so?"

"He found me." Sonia became distant, her eyes focused on a faraway point, only the movement from her fingers, busy playing an imaginary piano on her leg, proved she was awake. Then all of a sudden she said, "Pax, I'm not sure this is the right place for you."

"What do you mean?"

"You don't look like a maid. You don't talk like one. You're different from me and the other girls."

"You don't want me here?"

"Sooner or later, someone's going to look for you. You've that kind of aura about you. You're loved. You're missed. And I know you weren't fathered."

"You're throwing me out, then," Pax stated in a flat voice.

"No, I told Lucas that, in my opinion, the man who brought you here should take full responsibility for you."

"What?" Pax couldn't believe her ears.

"That's what I think." Sonia finally took another bite from the sandwich.

"Thanks, I guess," Pax murmured under her breath.

"Don't thank me, yet. Lucas said he's going to think about it."

"Did you see *him*?" Pax couldn't help but ask.

"Hmm. He's a melancholy guy." Sonia didn't pretend not to know whom Pax had asked about. "Lucas put him to work at the wind plant." She finished eating and then went out again, leaving Pax alone in the house with too many thoughts to keep her company.

The rest of the day was a nightmare for Pax. Her routine had been devastated by Sonia's mention of Prince and the admission about her past and she couldn't seem to find a way to reestablish some peace in her mind. She checked the dough one time too many, and the cold air, infiltrating inside the cupboard each time she opened the drawer, ruined the rising. She prepared another batch and let it rise longer than was necessary. After trying to salvage the dough—wasting ingredients was something she now deemed as morally unacceptable—she decided to bake something that didn't require any yeast.

Pax had come to enjoy dinnertime with the girls. It was the only time of the day when everybody was in the house at the same moment, and they spent the evening chatting about the workday in the City of Men. But that night, her thoughts were scattered and she only half-listened to what they were saying.

Sonia was talking about the Priest's health, a topic that was discussed every night. "No, he isn't responding to therapy anymore," she answered someone's question.

"I feared this moment would come. I didn't expect it to be so soon." Cordelia sighed and proceeded to serve the soup Pax had prepared. A moment of hesitation on Cordelia's side and the wooden ladle fell on the table, waking Pax from her reverie.

"Why the name?" Pax had been wondering for a while about the title.

"Everybody calls him that." Tai was cleaning her dirty hands on a towel. She had come back from the shop too hungry to shower.

Pax cringed at the thought of having to clean the black grease from the towel. Tomorrow was her turn to do laundry and she wasn't looking forward to it. "But there's no church for men on Ginecea."

"Not that you know of," Cara rectified her.

"I don't know lots of things." Pax made a conciliatory gesture and smiled, trying to melt Cara's walls. "Is he the men's priestess?"

"The title 'Priest' was given to him years ago, but he's nothing like the Priestess." Cordelia had the last word. For some reason, the Priest was a touchy topic for her, but then again, with so many untold stories, one was bound to step on someone else's toes sooner or later.

"Is the new prototype ready?" Cara asked Tai.

"Almost. I spent the whole day fabricating a piece that ended up being too short, and I had to toss it away. A colossal waste of time we don't have." Tai seemed seriously upset by the problem.

"Lucas must be pushing all of you to finish as soon as possible." Cara helped herself with another serving from the big, steaming pot. "I know because Krasinsky is complaining everyday about the crops. They are withering before reaching maturation. I heard the old man calling Lucas at least twice today."

"I was in the office when one of the phone calls came. Lucas was furious. But what can we do? I can't build pieces fast enough to finish the engine by tomorrow, and neither can the others on the team," Tai answered, lowering the spoon to the bowl.

"The Priest's hoping you can make it work before famine comes," Sonia said in a subdued voice.

"Don't you have one already?" Pax asked. She had heard a lot about the project of building a machine that could find water several hundreds of meters deep and act as a pump, but she couldn't believe that anybody was able to survive in the middle of the desert without a similar device already working.

"We do, but it's almost forty years old and breaking down a little more day by day. We expect by the end of the month, it will breathe its last breath. We're running out of time," Tai explained.

"The first to suffer will be the *families*." Cordelia referred to the more elusive inhabitants of that already elusive world. The City of Men was densely populated by men, of course, but at the outskirts there was a community of women, and even more surprising, nested deep inside a not-so-distant canyon, there were several families living very reclusive lives. Families composed of different genders. Nobody knew, or wanted to know, how many groups were hiding there, but almost everybody was willing to respect them. At least, as long as they kept to themselves. Cordelia wasn't the only one, who, for obvious reasons, had a soft spot when it came to the *families*.

"I know that some of the babies are sick," Sonia added with a sigh.

"I wish they could be integrated in the city," Cordelia said.

"*We* are barely tolerated, and only because some of us are highly skilled. And you know, I can't even find the courage to blame the men completely, after what we've done and still do to them." Cara put aside her plate and went for the cupboard. "Something sweet to alleviate our mood." She brought back some of Pax's creations.

"Looks interesting." Tai gave a curious look at the tart lying on the table.

Pax watched as the other women ate it, hoping it was sweet enough, given that she had already used more than the allotted quota of sugar for the week. "What kinds of skills are needed? How did you manage to be accepted by the men?" she asked. The questions were burning inside her mind. She had to know because she couldn't stand another day without seeing Prince.

"Being fathered women, we're trained to do everything. Our job descriptions go from plumber to nurse to teacher. And, as Cara just said, we proved they needed us. When they tried to be selective about it, we stopped working for them. It wasn't pretty. It happened two years ago, so it's still fresh in everybody's memory. Mine for sure, since I had just arrived when all hell broke loose." Tai shivered at the memory.

"Cordelia's parents, Guen and Arias, fought for our rights and paid dearly for it." Sonia squeezed Cordelia's arm in sympathy. "We'll be forever in their debts."

"Let's talk about something else, shall we?" Tai suggested.

"I admire you. All of you," Pax whispered. Four pairs of eyes looked at her with mixed expressions. "You dare to see, when other people just accept what they are told they are watching."

"Maybe it's easier when you're denied true freedom," Cara cautiously commented.

Pax nodded in agreement. She had lived such a sheltered life that for her, reality had been just a giant screen showing happy-ending reruns. What lay beyond that screen was mind-boggling and devastating. Maybe it really was easier to fight if you could see at least part of the bigger truth. She hadn't known.

"Nevertheless." Pax would have loved to repeat what Lexi had drilled in her mind about the fact that being ignorant wasn't an acceptable excuse. Her friend would have enjoyed this conversation, commenting and giving her opinion at every occasion. Pax opted for a safer silence. There wasn't a lot she could add to Cara's words without explaining where she came from. Several knocks on the metallic door echoed in the room and interrupted her woolgathering. She was the closest to it and went to see who it was.

"Pax!" A whirlwind of arms, hands, and lips crushed her in the most welcome and sweet embrace. She was filled with his scent before she could take a look at his face.

"I missed you," she whispered in his ear, forgetting the rest of the universe and melting in his arms.

"Hmm… do you mind?" Lucas's voice burst Pax's bubble. "Can I get inside?" he said when she didn't seem to realize she had to release Prince to let the other man in.

Pax blushed and then stepped aside. Lucas took a moment to scrutinize her; his eyebrows corrugated in a silent question, and then he left, called in by Cordelia. She forgot about the man as soon as he passed through the door. She leaned closer to touch Prince to make sure she wasn't dreaming.

"I'm sorry it took me forever. I tried to come earlier, but they kept me under surveillance the whole time. They're worried about people leaving the city and being found by Ginecea. Nobody can be trusted to keep quiet under torture." Prince walked inside the house with her.

Lucas was already sitting at the kitchen table, talking to her roommates, but Pax couldn't hear a word he was saying. She was looking at Prince as if she had never seen him before. And she hadn't. Not really until that moment.

"What is it?" he asked, his brow arched.

"You're healed." Pax couldn't look anywhere else. "You're beautiful."

"Pax, you should come here. Lucas wants to talk to you," Cordelia called from the kitchen nook.

"We'll talk later." Prince gave her a soft peck on her lips.

Pax wanted to cling to him and never let him go, but she recognized the urgency in his voice and reluctantly walked to the table.

"I should've known who you were immediately," Lucas said without preamble, looking at Pax with a long, unblinking stare. His words silenced everybody. "How I didn't see the resemblance right away is beyond me; and to think I've seen your pictures so many times."

Pax felt her extremities going numb. She sat down and looked at Prince, waiting for a clue. She didn't dare to turn her head toward the other women.

"Pax, it's okay. I told him you have special connections with a powerful family." He took her hand and slowly caressed it under the table.

"The Priest wants to see you," Lucas said.

"Why?" Pax had a sinking feeling in her stomach. *So, this is it.* Despite Cordelia's reassurance she was safe at the Sanctuary, she had the feeling her life was in danger since the moment Lucas had found her and Prince.

"Because he has something to say to you," Lucas answered after a long pause.

"And, what if I don't want to see him?" Fear made her brave.

"Trust me, if I were you, I'd go." Lucas smiled.

Pax found his reaction strange and looked at Prince again for guidance.

"The Priest is a great man. You'll like him," Prince said.

"I have a request." Pax tried to muster a hard expression.

"What do you want?" Lucas asked, seemingly amused.

"I want to work in the city; I'll meet the Priest if you find something for me to do in the city," she said in one breath. She knew she didn't have any bargaining power, and if Lucas wanted her to meet the man, she didn't have any choice but to comply, but she still had to try.

Lucas seemed to think about it for a second, his eyes bright with mirth. "I guess it can be arranged." He chuckled softly, as if he just told a joke.

"*I guess* it's a deal, then." Pax looked straight at Lucas to be sure he wasn't making fun of her, but the man nodded and she relaxed. "When do you want me to see the Priest?"

"The sooner the better. I'll wait for you at the main gate, tomorrow morning at seven. Please be punctual."

"Seven it is." Pax knew the rest of the room was looking at her for answers, and so she kept her eyes on a speck on the wall.

"Time for me to leave," Lucas said to Prince, "See you soon," to Pax and then left the room, with Cordelia in his wake.

"Come with me," Prince whispered to Pax.

She followed him without sparing a look for the remaining women. She was so focused on the way Prince's fingers were wrapped around her wrist, sending thrills up and down her arm, that she would have stepped over Lucas and Cordelia if they had not moved out of the way. Once her eyes were on Prince again, she forgot anything else, even that she was walking outside without a sweater and that she was only wearing a tank top. Prince led her to a secluded corner between two boulders, far away from prying eyes.

"Pax..."

She heard her name repeated at least a million times. And it was a good thing, because she would have forgotten even that. Prince's lips took possession of her mind and she ceased to exist as a conscious being. She was only aware of him and the way he made her feel. Her body was suddenly pressed against the cold sand and the stars in the sky went dark as Prince's eyes replaced them. Prince caressed and kissed her until they couldn't breathe, and still he didn't let her go. His hands followed the lines of Pax's body leaving her cold and burning at the same time. Her tank top stretched under his hands. Prince brushed the side of her breast and his lips left her mouth to kiss her nipple. Pax's hands took hold of him, pulling his head closer to her. She slowly traced his shoulders and then came back to focus on his chest, following the rising and falling of his breathing. Her fingers found the hem of his shirt and yanked it over his head, then resumed their journey along his body, only to pause at his pants. Following her instinct, she loosened the belt and opened the first two buttons, only to stop when he gasped. Her first reaction was to blush, she'd never done anything so brazen before and hid against him, but soon her heart matched Prince's erratic heartbeats and she was the one gasping. Her hands circled his back to brush the line of his shoulder blades and then continued down the ridges on his spine. Her fingers found the memories of countless mistreatments etched on his skin.

"I missed you so much. I thought I was going mad." He was shaking.

Prince, the man Pax had seen withstand a beating without as much as a whimper, was shaking at her touch. Pax felt humbled and powerful at the same time. She felt adored. "I don't want to live without you." That was it. It was her turning moment. There was no going back. Pax wanted him to understand what she meant.

"I know," Prince said and put her hand over his heart. He hooked one finger under the waistband of her pants and pulled them down slowly, waiting for Pax to stop him. She didn't. She removed the tank top completely and then helped him out of his trousers.

"I have thought of nothing else," he said with an uncertain voice. "I want you. Only you." He leaned until his mouth brushed against her ear.

Pax felt the fear in his voice and shivered in anticipation.

"Tell me; is it the same for you?"

"Kiss me. Hold me. Never let me go again," Pax pleaded, her voice so soft she didn't think he had heard her. Intense joy filled her when Prince covered her shivering body with his. She let him guide her as they were kissing each other, their hearts beating so fast that was hard to think and breathe at the same time. Their hands intertwined, their legs finding their natural place until Pax was cradling him as close as she could.

Pax was overwhelmed to see that Prince's eyes were lost in hers when she reemerged from the depth of a kiss that left her dizzy. Prince seemed to be equally dazed by what was happening to them. She saw the light changing in his eyes and something stirred inside her as well. All of a sudden, her legs were pressing him to her, but it wasn't close enough. Skin to skin wasn't enough. Prince was murmuring something in a language she didn't understand. His voice was beautiful; the foreign words he was breathing in her ear were like liquid fire. The burning pleasure traveled from her ear to deep inside her very core.

Pax felt his love and trusted Prince at the threshold of something that was new to her. She let her body accept his in a way she would have never thought possible. When the pain came, she tensed for a second and he froze.

"Please, don't leave me now," she whispered.

His lips gently traveled from her neck to her mouth and answered her prayer without words. Their bodies started dancing to their unique rhythm and it was beautiful. It was glorious. It was the reason why they were both alive. She finished where he started, pieces of a design that only made sense united. When Prince's breathing became so ragged and his body seemed to have found the end of hers, Pax blessed the earthquake that rumbled through her and finally swept both of them away to a place full of peace.

They stayed like that, embraced and united, under the stars. When a gleam of consciousness repossessed her mind, Pax went to caress his face with shaking fingers. She looked at Prince and his eyes were shining with the same tears she was crying.

"I didn't know..." Pax's voice was too broken to finish her statement, but Prince nodded in response.

He moved slightly and propped his head on his bent arm to better look at her. His other arm slid around her waist, ending at the small of her back. Pax found that she loved the feeling of his hand radiating warmth, lightly pressed, with his fingers possessively splayed on her skin. When Prince pulled her to him to kiss her lips, she thought there couldn't have been a more perfect moment in her life.

"I can't be with anyone else but you." Pax had to tell him. He had to know. The rest of the world wouldn't understand, and it would have been easier if they were both women. But she couldn't command her heart.

"You deserve better than me." Prince kissed her lips. When she tried to complain, he shushed her with his mouth pressed against hers. "I know I'm condemning you to a life a misery. But I'm too selfish to let you go. There can't be anyone else for me, either," he said and tears fell from his eyes to her cheeks. "I can't let you go. I'm not strong enough to live without you." Prince hid his head against her chest.

"Look at me," Pax softly commanded him, and when he didn't move, she gently raised his head with her hands. "Don't let me go. My biggest fear is losing you." She locked her mouth on his, and the intensity of what she was feeling was so powerful she started shaking in his arms. And being so close wasn't close enough, again. Pax lay down, and her whole body implored Prince to eliminate that gap between them, until they were one and the universe was singing in her ears once more.

CHAPTER 12

The morning after, Pax woke up after a short, although peaceful, slumber. The sun was already high in the sky when Prince had finally given her one last kiss before letting her go home. In fact, there had been several last kisses.

Pax looked in the mirror and the face staring back at her was disheveled with two big, blue circles under her eyes. She smiled. She had never felt so beautiful. Her body was aching; she was sure she had a sore throat, and she smiled.

"Big day, eh?" Cordelia was leaning against the doorframe.

"The first of my new life." Pax wanted to scream to the four winds that she was the happiest woman alive. She knew better.

"Wow, I hadn't realized you could be so enthusiastic. Although I agree with you; today your life will change." Cordelia kept looking at Pax, her lips curved up.

Pax blushed under the scrutiny, but held her ground and didn't say anything that would betray her. "Are you going to accompany me to the gate?" Pax washed her face with cold water, cleaned her teeth with a brushing twig and a pinch of ashes, and then tied her long hair with a rubber band.

Cordelia's eyes traveled to Pax's collarbone, where there were several telltales of her night, but didn't elaborate on what she saw. Pax closed the sweater to hide her neck and turned around to face the other woman, who hadn't answered yet.

"This is why I actually came to talk to you. Do you want me to walk you there?" Cordelia was still looking at her with unfathomable eyes.

Any other day, Pax would have shivered. "Off we go, then, or I'll be late." She led Cordelia out.

Although Pax had the feeling the woman was dying to say something to her, they didn't talk much during the walk, just civilized comments about the beautiful crisp air of a summer morning in the desert. Pax took in the colors surrounding them and thought she had never seen such shades of oranges and burnt earth tones. A few scattered flowers growing between cracks in the dried dunes surprised her eyes with a splash of bright azure.

"Amazing, isn't it?" Cordelia asked.

At first, Pax thought she was talking about the miracle of life in the middle of an unforgiving nature. Then she followed the woman's gaze and found it was exactly what she was talking about. Except that they had different subjects in mind.

"Speechless? I know. Even I, who was born here, am at loss for words when it comes to describing the city," Cordelia said, and Pax would have sworn she heard pride in her voice. "Everybody should know about this. It's such a loss that we have to keep it hidden." Cordelia kept walking slowly, almost reverentially.

"You're right," Pax admitted in awe.

They walked along a well-beaten trail that switched back and forth on itself, winding down and disappearing inside the flanks of a high canyon. Pax had already had a look of the city from afar, the day Prince and she had been brought there. But she wasn't prepared for what she was seeing now. The city lay inside an enormous bowl, completely surrounded by a natural-looking wall. The closer they came, the more was revealed. The whole city was built like a tiered cake; the roofs of the first layer of houses and shops creating the streets of the second layer, and so on and so forth up until the last layer. The predominant color was a rich reddish brown, and the morning sun gave the whole city an orange glow.

"I used to build sand castles when I was a little girl," Pax thought out loud.

"That's exactly what my mother told me when she tried to explain to me what the city resembled." Cordelia nodded and smiled as the sunrays finally reached the topmost layer. "Look." She took Pax's hand in hers and stood there, watching the open window of the highest building of the city become a beacon of light.

"Oh!" Pax felt overwhelmed.

"Every morning the Priest opens that window to let the sun in and purify the hearts of the men living in the city. It never fails to humble me," Cordelia said after a few moments of eerie silence. The whole bowl had been swept by the light and was now back to the earthly colors that composed its natural palette.

"Cleansed. I feel cleansed," Pax murmured.

"Yes, that too." Cordelia smiled a secret smile.

"But when the Priest... is gone, who's going to take care of it?" Pax closed her eyes for a second to memorize the image of the city shining like a sun.

"He's looking for a successor to keep the tradition alive. He knows that the end is near." Cordelia's eyes became bright. "Let's go down." She led the way methodically, warning Pax of false steps and treacherous hidden holes.

Pax hadn't said much earlier, but now, she was so focused on taking in all the details of the outlandish landscape that she didn't utter a single word for the rest of the walk. Cordelia seemed as mesmerized because she didn't try to start a conversation. Toward the end of the hike, descending toward the city, she noticed a series of dunes bordering it at intervals that looked too regular to be natural. She raised one eyebrow and Cordelia smiled at her.

"The men call it the Great Wall," she said. "In the past, during sand storms, people got swiped away by sudden avalanches. So, the Priest has thought of a way to dam the desert around the city. They've been building this wall for a while now by putting together wooden planks and anything else they can spare. They keep adding to the scaffolds any time parts of the wall give way."

"It's incredible what they've done out here with so little." She gave one last look at the Great Wall and then focused on putting one foot after the other on the steep descent. They reached the bottom of the bowl after a long hike accompanied only by the cooing sound of the owls going to sleep. Meanwhile, the temperature had risen to toasty warmth, the earlier crispness already a memory.

"Ready?" Cordelia asked before tapping softly on a wooden gate with her knuckles. Pax smiled and shook her head.

"As ready as I'll ever be," she answered.

Cordelia stepped aside to let Pax in first when the gate opened with a whooshing sound. "They're watching us." She looked up and waved her hand to someone Pax couldn't see.

"Lucas is waiting for you," a voice resonated close. Cordelia muttered a thank you to the thin air and moved ahead, leading Pax in her wake.

"Up we go," Cordelia commented as they entered a covered hallway that ended with a stairway. They climbed several floors and emerged on a balcony facing an internal garden. Pax didn't have time to take a good look at the variety of plants adorning the perimeter of the central koi ponds because Cordelia had already knocked on a door.

"Good, you're here." Lucas's deep voice greeted them both, but his eyes were only for Cordelia.

"Helped her find the way," she said, reciprocating the gaze.

Pax felt like the proverbial third wheel.

"Let's hurry. The Priest's been waiting for you since dawn." Lucas finally broke contact and looked at Pax.

Somehow, she would have preferred to be ignored for a while longer. Lucas still unnerved her. Despite all the talk about how he had saved her life, she was wary of him.

"I'll come along. It's been a while since last time I visited him." Cordelia entered Lucas's apartment and then turned around to indicate Pax should have done the same. She didn't have the time to ask where they were going because Lucas opened another door.

"What—" Pax stood at the edge of a balcony that opened inside the city.

The City of Men was completely hollow at its center, from the very bottom to the very top of it. If, from the outside it resembled a sand castle with its stony walls, the inside was like a big funnel. The whole city opened inside on the empty space in a triumph of colors. Where the outside was monochromatic and easily confused for a trick of nature, the inside was sculpted like a filigree of windows, arches, bridges connecting buildings from one side to the other of the void, balconies, and suspended gardens. And the colors. The colors were magnificent, joyous, and psychedelic.

"It's like the festival of light in Trean." Pax was comparing the reds, yellows, pinks, greens, and blues to something she had seen only once when visiting her grandmother, but the vision had remained engraved in her memory.

"Yes." Lucas laughed at Pax's comment. "But, here, it's an everyday occurrence."

"How do you know about Trean?" Pax couldn't help her curiosity.

"My parents told me about it." Lucas's smile had died.

Pax was going to reply with something along the line that she was sorry, without knowing what she was sorry for. Cordelia helped her out, asking Lucas about the pump. Pax listened for a few seconds and then kept following them—the sight before her eyes compelling her attention. Lucas's and Cordelia's voices became a low buzz while the city's own soundtrack grew louder. There were men everywhere. That fact by itself would have been noteworthy. Pax was fascinated by the way they physically owned the place.

Up to that moment, she had only seen men enslaved, barely living, at the fringe of a world made by women and for women. Here they were busy creating a life for themselves. She watched as nobody moved out of her way in deference. She barely noticed that Lucas and Cordelia were leading her to the upper levels of the city. They used a series of spiral staircases that jutted out onto the central void. Pax leaned out over the wrought-iron fence shielding the stairs and a strange euphoria conquered her heart. The whole city lay before her eyes, and it was vibrant and full of life.

"Why are you smiling?" Lucas asked Pax.

"I like it here," Pax admitted. "Where are we?" she asked, once her eyes focused on the dimly lit landing at the end of the flight of stairs.

"Halfway to our destination." Lucas was already out of sight. Pax gave Cordelia a questioning glance.

"We're going to take a ride on the elevator." Cordelia stepped off the last step and seemed to disappear, engulfed by the darkness.

Pax followed her to a landing that was big enough for the three of them to stand side by side. Before her was a wrought-iron gate of the same design as the fence. Lucas opened the gate and held it with one hand to let the two women inside the cabin.

"Enjoy the view." Lucas smiled while taking his position close to Cordelia. "We're ready," he called, banging on the wall by his side.

"Okay," someone called back and the elevator first fell a bit and then lurched up with a sudden jerk.

Pax readjusted her body and grabbed a bar.

"Easy, guys!" Lucas said, hands cupping his mouth to propagate his voice outside. "Forgive the boys; they've lots of energy." He smiled at Pax.

Pax imagined a horde of young men pulling and releasing a rope to make the elevator cabin go up and down. She leaned to see if she could find them, but another jerk send her against the back wall.

"When they behave, it's a nice ride. It's like being suspended in the sky." Cordelia was looking straight ahead at the other side of the city walls.

"The Priest lives in the Tower. It takes forever to reach him from this level," Lucas said. "I do it at least once a day, just for the pleasure of it. It relaxes me. But don't look outside or down if you are scared of heights." He patted Pax on her arm.

She looked down. "Oh. My. Heavens." It was like falling up, toward the sky.

"I know. I can't understand why the Priest chose to live in the Tower when he can have any space he wants, downstairs." Cordelia had her eyes shut.

Pax followed suit immediately. And although it made talking rather unpleasant, it saved her from throwing up.

"Here we are," Lucas said as the cabin settled down rather abruptly several minutes later. He opened another gate and Pax stepped out with wobbling legs. "One word of caution, the Priest didn't sleep well last night; please, be nice and respectful, and try not to hurt his feelings."

She didn't understand why he had said so, but saw he was waiting for her to acknowledge his words and nodded in consent.

"He has little time left... " Cordelia started, shook her head, and sighed. "Not my place." She took Pax's arm and they walked toward a door at the end of a hallway that opened onto a small rock garden.

"He doesn't meditate here anymore," Lucas said to Cordelia. He knocked gently on the wooden door, and a young man with a scarred face opened it. Lucas seemed surprised to see him.

Pax found the young man's face familiar, but couldn't remember where she had seen him.

"Hi, Horace," Lucas greeted the young man, who saluted him back with some sort of deference, but barely acknowledged Cordelia. They proceeded to exchange a few hushed words, and then Horace tipped his head on the side to talk to Pax and Cordelia.

"He needs to sleep," he said unnecessarily loud.

"What happened to Carl?" Cordelia asked the young man.

"His father fell and broke his leg yesterday. So today, I'm taking care of the Priest instead. Got a problem with that?" Horace looked at Cordelia with an angry stare.

"As long as you do your job, no," Cordelia answered.

"Follow me," Horace ordered Pax.

She moved only to stop when she saw that Lucas and Cordelia weren't coming along.

"I'll say hi to him later. I know he wants to see you first thing," Cordelia answered her silent question; her voice broke at the end.

"Go on. Don't worry." Lucas's eyes had a shine that hadn't been there before.

"Go," Cordelia said with a smile, openly crying now.

Pax felt ill at ease, but obeyed them.

"This way." Horace didn't even bother to see if she was following.

Pax found the young man too commanding for her taste, but she didn't say anything back. Instead, she hesitantly moved through a narrow room that looked like an antechamber. On the walls there were paintings, hundreds of them, covering any available space. They were mostly seascapes, shores and waves running from one canvas to the other.

"Here." The young man gestured toward the door he had opened for her.

From the look on his face, Pax gathered that he liked the idea as much as she did. She was pushed to the other side without as much as a *please*. "Hey!" She would have said something else, but her mouth hung open in surprise for a few seconds. A shadowed figure was looking at her, commanding her attention.

"Hi, Pax. It's so nice to finally see you. I've been waiting to meet you for so long that I'd almost lost hope." The Priest, a man whose age was hard to define, spoke slowly and with a beautiful lilting accent. His eyes seemed to brighten as he saw her.

"You were waiting for me?" Pax repeated in confusion. The Priest's words didn't make sense, and to add to the mix, his voice and his countenance were familiar.

He nodded. "I'd say that I've been waiting for you all my life, but it wouldn't be true. It has been a long wait, nevertheless." The Priest raised one thin arm and gently patted the cushion beside him on the low couch he was resting on.

Pax noticed his long legs lying at an angle, covered by a cotton blanket. She also saw the pillow propped against the wall where the Priest's head had made a shallow indentation.

"I don't understand," she said, trying not to stare at him. She didn't move, leaving one hand firmly on the doorjamb.

"No, I'm sure you don't." The Priest smiled sadly and put his hand back on his lap, his fingers playing with the blanket's fringes.

"Why did you want to see me?" Pax evaluated the idea of politely excusing herself and leaving.

"As I just told you, it's a long story, but I'd like to have your full attention before I start. Our time together is limited, I'm afraid."

"I'm listening." She hoped the conversation was going to end soon. She couldn't wait to see Prince again. Memories of the night before dominated her thoughts, leaving little room for anything else. *Get to the point already, so I can go find Prince.*

"What if I told you that I know your family?"

"Everybody knows the—" Pax wasn't sure what Lucas had told the man. For a moment, she regretted not having asked Prince what he had revealed to Lucas.

"You're right; the Layans are well known in Ginecea." The Priest's fingers stopped playing with the blanket for a moment.

Pax stared at him, deciding what the best plan of action was.

"Your housemate, Sonia, talks highly of you."

"But she doesn't—" She bit her tongue.

"No, don't worry, she doesn't know who you are, but for me, it was easy to put the pieces together once Prince told me your name was Pax."

"What are you talking about?"

"Well, it was too big of a coincidence that you, a girl named Pax, escaped from Sundial, where Maurice Layan's daughter, whose name is also Pax, went to summer camp."

"It could mean nothing."

The Priest's lips curved up as he bent to retrieve a magazine from under the couch. "I've looked at those pictures so many times... You're extremely photogenic. I have a box full of pictures of you when you were younger." He showed her a glossy image of Maurice, Claudine, and herself smiling for the camera.

Pax didn't take the proffered magazine. She remembered when the picture had been taken, only a day or two before she left for Sundial. "Why do you have pictures of me?"

"What if I told you that your family and I have lots in common?"

"I'd tell you that's highly improbable."

"Nevertheless, the Layans and I go back several decades."

"I don't understand."

"How could you, sweet child?" The Priest sighed, his eyes unfocused.

Pax wondered if the man was whole. The women at the Sanctuary spoke highly of him, but maybe his illness had compromised his brain. She almost hoped that was the case, because he knew who she was and she didn't like it. "Go on," she said eventually, making two small steps forward.

"I met your grandmother when I was slightly older than you are now."

"She went to visit the facility where you worked?" Pax was momentarily drawn back to the conversation.

"Yes, our paths crossed when she came to the Temple to have your mother Maurice. But, make no mistake, I didn't work there. I was a semental, a slave. I understand women have spruced up their vocabulary, but the truth stays the same. There are no workers in Ginecea."

Pax let the Priest pontificate on the subject, but when he paused, she asked, "Why are you telling me this?"

"Because it's relevant."

"Relevant to what?"

"To explain how you and I have a lot in common."

"How so?"

"For starters, your grandma and I were... friends."

Pax looked at him with pity. Her grandmother wasn't friendly with her own race; to contemplate the idea that Rosie Layan, known as the haughtiest of the pure breeds, had befriended a man was ludicrous. *As if Grandma would come close to a man... like I did.* She almost said so to the Priest, but then closed her mouth. He was lost in his thoughts once more. She almost felt sorry for the stranger she had heard so much about. However mighty the man had been, he wasn't there anymore. Before her eyes stood a dying, deluded old man.

"Why don't you sit down? So I don't develop neck pain on top of everything else I already have."

"I think you're confused and in need of rest." *And maybe by tonight you'll have forgotten about me.* She made to move, but the Priest's hand grabbed her arm with a strong hold, an unexpected display of strength for someone who looked so frail.

"Resting is all I do, nowadays. Give me a few minutes—" he said with a soft tone that was at odds with the grip on her hand.

I'm sorry, but a few minutes aren't going to make me believe anything you say. Pax thought as her patience was wearing thin. But, the Priest's sad look made her feel guilty, and she cursed herself for saying, "Just five minutes." *Not that one hour is going to make any difference.*

"They'll suffice." The Priest released her hand and patted the cushion again. "Please, sit down. And breathe. I'm very sensitive to people's emotions. You are... intense."

Pax's retort choked in her throat. She steadied her back against the wall and flattened her hands by her side, though.

"Okay, fine. You can stand. I'll stand as well." The Priest raised his hand for her to help and waited for her to decide what to do.

Pax saw how the man's body was shivering and sat down on the floor as far away as possible from him.

"That works, too," the Priest whispered and repositioned himself on the couch with great pain.

"Talk," Pax commanded with a clipped voice. She didn't like to be rude in general, and her tone wounded her because it made her feel like a horrible human being. "Please," she added under her breath.

"Coming to that." The man repositioned the blanket that had slipped away from his legs. Then, to further aggravate her, he poured some tea from a tray balancing on the couch. "What do you know about the Tarin accident?"

Pax wasn't prepared for the history question and she blankly stared back at him. *What about Tarin now?*

"Do you know what happened at Tarin?"

"Off course I do." She raised one eyebrow. *I don't have time for this.*

"Yes, but *what* do you know?"

Irritation was getting the better of her, but she was willing to play along to be done soon. "Pure breed women died, slayed by men. The accident changed Ginecean Laws regarding safety procedures in factories, farms, plants, etc.," she recited. "Every year, we remember the heroic actions of the women who lost their lives during the Tarin massacre." Being a senator's daughter, she had brought flowers to the monument erected in Ginecea every single commemoration since she was three years old.

"I was there when it happened."

"Didn't you just say that you were at the Temple?" Pax heard a man's voice coming from outside and her heart raced faster for a moment, only to be disappointed to recognize Lucas talking. She felt the Priest looking at her.

"I was sent to Tarin later. Someone warned the Priestess about Rosie and me—"

"You and my grandmother, what?"

"She talked to me, a brick wall between us, and that was crime enough to send me to my death," the Priest explained.

Pax couldn't help but shiver at his words. Until a month ago, she wouldn't have believed him. Ginecea was careful in giving edited information regarding the men. She hadn't known a man could be beaten to a pulp and nobody would raise a finger to stop it. And then she imagined herself and Prince having to talk without seeing each other, without being able to touch each other, and sadness mixed with despair filled her heart. "So, about Tarin?"

"Things didn't go the way you were taught."

"There was no Tarin massacre?" Pax was glad to return to a topic she could make a joke of.

"Women died, it's true, but they weren't killed by men."

The Priest looked at Pax with his liquid eyes and she knew he was waiting for her to stop him. "How did they die?" she asked instead.

"They were killed by other women."

"How do you know?"

"I told you I was there—"

"Yes, you were at Tarin—"

"No, what I'm saying is that I was *there* when the massacre happened. And so were your grandmother, her mother, her mother's publicist, and several other women who got caught in something much bigger than they."

She was stunned. He sounded lucid and yet, was talking nonsense. "My grandmother, Rosie, was at Tarin when it happened?" Pax couldn't imagine her grandmother, the most proper of the proper pure breeds, getting involved in something like what had happened at Tarin. "What was she doing there?"

"She was trying to help me escape. We didn't get far. Women were killed to cover the truth. I was shot."

"But, I never heard of this…"

"Of course not. The president was there and she couldn't afford a scandal involving her daughter. The whole story was tailored to fit what the public was eager to believe. 'Savages on a Killing Spree,' makes a better headline than, 'First Daughter Found Guilty of Perversion; Tries to Free Slave.'" The Priest readjusted his body and cocked his head slightly to one side as if asking her opinion on the matter.

The word 'perversion' resonated longer than the others in Pax's already crowded mind. She shook her head.

"No? You don't think so?"

No, I don't feel... perverted. "What I think doesn't matter."

"What does matter, then?"

"The truth matters."

"The truth is that I'm one of the few who survived the Tarin massacre and it's thanks to your grandmother."

"Give me a proof you really knew her."

"You ask for a proof... here it is. Your grandmother's name is Rose, not Rosie."

Pax was taken aback. The only person outside her immediate family who knew that was Anna. It wasn't a big secret by any means, but it was something he couldn't have known under normal circumstances. "Let's start from the beginning, again. Exactly, how did you meet my grandmother?" She was now looking at him with different eyes. For the first time since she had entered that room, she was ready to listen.

His lips curved in another of his small smiles. "I met Rosie when she was twenty-one, and I was twenty-two. Her mothers had decided it was time for her to find a suitable bride and have children. Your grandmother had decided things shouldn't necessarily happen in that order. She went to the Temple and asked the Priestess to be blessed with child."

"But it doesn't work that way. Nobody goes to the Priestess with that kind of request!"

"If you have money and noble ancestry, you can get away with a lot more than that in Ginecea. Ultimately, you're the proof of what I'm saying," the Priest stated. "As you can imagine, the Priestess was, at first, put out by Rosie's childish request, but later decided to indulge her. Rosie was the president's daughter, after all. It also helped her cause that she knew something about the Priestess that—"

Pax interrupted the Priest in mid-sentence. "I'm not interested in old gossip, and I also know how kids are conceived."

"I'm afraid to be the bearer of uncomfortable news, but everything you know about how kids are conceived is a lie." The expression on his face was gentle, a strange contraposition to his words.

Pax looked at him and couldn't suppress a shiver. She didn't want to listen to what he was saying, but couldn't help to stay, mesmerized by the calm emanating from him. There was something in the way he talked that made her almost want to stay.

"Every woman born on this planet is fathered. The Temple is a fertility clinic. The Priestess, a skilled obstetrician. The ancillae, qualified nurses." He paused for a second and then started again, his voice sadder and tired. "Why do you think we, *men*, are still alive, even if kept in slavery? Women loathe us so much that it would only make sense if they had wiped us out centuries ago. But we're still here. Treated like animals. No, I correct my statement. We're treated worse than animals, but we're still here. Why do you think that is?" he asked her, bittersweet words made painful by the strained look on his face.

"I'm... not sure." The blasphemy about every woman being fathered was making her feel uncomfortable.

"The Priestess can't create life from nothing."

"Of course not, she mixes the DNA of the mothers. Every mother decides how much of her she wants to be in her daughter. Then the Priestess adds a third component, the *incognito*, which is what makes everyone different and unique. It's how pure breeds get their souls, according to religious people," Pax interrupted the Priest with the trite tale she had learned at school, adding the last statement as her own spin on it. She had grown skeptical.

"Your *incognito* is the semen from your biological father." The Priest ended her tirade with a wave of his hand.

"It's not possible," she said, a dogma engrained in her mind since she had use of reason.

"Why not? It's actually more plausible than the story they have fed you." The Priest looked at her and shook his head as if he was remembering something. "Would you like to hear how I met your grandmother?"

"I thought you already told me." Pax's head was heavy with thoughts she didn't want to think. And the more her mind lingered on them, the more she felt uncomfortable.

"I didn't tell you *how* it happened." He paused, and then he slowly started to talk again, without hurry. "It was only by an incredible chance that Rosie and I met. Unbeknownst to both of us, I had been chosen to be her semen donor."

Pax gave him a shocked look, but he raised one long finger and she choked back whatever she was going to say.

"A guard made a mistake and I ended up in a room I wasn't supposed to be in. I listened to Rosie's voice, and I fell in love with her even before laying eyes on her beautiful face." His eyes sparkled at the memory.

Pax felt something, but she didn't want to acknowledge it. She could see, though, that he was somewhere else entirely.

"In retrospect, it really was as simple as that. We started talking through a wall—she used to take a walk outside my cell every night before going to sleep—and something happened during those conversations. Little by little we came to know each other. I remember waiting the whole day to hear her voice at night and how disappointed I was the time she couldn't come."

Pax felt it again, but one more time, she pushed away the recognition of what that feeling could be.

He looked away for a second and then came back to the present and waved his fingers in the air. "Anyway, soon enough, the expected happened. As I already told you, someone discovered us and I was sent to Tarin to die. My only luck was that I was too valuable to be disposed of right away, and Rosie managed to find a way to follow me there."

"It's hard to believe she did something like that... following you to Tarin."

The Priest's lips curved up at her words. "But she did. Of all the things she did for me, following me to Tarin was the most incredible. You see, she didn't have to. She could have forgotten about me and gotten along with her already complicated life. But she did come to Tarin, and she saved my life."

"How did she do it? Save your life, I mean," Pax asked.

"It's a long story that I know only partially, but to make it short, she bargained my freedom with hers, as I came to realize only much later."

Pax felt a deeper tug this time. Something she couldn't easily dismiss. "Did you really fall in love with her?" she asked, her heart jumping unexpectedly at her own question.

"Yes, I did."

"Was it worth it to... love her?" She heard herself uttering the words.

"Was it worth it, you are asking?" The Priest's eyes went wide, and for a moment, Pax thought he wasn't going to answer. "I'd have stayed in Tarin, just to be with her. I'd have voluntarily chosen to be a slave all my life. I existed only for the few minutes Rosie's bribes got us. We never had any privacy. I was chained to the wall. She used to reach through the bars and stretch her fingers just to touch mine. We talked for hours about us, about our... about the life we would never have. We dreamed." The Priest paused, his eyes lost in the memory. "We had a few precious moments of stolen bliss. And, yes it was worth it," he added as an afterthought and paused again, this time longer than Pax could bear.

"What happened in the end?" All of a sudden, she wanted to ask why they had separated, but somehow, it sounded too personal. Meanwhile, she had moved closer to him without realizing it.

"Rosie knew my days in Tarin were numbered and she arranged to set me free with the help of one of the guards. She promised me she was going to join me as soon as our baby was strong enough to survive in the desert," he finished almost hurriedly. A new pain strained the Priest's fine features.

"But, you didn't try to contact her? She didn't reach for you?" Pax couldn't help but ask. She had asked, but she didn't want him to answer. She already knew what had happened to them. Nothing.

He shook his head slowly. "I still love her, you know? I love her now with the same intensity I loved her then." He paused for a long time.

Pax didn't try to fill the silence.

"She married soon after I settled here. I didn't know it immediately. Then I realized what she'd done for me, and that she wanted me free more than anything else."

"Have you ever heard from her in all those years?"

"No. Never. If she tried to send me messages, they never arrived here. But I doubt that. She has been doing everything in her power to protect Maurice… and me."

Pax thought of saying something, but she couldn't. Her head was spinning.

"I tried to follow Rosie's life as best as I could through magazine articles I had smuggled here. But she kept to herself, and for being a first daughter, she never stood under the spotlights. I know she never divorced her wife, and when she became a widow, fifteen years ago, she went to live by the sea."

"Where she still lives in a secluded cove, away from everybody." Pax thought of her grandma and her reclusion. She had always loved the austere, little woman, but never understood her penchant for solitude.

"I know she never remarried. I like to think that Rosie has never forgotten me," he said.

Pax couldn't help staring at him.

"I never had anyone else in my life." The Priest's eyes were bright. He wasn't talking to her anymore.

"It's something…" Pax's throat closed on the remainder of the sentence.

"What is it?"

"To love the way you did. It's something not everybody gets to experience," she finished.

"No, I guess it's not." He took her hand from the floor and gently caressed it.

She let him. "How did you survive?"

"Well, the physical part was easy. After a few years, my body was whole again. My heart, on the other hand, has never healed," he answered. "But I have had a life full of love, and now I even got to see you, my… Pax. Today is one of the happiest days of my entire life."

Pax was confused by the old man's words.

"*Pax*, I like your name. You know you are the only one with that name?" he continued.

Pax wondered how he could know she was the only one named so, but instead, she said, "Grandma Rosie wanted me to have this name. I don't know why. My mothers thought it went well with the family's last name, and it was original. What's your name?"

"Oh, my. Almost nobody knows my name." The Priest seemed to think about whether to tell her or not.

After a long silence, Pax decided that she wanted to know. "Why?" she asked.

"Rosie was the last person to call me by my given name," he said and a tear fell to the blanket. "At the beginning, I couldn't stand the sound of my name from any other mouth that wasn't hers. And then life happened, and I became the Priest."

Pax waited for him to elaborate on what he had just said, but he had withdrawn into himself, which gave her a moment to collect her thoughts. The whole exchange had been surreal. She replayed some of the most absurd passages and almost smiled. But then, something else he had said made sense, and the smile disappeared from her face to be replaced with a deep frown. If part of the speech was true, why not everything else? Her head hurt. Finally, she connected some of the dots and a question emerged from the chaos. "But, if my mother was… fathered—" She couldn't help but lower her voice on the last word. "—it means that you're…"

"Your grandfather." The Priest's expression changed to one of pure delight, as if a weight had been lifted from his shoulders.

Pax's eyes went wide at his words, unable to fake a calm she didn't feel. "I need time to digest this." She tried to sound gentle.

A gentle knock on the door interrupted them. "It's okay. We'll have time to talk later. For now, it's enough." The Priest patted her hand and then released it. "Come in, Horace," he called, turning toward the door.

The young man came in with an apologetic look on his face. "Sir, I must remind you of your nap," he said, looking back and forth between Pax and the Priest.

"Thank you, Horace." The Priest nodded and then looked at Pax. "I'd love to see you tomorrow morning, if that's okay with you."

"Yes, I've so many questions—"

"I promise I'll answer all of them." The Priest's voice was weaker than a moment before.

Pax didn't want to leave, but saw the strain on his face and the light shaking of his hands. "Tomorrow then." Horace held the door for her, and she reluctantly stood up and made to follow him outside.

She was already outside the door when the Priest called her. "Pax?"

She turned to face that man who looked so much like her, her heart squeezing in her chest. "Yes?"

"Your mother was named after me," he said and waved good-bye.

CHAPTER 13

Pax had left the Priest's house, her *grandfather's* house, in a haze. Cordelia and Lucas had asked her questions, and she had probably answered, although, she wasn't sure of what she could have possibly said back. After Cordelia had briefly visited the Priest, they had taken the elevator back to the lower levels and walked her outside the city. At some point, Lucas had disappeared, and she and Cordelia had found their way back home.

"Are you going to cook any dinner at all?" Tai finally asked, after having already asked if there was anything left from lunch.

"Working on it."

Pax was looking outside the window. She was staring at a point presumably in the direction of the City of Men. Her mind had never left the Tower. In her mind, she had never stopped talking to Mauricio. Her grandfather's name was Mauricio. He was dying and she could only imagine all the conversations she wished they might have. Her mother Maurice was fathered. Actually, if what Mauricio had said was true, every woman in Ginecea was fathered. Pax had slowly come to the conclusion that she had a biological father. She didn't really have two mothers. She had one mother and one father. But Maurice and Claudine were both her mothers; she couldn't think otherwise. She felt like screaming.

"You're moving a wooden spoon inside an empty bowl." Tai touched Pax's elbow with a pen.

"No need to poke me!" Pax snapped back.

"I can help you," Tai offered.

"Help me with what?"

"With the dinner?" Tai looked at Pax with a mix of frustration and curiosity.

Pax looked back and realized she had to calm down a notch or two. It wasn't Tai's fault she wasn't the person she wanted to talk to. The person she was longing for was working at the wind plant, and she had no idea where the wind plant was. Or even what one was supposed to do at a wind plant. Tai poked her again with the pen, and this time Pax held her tongue in check.

"I... I'm sorry. Yes, please. I could use some help," she admitted, giving a last tuck at the imaginary cream she was whipping inside the empty bowl.

"It's okay; I tend to lash out at people when I'm angry. Or sad," Tai said, putting on a white apron.

"I'm not angry," Pax replied with too much conviction.

Tai raised one skeptical eyebrow and then smiled.

"Okay, I feel... strange today." Pax let the words hang longer than was proper, but Tai understood her request for privacy.

"Your *friend* intercepted me at the end of my work shift," Tai said.

"You saw Prince?"

"Prince? Is that his name?" Tai asked incredulously.

"Yes. So, you saw him." Pax raised her hands and prompted the girl to keep talking.

"*Prince* gave me a message for you."

"Yes?" Pax's mood was having a relapse into the darker side.

"Do we need the grayish flour or the other one? What do you call the brownish one?" Tai moved away from the floating table and went to the pantry.

"It's rye flour. And no, we don't need it."

"So, which one do you want me to use for the bread?"

"The one that says on the bag 'bread flour.' And don't forget to sift it." Pax wanted to choke Tai.

"All right, I'll tell you what he said; he's coming later tonight." Tai brought the bag of flour to the floating table and started measuring it for the bread. "Be careful," Tai added seriously. Pax wasn't listening anymore.

After having baked restlessly, having endured Tai's company first, and then the cheerfulness of the other women, Pax resigned herself to wait for Prince to arrive. As soon as dinner was done, she put a sweater on and went outside in the courtyard. She played with her dead cell phone for a while. She flipped it open and then snatched it back closed to hear the clipping sound. The cell phone battery had died soon after she had left the farm, but she was used to its weight inside her pants pockets. It was the only familiar thing left to her. Her cell phone was the only constant in her life.

Pax was upset with the entire world. Everything she knew seemed like a lie. She, and every other woman on Ginecea, had been raised on principles that were wrong. Society had made her believe she couldn't possibly develop any sentiment toward a man. And if that happened, she must have been a pervert. Society was keeping Lexi apart from her true love, under the assumption that Lexi was of a superior breed. They were all the same. Women. Men. Pax's head was heavy with thoughts she never had reason to contemplate before. She had been so mad at the Priest, she still couldn't bring herself to call him *grandfather*, because he had forced her to face a reality where her mothers were wrong. She had been ready to antagonize them, and she had done that successfully by saving Prince from certain death. But it was easier to think she was trying to change a system in which she had believed for the best part of her first nineteen years. It was much harder to discover their system was based on prevarications and it was rotten from the inside out.

Pax had never believed the fathered women, who normally were employed to serve the higher breeds and who also gave birth to men, were inferior. Lexi's words had found fertile ground in Pax's conscience. *But* she had accepted the social hierarchy without further questioning. She felt sick. Her mothers were the paragon of everything that was wrong with the Ginecean society. Maurice, whose mother had known the truth about her conception, was running as president. Pax almost laughed at the irony.

She started feeling cold and suddenly realized it was getting darker. Pax couldn't tell how long she had been waiting, but the layer of dew on the brick wall she was using as a seat was revealing. She hugged herself, anticipating the moment she was going to feel Prince's arms embracing her in his warmth. She was going to tell him everything she knew. Prince was going to make her feel better. That certainty kept her waiting, even when the night grew too silent for comfort. Finally, she saw a dark figure emerge from around the corner.

"Prince!" Pax wasn't going to stay put, so she broke into a run toward him. She flew into his arms before he could say anything. She had missed him so much during the few hours they had been apart. "Prince?" She didn't have the chance to say anything else. Black shadows obscured her eyes, and she felt dizzy. Her last thought was that Prince was going to wait for her in vain.

She was moving or rather she was being moved by someone or something. Pax couldn't be sure. Her head was undulating at a strange angle, and she couldn't see anything. Her chest was crushed by a hard surface. Her lungs were pumping in stale air. Pax opened her mouth to speak, but no sound came out.

"I knew she was trouble the moment I saw her with the rescued man." A man's voice echoed in Pax's muffled ears. Coarse fabric chafed her skin. She fought the urge to spit out the hard filaments insinuating their way between her lips. She was trapped inside a sack. From the smell and the texture of it, it was probably the horse's forage bag. "But I could have never imagined what kind of trouble she was bringing to us."

"Neither did I," a familiar voice said.

Pax had heard him somewhere before.

"Maybe we should leave her in the desert and be done with her. Lucas isn't going to risk his men to launch a full-scale search for a woman. He has better things to do," the first man proposed calmly.

"You forget that she's not just *any* woman. She is worth more alive than dead."

"I have a bad feeling about this—"

"Nonsense. If we don't act first, we're going to have the whole Ginecean Army stomping across the City of Men. She's Maurice Layan's daughter, for Heavens' sake. Do you think the Layans are not already combing the desert for their spoiled brat? I wouldn't be surprised if we find them around the corner."

"I'm still concerned. If we leave her to the mercy of the desert's animals, there's a good chance nobody is going to find her, anyway."

Pax was getting rather worried with all the talk about killing her, but realized her situation wasn't going to improve if her captors knew she was awake. A hand rested heavily on her thigh, and she forced a few shallow gulps of air in and out, hoping the man didn't realize she was listening.

"Did she move?"

"No, I was just checking that."

"Horace, I think I see something."

The horses stopped moving. Pax suddenly realized why one of the two voices sounded familiar. Horace. The rude man attending the Priest. He must have been eavesdropping on her conversation with her grandfather.

"I see something, too. Go ahead and scout what it is," Horace ordered with the attitude of someone who had everything under control. Pax heard the other horse galloping away. The hand resting on her thigh gave a hard squeeze, and she couldn't help but yelp in surprise.

"I thought so." Horace grabbed Pax through the sack and set her upright.

"Now, tell me how your ride was." He pulled the sack off of her head with a yank.

Pax gasped for fresh air and then found herself facing the young man closer than was comfortable.

"You don't look half bad," Horace said in a way that made Pax shiver. "Maybe we could get better acquainted, don't you think?" He stroked her cheek roughly.

"Don't touch me." Pax's body was shaking with rage.

"I'm not good enough for *mistress*?" Horace's hand crept around her back and pulled her hair with a vicious tug.

Pax didn't give him the satisfaction to cry.

"I think there's time to play with you." He pulled her off the horse and let her fall on the ground. He dismounted right after and pinned her down, sitting on her back.

"You know, it wasn't a coincidence I came back to check on the Priest when he said your name. Your demeanor gave you away from the beginning. I knew there was something about you. And then the Priest called you Pax. What a unique name. I'm sure everybody tells you that. So I kept listening from behind the door. I was already intrigued by you. The circumstances that brought you here were so... vague. Then the Priest said your mother's name. It eluded me at first, but I kept thinking about you during the day, and finally it hit me. There aren't lots of girls named Pax with a mother named Maurice. Only one, Pax Layan." Horace yanked Pax's sweater from the neck and tore it open.

"What do you want from me?" Pax's mouth was full of dirt, and she was starting to panic.

"Now? Isn't it obvious? Or hasn't your kidnapper *explained* to you some basic comparative anatomy?" Horace laughed at his joke and Pax felt the urge to puke. "You know, I never had a superior breed before. Let's see how different you're from the other women."

"No!" Pax screamed, trying to free her body from his grip.

She thrashed with all her might, but he didn't move. Horace shoved her head hard on the ground in retaliation, and he moved his hands to lower her pants. Pax felt his rough fingers probing her skin and screamed. Horace laughed at her cries. She heard the man working on his own clothes and tried one last time to free herself. When every effort was welcomed by the man's dirty words, Pax closed her eyes and hoped it was fast.

All of a sudden, the ground started vibrating. Horace stopped digging his fingers in her thighs. Pax took advantage of his temporary distraction and used all her strength to turn around and throw him off. Horace was back by her side in a second, but meanwhile, the source of the commotion was revealed. One man riding a horse was followed by two armored cars, chasing him closely.

"You're a lucky bitch," Horace barked.

Pax sagged on her hands and knees, feeling ill. Horace moved out of the way while she cast out all the contents of her stomach.

"What the—" He didn't finish his sentence, but started swearing instead. "Not like this. This is not what I planned. Damn you, Marcus," Horace repeated under his breath several times. "Not like this!" he yelled.

The man on the horse was a few yards away and had a scared expression on his face. Pax instinctively reached around to close the sweater on her back, but had to give up and brought her knees under her chin instead.

"What did you do? You idiot!" Horace spat on the ground.

The armored cars were approaching fast; Pax tried to make a run for it, but Horace took her by the shoulder and held her by his side.

"Horace, they ambushed me. I'm sorry." Marcus looked at Horace and then at Pax, disheveled and sick. He paused for a moment, trying to assess what had happened.

"And why did you come back here?" Horace gave Pax a jerk to keep her in place. She was feeling faint.

"You haven't touched her. Have you?" Marcus asked, terrified.

Pax started hoping again. Whatever the reason was for the man's discomfort was good news for her.

Horace didn't have time to answer; the armored cars skidded to a halt before them, creating a cloud of dust. He let go of Pax and she sagged down on her knees and started coughing. Her stomach painfully cramped and she retched again.

"Raise your hands above your head and kneel down," a woman's voice resonated in the air.

Pax looked up, wiped her mouth with a dirty hand, and tried to say her name. She managed to emit a comprehensible sound after several tries. Meanwhile the dust had settled down. A woman in military gear was standing by the side of the armored car, aiming a gun at them. Pax moved her head slowly to show her long hair. She said her name again, this time louder and clearer.

"Pax Layan? Are you Pax Layan?" the woman, now a shadow towering over Pax, repeated.

"Yes."

A hand raised her chin, and after a brief examination, the woman shouted a few commands. Four women came out from the two armored cars.

"Mistress Layan, I am Captain Larouche. Are you okay?" The woman was looking at her with worried eyes.

"Yes." Pax's legs were trembling and her breath was shallow and ragged, but she was fine. She tried to stand up, but staggered a few steps and went down.

"It's really her, Captain?" Another woman came close and helped Pax up.

"Yes, it's her. We can finally go back," the captain replied. "Throw the men into the other car."

"You promised me—" Marcus was hit by the captain's aide.

"I don't make promises to slaves." The captain kept her concerned face on Pax while waving her hand at the aide. "Let's move!" She gently accompanied Pax to her car. "It's a long trip to Ginecea; we better get started."

"I—" Pax held her tongue before she said she never intended to go home. She realized in time she had almost revealed the whereabouts of the City of Men. She thought of Prince and the end that would befall him if caught, and she shut her mouth tight. "I can't wait to see my mothers," she finished with a long stare at Horace and Marcus, who had been waiting for her words in trepidation.

"Of course. Let's get inside, where you can relax." The captain opened the passenger door for her. "I'll call your mothers; I'm sure you wish to—"

Pax put a hand on the captain's. "Not yet, please. I'm too shaken…" Her feelings were still raw and she didn't want to talk to them before Larouche.

"I understand, Mistress Layan." The captain helped her inside. "We have to inform your mothers we found you, but maybe you can talk to them later?"

"Yes, thank you. I don't want to scare them."

"Of course," she said and then called to the front of the car, "Fary—" The woman at the wheel tilted her head in response. "—call the capital with the good news." She gave Pax a small smile. "Just tell us when you're ready."

"Thank you." Pax turned around to see the two men being unceremoniously hauled inside the other armored car. *Good riddance to you,* she thought. And then she started worrying about their moral fiber. She didn't have time to brood over her thoughts, because Captain Larouche started asking her questions right away.

"I don't know anything. I was kept in a dark place the whole time," she said with the right amount of breaking in her whispered words.

"Can you tell me how many men were there?" The captain was gentle, but she had a report to compile.

"Only two." Pax realized she had sounded too sure. "But I was blindfolded the whole time."

"Did they harm you in any way?" Captain Larouche put a hand on Pax's arm.

"No—" Pax shivered at the thought of what had almost happened to her.

"You can talk to me." The woman had lowered her voice and was looking at Pax with sympathetic eyes. "Back there, when I first saw you, you looked terrified. Did that man—" She paused for a second. "—Did he do anything to you?"

"He was going to... but you stopped him," she said, without having to fake feeling sick. She turned toward the window and secured her hands under her legs to stop the trembling. A blanket was put around her shoulders. "Thanks," she murmured.

"Can you tell me where they kept you?" The captain changed topic. "I know that you couldn't see anything, but maybe you heard something your captors said."

"They were careful around me. They let me out, once in a while, to stretch my legs. They never removed the cap on my head. This time they brought me on a ride, but I wasn't on the horse for long, so I guess their camp was close to where you found me." Pax didn't know how much she could lie without saying anything that was going to contradict her words later. "I'm tired," she said, lowering her eyes.

"Of course you are. We can continue this conversation later. Now rest." The captain patted Pax's leg and then dimmed the light over their heads.

Pax thankfully nodded and turned her head toward the window. Her eyes searched the night, looking for the distant spot where Prince was. *When am I going to see you again?* When dawn's pale light revealed the change in the scenery, the harshness of the desert mollified by a gentler landscape, she wept. Her heart was breaking at the realization she was now a life away from Prince.

"Captain?" Fary, the woman in the front, turned around to interrupt Pax's hours of restless thinking. "We are three hours away from Ginecea."

"How do you feel?" the captain asked Pax.

"Better." She couldn't put that off any longer. "Can we make that phone call now?"

Fary put them through and Captain Larouche took the call on the speaker phone, and a moment later, Pax was talking to her mothers. Claudine and Maurice kept her, and the rest of the car, company for almost two hours. Only the captain's polite request to keep the line free for the last stretch of the ride gave Pax a much needed respite from the onslaught of maternal worries. Fortunately, neither Claudine nor Maurice said anything that would compromise the tale Pax was painstakingly fabricating. Pax wondered about that while she repeated her story for the second time around, and her mothers kept listening to her without a single question about Prince.

When Claudine and Maurice were forced to free the line, Pax rested her head on the cushion and closed her eyes, pretending to sleep. Her intent was to deter the captain from resuming the questioning and be free to check the car compass to see the route they were taking to drive back to Ginecea without arousing any suspicion about her interest. The armored car, a jet-car, the captain had called it, had been traveling at a dizzying speed, and with great difficulty she had tried to keep track of what she was seeing.

She slowly slipped into a warm dizziness and fitfully slept for the last part of the trip. She had a nightmare about Prince being murdered before her eyes and woke up crying. The captain and her team fussed over her and assured her the two men were going to be punished severely for whatever they had done to traumatize her so. Although Pax didn't like the idea of any human being tortured, she couldn't help but think of what Horace had planned on doing to her if the captain hadn't showed up. Her body started shivering again.

The captain offered Pax a thermos with some hot tea and then left her alone. Since she didn't know what the official story was regarding her *kidnapping*, she committed to looking shell shocked to avoid further talking. Pax realized the depth of the cover up Anna had been working on when instead of bringing her directly home, the captain went to switch the armored car with a civilian non-descriptive van. Then, instead of entering the Layan Mansion from the main entry, the captain directed the vehicle to the back of the property. Pax noticed that everything looked normal at the main gate. No frenzy of newspaper sharks.

"Pax, oh my Heavens, my sweet baby," Claudine kept repeating for several minutes before any coherent sentence would come out of her mouth. Maurice and she were all over Pax as soon as she stepped inside the house.

"Honey, never do anything like that again. You almost killed us." Claudine was crying profusely on Pax's shoulder. Anna immediately came close to show her support and softly whispered in Claudine's ear to be careful with her words before the captain.

"You're here now. Everything's fine. You're here, safe and sound. Nothing happened to you. You look fine. Right?" Maurice blathered about for a few seconds, holding Pax tight and looking at the captain.

"She's fine. The two men she was with hadn't touched her," Captain Larouche confirmed.

"Is it true?" Maurice asked Pax while shielding her from the rest of the room.

"Mom, nothing happened to me. I swear."

"You were kept hostage by two men, the whole time?" Claudine was looking at Pax, who couldn't bear to look back. Anna softly squeezed Claudine's forearm.

"Yes, there were only two men where we found her. One foolishly went scouting for us," the captain said with a derisive scoff. "They had this crazy idea to ask for a ransom."

"A ransom?" Claudine turned around and looked bewildered at the captain. Anna touched her again.

"Yes, can you believe their brass?" Captain Larouche shook her head.

"I don't know how they could think to survive after having escaped from the farm with such an important hostage," Anna, who had kept quiet since Pax's appearance in the house, commented with her official matter-of-fact voice.

Pax nodded absentmindedly. She was starting to see where all the lies were going.

"Have you already notified the farm that the fugitives have been found?" Anna, ignoring Pax, asked the captain.

"I will now. If you'll excuse me for a second." Captain Larouche disappeared after Anna into the adjacent room.

"We have to talk," Maurice said in a low voice meant to remain inside their embrace. The rest of the captain's team was a few feet away, waiting for orders.

"You won't say a thing. Let Anna deal with the details," Claudine added between kisses on Pax's forehead.

"Thank Heavens, you're safe. We haven't slept since you left the farm. What were you thinking? No, I don't want to know. I only want life to resume. Our normal, beautiful life." Maurice alternated kisses and scolding with the same vigor. "I've been so worried about you. The idea of you, all alone with that man, was terrifying." She couldn't stop talking.

"And he also had an accomplice. They didn't…" Claudine didn't finish her thought; her voice broke and she hugged Pax even tighter.

"Moms, nothing happened to me. Prince doesn't have anything to do with the two men who kidnapped me." Pax disentangled herself from her mothers and looked around. "Why don't we continue this conversation in my room? I don't feel comfortable here."

"What do you mean?" Claudine asked, loud enough to make one of the captain's women turn around.

"I think that Pax is right. We should go upstairs." Maurice gently squeezed Claudine's arm and imperceptibly nodded toward the women.

"I'm tired," Pax announced.

"Can you ask your captain to come back so we can thank her? Our daughter would like to go up to her room," Maurice asked the closest woman.

Less than a minute later, the captain was saluting the Layans. "I'll come back when it is more convenient for you. I have a few more questions, but they can wait," she said to Pax.

"We'll call you as soon as Pax feels better," Anna promised.

CHAPTER 14

Pax reached her room with a strange feeling of not belonging. She climbed the majestic staircase, flanked by her mothers, and felt like a ghost visiting a place that once had been important to her. Every step was both familiar and strange. Pax recognized the spot of ink on the marble tile. She had been seven when, while chasing Lexi up and down the stairs, she had stepped on a pen and smashed it, staining the tile. Walking through the hallway that led to the bedrooms, Pax saw the nick on the wall under a low coffee table caused by playing indoor soccer with Lexi. She had put a small statue before the indentation and never told her moms. Some of the maids had moved stuff around to dust, and since then, the incriminating mar in the wall was out for everybody to see, but Maurice and Claudine had never noticed. The wallpaper, the lightest azure with white bird silhouettes, was exactly the same it had been at the beginning of the summer. Pax looked at it as if she had never seen it before.

The real shock for Pax was her room, her beloved bedroom, which she had remodeled with Lexi's help with ivory furniture and dusty pink draperies. They had watched a movie where the main character lived in a house painted in those two colors. Pax had begged her mothers for weeks until they had caved in and had allowed her to change her room any way she wanted. It had been her sixteenth birthday present.

Pax stepped inside and hated it. Immediately.

"I can't sleep here." She was out of her bedroom in no time.

"I don't understand." Claudine, who followed Pax, looked at her daughter and then at her wife with a weary expression. "I can ask for some chamomile tea. Maybe you need to relax. That's it. You drink some calming tea, and then we'll talk about sleeping somewhere else," she said after a brief pause.

"Excellent idea. I could use some tea, too." Maurice went to the interphone in the hallway and asked for some light breakfast to be brought upstairs. "You traveled the whole night and the better part of the morning. You probably didn't sleep, and Heavens knows when the last time was you had a proper meal." Her voice was getting steadier.

"I slept a few hours." Pax pondered what she could safely say and what she better keep to herself. Her eating habits in a house full of women who had decided to flee society to live at the fringe of a city full of men, *free men*, did seem the kind of thing to keep secret. So she kept it at that—she had slept a few hours inside the armored car. She was hungry, though. Pax's stomach rumbled at her last word.

Mothers and daughter had their late breakfast in the library. Pax had gone there and refused to go back to her room. Maurice tried to reason with her. Claudine asked why she was reacting that way. Pax would have loved more than anything else to speak freely to her mothers, confess she couldn't bear the idea of going back to who she had been before leaving Ginecea and her comfortable, beautiful house. She wanted to say that the Pax they knew and loved, the Pax who had remodeled that bedroom, was dead. Once or twice she almost went as far as to ponder the idea of telling them the truth about her and Prince. Almost.

"You seem in good condition," Maurice started tentatively.

"We… need to know what happened to you during the two weeks you were… there with him," Claudine ended.

"Fifteen days—" *And, I've only seen him once.* It was a painful realization. Two tears escaped her eyes, and she was fast enough in wiping them without her mothers noticing. Or so she thought.

"Sweetie, I didn't mean to make you cry. I'm sorry. It's just that it killed us not knowing, all this time, wondering if that man was harming you… if he was forcing you—" Claudine was already silently crying and Maurice put an arm on her shoulder.

"If you don't want to talk, it's okay. Anna can buy you some time. We'll stick to whatever story she has put together. You won't have to talk to anybody. No journalists, anchorwomen, or police officers will bother you. I promise. The press will never know what happened. The farm is interested, as we are, in keeping everything hushed. But something happened to you, and it's going to break our hearts if we don't do anything. Sooner or later you'll have to confide in us and let us help you." Maurice did the talking, and Claudine nodded between sobs.

"You know that I wasn't kidnapped. You were there when I helped Prince escape from the farm. You understand that I knew what I was doing. Right?" Pax was holding her cup of tea like a shield.

"We thought about that. A lot. And we came to the conclusion that you were suffering from a trauma. Sometimes it happens, you know? We talked with your therapist about... your situation. Doctor Cassandra explained to us that in extreme cases of distress, the abductee can forge a bond with the abductor." Claudine managed to get hold of a handkerchief and cleaned the running mascara from her cheeks.

"You believe so?" Pax asked both her mothers.

"Of course we do, sweetie. What else could it be? It makes perfect sense," Maurice answered with her softest voice. The exact way she used to talk to Pax when she was a child and she was throwing a tantrum over some toy she swore she couldn't live without.

"It makes perfect sense. Doesn't it?" Pax said slowly, looking at some distant space outside the library.

"I think we should schedule an appointment with Doctor Cassandra as soon as possible. She understands the situation and she'll find a spot for you right away." Maurice was already walking toward the desk where there was an antique phone.

"Wait. I need to rest. And then I want to see Lexi," Pax ordered, but she did it with her sweetest tone and yawning in the process.

"I guess you're right about resting. You must be exhausted," Maurice said slowly.

"But I'm not sure about seeing Lexi. I don't think it's a good idea," Claudine interjected.

"I need my best friend."

"Sure, it's understandable, but—" It was obvious that Claudine didn't want to say anything to burn the bridge of communication they were slowly building with their daughter. Pax was counting on that to get away with what she wanted.

"I think you should be careful with what you say about... what happened to you. And with whom." Maurice had the phone in her hand. "Maybe you can rest, then talk to the doctor, and then we can invite Lexi tomorrow morning." She raised the phone and started dialing.

"I won't talk to the doctor today. I'll rest and then I'll see Lexi." Pax put down her cup on the coffee table by her couch. She stood up and went to the desk where Maurice was still holding the phone in midair, gently removed the phone from her mom's hand, and quickly dialed Lexi's house.

"Think twice about what you are doing. Please." Maurice stepped back and let Pax call without interfering. Claudine silently questioned Maurice.

"Lexi?" Pax turned her back to her mothers, regretting the decision of coming to the library where she had no privacy. She kept the conversation short and invited her friend right away for a sleepover. As soon as Pax had heard Lexi's voice, she realized she couldn't wait another minute to see her. Resting could wait. Maurice and Claudine stayed with her until Lexi burst inside the library only half an hour later, and then they reluctantly left them alone.

"Pax! I missed you so much!" Lexi had lost some weight since last time Pax had seen her. She still wore her long blond mane wild, but her blue eyes were sad, and her hands moved constantly. She ran toward Pax and embraced her, unable to say anything else.

"Missed you." Pax reciprocated the fierce hug.

"Pax, never leave me alone again. I don't know what to do with my life without you. And I have so many things to tell you." Lexi was still holding Pax. Warm tears rolled down her cheeks while she tried her best to hide them from her friend.

"Same here." Pax stepped back when she realized that Lexi was crying. "Don't get emotional on me. You know I can't stand you all teary eyed and stuff." She smiled and gave a soft pinch to Lexi's arm. "You see I'm here. You aren't dreaming!" Pax's words were immediately rewarded by a smile.

"You're more a nightmare than a dream, but I'm so happy you are alive and all in one piece that I'll even laugh at your poor sense of humor." Lexi emitted a choked sound and Pax pinched her again.

"I *am* funny," Pax complained.

"No, you aren't," Lexi stated, openly laughing now. She wiped the tears from her face and hugged Pax again.

"I really missed you. If only we had fallen in love with each other, our lives would be much simpler." Lexi sighed and laughed at the same time, tears betraying her again.

"You have no idea," Pax murmured, too low to be heard. "You snore in your sleep. And my moms wouldn't approve of our union," she added louder.

"Right, and you always do what your moms tell you." Lexi snickered.

"Only if you're involved," Pax retorted.

"You're mean." Lexi chuckled, amused, and then looked around the library with puzzled eyes. "Why are we here?"

"Long story short, I can't stand my room." Pax waived away the topic with a flourish of her hand.

"Okay. So... how are you?" Lexi suddenly asked, with eyes more worried than she wanted to show. The easy bantering of a few seconds earlier was already forgotten.

"I'm well enough, I guess. Given the circumstances and everything," Pax said, attempting some humor that got lost somewhere in the big room.

"Do you want to talk?" Lexi asked, holding Pax's hand.

"I don't know where to start." Pax shrugged.

"How about the beginning?"

"I'm in love." Pax smiled unwillingly.

"Tell me about her."

"Him."

"Hmm?"

"Him. I'll tell you about *him*. Prince." Pax waited patiently for Lexi to say something. Anything. Words never came. Lexi simply stared at her friend with her mouth open. "You can leave. If you don't want to be in my presence, I'll understand. I'll invent something for my mothers. Don't worry," she said with clenched teeth. Lexi's silence was painful to bear, and she was tired. Pax removed Lexi's hand from hers and scooted on the couch to put some distance between them. Angry thoughts filled her mind.

"No, it's not what you think. I'm surprised, yes, but I wouldn't leave you for anything in the world, not now that you're finally back." Lexi moved closer to Pax and hugged her. "I'm with you, one hundred percent. I don't care about your sexual orientation. I'm your friend. Your twin, remember?"

"Thank you, thank you... thank you." Pax was sobbing loudly. Anger was immediately replaced by relief. She had held the tears in while in her mothers' presence, but she couldn't contain them anymore. "I can't breathe at the idea that I'm not going to see him again." Her words were broken and whispered.

"I know. I know how you feel," Lexi said. "*I know exactly how you feel.*"

"We've made such a mess of our lives, haven't we?" Pax sniffed in her sleeve and then sighed.

"Yes, we did." Lexi put a hand on Pax's shoulder. "But we have each other. Never forget that."

"I missed you so much. You have no idea how many times I've imagined this conversation in my head." Pax finally smiled.

"Let it out, then! Tell me everything about your... Prince?" Lexi smiled, too.

"I know. It sounds funny." Pax laughed a little, and all of a sudden she realized the sun was shining through the big windows of the library. "Let's go outside. Some fresh air is going to wake me. I'm about to crash, but I really want to talk to you first." She was already yawning, but led Lexi downstairs and out to the vast expanse of luscious flowers and plants of the backyard. The sunlight hit her eyes and gave her the jolt she needed to stay awake long enough to narrate her story to Lexi.

The gardens at the Layan Mansion were in full bloom in late summer colors. Pax breathed in and out slowly for a few seconds, taking in the scents coming from the small orchard that was Claudine's pride. Apricot trees and lavender plants created an interesting palette for the eye. "I came here so many times in the past, and only now I see the colors," she commented, lightheaded.

"You sound... different," Lexi said.

"Because I'm a different person." Pax sat down on a stone bench shaded by a wisteria. She looked at the vines, weighed down by a cascade of flowers, and remembered something her grandmother Rosie had explained to her about wisteria plants. "It takes ten to fifteen years for the vines to blossom, and they normally do it in spring. We force them to blossom at the end of summer as well," she had explained, braiding a flowery necklace for her in that same spot. *We are a controlling race. Not even nature escapes our whim,* she thought and sighed out loud.

Lexi looked as if she wanted to say something, but thought better of it.

"Sit here." Pax patted on the cold stone.

Lexi was immediately beside her and promptly removed her cell phone from the back pocket of her jeans. "Nobody is going to bother us." She smiled at Pax while turning it off.

"I think I lost mine..." Pax saw the question in Lexi's eyes and hastily added, "Somewhere." She couldn't talk about Horace's hands roving over her body. Not yet. Maybe never.

"We could ring for some tea or something to eat?" Lexi asked. Once on the bench, she carefully adjusted her body with her legs underneath her.

"I hadn't realized how much I needed this. You. Something unchanged in my life." Pax relaxed her chin on her bent knees. She intertwined one trembling finger with the trailing purple flowers, and the scent of the wisteria filled the air. "Yes, we can ask for refreshments. Isn't it strange how accustomed we are to privileges when lots of people do without?"

"I'm glad you realized that." Lexi moved on the uncomfortable stone.

"When my moms called for the tea earlier, I was almost surprised that someone prepared it for us. I mean, it's not that in the time I was out, I forgot how life is around here. Very comfortable. But for the first time, I was really glad I didn't have to do it myself. Not that fetching tea is so difficult, but still, I was glad I didn't have to. Does this make any sense?" Pax looked at Lexi with pleading eyes. She wanted to be able to communicate with her friend. The things she was going to say were hard to utter out loud, and she was already tired of the small talk.

"I think I do. Although I'm not sure I have even the faintest idea of what you've been through out there." Lexi put a hand on Pax's arm and squeezed softly. "Why don't you tell me?"

"Everybody thinks I have endured hell at the hands of some man, but the truth is that *he*, Prince, ran away with me." Pax was frustrated by her inability to explain better. She called one of the servant girls discreetly roaming the garden to see if Mistress needed anything. Lexi asked for tea sandwiches and chai. Pax didn't want anything.

"We are like them," Pax muttered, shaking her head slowly.

"What did you say?"

"I must tell you something."

"Okay."

"You should fight for your love," Pax started, hoping to find the right words to say what came next.

"I know that—"

"Aria is as worthy as any pure breed."

"Don't say her name out loud!" Lexi frantically looked around, searching for indiscreet ears. "Do you want her deported? Of course she's as worthy as me," Lexi said, once she saw nobody else was around.

"No, listen to me. I mean it, literally. Aria—" Lexi's eyes shot her a terrified glance and Pax amended her error. "—*she* isn't different from you, or me. We are all born the same way."

"Of course we are the same. We're women, after all." Lexi looked perplexed by her friend's words.

"Not only that. We all have a father. Aria, you, and also me. Every woman on Ginecea is fathered." Pax dropped the bomb and didn't pause to see Lexi's reaction to her blasphemous words. "I met my grandfather, and he explained it to me. The Priestess and the Ancillae are not who we think they are. The *incognito*, the mysterious factor the Priestess supposedly implants in the mother's womb, is none other than the father's seed. I know, I know, it's not easy to digest. But don't you see? It makes perfect sense, once you know it. We're kept in the dark for our own good, so we can keep

172

exploiting the men and using the fathered women as lesser citizens. I'm so ashamed of who I am. I've never thought of one day feeling nauseated by what my mothers stand for. But here I am. I'm shocked. I'm devastated." Despite her words, Pax was elated. Something good was coming from being forced back to Ginecea.

"I want everybody to know what a shame we are. We are jackals. Parasites, who don't know how to care for ourselves. We need slaves to do the hardest jobs, the ones we don't even force the fathered women to do, but we call them workers, as if changing the name makes it less wrong. And then we have our servants for all the things we are simply too lazy to do. I hate myself—I hate the society I live in," she finished, just as the servant girl came with a tray full of food and assorted teas. Pax gave her a thorough look. "Would you like something to eat or drink?" she asked the servant girl.

"I beg your pardon?"

"Come here. I'll serve you for once. Do you want sugar in your tea?' Pax asked, already pouring the water in the cup.

"I don't understand—" The servant girl looked ready to bolt and was clearly scared.

"Pax, I don't think she wants anything now. Right?" Lexi talked for the girl's sake, but kept her eyes on Pax.

"No, thank you, Mistress, but I need to go back." The servant girl was already several steps onto the main trail and was moving backward.

"But—" Pax tried to stop her.

"I'll get in trouble. Please?" The servant girl looked at Lexi with pleading eyes.

"Let the girl do her job. You are putting her in an awkward situation," Lexi said softly.

"It was just a little social experiment," Pax said and then dismissed the servant girl. "Don't worry." She watched the girl go before adding, "You see? We're all programmed this way. She doesn't know we're born with the same rights. I need to do something. I can't stand knowing and not doing anything."

"Pax, I think you had a traumatic experience and you need to see someone." Lexi spoke slowly.

"Did you listen to what I have just said to you?"

"Yes—"

"YES? Have you, really?"

"Pax…"

"No, I don't think you have. Because if you had, you would already be doing something." Pax was angry and Lexi's sympathetic expression was an insult to her feelings. "Don't."

"What?" Lexi raised her hands in surrender.

"Just… don't pity me." Pax felt a pang of pain. She had heard the same words in another context.

"What do you want me to think when you act like this?"

"Think for a second that I could be right."

"Of course, but listen to yourself first. Then we can have this conversation again. After you have rested."

"Even if I sleep ten years, reality isn't going to change. Talking to Doctor Cassandra will only make things worse." Pax was tired though, and the conversation with Lexi was taking its toll. But she didn't want to leave before having reached some understanding with her friend.

"Try. Everybody is so worried about you. Please, just give it a try," Lexi pleaded.

"Everybody is worried about me." Pax sighed. "You were warned beforehand. You talked to my mothers before coming here." She felt betrayed. Lexi was her *friend*. "Are you going to report soon after you leave?" It had finally dawned on her that earlier Lexi had let her talk without interrupting and without showing any emotion, even when she had challenged the holiest of the precepts the Ginecean society was built on. "Do you think I lost my mind?"

Lexi dismissed the last question, arching her brow and shaking her head. "I've been pestering your mothers with calls since you disappeared. At first, they didn't tell me anything, but as the days passed and there wasn't any sign of you, they asked for my help. They'd been hoping the whole time you would communicate with me. At that point they had to tell me what was going on, otherwise I would have never, ever, betrayed you. They told me a man kidnapped you, and you disappeared into the desert. I waited for your call to tell me that you were okay, but it never came. I thought the worst had happened. So excuse me if I care, and if your mothers care. And excuse me also if I talk to your mothers without your permission. I think that we, your mothers and I, have all the rights to use whatever stratagem to help you." Lexi stood up, towering over Pax.

"I—" Pax was confused by Lexi's outburst. They rarely had confrontations.

"You what? You think that your actions have no impact on the people who love you? Are you so spoiled?" Lexi kept pouncing.

"I didn't mean to upset you. Pardon me for my shortsightedness. I was trying to save a human life when I ran to the desert. And I didn't call you because my cell died. Is that enough for you?" Pax could stand anything, but not Lexi's insults.

"Your cell died."

"Yes, without a charger, cell phones tend to stop working after a while." Pax was so tired she didn't care anymore to keep her tone from being overly sarcastic.

"That explains several things," Lexi admitted, and then after a long silence, she sat down again. "Okay, I still think you need to sleep, and I promise not to say anything to your mothers before I listen to your story."

"Truly listen?"

"Truly listen."

Pax wanted to say much more, but her head was exploding and there were dark blobs dancing at the side of her eyes. Lexi accompanied her back to the library where a makeshift bedroom had already been created by putting together two beds.

"We would be so much more comfortable in your room," Lexi commented with a grimace.

"Suck it up." Pax was already out at "up."

She slept dreamlessly and tossed and turned the whole time. Light was inundating the room in an orange shade when she woke up.

"Good day to you." Lexi's voice came from somewhere in the room.

"To you, too." Pax propped herself on her elbow, looking for her friend. She scanned the orange shadows until she found her. Lexi was sitting at the desk reading a magazine.

"I've been waiting like forever for you to re-emerge from your coma," Lexi said, leafing through the pages.

"What time is it?" Pax asked, sitting on the bed.

"Two o'clock in the afternoon. You slept almost twenty-four hours. Congratulations." Lexi looked at Pax and smiled.

"I was tired."

"That I never doubted."

"So, here we are again." Pax looked for something to wear. She didn't find her clothes where she had scattered them on the floor the day before.

"Your maid has already brought a fresh change. She said to call if you don't like what she chose for you." Lexi pointed at the neat pile sitting on the desk. "Right, listen. I'm sorry about the way I spoke to you yesterday, but I was worried." Lexi scooped up the clothes and brought them to Pax.

"It's okay. I guess that I should have tried another approach instead of shoveling what I had to say down your throat," Pax admitted, accepting the perfumed bundle from Lexi's hands.

"I—as promised—didn't talk to your mothers. They asked, of course. I was vague." Lexi sat down at the desk.

"Thanks."

"You know you can count on me. Always," Lexi said with enough enthusiasm to make Pax nod in consent.

"I know! It's just that… never mind. I don't want to start fighting again." Pax donned a freshly laundered shirt with matching skirt. "All I want is for you to listen. And open your mind." She tried to be soft-spoken.

"Shoot."

Pax ever so slowly started to relax her jaw, and word after word, she told her story. From her first day at the farm, to her real abduction the night that she was waiting for Prince. It took several hours to navigate through all the details, but later in the afternoon, when the sun was already going to sleep, Pax finally ended her tale with a sense of relief.

"It's a lot to digest," Lexi commented after having said almost nothing the whole time Pax had talked.

The silence had unnerved Pax, but it had also helped speed the narration, which had proved long enough without interruptions.

"I'm only considering *this* whole scenario of yours because *you* are telling me. But I have to be completely honest with you. Although on a deep, selfish level I want to believe everything you say, I still doubt that priestesses have been conducting a fraud so well disguised for so long without ever being caught." Lexi shook her head thoughtfully.

"But don't you see? The beauty of the whole scheme lies in the fact that no woman in power is ever going to release such information." Pax sighed.

"I give you that, but what about the fathered women? If there was even the slightest chance that what you are saying is true, don't you think they would have started a revolution already?"

"Maybe they did, and we never knew."

"It's not possible."

"It actually is. The Priestess could have silenced the uprising before it became public," Pax counteracted. "My servant girl at the farm, Celeste, was murdered because she tried to rebel." Pax's eyes became bright.

"That's... horrible." Lexi shivered.

"Who knows how many Celestes have lost their lives to maintain this secret?" Pax asked bitterly.

"It's not that I don't want to believe you just because, but we've studied in school how reproduction works. There are tons of books where the science behind the propagation of the woman species is explained in great detail. Why bother to invent anything when we could have accepted the whole thing as a dogma?" Lexi reasonably asked.

"Because we are a complex and sophisticated society. Maybe centuries ago, women even prayed at the Temple. You've heard all this crap about going back to our origins and embracing a more spiritual life. The majority of the women on Ginecea are well educated. Even a large portion of the fathered women are allowed to finish the primary studies. Obviously, they aren't given the instruments to reach any personal growth, but they are not completely ignorant." The more Pax talked, the more she realized how obvious the truth was.

"Well, pure breeds couldn't stand to be served by fathered women who couldn't write and read," Lexi resumed one of her favorite arguments.

Pax stopped Lexi right there and said, "Only the men are kept completely in the dark. We need our slaves to remain such. If we let them better themselves, we lose them. We can't afford to have them organized and belligerent. But even the best plans have flaws. The City of Men is the result of those flaws. And the most incredible thing is that there aren't only ex-workers living there, but also women. And even families composed of parents of different sexes," Pax added the last part and watched carefully how Lexi was going to react.

"There are kids raised by mothers and fathers? Living together, you mean?" Lexi seemed perturbed by the last bit of information.

"Yes."

"I've never heard of anything like that before." Lexi was going to say something, thought better of it, and waited for Pax to resume the conversation.

"I'd never heard of lots of things before I saw them with my own eyes. And then it wasn't a matter of hearing rumors anymore. I could show you the City of Men." Pax left the last sentence hanging. Less of a question and more of a hope.

"Do you want to go back there?" Lexi looked as shocked as she sounded. She didn't even try to hide her surprise at Pax's suggestion.

"If you love Aria one fraction of how much I love Prince, you know I have no choice." Pax regarded her friend with her most stern expression.

"Pax, it's not a problem of who loves whom more! You can't be serious. Your mothers are never going to let you out of here unsupervised again. Even in your love-struck state you must realize that."

"I'll find a way."

"Pax—"

"I won't repeat my grandmother's error. Maybe she didn't have the power or the strength to bring down this rotten society, and probably I'm cut from the same cloth, but I won't live my life as she has done. She could have fought to be with Mauricio. I won't become her, sad and lonely, when I can at least try to be happy." Pax looked Lexi in the eyes and dared her to say something back.

Lexi surprised her as she usually did. "Your grandmother!"

"What about her?"

"You must talk to her. She's the only one who knows the truth behind your... Priest's words."

"I don't need my grandma to validate Mauricio's words. I believe him."

"I'll come with you. We'll say that you need to relax in a stress-free environment before college starts. What better place than your grandma's isolated retreat by the sea?" Lexi was already planning.

Pax knew better than to try to stop her, but she still had something to say. "I'm doing this for *you*. You're the one who needs some sort of validation. I'm ready to accompany *you* to my grandma's, but rest assured that by the time college starts, I'll be on my way back to the City of Men." Pax spoke gently, but her tone didn't give rise to any doubt she was going to act upon her words.

"Okay, I'll even accompany you, if what the Priest told you has any resemblance to reality," Lexi conceded.

"I warn you, even if my grandmother doesn't confirm his words, I'll still run away to Prince. Do you understand that?" Pax asked Lexi, raising her voice without noticing.

"I had that feeling, yes. But putting things in perspective can only help at this point." Lexi finished the conversation, offering her right hand to Pax.

"Okay, but I won't change my mind." Pax shook Lexi's hand and added a smile at the last second. "And to think you were the wild one."

"'Beware of the quiet ones,' my mom always says." Lexi smiled back and stood up to hug Pax. "I'll be here for you always. No matter what."

CHAPTER 15

Lots of pleading by a progressively more annoyed Pax and a less belligerent Lexi didn't soften Claudine's and Maurice's hearts over the seaside-vacation plan. Only a chance intervention forced them to change their minds. They were still traumatized by having lost Pax once to let her out of their sight again anytime soon. Several conversations started nicely enough, then escalated into loud discussions. Once or twice even Anna was thrown in the middle to give her opinion about how senseless Pax's request was. In less than a week, the Layan household couldn't go an hour before people started yelling at each other. Pax and her mothers reached a point where they didn't talk at all to avoid unpleasant confrontations.

Captain Larouche happened to come back to ask Pax a few questions during one of these silent sessions and left without accomplishing much. It actually worked for Pax, since she really didn't want to be asked anything, but she had a few questions of her own. She didn't have any better luck than Captain Larouche. She asked what had happened to her kidnappers and obtained a vague mention of a facility where they were being interrogated. She noticed how Anna put an end to the conversation with the excuse that Pax was still suffering from shock. The captain was told not to come back after that visit. Unfortunately, the series of unwanted visits didn't end with Captain Larouche's.

Three days later, the Priestess herself decided to grant the Layans a surprise visit. Anna almost had a stroke when the most revered person in Ginecea knocked at the door accompanied only by two of her personal guards. The two highly trained soldiers, dressed in their black and gold livery and looking very martial, stood by the door of the formal living room. Pax was more interested in them than in the dramatic figure of the Priestess, who sat ramrod straight on the sofa and smiled incessantly.

The older woman was used to being the absolute center of attention, and it was immediately apparent she wasn't amused by Pax's lack of interest in what she was saying. Anna gave Pax a kick under the coffee table, and she decided to recite from the script. The Priestess had a lot of questions regarding her captivity and seemed very interested in knowing the details of what had happened while she was kept in the desert. Pax found the twenty questions game not to her liking, but answered them with a plastered smile on her face, while trying to remember what she had already told Captain Larouche.

After the visit from the almighty Priestess, Pax was finally left alone. Anna and her mothers built an effective security line all around her, and nobody else was allowed in the house. Worried family friends were kept at phone call's distance with various excuses. Although Pax didn't have any interest in seeing anyone who wasn't Lexi, she still found the situation annoying. Her temper grew rather ill at being kept isolated from the rest of the world as if she were a porcelain doll that could break at any time. She could handle real life better than they thought. She was also tired of trying to convince her mothers she was fine and that she could have a little field trip.

Unexpected help came from Rosie, the reclusive grandmother who had been the center of all the discussions without being asked once what she thought of Pax spending time at her place. At the end of the second week of the siege, she called. Claudine happened to be closest to the phone and answered before Pax could grab the speaker head. Pax pressed the conference button and hijacked the conversation.

"Hi, Grandma Rosie, how are you?"

"Rosie, what a pleasure hearing from you," Claudine said, sending her daughter a warning look.

"I'm fine. What about all of you?" Rosie's tone was curt.

"We're well and—"

"Great. Can I talk now to my favorite granddaughter?"

Pax couldn't repress her chuckle. *Favorite granddaughter*. It was a long-standing joke about the Ginecean law about the one-daughter policy. Rosie loved to make people cringe uncomfortably.

Claudine wasn't immune to her mother-in-law's poisonous streak. She sighed and silently bowed to Pax. "All yours."

"Would you care to come visit your grandma?" Rosie asked without preambles.

"I'd love to." Pax smiled a smug smile, looking directly at her mother Claudine. "I can leave today," she added with a wider smile.

Claudine became an unhealthy shade of white. "Pax needs to take care of several things before she leaves for college." She tried to take back the reins of the conversation. Pax stood by with an angelic expression on her face. Claudine couldn't hide the rising panic in her voice.

"I'm not inviting her for a month! It's just this weekend. I haven't seen her in a while, and when she starts college, I'll see her even less, and I hardly see her already. I'm old and dying." Rosie used her mother-in-law voice that normally irritated Claudine to no end.

"You'll live forever, Rosie, and Pax has already lost too much time and she hasn't bought anything for her dorm," Claudine said out loud and then whispered, "You'll outlive me."

"Nonsense. It's Friday afternoon, and stores are closed on Sundays anyway. Do you think tomorrow is going to make any difference? I can be dead by Monday for all you know." Rosie was on a mission. Pax silently thanked her grandma's desire to win the usual battle of wills against her daughter-in-law.

"Mother, please, it's not that I don't want Pax to visit you…"

"I'm glad to hear that, so it's decided. Pax, I'll wait for you to have dinner together tonight. See you later." Rosie hung up before Claudine could say anything back.

"You heard her. She could breathe her last breath any moment now. I better hurry." Pax kissed her mother on the forehead and went to call Lexi. While she was packing her bags, she heard her mothers discuss the situation. The servant girl who was helping her fold her clothes couldn't help but snicker at the name calling that took place afterward. Pax thought her grandma deserved most of the epithets Claudine bestowed angrily upon the meddling mother-in-law, but for once, Rosie had really helped her.

* * *

"Did I tell you to bring your friend?" Rosie asked as soon as she opened the door. Two smiling girls beamed at her words.

Claudine and Maurice had tried their best to cancel their appointments for the weekend and accompany Pax. A dismayed Anna had informed them that Maurice's political campaign was at a sensitive stage. Maurice had several interviews and Claudine's presence by her side was pivotal to give the right impression. Pax had graciously accepted the idea of being escorted by the Layans' chauffer, who was also a skilled bodyguard. Floria, the martial artist who doubled as limousine driver, drove her first to pick up Lexi at the Corelli mansion and then slowly extricated them from the crowded streets of Friday-afternoon Ginecea to reach the isolated cove where Rosie lived.

Pax had always loved the three-hour drive to Silence Point. The city's busy life gave away almost immediately to the rolling hills of the countryside, covered with miles and miles of fragrant orchards and dark green rows of vines, rectangular patches of colored sunflowers, and parallel lines of violet lavender fields. Pax never had enough of that summer view. Two hours into the drive, the gentle rolling hills lost their softness to become more angular and rugged, the green shades darkened, and trees grew in contorted shapes. Even the air had a different quality. Pax rolled down the windows and stuck her tongue out to feel the cold saltiness. Finally, a mere twenty minutes from their destination, the majestic sight of the ocean appeared after a sharp curve in the road. It never ceased to make Pax feel small.

"Grandma, it's so good to see you." Pax hugged the older woman with great affection.

Rosie was agelessly old, a small woman with a regal countenance. She wore her long white hair in a severe ponytail that accentuated her patrician features. Two bright, dark brown eyes dominated a slightly wrinkled face with a small nose and a smart mouth.

"You know I'm not really dying tomorrow?" Rosie asked, taking a better look at her granddaughter.

"You look splendid as usual, Ms. Layan," Lexi said, still smiling.

"You can stay." Rosie hugged Lexi and smiled back.

It was a rare treat to see her smile. Pax actually got slightly worried.

"But don't try too hard or I'll get annoyed," Rosie finished with a *mph* sound. Pax relaxed.

"I'm hungry. It took you forever to arrive. Did you make her wait?" Rosie raised an accusing finger to Lexi's face.

"I was ready the moment she knocked on my door." Lexi, who years before had spent a summer at Silence Point with Pax, was used to the woman's antics and lack of social skills.

"Floria *drove* us here," Pax explained patiently.

"It's about time you get your pilot's license." Rosie saluted Floria with a nod.

"Working on it. You'll be the first to test my flying abilities," the chauffer answered with a deadpan tone.

Lexi and Pax started laughing.

"I can only imagine what you'll become at my age," Rosie muttered.

"Your spitting image," Pax couldn't help but say.

"Bring their stuff inside. You know the way. The usual rooms for the girls and for you, although you deserve the dog's house," Rosie commanded Floria with her words, but her tone was playful. She had a special bond with Floria. Rosie had found her in a facility for troubled fathered women and paid for her instruction. Later, she had insisted that Maurice employ her.

"Dinner is getting cold," Rosie reminded Pax and Lexi. Floria came back and said she had received a call from Claudine, and she couldn't stay.

"I'll come back Sunday to pick you up." She saluted the three women and was out.

Pax felt a gush of relief that the chauffer had left. She meant to prove once and for all to Lexi that everything she had said was true. Having Floria in the house would have complicated things since Grandma Rosie treated her as part of the family. Pax didn't think it was a good idea to let Floria in on this.

Later, with their stomachs full and their hands warmed by steaming cups of tea, Rosie, Pax, and Lexi went outside on the balcony to look at the starry sky. The tiled deck overlooked the sea from a cliff and gave the impression of being suspended atop a cloud. The transparent parapet separating the onlookers from the void completed the effect.

"I bet you can't see the stars anymore in Ginecea," Rosie commented.

"I haven't checked in a while," Lexi answered while Pax remained silent.

"Why do you live here alone?" Pax asked after a few minutes.

"I don't like company." Rosie didn't seem surprised by Pax's abruptness.

"Aren't you scared at night?" Pax had morose thoughts, probably induced by the nocturnal sounds. Howls living above the canopy of trees bordering the property and furry animals below created a stream of eerie calls through the otherwise silent night.

"Only my dreams are scary," Rosie answered with the sadness that was her trademark, when she wasn't being smart.

"Maurice told me to ask you if you need any help. We've a few girls who could come here and stay with you," Pax remembered to ask. Her mother had stressed the request several times.

"I don't need anybody," Rosie clipped back.

"But—"

"But thank you very much. Report my gratitude to your mom." Rosie put a conciliatory hand on Pax's arm and squeezed softly.

"I will." Pax sighed, knowing her grandma's words were final on the subject. She had never given any second thoughts to the fact that there weren't servants in Rosie's home. She had accepted that as another eccentricity regarding this unique person. Now she was looking at her grandma with different eyes.

"Don't you grow tired of caring for the house all by yourself?" Lexi asked.

"I bought this house because it was small." Rosie turned around and looked inside through the window glass. "And because it's far away from nosy little girls." She took a sip from her now lukewarm tea.

"Mine is cold, too. I'll go warm it up." Lexi promptly took the cup from Rosie, who muttered a thank you, and went inside.

"Grandma?" Pax had been waiting for the right moment to start the conversation.

"Yes, granddaughter?" Rosie turned her bright eyes on Pax.

"I have something to ask you…" Pax's tongue was dry and stuck to her palate.

"I've already left this house to you. I've nothing left," Rosie said in a mocking tone.

"Well… thank you. Aren't you the nicest grandma?" Pax was taken aback for a second.

"You're welcome."

"But, you see… you still have something left to give me." Pax didn't know how to introduce the subject without scaring her grandmother to silence.

"And what could that be?" Rosie asked, finally engaged in the conversation.

"I met a person a few days ago, who met you when you were young." Pax was looking for the perfect wording.

"So?"

"This person still thinks fondly of you." Pax hesitated.

"How nice to hear." Rosie gave Pax a puzzled look. "Do you remember her name?"

"Mmm hmm." Pax nodded cautiously.

"I'm old. Spit it out while I'm still here." Rosie turned around and relaxed her body on the chaise longue. "How long does it take to warm a cup of tea?" she asked into the night.

"Mauricio," Pax whispered. She was anxiously waiting for her grandmother to react to the name. Fear and hope got mixed in her mind and she started sweating. A long silence followed that single word. "Grandma Rosie?" Pax finally mustered the courage to say something.

"I heard you," Rosie answered with a tone that didn't carry any inflection.

Pax noticed her grandmother's hands went to her necklace, the only jewel she had ever seen her wear.

"How did you meet him?" Rosie's voice was still cold, but some feeling was showing beneath the composed mask, her fingers caressing the pendant, a smooth pebble, dangling from the necklace.

"It's a long story—"

"We have the whole weekend." Rosie was now looking at her granddaughter with great intensity.

"As you know, I was sent to a farm for the summer. From there, I reached the place where Mauricio lives." Pax wanted to trust Rosie, but she needed to know her true sentiments first.

"I see…" Rosie kept her voice controlled, but one hand grabbed the hem of the blanket, her fingers playing nervously with the fabric. "How is he?" she asked, her other hand cupping the pendant over her heart.

Pax thought a few seconds about the answer and then decided to tell the truth. "Mauricio is dying." She wanted to add, *I'm sorry*, but waited for Rosie's reaction.

"He—" Words failed Rosie, and her voice choked. Another long silence was broken only by the howls in the night. "What do you know?" She lowered her head.

"He told me everything." Pax took Rosie's cold hand in hers.

"So you know who he is." She wasn't asking.

"I know he's my grandfather," Pax said, relieved they had reached that point so early in the conversation. She wasn't sure of how long she could stand waiting for the truth to come out.

"I've never thought this day would come." Rosie's eyes were focused on the dark sky. "All these years I've never dreamed I could talk to someone about Mauricio." She took away her hand from the warm embrace of Pax's. "Do you despise me? Are you shocked?" she asked, looking ahead of her, her eyes focusing on the faraway stars.

"For what?"

"For having befriended a man. What else?" Rosie seemed angry.

"Mauricio is only that for you? Someone who was once an acquaintance?" Pax was disappointed.

"What did you expect me to say?"

"Something different," Pax said in her lowest voice.

"He's the love of my life." Rosie was now defiantly looking at Pax. "Mauricio has been the one. I never betrayed Lavinia, and I took care of her, but I never felt anything more than affection for her. I've never desired my wife." Rosie didn't lower her eyes again.

"Oh, Grandma…" Pax was going to say it was the most wonderful news she had ever heard, but Rosie interrupted her.

"Are you shocked now?"

"No, I'm not. But I have to ask you something."

"Okay, what else do you want to know?"

"Why you never tried to reach him?"

Rosie's eyes became brighter at Pax's last sentence. After a few seconds, she resumed her position, looking straight ahead and speaking with a distant voice. "Oh, I tried. Heavens know I tried. I even dishonored my word in the process. As soon as I had Maurice, I ran away from my family. I had sworn to get married to the girl of my mothers' choice, if Mauricio was left free. But I couldn't live without him. I didn't want my little baby to live without her father.

"So, at the first occasion, I ran away from everybody and everything. It was Maurice's Dedication Day. My mothers were so happy, parading the Layans' impending union with my future wife's family. I left while my mother, the president, was giving a speech for the press. I didn't look back. I betrayed my mothers without thinking twice about what I was doing to them. My only thought was reaching Mauricio. I was young and naïve. I drove for days in the desert. The realization that I wasn't going to find him hit me only when the fuel indicator reached low. And then I stopped producing enough milk for Maurice to survive. Probably a combination of stress and dehydration. I remember the precise moment when I had to decide. I looked at my baby girl sleeping in her car seat, and I saw her pink lips were chapped and her breathing was shallow. Maurice was born premature and was so small. I was scared she was going to die because of my foolishness. I called for help. My mothers took me back, but they made me promise to never look for him again." Rosie's deep emotions were now etched on her face.

"You didn't have a choice."

"No, I didn't. My mothers threatened to challenge Maurice's custody on the grounds that I was mentally unstable. I was allowed to raise Maurice at the cost of being their puppet. I was also told that Mauricio had a better chance of living if I forgot about him. I was the daughter of a president. I didn't have friends with whom to confide my sorrow. Instead, I had a staff of people who hid the truth I had discovered from the rest of the world. There isn't a day that doesn't goes by without asking myself what if..."

"Grandma, I'm sorry." Pax tried to read her grandmother's eyes in the dark.

"At least they kept their promise; I've always wondered about that, but Mauricio has lived. I didn't cause his death through my actions."

"Mauricio has lived as a free man." Pax was now anxious to tell Rosie the rest of her story. She felt elated she could finally confide in someone else other than Lexi. But Lexi didn't count. She was her twin, after all.

"Where did you see him?" Rosie asked breathlessly.

"*Somewhere—*" Pax waived her hand in the air. "—in the middle of the desert. He leads a community of men, ex-workers like himself and some women who rejected our society." She didn't know where to start, and so she was trying to summarize in a few sentences two months' worth of talking.

"But how did you end up there?" Rosie finally asked the question Pax was waiting for.

"Because... I'm in love with a man." Pax smiled weakly and held her breath.

"*You* start talking." Rosie pointed a finger at Pax and then turned around toward the house and said, "And *you*, Lexi, come sit down and stop eavesdropping. Didn't your mothers teach you manners at all?"

"Here's your cup of tea." Lexi walked to the front of the balcony and sat by Pax. "I'm afraid it's cold again." She gave Rosie her cup with a sheepish smile. Rosie muttered something uncomplimentary about young age and brains.

Pax started from the beginning. At first she found it difficult to follow a straight line of narration and jumped back and forth. When she realized she had both Rosie and Lexi enthralled by her words, she relaxed and lost herself in the tale. The starry night was now silent, all the nocturnal life gone to sleep, and the first light of the morning was shining light pink over the silver sea.

"That's quite a story," Rosie commented after a long silence, punctuated by the sloshing sound of the waves crashing against the rocks several yards below them. "I'm at a loss for words."

"Isn't that a first, Grandma?" Pax's lips curved up.

"I suppose it is," Rosie agreed slowly; then as an afterthought she added, "I think we should rest now."

Pax was relieved and disappointed at the same time. She was tired. She thought that the only time she had slept well had been the last time she had seen Prince, just after they had spent the night together. But she needed to talk to her grandma. She had so many questions.

"Don't worry. We're not done talking." Rosie seemed to read Pax's mind. "But we need to sleep."

They all went to sleep, and by the time Lexi tried to say goodnight, she was already snoring. Pax wasn't so lucky. She stared a long time at her friend dreaming happily in the twin bed next to hers. Then she focused her eyes on the ceiling and thought of Prince. What was he doing now? Was he thinking of her? Was he worried for her? Did he wonder if she had left him? The image of the Priest, her grandfather, lying on that couch, at the end of his life, thinking of Rosie, filled her mind. Wet tears rolled down to her pillow. She didn't want the same fate for Prince. She missed him terribly and hugging the soaked pillow didn't fill the void in her chest. Pax said "I love you" to the sky outside the window and hoped Prince could hear her messages. "I love you, I miss you, I need you..." she repeated until her eyes closed and she dreamed of him.

By the time she rejoined the rest of the company in her grandmother's kitchen, the day was on its way to becoming a sunny afternoon. The salty air was crisp, but not pungent. The colors of the foliage visible outside the windows were changing into the warm tones of the end of summer. The tapas Rosie had cooked were a perfect mix of breakfast, lunch, and early afternoon tea.

"Keep the windows open. I like the breeze," Rosie said to Lexi, who was walking around the room, looking for something to do.

"Old ladies normally feel the cold," Lexi said, finally sitting at the kitchen table.

"And young ladies normally shut up," Rosie mocked Lexi's tone and then smiled.

Pax, who was silently enjoying the food, thought for a second that she had seen her grandmother smile more times in the last day than in all the times she ever visited her.

"Anyway, I'm not an ordinary *old lady*, as you gently put it." Rosie smashed Lexi's hand reaching for another helping of tortas. "I have no servants, as you can see. I do stuff for myself. In a word, I'm not an old incompetent ninny—" She raised one eyebrow at Lexi and continued with a supercilious tone. "—as I'm sure you are going to become."

"Ouch." Pax took a sip from her cup of cold hibiscus tea. "You don't like the idea of having servants," she added, more as an inner thought than something she wanted to ask.

"No, I guess not. When I realized the truth about our society, the mere idea of using a maid made me sick." Rosie went to refill the carafe with the tea.

"How could you stand it? I mean knowing what you know and…" Pax stopped before saying the condemning words.

"I couldn't, and I still can't stand it. I feel sullied for having let my mothers and society at large dictate what was expected of me. My only act of rebellion was to isolate myself here. I'm not proud of it. But I couldn't renounce my daughter. And I wouldn't have survived the pain of knowing that something, anything, had happened to Mauricio because of me," Rosie said with a tired voice.

"I'm sorry. I didn't mean to disrespect you." Pax went to hug her grandma.

"Thank you, honey, but I don't have the highest opinion of myself anyway." She reciprocated the gesture and then patted Pax's head.

"Don't. Don't punish yourself for having to compromise," Pax said in a whisper.

"I don't think I feel any better about myself." Lexi, who had heard Pax, came close to them. "I told your grandma about Aria," she explained. "While you were sleeping, we talked about my ill-fated love. I've never spoken to an adult about it, and I feel much better now. I'm not close to a solution, but at least I could be honest for once." She smiled sadly.

"So, what do you plan to do? Now that you know the truth," Pax asked gently.

"I guess I'll have to muster the courage I've lacked so far and fight for her. How, I still don't know." Lexi sat down in the chair next Pax's.

"You're clearly in good company." Rosie poured some tea for Lexi and then moved the plate with the tortas closer to her. Lexi mouthed, "Thanks."

"May I ask you why you never told my mom about her origins?" Pax put down her empty cup.

"I've been waiting for the right moment for the last fifty years. At first, she was too young. Then she went to college, and when I thought she was old enough to understand, she announced her interest in following her grandmother's steps. She's been working on becoming the youngest president ever since. She's married a wonderful woman, and as a mother, I couldn't ask for better for my daughter. Then you were born, and at that point, I didn't have any right to destroy Maurice's happiness. Imagine if she knew... it would end her career. And maybe even her family." Rosie spoke with great passion; Pax and Lexi stared at her for a few seconds before regaining their voices.

"I suppose now is the worst moment ever to divulge such truth." Lexi was the first one to speak.

"Mom's going to win this election. I can feel it in my bones. It's her time," Pax said.

"If anyone is going to make it so young, it's going to be her," Rosie finished proudly.

"So, what am I going to do?" Pax asked, bracing for a suggestion she didn't want to hear.

Voices from outside the window intruded in the conversation. Several knocks on the door followed.

Chapter 16

"Mom?" Maurice called, her voice muffled by the walls.

"What are you doing here?" Rosie asked the small contingent of women captained by a smiling Maurice. Claudine followed right behind, and then Anna, and Floria closed the ranks at the rear.

"Always nice to see you, Mom." Maurice hugged her mother tightly.

"It's nice to see you too, but you don't normally like to surprise me." Rosie looked at her daughter in suspicion.

"I wanted to see you, and since Pax is here, I thought it was a great idea to stop by," Maurice explained while marching down the hall to deposit her laptop bag in the small studio.

"How nice." Rosie hugged Claudine and Anna and then whispered something to Floria, who shrugged in response with an expression meant to say that she was going to know soon enough.

"I don't have enough beds for everybody; we'll have to share—" Rosie started.

"Thank you, Rosie, but we are *all* going back tonight after dinner," Claudine answered with a sweet smile.

"*All*? What do you mean all?" Pax asked, already knowing the answer.

"I was able to schedule an interview with the Penny Ron Show for tomorrow afternoon. Penny asked for Claudine and Pax to be present in the audience," Anna explained, extremely satisfied.

And she had good reason to be. The Penny Ron Show was a prime time talk show followed by millions of women. Penny was very picky in her choice of guests. It was short of an honor to be asked to the show, and no woman in her right mind would have denied any request made by the anchoress. Penny Ron was so influential in the Ginecean society that she had decreed political winners and losers by simply talking. Legend said she only endorsed the next president.

"Congrats, Anna." Pax saw no point in trying to argue her way out of that one.

"We can bring two guests with us." Maurice invited both Lexi and Rosie.

"No, thanks," Rosie answered, while at the same moment, Lexi yelled enthusiastically, "A Penny Ron Show invitation? Are you kidding? Of course I want to come! Thank you so much!"

Maurice laughed at Lexi's enthusiasm. "You're very welcome."

Pax didn't say anything else. She sighed and watched outside, hoping the sky could answer her prayers. She needed some help. She didn't know what to do and felt terribly guilty that her actions could cause so much pain to her mothers.

The rest of the afternoon was spent outside on the balcony, until it was too cold and everybody was shivering. They had a sensible dinner cooked by Rosie and Floria, and then Maurice announced it was late and they better hurry.

"I'll call you," Rosie said when she hugged Pax goodbye.

"Don't leave me alone; I need you," Pax whispered back.

"I know, sweetie."

On the drive back, Pax kept her nose against the window of the limousine, but it was too dark and the stars were covered by clouds. Lexi dozed off almost immediately and Pax wondered, as always, how her friend could sleep so peacefully in every circumstance. Maurice had a phone interview with someone on the other coast that was six hours ahead of them. Anna helped her prepare to answer the prickly questions, and Claudine stood enthralled by the exchange, looking adoringly at her wife.

Pax thought for a second of how lucky her mothers had been. They had found each other straight out of college and fell in love. They lived for each other and for their daughter. Maurice had built her career mainly thanks to the fact that the Layans didn't have skeletons in their closet. They were the perfect family. Lovely marriage, no lovers or ugly scandals. Good student daughter who had never courted danger or tried anything reckless.

"What's so funny?" Claudine asked Pax.

"You don't want to know," Pax answered. She couldn't say, "Mom, you know about that plan to assure I didn't do anything stupid with Lexi? Good news is that it worked on that account. But it kind of backfired. I ended up making love to the man I want to spend my life with." It sounded a little bit too drastic. But in its tragedy, it was outrageously funny.

"I'm always intrigued by a good mystery," Claudine probed.

"This is not the kind you like. Trust me." Pax was still smiling.

"Humph... you think I'm boring." Claudine always complained about that.

"So, do you know what Penny Ron is going to ask Mom tomorrow?" Pax decided to change subject.

"Actually, yes, I do. Penny wants to do a whole episode about fathered women's rights and betterment of the workers' conditions. It's all the rage now. Maurice's conservative, but humanitarian approach is going to win large approval. Her opponent doesn't have a chance." Claudine beamed.

Pax's heart sank under a mountain of rocks. She was living a vivid nightmare and every attempt at waking up was failing. Claudine went on for several minutes about all the reforms Maurice was going to propose to give the fathered women access to a better instruction and increment their power of vote. Maurice was also thinking of ways to make workers' lives more tolerable. Pax had to admit her mother would make an excellent president and her ideas, at least the ones Claudine was loyally reporting, weren't bad. Maurice, as a president, wasn't going to be cruel to the workers, but she wasn't going to start a revolution, either. Maurice was going to make her mark in history as the gentle president, the fair and magnanimous. The president who was good to the fathered women. She wasn't going to be remembered as the one who freed the workers. Pax fought the urge to start laughing. Again.

"Are you listening to me?" Claudine asked, tapping on the window attached to Pax's nose.

"Maurice wants to change Ginecea for the better."

"Yes! If elected she'll be able to grant free education for all the fathered women, not only for the ones who work for the pure breeds.

And, this is a big secret. Her ultimate goal is to fight for the fathered women to have power of vote."

"She'll increment the percentage of fathered women who can vote," Pax repeated what she had just heard.

"At the beginning, yes, but eventually, she'll give the right to vote to every fathered woman." Claudine couldn't be prouder if she had thought of it. "She also wants to push a law to insure them a pension when they are too old to work," she added with a big smile.

"That's... great," Pax finished lamely, for lack of better words. It was actually monumental. Lots of politicians had proclaimed their intentions to better the quality of life of the lowest cast of electors. Once elected, they usually forgot about the fathered women and their sad lives. After all, the multitude of the servant class, although they outnumbered the patricians ten to one, not only weren't allowed to own property, but they also had limited rights when it came to vote. For every ten thousand of them, they had to elect one spokesperson, who in turn, could cast one vote in representation of all of them. Ironically, more than once, elections had been decided by just a few votes.

"Is Mom going to announce it tomorrow night?" she asked, leaning against the seat.

"Yes! I'm so excited!" Claudine seemed on the verge of jumping up and down.

Maurice blew a kiss to her from across the seat. Then she put a finger on her mouth and shushed them with a smile. Her interview was starting. Anna counted backward and gave Maurice the signal to start talking on the phone.

Pax looked at her two mothers and a sweet sadness possessed her heart. She wanted what they had. Was it her fault that she had fallen in love with a man? If anything, it was entirely their fault if she was in that situation. This time she couldn't help but laugh out loud. Anna gave her a reproachful look and she excused herself. By the time Maurice was done with the interview, they had arrived home. It was too late to bring Lexi to her house, and she was going with them to the show anyway, so it was decided that she would sleep over.

Pax refused to go back to her bedroom, again, and Lexi followed her to the library with a resigned look.

"You can't punish yourself forever, you know. He's not going to sleep better at night if you're miserable," Lexi whispered in Pax's ears.

"Why on Ginecea do you think that?" Pax was startled by the accurate analysis Lexi had just made. But she wasn't going to say it out loud.

"Because I had a similar phase," Lexi answered honestly.

"Anyway, I still can't stand to sleep or even breathe in my room," Pax hissed back.

"That's okay, as long as you're not in denial." Lexi had to have the last world.

Pax tossed and turned several times, but she slept long enough to reach the following morning. The day was uneventful, but annoyingly full of little tasks having everything to do with the main event of the night. Pax didn't feel okay—she was slightly sick, but she was forced to see the hair stylist, the aesthetician, the makeup expert, and the tailor. Lexi loved the whole process, and Pax would have, too, if her thoughts weren't miles away.

"You look gorgeous, my sweet little thing." Claudine cooed over her daughter when she and Lexi walked down the stairs. "You, too, are spectacular," she said to Lexi.

"It's going to be a wonderful night for your family," Anna chimed in with bright eyes.

"It's mostly thanks to you. And… you are part of the family!" Maurice hugged Anna, who started crying in earnest.

"Imagine the night of the election…" Pax murmured to Lexi.

"Madame President." Lexi bowed to Maurice.

"I'm humbled by your devotion." Maurice acknowledged everybody in the room. "But let's wait for the actual winning, shall we?"

*　*　*

Maurice was actually right in her caution. Her passionate speech about the condition of fathered women received a lukewarm reception, while her mild proposal regarding increasing food portions for the workers was openly booed. Penny Ron had stopped her there, and she hadn't even tried to talk about giving men one hour of free time a month as rehearsed with Anna.

"It was to be expected on some level," Anna said for Claudine's benefit as they were driving back to the house. The atmosphere in the limousine was subdued.

"Don't worry, Claudine. People are fed up with promises. Let's give them some facts, and you'll see that the electors will warm up to our cause." Maurice embraced Claudine and gently brushed her forehead.

"They should kiss the floor where you walk." Claudine had been offended by the way the audience in the studio had reacted to Maurice's words.

"Thank you, my love. But don't get upset over nothing." Maurice straitened and sat facing her wife, then reached out to put her hand to rest on Claudine's knee.

Pax noticed the gesture and smiled.

"I know. It's absolutely nothing, but still," Claudine said with an apologetic expression. "You're brilliant," she added, to be clear on the subject.

"Will I ever find a nice woman?" Anna asked Pax and Lexi with a dramatic tone. Everybody started laughing inside the limousine, and the sad atmosphere dissolved into the night. Floria drove Lexi home—her moms had called, saying the sleepover had lasted long enough already—and then brought the rest of the women back to Layan Manor.

Pax went back to sleep in her new bedroom, the big library full of books, haunted by memories. She would have preferred to have Lexi move in, but she knew they were supposed to share a dorm soon enough. In less than one month, Pax's classes were going to start, and in everybody's opinion, her life, too, would start anew.

Pax knew better than to confront her moms with the disappointing news that she wasn't inclined to follow the written route. Her longing for Prince grew stronger every hour. It had become a physical necessity. She missed him in a way that left her body aching. She thought of him every waking minute and dreamed of him every sleepy one.

Days passed. Soon enough, Pax found herself unwillingly involved in a never-ending shopping spree. Claudine spent all her free time buying every possible dorm-related item she found. Pax knew her mom was getting frantic at the idea of her daughter leaving for college, and she didn't have the heart to deny her anything. Not when all she could think about was the sorrow she was going to cause the moment she left, but not for college. Her promise to run away to be with Prince was weighing down her heart, but she couldn't think of anything else. She felt as if she were the worst of daughters to even contemplate that. Every time Claudine reassured her that she was going to visit her at the campus at least once a week, Pax wanted to cry.

Her mother was doing her best to let her go after what had so recently happened, and she was going to rip her heart apart. Only repeated reassurances from the college's head security about the safety on campus had convinced Claudine to at least consider the idea of letting Pax sleep outside the house. And she still wasn't completely sold on that. Anna had done the possible and the impossible to relocate Pax, and Lexi with her, close to the rector's apartments. It was highly irregular and also meant much grief to the two friends when the rest of the students learned about their arrangement. Maurice had promised a substantial donation for the college library, which it was going to be anonymous, and Pax and Lexi's room had moved three floors up and an entire building to the right.

"We're going to die," Lexi commented when Pax called to give the news.

"I don't see anything good coming from it either, but dying seems rather excessive, even for you," Pax answered with a lack of real interest in the topic. She actually wondered why she had called her friend in the first place, when she didn't feel the need to talk. Habit. She had been reporting to Lexi whatever happened in her life since she was a little girl. It was ingrained in her brain. She was sitting in her new favorite chair, a swiveling monstrosity that belonged to the library's desk. She didn't go out anymore. Her only bridge to the outside world was Lexi.

"You aren't being as mean as usual. Are you okay?" Lexi asked.

"Just a little headache." Pax felt tired. Claudine had already asked twice if she wanted to take the call outside in the garden, just to breathe some fresh air.

"*You look too pale,*" Claudine had said, worried.

"And yesterday you ate something bad," Lexi commented with a pensive tone. "You sure are a frail little thing, my friend."

"It's nothing." Pax dismissed the talk about her health with an annoyed wave of her hand that Lexi couldn't see.

"There's a meeting with the other girls from our dorm. Ex-dorm, I believe now." Lexi made a choked sound, but she didn't comment further on the subject. "They're going to watch a movie or something. What do you think?"

"I'm too tired. I'm going to sleep early," Pax said without thinking and then bit her tongue.

"What do you mean you are going to sleep early? It's six in the afternoon. You must be kidding. Right?"

"I meant to say that I'm going to take it easy. I have a book to finish." Pax dropped her head on the desk and left it there.

"Mhhh. Do you want me to come over?" Lexi had already tried the same technique for the last three days.

"Tomorrow—I'm sure I'll feel much better. Maybe I'll even come visit you," Pax said immediately.

"Are you sure? I don't have to go out with the girls," Lexi tried again.

"No, don't worry. Go out and report tomorrow." Pax yawned and moved her head to lie more comfortably on her arms.

"Tomorrow, then."

"Yep. See you. Bye." Pax hung the phone on its cradle and yawned again, louder this time. She opened and closed the book she had mentioned, and then she put it back beside another stack of books. The desk was completely covered with books, magazines, and clothes she had meant to fold herself. She had decided to refuse the servants help, if not strictly necessary. It was a laudable endeavor, but not a realistic one. She didn't know how to do lots of things, more so than she had realized. She had thought the days spent in the desert with Cordelia and the other girls had been enough to teach her everything she needed to know. But it was far from being the truth. And she was constantly tired. She found, all of a sudden, she didn't want to do anything at all. She only wanted Prince. Pax wiped a solitary tear from her eye just in time to face Maurice.

"Sweetheart, what's with all this melancholic nonsense?" She materialized at the door of the library with a tray. "I asked Louise to prepare your favorite cookies, and I, personally, brewed your tea the way you like it." Maurice walked carefully inside the room. She managed to avoid all the debris Pax had left behind in her quest to alphabetize the books. She deposited the heavy tray on the desk, moving everything on it to the side.

"Thanks, Mom." Pax felt an inexplicable urge to cry, but she steadied her face, breathed slowly, and regained her composure. Then, finally, she looked at her mother to see if she had seen her.

"You should go see Doctor Cassandra. You clearly have some sort of post-traumatic stress disorder. Heavens know, I would be a wreck in your place. Why don't you let us help you?" Maurice attacked the matter from another angle compared to Claudine's emotional tactic. Maurice was trying the sympathetic card.

"I've repeated it a thousand times already. I don't need to talk to the good doctor. I'm fine. I have the flu. I have flu-like symptoms. Therefore, I'm tired, nauseated, sore, etcetera, etcetera. Nothing more, nothing less." Pax kept her voice under control. She didn't want to sound irritated. She didn't want to have another discussion about the necessity of scheduling another appointment with her psychologist. Soon after coming back from the seaside visit, she had agreed to have a few psychoanalysis sessions. She had done so more to appease her worried mothers than for her own sake.

After the Penny Ron Show, Maurice had had to deal with a decrease in popularity, and Claudine had been worried on two fronts: her wife's political career and her daughter's sanity. Pax, who at the moment didn't feel exactly like the daughter of the year, had finally said yes after the nth time she had said no had reduced Claudine to tears. Doctor Cassandra was a fine doctor with excellent bedside manner, but she wasn't the person to whom Pax could confide her secrets. There was only one such person, and he was far away from the psychologist's office.

"I think you should reconsider. Four sessions are not enough for the doctor to make a sound diagnosis." Maurice had also decided to be the voice of reason.

Pax thought they made a funny tableau, the perfect mother and the good daughter having biscuits and tea, catching the last sunrays of the dying summer. She almost said it out loud. "I'll think about it, if I feel blue again. Thank you, Mom." Pax ended the conversation with a hug, when she would have preferred to start talking to her. Really *talking*, not that civilized exchange of niceties that passed as conversation. Pax was well aware she was the one who had started it. She hadn't seen any other solution after having yelled and screamed her intentions regarding seeing any doctor at all. She had offended both her mothers in one single nasty turn of words and decided, once her hot head had cooled down, to change things. Or at least her behavior. But she wasn't satisfied by it. She missed talking to her mothers. Last time they'd had a meaningful conversation was before the summer. Before the farm. Before Prince. BP. AP. Pax's world was divided in two temporal slots, before and after Prince.

"Is there anything you want to talk about?" Maurice's customary ending to their afternoon conversations.

"I…" Pax didn't even know how her mouth had started talking without her brain being the wiser. At the same time, Maurice's cell phone rang. She gave an annoyed glance at the screen and then raised her eyebrows in surprise.

"Just a sec. I need to take this." Maurice went outside in the hall.

Pax heard her mom's voice become more and more excited; then she finally hung up and came back inside.

"It seems that someone actually appreciates my ideas about the fathered women. Anna just told me I have been asked to give a speech during the opening ceremony at your college. The rector is sympathetic to the cause," Maurice said, happy about a break in the wall of not-so-good news that had followed the Penny Ron Show.

"I'm glad to hear that. The rector must be a smart woman." Pax also thought the rector was enjoying the new addition to the library very much. She didn't say anything. Her mom deserved the moment.

"What did you want to tell me, my love?" Maurice asked, still smiling from the phone call.

Pax looked at her and felt small and selfish. "Nothing serious, Mom. I'm sure you have an important speech to write. Go. Don't worry about me." More or less what she normally responded at the end of every polite exchange with her moms. Situations varied every day, but the play followed the same routine. Only this time she felt hollow inside. After her mom had hugged and kissed her and left the room, Pax had an imaginary conversation with her. The conversation that almost happened. Every day.

"Mom, I'm so glad you are here. I want to tell you something, and I know you're going to understand me. I love Prince. And I miss him. And I want to go back to live with him. Don't worry. I won't create a huge scandal. Your career is not going to be affected by my actions. I'll be very discreet. I'll leave one night and disappear.

"No, I'm sorry; I can't tell you the exact location where I'm going. But I'll be fine, I promise. Prince would never let anything happen to me. I'm pretty sure he loves me, too. And, by the way, there are 'different sex' couples living there. I know it sounds dreadful, but they are nice people. They are like me. I understand it's difficult to accept my diversity now, but I know you love me as much as I love you, and you'll overcome the initial prejudice against my sexual orientation. I'm the same I was before. I discovered that I love a man. Just that. It's not as awful as people think."

Pax looked at the empty space in front of her and cried. And then she almost laughed. She realized that not even in an imaginary conversation had she dared to tell her mother about Mauricio and everything he stood for. It wasn't that Pax was afraid of the Priestess. She had met her and she had never liked the woman. Pax was worried about what was going to happen to her mother once she told the truth. She knew Maurice would end her career immediately. She was a woman of the highest moral standards. She would have never, ever, gone through the presidential campaign knowing that the Ginecean society was a complete scam. And her sacrifice would be to no avail, since some other candidate would take advantage of Maurice's failure. Some unscrupulous woman would obtain an easy victory based on lies. Ginecea was better off with Maurice, clueless and in the dark, governing it, than without her.

Pax's head was exploding. Since she had decided the four sessions of therapy were more than enough, she spent half of the time thinking she ought to tell her mothers about Mauricio, and consequentially what she knew. But the other half of the time, she thought of why it wasn't the greatest idea. Deep inside, she was terrified of being rejected by her mothers. If she insisted on talking, they were going to realize they were in flagrant denial where Pax was concerned. They had accepted too easily a theory that fit their need for normalcy. Pax couldn't be emotionally attached to a man. Therefore, she hadn't escaped with him, saving his life, intentionally, fully knowing what she was doing. Instead, their daughter suffered from a conveniently tailored syndrome that explained her erratic behavior. Because no girl from a good family would do what she had done. No. Absolutely not.

CHAPTER 17

So here she was. Lonely. Lovesick. Days passed and then weeks. It was time for Pax to start college. All her plans to escape from Ginecea had been put to a halt by tedious reality. Maurice's run for the presidency had seen both good and bad days. Anna and Claudine had both been busy with the campaign. Pax had faked good health any time one of them came to pay a visit. Thankfully, her temporary bout of blues got better, and she realized she had acted strangely toward Lexi. Pax apologized to her friend, feeling she had been unfair to her. Lexi didn't make a big deal out of it, and everything resumed as usual between them. Except for the part where Pax hid, even from Lexi, that she was still sick every day and that she still wanted to leave and be with Prince.

"So, today is the *day*, yea!" Lexi had called Pax first thing in the morning.

"You sound enthusiastic to start studying again. It's disgusting." Pax was sipping some chamomile. She had eaten something the night before that had disagreed with her stomach twice since waking up.

"I'm thrilled." Lexi sounded offended. "Be ready. We're on our way to pick you up." She hung up.

Lexi's mothers had offered to bring the girls to school since Maurice, and therefore Anna and Claudine, had driven to the college earlier in the morning to prepare for the speech. A presidential candidate's presence had stirred the curiosity of the media, and the college grounds were a circus of cameras and anchorwomen. Claudine had gone to supervise the security measures. She was worried both for Maurice and Pax. They had received a few threatening anonymous letters, which according to Anna was rather normal given Maurice's apparently controversial stands. But Claudine had freaked out, nonetheless.

Lexi's mothers had saved Pax's morning nap by offering to escort her to school with their armored car. Claudine had capitulated and Pax had slept four hours more that morning. It wasn't that Pax wasn't concerned for Maurice's life. She was somehow distracted. She had passed from a self-described mourning period, when she couldn't tolerate Lexi's presence, which by itself should have worried her, to a mere I-am-here-but-not-really period.

Pax knew her current feelings toward the rest of the world weren't normal, but she didn't have any energy to change that. She knew her moods were swinging with the same easiness as the leaves were falling from the trees. She knew that, at least for the time being—she had reached that compromise with herself—she wouldn't do anything that could ruin her mother's election. Maybe, hopefully, she would go crazy before she had a chance to ruin someone else's life.

Pax looked at herself in the mirror. In her imagination Prince was behind her, resting his hands on her shoulders. How much longer could she go before really going insane? She looked again and Prince was gone. She felt a surge of panic swelling inside her. What if she was going to forget the exact color of Prince's eyes? Or the curve of his lips when he smiled? Or the gentle pressure of his fingers on her face? The idea was painful. Memories were all she had left. She couldn't lose them. The mere thought that life was going to erase Prince's memories, day by day, inexorably removing bits of him from her heart, was a cold dagger in her chest. Her cell phone vibrated on the vanity table she had moved to the library.

"Come down. We're outside the back entry." Lexi's voice resonated in the big room.

Pax donned the college uniform in haste. She ran downstairs and entered Lexi's car without having given a second look at the mirror. She greeted the prime minister and her wife with the usual deference, although she had known them forever, and then hugged her friend.

"You look a mess." Lexi immediately dug inside her bag to fetch a comb. "Here, get acquainted with this ancient instrument."

"Good morning to you, too, and thanks." Pax took the proffered comb and disentangled her long mane. "Better now?"

"Better than before." Lexi left it at that and then plunged into a long conversation about all the things they were going to do during college.

Pax smiled at first, trying to follow Lexi in her flight of fancy. "I won't be there for long," she stated with a calm she hadn't possessed in a while.

"Pax—"

"I'm leaving after Election Day," Pax said, lowering her voice. The last thing she wanted was to warn Lexi's mothers, sitting in the second row, about her plans. It was the shortest way to announce it to her mothers without telling them herself.

"But, why? I mean, I know why. But... how? And when?" Lexi threw her hands in the air in a frustrated gesture, still managing to keep her voice low enough not to draw any suspicion from her mothers.

"I don't know, yet."

"Let's talk about it first. Okay? Don't shut me out again," Lexi pleaded, resigned already.

"Maybe the less you know, the better it is for you... and me," Pax said slowly.

"You don't trust me? I didn't say anything to your mothers, after all." Lexi shifted uncomfortably on the seat.

"And I haven't thanked you enough for that, but..." Pax paused for a moment, looking for the right words.

"I want to help you."

Meanwhile, they had arrived at their destination. Lexi saluted her mothers with a fierce hug and they promised to see each other later after the Opening Day speech. Pax waved at the two women and turned back to her conversation with Lexi, only to be interrupted by senior students eager to help them find their way around the college. Due to safety reasons, both Pax and Lexi had had their private tour in advance two days earlier, but they didn't say anything to the volunteers and went along with them.

Lexi had asked Pax to minimize the difference in treatment they received. She didn't want to attract unwanted attention, and revealing they had already strolled at leisure through the whole college and their personal items were already neatly arranged inside their cozy room on the third floor by the rector's apartments, wasn't going to make them well-loved. "I feel like I couldn't get lost even if I wanted to," Lexi commented tersely.

Pax didn't say anything. She went through the motions just to make Lexi happy. She didn't care one way or the other. If she had felt detached at home, her own home, where she couldn't stand to sleep in her room, here at the college everything seemed even more surreal. She didn't belong anywhere anymore. She was biding her time.

"Let's go to the auditorium. Your mom is almost ready to start," Lexi said.

Several heads turned around, but nobody dared to ask anything. Pax and Lexi ignored the stares and followed the other students slowly descending toward the auditorium. They sat as far away as possible from the podium and the first row where all their mothers were sitting along with the teachers and the rector.

Maurice's speech went very well. It didn't surprise Pax, since she knew her mother was an excellent orator, but a standing ovation was a great accomplishment, even for her. Pax traded her usual apathy for some pride in being the daughter of such a woman. The moment lasted long enough for Pax to congratulate her mother and even shed a tear. Later that night, while Lexi was taking hours to shower in their shared bathroom, Pax reflected she had probably cried for more than a good speech. She had cried because she knew her path was going to separate her from Claudine and Maurice and that had probably been their last good moment together.

"I need a tampon. Do you have any?" Lexi emerged from the bathroom, dripping water everywhere and fogging the bedroom windows.

"I don't think I put any in my toilet bag..." Pax felt something nudging at her brain with insistency, but shrugged her shoulders and went on. "Maybe there are some in the welcome basket over there." She waved her fingers at the table where a housekeeper had left some feminine items for them.

"Nice. Yep. Here they are. Saved." Lexi picked up a small cardboard box from the basket and went straight back to the bathroom.

Pax was left alone, again, with nothing else to do but think. "What day is today?" she asked through the thick veil of fog and hot vapor coming from the bathroom.

"Tuesday," Lexi answered.

"What date is today?" Pax asked again, irritated.

"You're kidding." Lexi actually came out of the bathroom to answer that.

"What date is today?" Pax repeated.

"We've been talking about today for the last month. The first day of college. The day you mother gave a memorable speech…" Lexi went on and on. Pax wasn't listening anymore. Even without actually saying the date, Lexi had answered her question.

They had been talking about that date for over a month. Pax tried to remember when she'd had her last period. She tried some more. Finally, a memory of Cordelia brewing some chamomile tea for her menstrual cramps emerged from the confusion that was her mind. It was at the beginning of her staying at the Sanctuary—if she remembered correctly, the second day. Pax sat down heavily on her bed. Almost two months since her last period. She wasn't regular, but still.

"Okay, I'll tell you! Today is—" Lexi was smiling.

"I'm late," Pax interrupted her.

"No, there's still plenty of time for dinner. I'm going to wear something clean—" Lexi was still smiling.

"No, *I am late*." Pax was finding difficult to talk.

"Okay, understood. Next time I won't take so long with the shower, but I think you're exaggerating a bit." Lexi was now slightly annoyed.

"Lexi, try to listen to what I'm actually saying. I had my last period more than a month ago." *Actually, almost two months ago…*

"So? It happens to me all the time. Once it came after three months. I had to take those horrible pills that made me fat. You remember that." Lexi dismissed Pax and sat on the chair by her little desk.

"My case is… different."

"Okay, maybe it's not hormonal. You've lost lots of weight. It can be related. You've been under a lot of stress." Lexi was opening drawers and moving around pencils and pieces of paper. Pax went to her and put a hand rather forcibly on the desk.

"Pay attention to me."

"Okay."

"I think I'm pregnant." Pax exhaled loudly.

"What a silly thing to say."

"I'm serious."

"How can you be? Did you go to the Priestess without telling me? And when?"

"I didn't go to the Priestess."

"And how can you be pregnant if you didn't go to the Temple?" Lexi's eyebrows arched and Pax answered with a sad smile. Lexi looked at her with a puzzled look on her face, then recognition dawned on her and she gasped. "No!"

Pax didn't lower her eyes, but remained silent.

"You're kidding!"

"No…"

"You couldn't possibly have…" Lexi's mouth stood hanging.

"I did." Pax felt strangely better.

"Pax!" Lexi's voice was shrieked.

"I told you. I love Prince." Pax relaxed with every word she said.

"But, I read the biology book… I know the dynamic of how the fathered women are conceived."

"It was beautiful."

"From what I read it sounds… crude, not beautiful. That's why there're semen factories where they use more… humane methods to procreate fathered women. They do everything in a lab. Was he violent?" Lexi wasn't listening to Pax. She was too lost in her thoughts.

"Prince was so attentive." Pax was following her own inner dialogue when she heard what Lexi had just said. "Violent? No! Prince would never hurt me."

"It's difficult to believe a man could be *attentive*," Lexi commented.

"You said you weren't going to judge me for my sexual orientation." Pax's temper raised several notches.

"And I stand by it. But I didn't know that you had done… what you've done with him. It's different than just proving affection for him," Lexi finished lamely.

"Well, now you know the whole truth. What's it going to be?" Pax was giving her friend an ultimatum, and if outside her voice was cold, inside she was burning with fear.

"Nothing changes. I just need a moment to digest the news." Lexi looked straight at her friend and added, "I told you. I won't leave you alone."

"I thought—" Pax was feeling queasy.

"You thought wrong, as usual. Now, let's think what we're going to do."

"What do you mean?"

"I can ask Aria if she knows of a place where you can be helped with this problem. I'm sure the fathered women know more about the subject than we do." Lexi was all business.

"I don't want to do anything," Pax said in a low murmur. Lexi was already dialing a number on her cell phone. Memories of eavesdropping on some of the maids' conversations came back to Pax and she shivered. Not all the fathered women willingly accepted to carry fathered children. There were places where they went… "I'm not going to terminate my pregnancy," she said louder.

"What?" Lexi put down the cell phone on the desk with a clank.

"I love Prince," Pax said.

"I understand that, but have you thought of what is going to happen if you persist in this folly?" Lexi was talking very slow, her face the picture of worry.

"No, obviously, I haven't thought of anything yet. I've just realized I might be pregnant. I don't know anything yet," Pax explained.

"I don't understand."

"I love Prince. I want his child. It's not that hard to understand." Pax smiled at her friend.

"I think you've lost your mind."

"Probably. Most certainly. Are you going to help me anyway?"

"I'm already regretting it, but yes." Lexi came close to Pax and sat on the bed beside her friend.

213

"Thanks, as always." Pax hugged Lexi.

"Did you even think something like this could happen to you?" Lexi asked softly.

"The truth?"

"Yes."

"Honestly, I never thought I was going to make love to him. It happened." Pax shrugged and smiled again. "We were lost in the moment and it simply happened. We hadn't planned it."

"Maybe we should have studied biology better. You could have prevented it," Lexi commented.

"Not the kind of knowledge a girl thinks useful."

"Go figure," Lexi agreed.

"It changes everything," Pax thought out loud. Then, as if on cue, her stomach rebelled violently to the idea of keeping inside the afternoon tea.

* * *

"Now everything makes sense," Lexi said, while keeping Pax company in the bathroom. It was the morning after and Pax had started being sick at dawn. "Here it says you normally throw up the first three months. It's called morning sickness." Lexi was reading from a book she had borrowed from the library.

"Lucky me, my body decided it was morning several hours ago." Pax wiped her mouth on the wet cloth Lexi was offering to her. "What else does it say?" She indicated the book.

"I'm not sure you really want to know. There're gruesome details here." Lexi was making disgusted faces, and after a shocked expression, she closed the book with a slam. "No, you really don't want to know. Trust me on this."

"How bad can it be?" Pax's stomach was heaving again.

"Let's say that I've developed a whole new respect for my mom Paola. You should thank Claudine too," Lexi said with a thoughtful face, opened the book again, and shut it with the same rapidity.

The grimace on her face was enough to discourage Pax from asking for clarifications.

"You'll know soon enough anyway," Lexi stated. "You should've been done vomiting three or four times ago." She was holding Pax's head.

"I thought so, too," Pax answered from the toilet.

"I'll take notes for you." Lexi patted Pax's back and waited a few minutes to see how she was faring before leaving for the first class of the semester.

Pax lay still on her bed, worried that even the smallest of the movements could set off the nausea. "How much longer is this supposed to last?" she asked the ceiling. The ceiling didn't answer back and that was enough for her to stop asking questions. She had dared to leaf through the pregnancy manual's pages and regretted it right away. She should have trusted Lexi on the matter. Pax's notion of what was going to happen to her was a distant, and rather fragmented, memory of a boring biology class. The whole two interminable hours of the class, she had been busy sending Lexi notes about a girl she liked. Now she couldn't even remember the girl's name. *Lisa? No, Lucy. Linda?* It was pointless.

* * *

"Pax?" Lexi was still holding Pax's head over the toilet. "Do you think I can leave you now?" Another morning, another week, same scenario.

"I'll manage." Same answer.

"I'll bring you food for lunch. Rice porridge?" Lexi was trying her best to vary Pax's diet, but her stomach disagreed on principle with whatever she ingested.

"Sounds yummy." Pax even tried to smile. The gesture was lost on Lexi, who couldn't see her face admiring the ceramic plane of the toilet. "If I feel better later, I think I'll try to join you for chemistry lab." She turned her head around.

"You look... better today." Lexi wasn't good at lying.

"Thanks for trying." Pax sat down on the bathroom floor and leaned her head against the tiled wall.

"Well, someone has to do it."

"Go now, otherwise you'll be late." Pax dismissed her and waved a tired hand. "Please, write better notes today. I can't decipher your mangled writing," she added when Lexi was already out of the bathroom. She laughed at the rude retort. Not that Pax had any intention to study, but she had to maintain the charade for her mothers' sake. She needed to lay low until she could leave without creating any unwanted publicity that could ruin Maurice's run for the presidency.

Pax had done her best to be present at as many classes as she could. Although the operative word, she realized, was being present. She couldn't concentrate during the lectures, and her notes were accordingly useless. She spent hours doodling, daydreaming, and trying to stay awake. Pax would have slept the whole day if it were completely up to her. She was also losing weight at an alarming rate. She was actually looking forward to the rice porridge.

* * *

Another week passed.

"There's a notification for you, Pax." Lexi had just deposited their lunches on her desk. She was holding a brown letter she had found in the mailbox attached outside their door. She was weighing it in her hands suspiciously.

"What is it?" Pax asked from her bed. She was having a particularly bad day. It had started with the usual nausea, and it had progressed to acid reflux and then painful stomach cramps, all in a matter of hours. Once the pain and the nausea had ebbed, Pax had found peace on her bed and stayed there. Now the aroma wafting from the food containers was offending her nose.

"I don't think it's good news. It's from the faculty." Lexi was looking at the letter this way and that.

"Open it, please." Pax moved her hand, giving her friend permission to read it for her.

"Uh-oh…"

"What is it?"

"I'm afraid the rector is taking a personal interest in your health—"

"Go on, the suspense is killing me." Pax didn't even try to conceal her complete lack of interest.

"The rector has already notified your mothers that you've missed more classes than are allowed per semester." Lexi summarized the content of the letter.

Pax remained on the bed, breathing slowly.

"Pax, we can find a way out of this…"

"How can I explain my sudden penchant for the bathroom?" Pax finally said with a tone that wanted to be light, but failed.

"Your moms are going to call you any minute now. Think about something to say that can explain all the absences. And the grades." Lexi was still looking at the letter with wary eyes.

"Or better said, the absence of grades," Pax whispered.

CHAPTER 18

Pax was looking outside the window, but whatever landscape passing by was lost to her. She had run away and took the first train to Silence Point, thinking it was for the best.

"*I can't ruin them. If anyone finds out...*" Pax had said while furiously packing.

"*Anna can help you to keep it secret.*" Lexi had tried to reason with her.

"*You don't understand—*"

"*Wait and see; don't do anything in the heat of the moment. There's a solution to everything. Even when you think it's the end of the world. You can raise your baby girl here. I can help you. Your moms will help you. They won't abandon you.*"

"*And what if I don't have a baby girl? Have you thought about that? Because I have.*" Pax had repressed a sob, and after shaking her head, she had thrown another shirt in her bag.

Now, alone in the train car, she let the tears out. She was sick again, and her head seemed on the verge of detaching from her neck. Pax closed her eyes and filled her misery with the memories of Prince. She put one hand on her flat belly and imagined that hand was his. "I love you already," she said, moving her fingers in a slow caress.

Once at the Bayview's train station, Pax hired a cab. It took almost two hours to reach her grandmother's secluded home. She waited patiently the entire time, eyes closed, breathing in and out in the hope of avoiding casting out her last meal on the car's floor. She barely succeeded. Pax had just finished paying for the ride when she had to excuse herself behind a tall bush.

"You look... sick," Rosie welcomed her.

"Good to see you too, Grandma. Between you and Lexi, I don't know who's more supportive," Pax said while wiping her mouth with a tissue. Lately she hadn't gone anywhere without them.

"Lexi called. She said you were going to explain." Rosie regarded her granddaughter with an arched brow.

"May I come in?" Pax was tired, and now that her stomach was food free, she was also hungry.

"Please." Rosie moved aside to let Pax in.

"Do you have a piece of bread I can eat?" Pax asked, moving toward the kitchen after having dropped her bag at the entry. Had she eaten any of the food Lexi had brought for lunch? She couldn't remember. She had eaten something in the recent past, though. The bush could attest to that.

"As I mentioned, Lexi called. Dinner has been ready for some time now. I'll warm it up." Rosie moved purposefully to the oven and turned on the heat. Then she went to the fridge.

"Orange juice or cold tea?" she asked without turning, her head hidden between the fridge doors.

"Cold tea?" Pax wasn't sure tea was the lesser of two evils.

"I'm asking you."

"Maybe some hot tea and crackers." Pax went to the pantry and found what she was looking for.

Rosie didn't say anything, but moved to the sink to fill the kettle with water and put it on the stove. After Pax had finished one package of saltines, Rosie finally talked. "How many weeks are you?" She poured the hot water in a cup and chose one tea from the many she had stored in the pantry.

Pax almost choked on the cracker.

"So?" She put the steaming cup of tea before Pax. "Drink some."

"How do you know?" Pax managed to ask after having soaked her throat with the scalding drink. *Lexi, I'm going to kill you.*

"I had the same symptoms with your mom." Rosie drank from her cup and then went to check the oven.

"Are you going to tell on me?" Pax felt stupid and embarrassed for having to ask it.

"It's legal to have kids at your age." Rosie stared intently at her granddaughter.

"This baby is Prince's." Pax lowered her eyes.

"Who else's?" Rosie put a warm hand under Pax's chin and gently raised her face. "It's not my business to tell your mothers. You should do it." Rosie's words were typical Rosie, but her tone was soft.

"I can't. I don't want to be the one to stop Maurice's candidacy. She's going to be a great president. I'd never forgive myself if..." Pax started crying and dropped her head on the table. Rosie patted Pax's back and shoulders.

"It's okay. Please, calm down." Rosie fiercely hugged Pax's trembling body until she started relaxing.

"I need to go back to Prince. And once we're together... we'll disappear somewhere. Away, where I won't be a problem to anyone. But I want this baby. And I want to be with Prince. I can't live like this," Pax said all in one breath.

Rosie looked at her as if it was the very first time she had seen her granddaughter. "Okay."

"Okay?"

"You're right. One can't live like this."

Pax looked up with a puzzled expression.

"I'll help you go back."

"Really?"

"Yes, really. And I'll come with you." Rosie caressed Pax's head with a tenderness she had never known her grandma possessed. "We'll have to leave first thing in the morning before your mothers come charging here, worried about you." Rosie smiled at Pax, and then she went on with the menial task of putting the dinner on the table as if nothing had happened. Pax wasn't fooled by her grandma's apparent calm.

"Tomorrow morning?" She wanted to leave, but even in her impulsiveness she knew it was soon. "Don't we have to plan for it?"

"The sooner the better."

Pax could feel something was amiss. "I agree, but—" She had just noticed the pallor in her grandmother's face and the slight tremble in her hands. "Grandma? Is there something *you* aren't telling me?"

Rosie made a noncommittal sound and then fussed some more with the food. She tossed the salad for a full minute before putting the bowl on the table.

"Grandma, please." Pax saw the little details she had missed at first. There were several medicine containers on the counter. More than she remembered she had seen the last time she was there. Pax also noticed the house wasn't as shiny as usual.

"I didn't mean to tell your mom, and you, until… well, until I had to." Rosie was looking outside straight through the window glass.

Pax didn't ask the rhetoric question. The presence of the medicine alone was enough.

"You have the gift of timing." Rosie put one hand on Pax's.

"How long do you have?" Pax's voice broke.

"I think I just asked you a similar question. It's funny, isn't it?" Rosie smiled at her granddaughter.

"No, it isn't." Pax didn't want to cry again; her head was hurting so much already.

"No, I guess it isn't. I have long enough to accompany you on your journey."

"I don't think it's wise—" Pax looked again at the medicines, trying to decipher what they were for.

"Since you told me about Mauricio, I've been planning to go looking for him."

"You've been planning to go to see Mauricio? But—" Pax said and then tilted her head toward the medicines.

"But nothing. I'm not taking the medicines, anyway. More side effects than benefits. I want to see him one last time. And I want to be lucid when it happens." Rosie was preternaturally calm. "And I don't have a choice now."

"Where we're going is not around the corner."

"I know." Rosie gave Pax a caress on the cheek. "But it doesn't take more than six months to arrive there."

"No, definitely not."

"So, you see? We're perfectly fine."

"No, we aren't. We're actually screwed." Pax wasn't sure if she wanted to cry or to laugh, or both at the same time. She opted for the last one.

"It's okay. After the doctor gave me the diagnosis, I spent the next three days passing from one emotion to the other. There's nothing like love or incumbent death to make you realize how many things you still want to do."

"What are we going to say to my moms?" Pax asked to change topic.

"It might be better to stick to the truth as much as possible. I'll elaborate along the lines of the excuse I've readied for my departure."

"You thought things through."

"I sure did." Rosie seemed to be on the verge of saying more, but went to open the oven without a word. A fragrant smell of baked pasta invaded the kitchen.

"Okay." Pax's stomach rumbled loudly. "Sorry, I haven't eaten a lot lately."

"You're all skin and bones. It was one of the clues when I saw you standing at the door like a lost puppy." Rosie filled Pax's plate with a heaping portion of pasta.

"And Lexi's call."

"And Lexi's call. Although, she didn't say a lot. Only that you needed help."

"She's a good friend." Pax attacked the plate with a ravenous appetite.

"Yes, she is. Maybe my life would've been different with a good and loyal friend by my side. But I was a president's daughter. Not the kind of person who has friends."

"I've never realized how lonely you must've been."

"I've had a good ride. Don't worry about me. Remember, everybody decides the life she wants. I decided what I thought was best at the time. And life is giving me another opportunity to set things straight." Rosie was spreading the food all around the plate without bringing any to her mouth. "When I called *requesting* your presence last time, I already knew. I wanted to see you and say my goodbyes while I still felt good. Then a miracle happened. You came with the most incredible gift I've ever received. Hope." Rosie's hand went to the stone pendant, her fingers slowly caressing it. "And now… fate has decided to play another trick on me."

Pax was overwhelmed by Rosie's words and realized she barely knew her grandmother. There was a whole other person behind the façade Rosie presented to the world. Pax saw she needed a moment by herself. "I'll go wash my hands." She needed it too. The hot water stung her skin, but she didn't mind. Her reflection in the mirror looked haunted and the dark circles under her eyes scared her. She was thankful her mothers hadn't seen her. They would have locked her away. She went to dry her hands. "Grandma? There're no towels in the bathroom."

"Linen cupboard," Rosie answered from the kitchen

Pax went to her grandmother's bedroom where the linen cupboard was. She was leaving the room with a set of scented towels, when she saw the folded clothes lying on the bed and the open suitcase on the dark hardwood floor. "Well, she doesn't waste time," she murmured. One notebook with several torn pages was on top of a stack of shirts already packed inside the suitcase. Curiosity won and she bent to take a look. "What's this?" She ran back to the kitchen.

"Is this what I think it is?" She showed Rosie one of the pages.

Rosie sighed and then nodded.

"Why didn't you tell me? And how on Ginecea do you have those coordinates? Are they reliable?"

"I was going to tell you tomorrow morning after you had a good night's sleep." Rosie showed her the chair, silently suggesting her to sit.

"Why?"

"I wanted to give you a chance to cool down. In your state—"

"Why?" She didn't know if she wanted to be angry at Rosie or not.

"Because, maybe, you'd change your mind and decide not to come after all. You'd be safe and back with Maurice and Claudine. At that point, it wouldn't have mattered."

"What wouldn't have mattered?"

"What is going to happen to me."

Pax wanted to yell that what happened to her mattered to a lot of people, but there was something else she couldn't quite point her finger at. Several half-said sentences Rosie had said came back to her. "How did you get the City of Men's coordinates?"

"Floria gave them to me."

"Floria?" She finally sat down. "What does Floria have anything to do with this?"

"She called me this morning." Rosie went to open the window to let some air in.

Pax put the piece of paper still in her hands on the table, then forced herself to relax and channel her frustration toward the leg of her chair that she slowly kicked with her shoe. She didn't want to raise her voice with her grandmother, but was close to losing her battle. "What did she say to you?"

"Floria happened to listen in on a conversation Anna had with Maurice."

"Floria did what?" She stopped kicking the chair, a sentiment akin to shock settling in. "I can't believe she could betray my mom like that, after all she has done for her."

"Don't go blaming the poor girl; I asked Floria to keep her ears open for me."

"And what did she report to you?"

"Captain Larouche called to inform your mothers your kidnappers have finally talked."

She had been wondering about them. "And the captain also told Anna the coordinates?"

"No, she didn't. Floria found out—"

"How did she find out?"

"She has friends in the right places." Rosie made a gesture indicating that how Floria had gathered the information wasn't important. "Ginecea is marching against the City of Men as we speak. I was leaving when Lexi called."

Pax stared at Rosie, panic displacing the shock. "We must leave now. We must warn them."

"That was my plan, but when Lexi said you were coming, I couldn't leave without seeing you one last time. I know I'm not coming back from this. And then I thought I could outrun the army anyway, if I left soon enough."

"We must go now."

"No, you must eat now and rest, as I said."

"But, how can I eat or sleep knowing Prince is in danger?"

"You'll have to." Rosie gently reached for Pax's belly and laid one hand on it. "You'll have to change the way you think now."

Pax didn't throw up the dinner, which by itself was great, but she also managed to sleep one or two hours. It wasn't peaceful slumber, but it was better than lying awake tortured by worried thoughts. When she sat at the kitchen table for breakfast the next morning, she was barely able to stay still the moment it took to eat the eggs and bacon Rosie had prepared. Her grandmother was nowhere to be seen. She went for the quickest of showers and was in and out of the bathroom in less than five minutes, having brushed her teeth and combed her wet hair.

"Claudine already called, twice," Rosie informed her as a good morning, once she came back inside the house. "I was preparing the car for the trip."

"I would've been surprised otherwise. So, what did you say to her?" Pax was storing some of the breakfast food inside a plastic container. Lots of it was untouched and cooling on the serving plates. Rosie must have cleared the entire fridge and a big part of the pantry.

"Not much. Just that you're still stressed after what happened to you and that you wanted to spend some time with me. I also said we are leaving today for a long overdue Grandma/Pax adventure. She was relieved I had everything under control and concurred that fresh air and a change of scenery are going to work miracles for you."

* * *

"Do you know how to drive?" Rosie asked an hour later. They had left her house in the truck she kept well preserved under the hangar. Once on the road, she had handed Pax a map and told her to be her navigator after showing her the notes she had made.

"No," Pax said, munching on a snack Rosie had prepared for the trip, and then as an afterthought, she added to explain, "Floria." Her mouth was already full with another morsel. Once in the car, she had realized she wasn't feeling nauseous and that is when she felt the first pang of hunger, even though she had eaten her breakfast. "I feel like I haven't eaten for the last month."

"Slow down, or you're going to be sick in the car." Rosie gave her a worried look.

"I've a hole in my stomach." Pax closed the container, though.

"You're probably halfway through your first trimester already," Rosie said, looking back at the road.

Pax didn't comment on that piece of information. She wasn't ready to talk about her pregnancy yet. There were so many things she didn't know, and so many others she wasn't even sure she wanted to know. She should have been grateful the only person on Ginecea who could understand her was available to talk. She knew that. But every word regarding her state brought back memories of *that* night. Her eyes had the habit of going liquid every time she thought of the last time she had seen Prince. *What if I'm late? What if something happens to you?*

"You could've gotten away with it almost until the end." Rosie pointed one finger at Pax's flat stomach.

Again, Pax remained silent. A few traitorous tears rolled down her face. Her hand went to her belly, and Pax realized how the little gesture had become second nature to her in such a short time. A smile crept to her mouth and made the tears disappear. She still didn't feel like talking, but the sadness was gone. And the snack was still inside her stomach. Pax was glad her grandma understood her need for privacy better than anybody else. So, she stayed that way, silent and free to worry about Prince without having to share, for a long while. The landscape had already changed by the time the conversation resumed.

"Out of curiosity, what was your plan?"

"Hmm?" Pax blinked her eyes and did her best to focus on the here and now. Rosie had kept the driving speed steady, but to her it seemed too slow.

"You were going to look for the City of Men on your own. What was your plan? I assume you had one, right?"

Pax looked outside. "When I was rescued, I tried to commit to memory every shrub, every dune, every copse we were driving by going back to Ginecea. I was going to follow my memories."

"How?"

"What do you mean, how?"

"I mean how were you going to cross the desert? You don't even drive."

"I would have figured that out. Millions of women drive. Lexi drives. I'd have asked her to give me lessons. I didn't expect to get pregnant and have to flee."

"But then you'd have followed your memories."

"Yes, that was my plan."

"Did you consider that the desert changes every time the wind blows and rearranges its landscape?"

"I would've gone anyway. Maybe I'd be lucky and my landmarks were still there." Pax shrugged, but hearing the words from someone else made all the small voices she had kept at bay become clear. *You didn't have a plan at all*, they were saying louder and louder. *You never thought it through.*

"I understand." Rosie smiled at her. "I went through the same thing. The urge of doing something, anything, was almost the death of me and Maurice."

"I would've gone anyway," Pax repeated, but softer. The implications of her choice now laid out before her.

"Thanks to Floria, we'll just have to follow directions." Rosie tapped the map with a finger. "Still think she's a rat?"

"She probably saved my life without knowing it."

"Yes, she probably did. Now rest. The road is uninteresting and I need you fresh when we reach the desert." Rosie didn't add anything else.

Although she had millions of thoughts crowding her mind and a headache starting to get noticeable, an uneasy torpor claimed Pax soon enough. Her body full for the first time in more than a month, she even slept at some point and dreamed. She knew it was a dream while she was dreaming because Prince and she were raising the baby as a family. A whole life made of diaper changes, visits to the grandparents, and thousands of little silly things. When she opened her eyes again, the sun was slowly disappearing behind the imposing ridge bordering the coastal region from the desert.

"You sure were tired," Rosie welcomed her back.

"I'm always tired, lately," Pax commented with a loud yawn.

"I remember that. With Maurice, I slept for the best part of nine months. When I wasn't vomiting, that is." Rosie laughed.

"Not vomiting is such a nice change." Pax yawned again and focused her eyes on the landscape. "You haven't rested since we left your house. Aren't you tired?" She was trying to determine where they were. The dots on the map didn't mean anything to her if not matched with her own memories of places.

"I'll have time to sleep later." Rosie laughed at her private joke and Pax scowled at her. "No, I'm not tired, don't worry. I'm excited at the idea of teaching you how to drive. Ready?"

"I guess it's now or never." Pax felt suddenly nauseated again. She hadn't thought she would be scared at the idea of driving.

"Relax. We'll start when we reach the desert. Although in the last two hours, I've seen no more than three cars. You'd be in no danger of hitting anybody even if you wanted to, but we'll wait."

"You're not the grandmother I thought you were." Pax wondered how many other things she had assumed about Rosie.

"Aren't you glad?" Rosie turned to her with a smirk.

"I am." Pax couldn't help but smile. She liked this Rosie so much better.

"Are you hungry?" Rosie gestured toward the rear seats where they had dumped the containers of food.

"Not hungry. I'm sure you're more tired than you want to admit and we need to hurry. Let's switch places and tell me what to do."

Rosie gave her a look and she must have read the decision in her eyes. "Very well then. The wheel is yours."

Pax waited for her to bring the car to a full stop, then went out and was at Rosie's door before she could change her mind. "Now I understand why lots of people like to drive. It can be relaxing, after a while," she commented several hours later. She had almost driven the car off the road, hit the brakes too hard when a rabbit appeared out of nowhere, and managed to stop the engine, all at once, but the worst was over.

"Especially since you didn't drive us into a tree." Rosie repressed a yawn.

"You should rest. We can't afford to waste any time, and in a few hours I'll need to take a break." Pax had already suggested it several times.

"I guess I can sleep now that you have mastered the art of driving." Rosie's hand absentmindedly reached for the necklace falling over her shirt.

"It's not my fault I was born in a rich family." Lexi's sermons resonated in her mind. She heard Rosie sigh, but neither of them was in the mood for talking anymore. She focused on the road ahead and looked on the radio for a music channel she liked. When she heard the first few notes of a song she used to sing with Lexi, the reality that she wasn't going to see her friend anymore hit her hard. It seemed surreal she had left her twin with barely a hug just the day before. Lexi had helped her to run away before Claudine and Maurice could arrive with Anna in tow to check on her. Everything had been a blur. Pax hadn't had time to realize she had bid farewell to Lexi, and that she hadn't said anything meaningful.

CHAPTER 19

She didn't care about leaving everything she knew behind. The moment she had acknowledged her feelings for Prince, her life had changed. Irrevocably. But losing a friend like Lexi, permanently, was a different kind of grief. Pax had never imagined a life where her friend wasn't present. She was going to have a child and Lexi wouldn't be around to be the aunt.

"Why are you crying?" Rosie asked with a tired voice.

"Grandma! Why are you already awake?"

"Because I can hear you sniff. What's wrong?"

"I won't ever see Lexi again."

"Are you having second thoughts?"

"No, it's not that."

"Because if you have, it would only be normal. You're making a tough decision. There's nothing to be ashamed of if you change your mind. I can drive you back. Just say it."

"I haven't changed my mind. I would never change my mind. It's only I've been friends with Lexi for such a long time. I can barely remember when I didn't know her. It feels wrong to think of a future where she isn't present. It's just that."

"Are you sure?"

"One hundred percent." Pax wiped the tears with the back of her hand.

"It's going to get harder." Rosie's voice was soft. "You're going to miss your mothers, and you're going to question your decision more times than you can possibly imagine."

"It's not that I could decide otherwise. I'm going to have this baby, and I want to live with Prince. I don't have any other option but running away." Pax was starting to feel tired, and her eyes weren't accustomed to driving at night. "And now that I know what I know—" She couldn't say it.

"I rested long enough. Let me drive." Rosie caressed Pax's cheeks. She drove the entire night while Pax tried to rest in the back of the car. She thought of Prince the whole time, and when she finally lost connection with reality, she had a vivid nightmare.

"Pax? Wake up—you're dreaming. It's nothing."

Pax heard her grandma's voice calling her from somewhere far away. "Grandma?"

"I'm here."

"Where are we?" Pax asked, disoriented. She shielded her eyes from the blinding light.

"We entered the desert a few hours ago." Rosie had stopped the car and was pouring tea from a thermos. "It's barely warm." She gave Pax a plastic cup.

"Better than nothing." Pax took the cup, drank from it, and made a face.

"Told you." Rosie smiled and then sobered immediately. "I've been following the directions on the map, but I'm concerned we haven't caught up with the army yet. Do you recognize anything?"

"It was night when I was rescued from my kidnappers. I know we drove northeast the whole time going back to Ginecea. I constantly checked the car compass," she said, looking around. Then, something caught her attention.

"What is it?"

"I remember that peak over there." Pax pointed her finger on the window toward a rock formation on their right.

Rosie started the engine and drove toward the peak.

"Have you thought of what are you going to do when you see Mauricio?" Pax asked all of a sudden.

Rosie shook her head. "I've fantasized so many times about being with him, and now I'm terrified it's never going to happen, and I can't afford to think about that."

"I know." Pax looked away, focusing her eyes on a dark spot on the window. "I can't go a full minute without worrying. My head is full of what ifs."

"Yes, exactly. And also in my case, deep inside, I don't think I deserve to see him again."

"But you did everything you could to save his life. You were forced by the circumstances to stay away from him." Pax looked at her grandma and saw how painful it was for her to talk about it. She felt guilty for having judged Rosie harshly and without knowing her side of the story.

"And still, I've been torturing myself all these years with all sorts of doubts. What if I had done this or that? I've never stopped asking myself what I could've done differently to be with him." Rosie kept driving, but Pax could see how her hands were clenching the wheel.

"Mauricio would've made the same decisions had he been in your position. You saved three lives, yours, his, and your daughter's. I don't think you should feel guilty." Pax wrapped one arm around her grandma's shoulders and then lay down her head. "I'm here thanks to you, after all."

"You and your mother are the only reasons I didn't go crazy or worse." Rosie leaned against Pax and turned to put a gentle kiss on her forehead.

"Don't talk like that." Pax felt a painful tingle at her grandma's words. Rosie had struck a chord close to Pax's heart. She knew very well that not fighting to be with Prince wasn't a possibility, even more so now.

"Ready to drive? I need to rest." Rosie suppressed a yawn and slowly stopped the car.

"Sure would be nice to have one of the armored cars that drove me last time." Pax was relieved to be at the wheel again. Here in the desert there were fewer obstacles she could crash against, and she needed to do something else than just think.

Another full day passed between driving, eating whatever was left in the basket Rosie had prepared before leaving civilization, and talking. Pax had followed directions and kept the car on a southwest route while mentally checking every landmark she recognized. They still had water, and Rosie had filled the large trunk with containers of extra fuel they used sooner than Pax had thought necessary. When they stopped to refuel the car, she was reminded of how her judgment about the whole endeavor had been unrealistic. Even though she had lived for several days outside of the comfort of Ginecean standards, and she thought she could handle adversities, she still didn't know anything about surviving in the desert. She still didn't know what she was doing.

"What if Floria hadn't called you?" Pax asked out loud, after driving for several hours without seeing anything the least familiar. The thought had been gnawing at her the whole time and she couldn't let it go.

"Why are you having these thoughts? They're no good for the morale." Rosie dismissed her with a shrug, but Pax knew better.

She could see the shadow on her grandma's face. "I didn't think at all about consequences. I simply acted on a whim," Pax murmured.

"It doesn't matter anymore. Floria called. Focus on that."

"Grandma, the fuel level is getting lower."

"We still have some in the back."

"And when it's finished?"

"And when it's finished, we'll see what happens next," Rosie answered calmly. "I'm going to ask you a question, and I want you to think about the answer for a few seconds."

"Shoot." Pax turned to better look at her grandma, but never got to hear the question because a loud noise interrupted her. "What was that?" She bent over the dashboard trying to determine where the sound was coming from.

"Turn off the lights," Rosie said with her hands already reaching for the buttons and then pointed at the ceiling. "It's a helicopter."

Pax followed the order and drove a few seconds in the sudden blackness of the night; then she slowed down and finally stopped the car to give her eyes time to adjust. "Did they see us?" She had to ask, just for the sake of letting out all her fears.

"Moving lights in the dark are impossible to miss."

"What are we going to do now?" Pax was still looking toward the sky, but she could only hear the noise. "I don't see the helicopter."

"I say drive carefully and find a good spot to hide the car. Can you see anything yet?"

Pax squinted and shook her head. A few minutes passed in complete silence and then she turned on the engine. "I think I see a boulder on our left."

Pax drove the car toward a dark, tall shape looming ahead, while listening the whole time to the helicopter's intermittent noises. She sighed in relief when, several minutes later, she reached the boulder which was considerably larger and taller than she had imagined. She drove around the rock formation and parked the car in what she hoped would be in its shadow when the sun was high in the sky. Pax took a sip of water from the bottle Rosie was offering her and angled her head toward the ceiling to check if she could hear the helicopter's engine breaking the desert silence. At first the flapping noise was closer, then it got softer, moved from left to right, got louder than before, which made Pax's heart skip several heartbeats, and finally it got softer and disappeared altogether. She took her time to breathe in and out a few times, and then she sighed again.

"Maybe they didn't see us," Pax said, lowering her eyes to her hands still attached to the wheel.

"Maybe they lost us."

"Let's put some sand on the roof now that it's still dark," Pax suggested and they immediately got out in the cold night to throw even colder sand on top of the car. After that, there wasn't much they could do, and Pax was tired. She forced herself to rest, even though her mind was racing through so many different scenarios and she felt she would never sleep again in her life. She managed to close her eyes and do some breathing exercises. Rosie didn't say a word, although Pax knew she wasn't sleeping, either. Her grandmother's thoughts were so loud she could almost hear them.

The sun was rising beyond a crest of ragged mountains when Pax was awakened from a fitful slumber by a vibration that shook the car. The tremor was accompanied by a repetitive metallic clang. She looked outside, but the boulder was effectively shielding the truck from whatever was happening on the other side. She got out and looked for a recess in the rock, and using the natural step to hoist her body up, she peeked at the vast expanse of sand. Pax almost fell from her observation post when she saw the army of beige tanks crawling up and down the dunes. She went back to the car to help her grandmother out and show her the sight that was at the same time terrible and comforting. "We finally found the army."

"They are coming from the Desertica region and not from Ginecea as I thought. That's why we didn't catch them earlier." Pax waited until the trembling on the ground became softer, counted to one hundred, and then slowly drove around the boulder, then waited some more until the rear end of the column almost disappeared at the horizon. She fervently hoped the helicopter wasn't coming back any time soon, but in all fairness, there wasn't anything else she could have done, if not pushing forward, toward the City of Men. She couldn't help but think they could get caught, but as her grandma had suggested, there wasn't time to dwell on unpleasant thoughts. And so she drove, following the serpentine trace the tanks were leaving on the immaculate sand.

"Imagine if it's all a coincidence, and the tanks are going somewhere else entirely." Pax realized the absurdity of her words and started laughing. "I'm going crazy."

"Hormones are getting the best of you. I remember I went insane for the first six months."

"And then what happened?" Pax wiped her eyes; they were getting tired of looking at the liquid plateau of heated sand.

"And then I lost it completely."

"Thanks a lot." Pax turned to look at her grandmother and found her playing with the pendant on her necklace.

"At least you haven't thrown up one single time since we left my house."

"It's true." Pax had forgotten. "And I haven't felt queasy at all." She squinted at the sun and closed her eyes for a moment. A loud hiss and the car sputtered. Pax opened her eyes to see a dark smoke coming out from the hood.

"I can't believe it," Rosie said, looking ahead at the thick fumes now obscuring the view. "Stop the car."

"What is it?" Pax asked, stepping softly on the break and turning off the engine.

Rosie gave a brief look at the dashboard. "Has that light been blinking for a while?"

Pax followed her grandmother's eyes and saw the bright red light she was talking about. "I don't know. I haven't noticed it; I was busy driving…"

"It indicates the level of the water."

"Is it bad?"

"Nothing we can do to fix it, I'm afraid." Rosie opened the door, got out, and stretched her legs, as if everything was under control and they weren't stranded in the middle of the desert.

Pax followed her outside and lay on the warm sand with her eyes pointed at the sky, the sun still high on the horizon. She wanted to cry.

"We need a ride," Rosie joked.

"We're so close. *This* is the real joke, you know?"

"Life and fate have a strange sense of humor." Rosie sat down beside her and started playing with the sand. "I will—"

Pax brought a finger to her mouth. "Listen."

"I can't hear a thing."

"Exactly. They've stopped. Maybe they're camping for the night." Pax sat up and scanned the horizon until she found the darker cloud formed by the tanks.

"I don't see how this changes our situation." Rosie raised one of her eyebrows.

"We're going to hitch a ride, like you said." Pax stood up and then pulled up her grandmother as well.

"We're going to do what?"

"Let's reach them, and I'll show you how." Pax looked so confident that Rosie didn't argue back.

They packed the remaining food, and all the water bottles left inside two backpacks. Pax took care to put the majority of the bottles in her backpack, and the weight was uncomfortably heavy on her shoulders. "Ready for the hike?"

"You look slightly insane."

"As usual, thanks."

After having covered the car with a thick layer of sand, they left it behind and started walking. It was soon evident to Pax that keeping a slow pace was going to be the key of their survival. She also thanked the Heavens her grandmother was in excellent shape, despite her age and illness. They slowly walked for hours, taking short breaks to eat and drink and rest their tired legs, but kept going until they came close enough to the encampment to see the first lights shining in the evening darkness.

"Okay, what now?" Rosie asked, setting her backpack on the ground with a sigh of relief.

"Now we wait until the camp goes to sleep," Pax answered, taking off the straw hat she had covered with a shirt and wiping the sweat from her forehead. Her hair was a tangle and weighed heavily on her shoulders. She braided it and raised it to expose her neck to the air.

"And then?" Rosie was massaging her calves.

"We rest for a few hours, and when they are going to move, we hop on the back of the tank at the end of the column." Pax explained it as if it were the easiest thing in the world to do.

"Okay then." Rosie made a sand angel on the ground and then lay still.

"Do you have a better idea?"

"Unfortunately, I don't," Rosie said with her usual sarcasm, and Pax was glad to hear that.

"We need to get as close as possible without being seen." Pax helped her grandma up, and then she started scouting for higher dunes, or any rock formation tall enough to hide them. They walked between the dunes and finally reached a spot that was at the border of the camp. There weren't boulders of any kind, but a recent windstorm had created a ridge that ran close to the camp. They nested against a compact wall of warm sand and prepared to spend a long night under the stars.

"Let's get comfortable." Pax rearranged her body several times. "How do you feel?"

Rosie had closed her fingers around the pendant, her eyes closed. "Well, all considered."

"I don't think I've ever seen you without that necklace of yours." Pax remembered one time when she had asked her grandmother if she could have it to play with. Rosie had answered it wasn't a toy, but let her wear it for a moment.

"You noticed, ah?" Rosie released her hold on it.

"What is it, anyway?"

"My most precious possession."

"I'm curious now."

"This pebble was a gift from Mauricio."

"Oh…"

"He gave it to me last time I saw him. I'd arranged his escape with the help of Guen, a guard working at Tarin—probably the only friend I've ever had—and she bought us one hour of freedom. Sixty minutes only for us. Alone. It was the happiest hour of my life. We went for a walk just outside the farm and talked, as any normal couple would do. We had our first kiss there." Rosie paused a moment. "Our only kiss."

"How was it?" Pax whispered the question. Rosie hadn't mentioned any of this when they had talked back at her house.

"Its memory has kept me company ever since."

A sudden noise made Pax jump. She was so enthralled by her grandmother's words she had forgotten where she was. "The gift?" she asked when the noise turned out to be nothing important.

"I told him how much I liked making stone sculptures and we made one together. The hour was already gone before I'd had any time to say all the things I wanted to say to him. My heart was breaking in a thousand pieces, but I had to be strong for him. I wanted him free and far away from Tarin. At the end of our date, he surprised me with this. Mauricio, who had never possessed anything in his life, gave me something he had taken great care to hide from the guards. This small pebble, a memento of his first time outside. For all the luxury my life has been, I've never received a gift more precious." Rosie brought the pendant to her lips and softly brushed it. "Later, I had it mounted and bought this necklace to showcase it the way it deserved…"

"Always close to your heart," Pax said after a moment of silence.

"Always."

The night was soon very cold, as if a curtain of ice had swept away the warmth of the day. Pax and Rosie cuddled together, trying to keep most of their bodies against the sand, but it was barely enough.

Pax had time to think, and her thoughts weren't pleasant. She wished she was in Prince's arms and dreaded it wasn't going to be. The cold seeped through her and left her with a sense of loneliness and desperation. *I am a fool*, she said to herself several times. But the bulk of her plan consisted exactly in the foolishness of it. Who would think two women would ride on the back of a tank? Nobody was fool enough to even think of that until she had, and it had seemed smart enough when the thought had been conceived. She closed her eyes for a few minutes and dreamed of something sweet she couldn't remember when Rosie's cold fingers tapped her on the shoulder.

"It's time already?" Pax asked before opening her eyes.

"They're leaving."

"We better hurry, then." Pax shrugged the sand from her clothes and shivered. She raised her head above the crest of the dune and looked at the camp. It was closer in the daylight than it had seemed at night. She slowly moved her head from left to right to scan the whole place; then she saw something that almost made her jump. Two soldiers were talking just a few feet away from their hiding place in the sand. Pax immediately put her head down. Rosie looked at her with worried eyes.

"Shhh," Pax whispered under her breath. The soldiers were called away after a few minutes and she started breathing again. "Okay, that was scary." She risked another peek and saw more than half of the convoy was already well on its way. "We must stay put until the last tank is moving and then we sprint and step, as lightly as possible, on the back of it." Pax pointed at the last vehicle slowly crawling in place after the others.

"Bulletproof," Rosie commented with a deadpan expression on her face.

"Thought so." Pax patted her grandma on the shoulder. She kept saying to herself not to overthink it, but the more she tried, the more she did think about it, until she reached a state of such nervousness her vision blurred. She wanted to cry out loud. "Need to tell you something—"

"Is it important?"

"I—"

"Breathe. In and out. And go." Rosie pushed her down the sandy steps of the dune.

Pax, after a moment of hesitation, went along with what she had explained a few minutes earlier. Crouching down low and trying not to stumble, she made a short run for the back of the tank. When she was close enough, she climbed on a step jutting from the lower part of the vehicle. Rosie easily followed her after a few seconds. Pax showed her a metal part where she could anchor her hands.

"Let's hope we're close," Rosie murmured.

Pax nodded in complete agreement while precariously securing her swinging backpack on her chest using one single hand. "*If they're going to the City of Men, we were very close according to the last time I checked on the map—just a few hours south of the Caves.*"

The position got uncomfortable immediately, and more than once, Pax looked at Rosie when they weren't whispering to each other, to see if she was still holding on tightly. After a while, time simply stopped having any meaning, and they moved from one cramped position to the other without finding one that wasn't painful. Pax had her back flattened against the ridged metal surface with her hands holding to the first step of a metal ladder, her fingers white and numb. She tried not to move for fear of warning the women inside the tank they had two hitchhikers. At any moment, the door on the turret could swing open and a soldier could come out for fresh air. Or the helicopter could come back. Pax had enough time to torment herself with every possible scenario of how they could be caught, and more than once her fingers lost their grip on the step. Fortunately, neither she nor Rosie fell from their ride. The tank progressed very slowly on the harsh terrain, but the hours passed even slower.

The sun was high in the sky, and the column was still conquering dune after dune without any sign they were going to stop any time soon. Pax had been peeking around, looking for clues they were on the correct path, but she couldn't hold out her head without exposing herself. She was at her wits' end when a sideways glance revealed several dark shadows ahead. "Are we even on the right track?"

"Yes, we are," Rosie stated with a conviction that made Pax turn. She saw her grandmother staring at the same shadows she had noticed. Now that they were closer, she realized they were structures emerging from the sea of sand. They varied in sizes and shapes; some were tall and thin, others were big and short, and others were a combination of the above. There were hundreds of them blossoming from the ground, composing in their randomness the idea of a garden.

"Do you know what they are?"

"Yes, they're stone sculptures," Rosie answered.

"Let's take a closer look, then. What do you think?" Pax let go of the metal step she had hung on to for dear life. Her legs didn't answer properly and she ended up breaking her fall with her head, but the sand cushioned her. Rosie dove soon after with more graceful results. They crawled toward the structures, but waited to get up until the tank was far off.

"They're beautiful." Rosie stood before a tall structure of rocks piled one on top of the other. Pax noticed the tears swelling in her grandmother's eyes and moved to look at another structure to give her some privacy. She kept at a distance, but couldn't help but look at her sideways. The intensity of the emotions playing in Rosie's face was impossible to ignore.

"These are Mauricio's. Each one of them is his. I can see his hands picking up the rocks to create the sculptures." Rosie touched the rocks with a reverent brush of her fingers. Pax shivered and had to look away for a moment. Her stomach filled with a hollow sense of emptiness.

"Rosie?" A deep masculine voice boomed from nearby. "Is it you...?"

CHAPTER 20

Pax recognized it and immediately looked at her grandmother to tell her, to prepare her. "Grandma—" But she didn't know what to say. Words seemed trivial.

"Mauricio." Rosie turned toward the voice, her eyes wide open, her hands both clutching the pendant.

"I never thought I would see you again." Mauricio came out slowly and uncertainly from behind one of the bigger sculptures. He walked helped by a young boy supporting him at the elbow. He acknowledged Pax's presence with the slightest of nods and kept looking at Rosie. He looked transfixed by her sight. "Rosie…"

"Mauricio?" Rosie was trembling and her voice was nothing more than a whisper.

"I can't believe it's you. I must be dreaming." Mauricio lowered his eyes and tears streamed down his face.

"I came here to see you." Rosie reached out her hand. "I crossed the desert to see you," she said, and then she repeated it softer, as if she had to say it again to make it true.

"Please don't wake me." Mauricio's voice was light, but his hand was shaking as he took hers in his and kissed it slowly. "I can't—" He looked as if he was going to finish his thought, but then closed his eyes and opened them again. "You're here." He gave her a smile, sought her lips and left a feather-light kiss on them. "My rose."

The young boy moved aside awkwardly, trying to avoid staring at the scene unfolding before his eyes. Pax stepped farther back, finding it more and more difficult not to cry.

"I waited so long to see you, to be with you." Rosie caressed Mauricio's face, wiping his tears away. "I can't believe it's finally happening."

"Neither can I." Mauricio leaned on her hand and kissed it while pulling Rosie in his arms. They stood silent and united in a long embrace as if they were another sculpture. Mauricio's tall body was curved around Rosie's tiny frame. She rested her head on his chest while he hugged her.

Noises intruded from the outside world. Pax turned around and focused her eyes on the horizon and the tanks' column, and she couldn't help but gasp out loud. "I'm sorry, but I think we should hide."

Rosie and Mauricio were snapped back to reality too.

"The column has stopped," Rosie said.

"George, run and warn the sentinels at the gate. Now." Mauricio didn't have to repeat it twice. The young boy was gone at "now."

"Follow me," he said to Pax and Rosie. Pax kept looking behind to see if the soldiers were coming. Mauricio never let go of Rosie's hand, and the three of them walked at a restrained pace. The terrain was hard to conquer, especially for two women whose legs were numb and tingly from being in the same position for hours, and Mauricio's condition was clearly worse; he could barely walk at all.

"Sorry." Pax put one arm under Mauricio's shoulder and pushed him to walk faster. Rosie did the same, and between the two of them, they managed to help Mauricio to speed up.

"Behind that boulder." Mauricio indicated a big rock several steps ahead of them with a nod of his head. "Here, let's go down." He showed them what at first sight looked like a hole in the ground.

Pax came closer and saw the hole was a passageway with steps carved in the rocky surface sitting just below the sand. She went down first, followed by Rosie and then Mauricio. Cold, dry air immediately hit her face as she adjusted to the dim light. Walking with her hands outstretched, she discovered a wall in front of her.

"Push it. It's a door to keep the sand out of the tunnel," Mauricio explained.

Pax pushed as told, and the door moved away from her with a whoosh. She stared for a few seconds at a tunnel lit by flickering lights and then she froze. The tunnel disappeared along with her breath. She heard the distant sound of running steps hitting the sand floor and blinked forcefully several times. When her heartbeats became so loud they drowned out all the outside sounds, her eyes stopped focusing properly and she only saw Prince's dark eyes staring back at her. And then she was wrapped tightly inside strong arms, warm breath tingling in her ear.

"Pax."

She heard her name and her legs gave out and she collapsed, only to be held tighter against a heart that was beating even faster than hers.

Pax almost fainted the moment his lips touched hers. "I missed you," she said in his mouth. "I missed you." A furious bump exploded in her chest. She was so lightheaded, spots of light burst inside the darkness of her closed eyes. She heard Prince gasping at the same moment.

"We must move. It's not safe here." Mauricio's apologetic voice broke their private moment. Prince put her down gently, but kept her hand firmly in his.

Pax walked in a state of haze. She saw and heard everything as if behind glass. She could only see and hear Prince. She didn't dare lower her eyes from him for fear of losing him. She clung to Prince like a lifeline.

"We're almost there," she heard Mauricio say while they walked farther inside the tunnel.

"Is the gate locked?" Mauricio asked Prince.

"Yes, I was there when George arrived at the gate and gave the news of your arrival. The sentinels were already securing it as I ran here to see if it was true." Prince was talking both to Mauricio and Pax at the same time.

Pax squeezed his arm to reassure him she was real.

"I kind of jumped past the sentinels," Prince said apologetically, when two heavily armed men appeared at the end of the tunnel.

"I'm fine." Mauricio raised his voice to reach the two men, who slowed down and finally stopped, waiting for Mauricio to reach them.

"He didn't stop—" One of the two men gave Prince a dirty look, but Mauricio stopped the complaining right away.

"I asked him to come here," Mauricio told the two men with a tone that didn't allow further questions. "What's the situation?"

"There's an army parked just outside the rock garden. The helicopter is still circling very close to the city," the man closest to Mauricio answered.

"I need to talk to Lucas." Mauricio was wincing, but when the two men stepped closer to help him, he raised one hand and waved them off. Rosie straightened against him. "Call him and tell him I'll meet him at the gate."

They hurried toward a small room situated at the end of the tunnel and waited for Lucas to arrive. The sentinels offered them the little they had—some water and leftover bread. It was enough for Pax; her skin was red and starting to itch, her whole body overheated. Eating was the least of her desires. She checked on her grandmother, but Rosie was beyond caring about physical needs. One look at Prince and she forgot the rest of the world as well.

"You shouldn't be here," Lucas said as soon as he walked in. "This place isn't safe. I already called for a stretcher." He acknowledged Pax's presence by Prince's side by asking, "You? What are you doing here? How did you—" Then his eyes moved to Rosie and he blinked. "Is she…?"

Mauricio nodded.

Lucas's expression changed from anger to surprise and finally to wonderment. "After all these years," he murmured and went on his knees before Rosie. "Thank you."

Rosie gave Mauricio a puzzled look. "Please, stand up." She helped Lucas on his feet.

"We're here because of you." Lucas took her hands in his and reverentially brushed them with his lips.

"I don't think that's necessary," Rosie said, some color flushing her face.

"The City of Men exists thanks to you." Lucas brought his right hand over his heart.

"It's true." Mauricio smiled at Rosie and mimed Lucas's salute.

Pax felt the intensity of the emotions playing before her and felt her own heart swell.

"There're no words to describe how honored I am to meet you, Rosie Layan. I only wish it had happened at a better time—" Lucas seemed to remember the reason why he was there. "I apologize for ruining the reunion, but you shouldn't be out of the safety of your apartment," he said to Mauricio and then escorted him and Rosie to the closest bench.

"This room is as safe as any." Mauricio sat without breaking contact with Rosie's hand.

"This room was built for the guards to relax every few hours. It doesn't have a single piece of furniture where you can comfortably lay and rest. As soon as we're done talking, you're going to leave with these guys." With a brief nod, Lucas greeted two men carrying a stretcher.

"Lucas, stop fussing over my health and tell me how bad it is." Mauricio leaned against the wall, and Rosie patted his hand.

"It depends." Lucas, who had been watching the two women, shifted his gaze from Rosie to Pax.

Prince tensed immediately and stepped closer to her. "On what?" he asked before Mauricio could open his mouth to utter the words.

"Pardon my question. I don't mean to be disrespectful, but I have to ask. How did you get here?" Lucas asked Pax, instead of replying to Prince.

"You can't think—" Prince started, but Pax stopped him.

"It's okay; he has every right to ask. We rode on the back of a tank," she answered concisely. Prince turned to look at her with a questioning expression on his worried face. Pax reassured him with a nod and then went on, telling the men of their journey. After a few minutes, she had successfully summarized her last five days.

Once they had a moment alone, Prince took her hand and squeezed it. "You shouldn't have come. This isn't a good time to be here."

"Can we go somewhere else to talk?" she asked, shooting a sideways glance at the human tableau just a few feet from them. She also saw her grandmother watching her and attempted a smile.

"Look at me." Prince's eyes were probing her.

Pax lowered her head automatically.

"I said, look at me." He put a finger under her chin and raised her face until her eyes were staring back at his. "What is it? What happened to you?"

"We need to talk, but not here." Pax was dying to tell him everything he wanted to know, and then some, but she needed time and privacy. A low rumble vibrated through the floor and the walls of the small room, and everybody stopped talking at once. The rumble was followed a few seconds later by an explosion. Pax lost her balance and hit her head against the corner of the bench where Mauricio and Rosie were sitting. She heard Prince screaming her name, but she couldn't see anything.

"Pax, wake up. We have to get out of here." Prince's voice was frantic. Pax tried to move her legs, but they weighed her down instead of lifting her up. Prince called her several times and then she felt herself being helped from the floor and into his arms. She thought of her grandmother, and she opened her mouth to ask, but no sound came out.

"Pax?" she heard Prince say, but she was too tired to answer. "Don't scare me. Wake up." She turned her head the other side, and a cold, wet blanket hit her face, making her gasp and open her eyes at the same time.

"Finally. Never do that again."

"Sorry I fainted." Pax tried to smile at him, but her head hurt. She wiped the water from her face and grimaced. "Did you need to drown me?"

"You weren't reacting and I was losing any hope of waking you."

"At least you didn't slap me." Although from the pain she was feeling every time she talked, she couldn't be sure of that.

"You hit that corner of the bench so hard you broke it."

"Well, that explains it." Pax winced when she passed a tentative hand through her hair. Then she focused on her surroundings. "Where are we? And where are my grandmother and Mauricio?" she asked when she was sure her eyes weren't playing tricks on her and she was looking at the outside sky. It was late afternoon.

"We're just outside the Caves. I lost everybody when the second bomb hit the gate. I took you and left the city."

"But what about my grandma?" Pax sat up straight and the rest of the universe started spinning in every direction.

"Easy, let me see your eyes." Prince steadied her. "We better get inside the Caves. You are in no shape to go anywhere."

Pax closed her eyes and inhaled. She registered the shift from light to dark while he transported her. The air had a definite smell inside the cave, earthy and damp, but it made her feel safer. Pax opened her eyes, but didn't try to move for several seconds to see if the spinning was going to stop.

"Did the water help?" a young voice called from the darkness.

"Yes, thank you, George. She's awake now," Prince answered. Pax tugged him on the arm and he slowly let her down until her feet touched the ground. At first the floor and the ceiling exchanged places before her eyes, but she let the moment pass and the natural order of things was reestablished soon enough.

"I can walk by myself," Pax told Prince, but he kept his arm around her waist to support her.

"She could have a concussion." A woman Pax hadn't noticed before was looking at her.

"Marie, can we use a room, just for tonight? I promise we'll be gone by tomorrow," Prince asked.

"I'll go fetch some medicine, in case she needs it. George, show them the way to the guest rooms." Marie walked away, immediately swallowed by the dark tunnel looming ahead.

"Yes, Mom." George gestured for Prince and Pax to follow him in the same direction his mother had gone.

Pax found the act of walking difficult and she leaned heavily on Prince. Once her eyes adjusted to the dim light, she saw the tunnel was decorated with stylized pictures depicting hunting scenes. Pax's head was pulsating with a throbbing pain and she had to lower her eyes on the ground to avoid tripping on the uneven terrain. Nausea overcame her after a few minutes of walking.

"You can use the first room. The bathroom is at the end of the hallway. You're lucky; today there's only one other family using it." George had stopped before the entrance of a tunnel branching from the main one and was waiting for them to reach him. "This door with the white garland." He pointed at the door and walked straight to it. When Pax and Prince arrived, he swung it open for them. "Mom will be back in a few minutes." And he left them, skipping away.

Prince helped Pax onto the low bed and sat by her. A torch lit the room, but Pax's eyes were blurring and she couldn't see anything clearly.

"Don't sleep." Prince nudged her when she closed her eyes.

"I'm so tired."

"You can sleep later. It's not safe until we know if you have a concussion." Marie returned as promised. Pax focused on the moving shape of the woman and saw she was carrying something.

"I'm thirsty." Pax pushed her tongue against her palate; it felt like sand.

"Here, you look dehydrated already." Marie gave Pax a water bottle, and Prince helped her drink. "How long since you had any water?"

"She had some just before the explosions, but she spent five days in the desert before arriving here," Prince answered for her.

"I'm fine," Pax squawked.

"I can give you something for your sunburns." Marie opened the satchel she was carrying. "I also have some herbal remedy you can take in case it's a concussion."

"What is it?" Prince asked when Marie produced several small flasks.

"I can't take anything," Pax said before Marie could answer Prince. She felt lucid all of a sudden and glad she had taken the time to read the book Lexi had checked out for her.

"But you don't look well. Maybe Marie can help." Prince tried to intervene.

Marie gave Pax a thorough look, a flicker of recognition showing on her face, and then stepped back toward the door.

"I'll give you some privacy," Marie said and gently closed the door behind her.

"I'm not sure I can take the medication." Pax sat with her back against the wall and took Prince's hand in hers.

"And why is that?"

Pax hesitated before answering. "I'm pregnant." She had thought of that moment so many times, and she had run every possible scenario, but not one of them envisioned what happened next. Prince didn't say a single word, but his eyes were bright with tears. He looked at her for a few interminable seconds and then he kneeled on the floor and bent to kiss her stomach.

"You've just made me the happiest man alive," Prince said.

Pax was overwhelmed by his reaction and tears swelled in her eyes. She stroked his head, now lying on her lap, while he gently caressed her stomach.

"Is the baby fine?" Prince asked suddenly.

"I think so. I haven't seen a doctor yet. I have just discovered it myself."

"You really shouldn't have left Ginecea." Prince was now sitting on the bed.

"There's no place for our baby in Ginecea." Pax scooped to fit in his embrace. "It could be a boy." She let the concept sink in and then added, "And even if it's a girl, she should be raised by her father."

"It's going to be tough for the two of you out here." Prince hadn't removed his hand from her belly. He circled it with his fingers in a lazy pattern, making Pax shiver. Her vision became unfocused once again.

"It was going to be impossible for the two of us without you. I was forced to leave you once; it won't happen again."

"It changes everything," Prince murmured out loud what probably had been a personal thought.

"What changes?"

"I was going to smuggle you back to the women's camp out there, and be sure that you were safe." Prince looked at her.

"But why? Why don't you want me with you?" Pax was in pain and everything hurt.

"Because, I love *you*. And I shouldn't." Prince went to kiss her lips, but she moved out of his reach.

"Don't."

"I only want what's best for you. And I know it's not me. I didn't want you to resent me one day." Prince moved alongside her, but Pax refused to be kissed. "When you disappeared that night, I almost went crazy with worry. I went to the Priest, and I begged him to help me look for you. I thought the worst had happened, and I wanted to kill the two bastards who had taken you."

"How did you know about Horace and Marcus?" Pax asked, despite the fact she was angry at him.

"They left the City of Men the same night." Prince managed to get hold of her hands. "I thought I was going to die when I followed their tracks and didn't find you. I wandered like a lost soul for days. I could only think of you and what could have happened to you. I had nightmares where you screamed my name, but I was always too late and couldn't save you. Soon, the men in my squad refused to sleep in the same room with me. Then the Priest let me read an article about your mother speaking at the inauguration of the college you were attending, and I realized you were better off without me."

"I'd never be better off without you." Pax wasn't angry anymore. She bumped her forehead against his and nudged his nose with hers.

Prince smiled and nudged her back. "As much as it pains me, it's the reality of our situation, and you know it."

"I don't have to accept it and neither do you."

"Well, we don't have a choice now. Do we?" He softly pressed his lips on hers. "And to think I had almost accepted you had a life in Ginecea, and I wasn't part of it. The Priest helped me a lot during those days. He told me his story with your grandmother, and I felt I wasn't completely alone in this world. My mind went blank when George came saying the Priest was with two women. I hoped against all odds it was you. I wanted to see you again if only for a moment."

"I never stopped planning to come back here. When the women came to rescue me from Horace, I had to go with them—"

"You don't have anything to apologize for." Prince interrupted her with a kiss and she let him. "I missed you." Prince kissed her neck. Pax sighed and melted in his arms while he left a trail of kisses along her collarbone and shoulders. "I didn't think I was ever going to touch you again."

"I never lost hope." Pax smiled at him. "I wasn't going to survive, otherwise. When those men kidnapped me, my last thought before I fainted was how to disarm them, because I was worried you were going to wait for me all night long."

"The idea that Horace and the other fool had in any way harmed you drove me crazy." Prince moved back to put some distance between them. Pax immediately felt cold. "Did they do anything to you?" He seemed calm, but Pax recognized the fury concealed by the restraint in his voice.

"No, they didn't." She didn't want to recount the details of what had almost happened that night. "I'm with you now, and that's all that matters." She kissed him to melt his anger. And then she kissed him just because it felt perfect.

"I'm really going to be a father," Prince said at last.

"Yes, you are."

"May I come in?" Marie's voice followed a discreet knock on the door. When Prince answered positively, she entered the room followed by George, who was carrying a wicker basket.

"How do you feel?" Marie asked Pax.

"Slowly but steadily better."

"I'm glad, since you can't take the herbal remedy I made for you. Good thing you were conscious when I tried to administer it to you. It would've been bad for the baby."

"How did you know?" Prince asked surprised.

"She's been touching her stomach protectively like any mother habitually does." Marie gestured to George to bring forth the basket. "If you feel better, maybe you want to try eating something later. Your pupils aren't dilated, which is a good sign. Drink some more. It'll help the process."

"I picked the food myself," George said, patting the basket.

"Thank you." Pax caressed the boy's hand.

"Do you have any news about the city?" Prince asked.

"No, I don't. None of us is going outside to verify what's happening. We've kids here to protect. We don't want to risk being seen." Marie looked uncomfortable.

"I understand. I truly appreciate what you're doing for us. As I told you, we'll leave as soon as we can," Prince said.

Marie asked if they needed anything else and then left with her son in tow.

"Where are we going?" Pax asked.

"I have no idea. My whole plan was to bring you back to safety and then go to the City of Men and help with the fight." Prince massaged his temples.

"I can't leave without knowing what happened to Grandma," Pax stated.

"I don't think that's a good idea."

They argued for several hours about it until Prince decided it was safe for Pax to finally take a nap. She didn't sleep for long, though, and woke up in the middle of the night thirsty. They had finished the two bottles of water Marie had brought them, and Pax couldn't go back to sleep. She decided to venture outside the room, looking for the bathroom. She was careful not to disturb Prince, who was deeply asleep, and tiptoed toward the end of the hallway. She drank from the bathroom faucet, a stream of fresh water falling into a hollowed rock and then started to walk back to their room, but by now she was wide awake. Instead of trying to get to sleep again, she settled for a stroll in the main tunnel.

Her eyes had completely adjusted to the dim light of the torches, and she stopped to take a look at the extensive paintings on the tunnel's walls and ceiling. There weren't only hunting scenes, as she had thought at first, but there were also daily life renditions. She walked slowly to better look at the stick figures narrating a fascinating story the like of which she had never seen.

"We don't know who drew the pictures." A voice from behind startled her. Pax turned and saw Marie cradling a baby in her arms.

"He wakes up several times every night, and I don't want my husband to be disturbed. He's normally very tired after a day in the fields. So I come here to look at the pictures to pass some time," Marie explained, slightly angling her body to let Pax see the newborn baby.

"How old is he?"

"He's just a month old, but already getting better at sleeping through the night, my little monster." Marie kissed the baby on the forehead, and Pax felt something stirring inside her.

"Have you already seen the family portraits?" Marie asked. "Come, I'll show you." They walked several minutes deeper inside the caves. Pax could feel the pressure in the air changing. "Here they are." Marie pointed at a group of drawings separated from the rest.

Pax stood before them, eyes wide in wonder. The first family group was a family composed of two female stick figures and two babies; the second group was composed of a male, a female, and two babies; the third group was composed of two males and two babies. The babies were assorted in gender. "How old are these paintings?"

"My guess is pretty old. I'm not a scholar, but they've been here for a long time before we claimed the Caves. And I mean a very long time. Before Ginecea's time, someone says." Marie was looking at the mixed family with bright eyes. "At the beginning, when I discovered I had feelings for a man who worked at the same facility where I was employed, I felt sullied and unworthy. I was a fathered woman, of course, but even so, my attraction for a worker was an abomination. I fought hard to regain any sense. I even got engaged to a nice girl, but I couldn't love her. I kept making excuses to go see him. One day, he told me about this City of Men where we could be finally free to love each other. I resisted, but then the fear of losing him gave me the strength to leave everything behind. And here I am. These pictures have given me so much strength through the years. They are proof that once my kind of love was accepted."

"Thank you," Pax said, while silently asking permission with her eyes to caress the baby. Marie nodded and she reached out tentatively to touch his soft skin. "If such a perfect baby is the result of love, there's still hope for our society. It shouldn't matter who the parents are." The baby cooed and moved under her caress and she smiled.

"When I held George in my arms for the first time, I felt the same way." Marie smiled back. "You could stay here, until the baby is born."

"Thanks, I'll think about it." Pax was touched by Marie's words, and for a few seconds, the idea of living in a safe environment, at least for the time being, made her feel hopeful for her future. But then she remembered who she was. "I'm not sure it's in your best interest to shelter me," she said, facing the stick figures on the wall. The sound of approaching steps made her pause, but she didn't need to turn around to see who was coming.

"Baby's sleeping; I'll go back to my husband." Marie politely excused herself and left.

"What are you doing here?" Prince asked, rubbing his face.

"I went for a walk and Marie found me." Pax walked into his arms and then turned around so they could both look at the paintings on the wall.

He bent to kiss her on the head and she leaned against his chest. "Look at us," she said and pointed at the family in the middle. She felt Prince shift his weight behind her, and then he tightened his arms around her.

"We're beautiful." Prince kissed her again.

"There was a time on Ginecea where men and women lived in harmony. Families were composed by people who loved each other." Pax snuggled inside his embrace to burrow some warmth.

"Things are going to change again," Prince said and his voice sounded so sure that Pax wanted to believe his words.

She turned around to look at him and was rewarded by a brilliant smile.

"We're going to fight for our baby's future. It's not just you and me anymore. We can't hide forever. Our baby deserves more than a life of hiding," Prince said and stroked her cheek with his fingers.

CHAPTER 21

The air outside the Caves was crisp and the sun was hidden behind a thick blanket of clouds. In the first hours of the morning, Pax and Prince left their refuge to let the families living in the Caves resume their normal activities. Marie had been nice to them, but both Pax and Prince understood she had more important things to do other than chaperoning them. And until they vacated the place, nobody else was going to get anything done.

They were sitting under a natural arch lying just outside the Caves. Pax was taking small, tentative bites from the sandwich she had found in the basket George had prepared for them. She sat up straight. Her head was still hurting, but she didn't have double vision or vertigo anymore. And even if she hadn't slept a lot during the night, she still felt rested. Prince's arms were better than any sleeping pill.

"I knew they would trade their lives for information on the whereabouts of the City of Men." Prince offered Pax a sip of warm milk from the thermos Marie had insisted on filling for them before they left. They were talking about Horace and Marcus again; Prince couldn't let it go.

"It was my biggest worry from the beginning." Pax licked the milk on her bottom lip.

Prince closed the thermos and put it back inside the backpack Pax had been carrying since she had left Rosie's house. "It was to be expected. I know for a fact that women can be persuasive when they want information."

"It would've been so much better if they'd been killed that night." Pax rewrapped the sandwich; she had lost her appetite and was feeling restless. "Let's go see what's happened." He was staring ahead, where the City of Men lay hidden to the naked eye, camouflaged with the rest of the desert. The army of tanks was parked a few miles north. From her vantage point, Pax could see the scene was completely still—nothing was moving. After the deflagrations had shaken the ground during night, the desert remained silent.

"They're fine," Prince said automatically. He had been repeating the same mantra every time she expressed her concern over her grandmother.

Pax thought it had become meaningless. "Why aren't they moving?" she asked, pointing at the dots littering the desert.

"I don't know," Prince answered, still absent-minded and then added, "It seems completely wrong the light is not shining today."

Pax followed his eyes and saw the top layer of the city, and she understood he was talking about the Priest's habit of using a mirror to catch the first sunrays of the morning to inundate the surrounding landscape with light. She had seen it only once, but Prince had been living in the City of Men for almost three months now.

Pax finally stood up, unable to sit and chat anymore. Prince didn't try to dissuade her from going back to the city. There was nowhere else to go for the two of them, anyway. As a family, they needed all the support they could find, and the City of Men and the Caves were the only candidates willing to accept them.

Prince silently led the way toward the city. The Caves were situated on a higher ridge, so it was easy to check on the troops stationed below. Once closer, Pax saw the city had been hit in several places, dark holes marring its exterior walls, but the Priest's creation was still proudly standing. She rejoiced at the sight. They reached the entry to the tunnel by the stone garden soon enough, after having descended the dunes riding them like ski slopes. There, the women had wiped out the sculptures in a senseless display of bullets. Rocks lay scattered everywhere, dotting the beige sand like tears.

Prince didn't pause, but she felt his rage at the desecration. "I made one for us..." He redoubled his pace. "Stay behind me," he warned her before pushing the door that opened into the tunnel.

Pax assented with the slightest nod and took his hand. They didn't find anybody waiting on the other side. "Okay, this is scary." They reached the end of the tunnel and entered the room they had left only the day before. "Nobody. This is the gate post. How can it be completely deserted?" She moved toward the door that connected the room to the rest of the city.

Prince walked past her and carefully opened it and peeked outside. "None. Not a single man in sight. Stay here." He went outside, closing the door behind him and leaving Pax alone in the room. "Come," he called a moment later, keeping the door ajar for her.

Pax looked at the big hallway opening on one side of the many indoor gardens the Priest had wanted while building the city. The atmosphere was dreamlike, as if at any moment people would come out from the dark nooks and greet them. Pax kept looking for any sign of life, but they walked from one hallway to the other without encountering another soul. "It's starting to get creepy," she commented after half an hour of what might have looked like a leisure stroll, if it weren't for the oppressive silence and the signs of fighting. The plants kept alive against all odds had been walked on by careless shoes. The walls had missing chunks, and there were stains she didn't want to look at closely. The air smelled of an unpleasant metallic aroma.

"Where's everybody?" Prince asked out loud. "Let's go to Mauricio's," he proposed, and Pax mouthed, "Yes." Before the explosions had started, Lucas had been adamant in bringing the Priest back to his apartment. "Probably Lucas thought it was the safest place to hide the Priest."

Pax kept her thoughts to herself. She didn't think escaping to the top floor was the best thing to do, if one was followed by an army. But maybe the women hadn't had time to go up. The City of Men was bigger at its base, and it would have taken some time to scout it. Pax didn't say it out loud and was fully aware her thoughts were as useless as Prince's reasoning if they didn't find anybody to talk to. She couldn't run, but did her best not to slow down Prince in their ascension to the top. She looked for any sign they were being followed or watched, but unnatural silence was their only companion. Prince opened the elevator door and she climbed inside, only to get out right after. "Nobody's here to man it." She sighed and looked at the flight of stairs with weary eyes.

"How are you holding up?" Prince asked, worried.

"I'm tired, and I don't like the idea of climbing all the stairs to Mauricio's apartment, but I can't sit still and wait to see what happens next."

"Tell me if we need to stop, please."

Pax reached Mauricio's slightly out of breath, but she hadn't complained once. She wanted to know what had happened to her grandma, and that in itself kept her going. She tried not to dwell on the scenes in the city; the evidence of the women's presence etched in every bullet encased inside its very heart. Prince hadn't commented once on the destruction and she knew he was trying hard to keep it together for her sake.

"Wait." Prince caught her hand in midair, ready to knock on the door. "It's ajar," he whispered, indicating the dark opening. The door sprang open one moment later, eliminating the problem of deciding what to do.

"Get in," a woman in a dark uniform ordered.

Pax noticed immediately the gold and black insignia of the Priestess's Army. She took Prince's hand and went inside the apartment, following the soldier through the hallway and into Mauricio's bedroom.

"Grandma." Pax saw Rosie as soon as she stepped inside the dim-lit room.

"What are you doing here?" Rosie's voice had an edge of panic to it.

"Looking for you." Pax tried to see if she had been hurt, but Rosie was shadowed by a soldier who kept her in a corner.

"I thought you took her somewhere safe," Rosie accused Prince.

Pax opened her mouth to answer back there was nowhere safe for the two of them, when she was blinded by a sudden flash.

"I think you have said enough already. Please shut up, sit down, and for Heavens' sake, stop touching this slave's hand. It borders on obscenity."

Pax's eyes couldn't see who was talking, but she recognized the public voice.

"I'm keeping this disgusting picture of Senator Layan's daughter holding hands with a man. I'm sure it's going to be of some use to me, don't you think, Rosie?" the Priestess said with a tone worth more than her sharp words and then snapped her fingers.

Pax was yanked away from Prince. She blinked her eyes several times and finally she could see again. The soldier who had invited them inside was holding Prince down, preventing him from getting any closer to her. Rosie attempted a step toward Pax and was forced to the floor by the soldier guarding her. The Priestess was still holding a camera in her hand and looked as if she were studying the lighting to take more pictures. Mauricio was sitting on the same couch she had seen him the last time she had been in this apartment. He looked terrible.

"Let me hug my granddaughter." Rosie was struggling under the soldier's grip on her bony shoulders.

"Only because you asked nicely." The Priestess waved her hand in a bored gesture, and the soldier let Rosie go. The Priestess sat down on a sofa and made a scene of flattening the wrinkles on her immaculate gown.

"Sweetie, you should've stayed away from here," Rosie whispered while hugging Pax.

"What's happening?" Pax asked over her grandma's head.

"This room is small. Even if you whisper, I can hear you." The Priestess laughed.

"So, you can answer me." Pax's blood was already stirring, but one squeeze of her forearm and she refrained from adding anything else in the same tone. She heard one of the soldiers hiss, "How dare you!"

The Priestess raised one arm in a pacifying gesture. "I *could*, but you don't deserve my courtesy." She was now looking at Pax with interested eyes. "You're a Layan through and through. Insolent to the bone."

"What's going on?" Pax asked once more.

Rosie applied more pressure on her grip this time. The soldiers moved toward Pax.

Again, the Priestess made a gesture indicating everything was fine. "We are waiting, if you want to know." She seemed amused by the situation.

"Waiting for what?"

"Whom." The Priestess was enjoying the game, but Pax wasn't.

"Whom?" she repeated with barely repressed rage.

"You're starting to annoy me. Your lack of manners is appalling." The Priestess sipped from a cup.

"Whom are we waiting for, please?"

"The rest of your lovely family. Your mothers and that horrendous woman who works for them should arrive soon. Care for some refreshment?"

"My mothers are coming here? Why?" Pax asked, looking for answers in her grandmother's eyes.

Rosie nodded sadly.

"Well, mostly because I asked them to," the Priestess answered.

"And why did you?"

"I'd enjoy teaching you some etiquette."

Pax looked at Rosie and saw the plea in her eyes. "Please…?"

The Priestess smiled at her act of submission. "See, it turns out your mother could really have a shot at the presidency, after all." Her voice was sweet and poisonous.

Pax physically recoiled at the meaning of her words.

"Even with my help in turning the public opinion against her, Maurice still manages to be a strong candidate with views way too liberal for my comfort."

Pax knew where the discourse was going, and she felt the impulse to laugh at the irony of the whole situation.

"You find it funny?" the Priestess said without changing her tone of voice, which had reached a shade of sweetness that was hard to bear. "Good for you. It will make everything easier if you could behave for a few hours. I'd hate to have to ruin that cute little body of yours."

Prince reacted to the Priestess's words, and the soldier hit him in the head hard enough to make him go limp. Pax screamed and was by his side in an instant, only to be not-so-gently put aside by the soldier.

"I told you not to touch the slave. You should start listening." The Priestess pointed her finger to the other corner of the room. Pax obeyed for fear of making it worse for Prince, but she kept her eyes on him until she saw his chest moving.

"Now, if you'll excuse me, I'm going to refresh myself. The desert doesn't agree with me." The Priestess stood up and disappeared in the adjacent room. The soldier assigned to check on Rosie gave her a meaningful look and then went to guard the door.

"Don't talk," the soldier said, and to make the order more official, she brought out a gun from the holster and started lazily playing with it while looking at Rosie. Pax sat down on the floor and tried to make eye contact with her grandma, but Rosie was now staring at Mauricio, who seemed to be having breathing problems.

"Don't get close to him," the soldier told Rosie.

"But he doesn't feel well." Pax couldn't help answering before Rosie could put herself in trouble.

"I said don't talk. And, let's not be ridiculous. He's just a man," the soldier answered back. She aimed the gun at Mauricio. "Since you seem so distraught, maybe I can help him end his suffering. What do you think?" She made to press the trigger, and both Pax and Rosie screamed at the same time. "I guess you're going to sit tight and be quiet now." The soldier lowered the gun. Pax mimicked to zip her mouth shut and raised her hand in surrender. Rosie simply lowered her eyes to the floor.

"Good girls." The soldier relaxed her stance against the door and resumed playing with the gun. Pax tried to inch her way toward Prince when both soldiers seemed distracted, but a sharp glance from the one guarding the door warned the other.

"Can you believe how low our society has sunk?" The woman kept her eyes on Pax.

"And the way she talks back to the Priestess! She must be in a great mood to let this scum address her without the honorific. If I were Her Holiness, I'd have slapped some manners into her already," the other soldier added.

"You're a perversion that should be eradicated from the Great Ginecea. You know that, right?" the guard by Prince's side spat out with such venom that Pax felt the sting of her words.

"From such a liberal mother, what else would you expect?" the other said.

"And what about this shining example of a grandmother here? Daughter of one of the greatest presidents Ginecea ever had, mother of a possible future president, and she's here in the middle of the desert doing Heavens know what."

Pax wanted to scream. They couldn't talk like that about her grandmother. They were as out of line as she was in her dealing with the Priestess. It was an unforgivable breach of etiquette at best to be disrespectful to an elderly pure breed, and Rosie was practically royalty among the Ginecean notables. A barely visible head shake from her grandmother convinced Pax that incensing the two soldiers wasn't a good idea.

"I'd never allow my daughter within ten feet of you. I feel dirty just by being in the same room with a man-lover." The soldier hit the door behind her with her booted heel.

Pax startled at the sudden noise.

"And to think she mixes with the highest pure breeds of the Ginecean society. It makes me sick to my stomach."

Pax, for once in her life, felt the urge to pull rank and put the two women in their rightful places, but she already knew it was better to let them talk.

"Fortunately, the Priestess knows how to deal with the likes of you. She's got plans." The woman checked her boot.

The soldier holding Prince down gave the other a warning look when she heard the statement.

"It's not like they aren't going to know it soon enough, anyway." The other shrugged her shoulders as if whatever was said in that room didn't matter.

Pax shot Rosie a look and found her looking back. She felt cold despite the rising heat. The Priestess chose that moment to come back. She was listening to someone on a two-way radio. After a few brief answers, she looked back at the rest of the room and smiled.

Pax felt a cold drop of sweat running along her spine.

"I'm happy to announce your mothers have just arrived on my personal helicopter."

Pax leaned on the wall behind her and let her head rest against it. Prince was still crushed on the floor, his head under the soldier's heavy boot, but he was fully awake. Pax blinked at him without moving her head, and he blinked back and raised the corner of his mouth as if to say: *Don't worry; everything is going to be fine.*

"Why are you smiling?" the Priestess asked Pax.

"I'm not," she replied without looking at the Priestess.

"You aren't going to smile much longer, you perv," the soldier closest to her whispered under her breath.

Pax noticed Prince trying to make eye contact again and then lowered his gaze on her stomach. At first she thought he was thinking about the baby, but when she saw the warning on his expression, she realized she was caressing her belly. She slowly moved her hand away before anybody else could see what she was doing and tried to steady her fingers on the floor. The sound of footsteps outside in the hallway broke the silence.

"Show time." The Priestess gifted her audience with another of her fake smiles.

A knock on the door, and the sound of several voices echoed just outside the room. Pax recognized the worried tones of both her mothers and Anna, who was loudly demanding to know where they were on behalf of the Senator.

"Let them in," the Priestess said with an amused tone, and the soldier by the door obeyed.

Pax looked at the scene unraveling before her eyes, and she didn't know if she wanted to cry or laugh. She did neither. Her whole body froze when she saw her mothers' faces. They had been thrown in the middle of something she had started, and they had no clue of what was going to hit them.

"Let's skip the whole greeting routine. I want to get away from this horrible place as soon as I can," the Priestess said when Maurice and Claudine, once their eyes adjusted to the half-light dominating the room, spotted Pax sitting on the floor. Their expressions were ashen, and Pax felt her heart lurching down to the floor between her feet. Claudine moved toward Pax, but the soldier who had opened the door put a hand out and stopped her.

"As I said, spare me the drama." The Priestess wasn't smiling anymore, and her tone had grown several degrees chillier.

"I don't understand—" Maurice was looking at her mother restrained by the soldier.

"Let me explain it to you. I have incriminating proof that your daughter is engaging in a blasphemous relationship with a slave and that she has been helped by her grandmother crossing the desert to reach him."

Rosie tried to say something, but the Priestess cut in. "My helicopter spotted a car driving in the middle of nowhere and reported it to me. How long do you think it took me to discover who was in that car?" The Priestess gave Rosie a disgusted look, then faced Maurice and Claudine. "Here there are pictures of her engaging in lewd behavior, ready for the press." She waved the camera in the air.

Pax saw the expression on her mothers' faces and had to look away to focus on thoughts that weren't painful. A sudden commotion in her peripheral vision brought her back to the room. Her mothers were furious and were trying to outmaneuver the soldiers. Anna stopped Maurice and Claudine before they could say anything at all.

"What do you want?" Anna asked.

"Forget something, secretary?" The Priestess shot a raised eyebrow in Anna's direction.

"Your Holiness." Anna bit her lips.

"Much better. I want the Layan family's full cooperation."

"You already have it. We've never been disrespectful to you. We've always followed your precepts." Claudine finally gave up her futile attempt at moving past the soldiers; her voice was croaked and low, her eyes fixed on her daughter.

"Oh, I'm sure you're going to be the most religious family in Ginecea after we're done here today. I don't need just respect or appreciation for what my church has done for this planet. I simply need your unconditional support in everything I decide, without question," the Priestess answered Claudine, but she faced Maurice the whole time.

"You don't expect me to simply follow whatever you say without question?" Maurice joined the discussion, a deep frown set between her eyes.

"It is exactly what I expect you to do once you are elected president—" The Priestess stopped Maurice from replying to the last statement. "—because if I say so, you will be elected. Rest assured of that. So, what is it going to be? Mutual help and a stellar career as the youngest president in Ginecea, or public disgrace as the mother of a depraved daughter?"

"What you're asking is immoral," Claudine intervened, her body language saying what her words hadn't.

Anna couldn't suppress a gasp fast enough. Pax slowly bumped her head against the wall. Rosie emitted a moan, echoing her granddaughter's thoughts.

"What I'm asking is the right price to keep your family alive. You think I'm being greedy? You should take a moment and ponder your options. The way I see it, you have no choice. I'm actually doing you a favor. Any other person would have thrown you to the wolves," the Priestess answered.

"The senator and her wife have been collaborating with you since their daughter came back." Anna tentatively moved toward Rosie, but the soldier raised the gun in warning.

Pax wasn't surprised by Anna's words. Things had gone too smoothly for her back in Ginecea. She should have questioned the whole policy of don't ask, don't tell issued by her mothers. She had been too comfortable with the silence and not having to answer questions she didn't want to be asked about Prince.

"And thanks to them, and their daughter's lack of morals—" The Priestess tilted her head in Pax's direction, and another sick smile graced her face. "—we are here today. Now, I don't have time to waste, and I'm late for my next appointment, so you should decide." She stood up and went to the window and looked out. "They really built something for themselves," she added, lost in thought. A fleeting gaze at Mauricio explained her words. When he raised his head, she immediately looked somewhere else, disgusted.

"You said you were concerned about Pax," Claudine said and shot an apologetic glance at her daughter. Pax shook her head and tried to lift the corners of her mouth.

"I was, and I still am, very concerned about your mentally ill daughter and the necessity of rendering her harmless. Obviously, if you're under my protection, we can find a better solution for her. She would be treated in the Temple, of course. I'm sure my talented therapists can find a cure for her *affliction*." The Priestess physically recoiled when she pronounced the last word, and her eyes settled for the briefest moment on Prince. "Nothing a good dose of electricity can't fix."

Pax felt her stomach churn at the Priestess's final threat. "What about them?" She indicated the two men in the room.

"Are you suggesting we discuss the slaves' future?" The Priestess was incredulous.

One of the soldiers exclaimed something under her breath. Pax looked at her defiantly.

"You—" The Priestess paused for a moment, as if at a loss for words. "—you can't believe I'm going to even contemplate answering your preposterous question."

"I know the truth about the farm," Pax said, keeping her eyes locked on the Priestess's, who in return remained silent.

"You don't know anything."

"You want me to go into details?"

"You don't know what you are talking about."

"Oh, I do, and I can prove it to you."

"Liar."

"Funny, your word choice used to insult me suits you perfectly." Pax indulged in the luxury of teasing the Priestess, despite the fact she was wagering with everybody's future. She couldn't help it. "Ginecean society is built on a gigantic lie. And you, and all the priestesses before you, are the ones spreading it," Pax added before Anna, who was inching toward her, could stop her.

"Pax—" Anna said tentatively, when it was clear that Claudine and Maurice were under a spell.

"Do you know the difference between a pure breed and a fathered woman?" Pax faced Anna directly. "No? It's not a joke," she said when Anna stared back at her with a worried expression. "It's actually so serious that if the truth left this room, Ginecea would probably crumble in a few hours. Am I right, Priestess?" Pax turned around to meet the older woman's gaze. "The answer to my question is: none." She kept her chin up to lock her eyes with the Priestess. "There is no difference between a pure breed and a fathered woman. They were both born from a mother and a father." She finished with a triumphant smile. Nobody had interrupted her.

She noticed Prince shaking his head slowly, and his eyes lowering to pause on her stomach.

"You are completely insane," the Priestess said, but her voice wasn't as steady as it had been before. "And I'm done with you."

Pax smiled again, but the moment lasted less than a second. One of the soldiers hit her repeatedly with the butt of the gun. The first hit reached her head, but when she went to instinctively protect it with her hands the soldier aimed for her stomach. Pax flopped down on the floor with a cry that echoed Prince's. "No, my baby, my baby, my baby." She rolled in fetal position, sobbing.

"Pax, what are you saying?" Maurice went to her side before the soldiers and the Priestess could stop her. They wouldn't have anyway because the Priestess had raised one hand.

"What did you say?" the Priestess asked loudly.

Pax kept sobbing, but didn't say anything.

"What. Did. You. Say?" the Priestess repeated, coming closer to Pax. She yanked away Maurice and pushed her shoe against Pax's hip. When Pax didn't answer, she kicked her. Everybody screamed at the senseless act of violence. "I will kick you again, and again, and again. And when I am tired, I will ask these women to do it for me." The Priestess immediately demonstrated the merit of her own words. Pax raised one hand in surrender.

"I'm pregnant." She hadn't planned to say it at all, but she wasn't going to lose the baby under torture. Prince was crying silently. The rest of the room reacted to the statement with a degree of despair that ranged from shocked silence to anger.

"Who is the mother?" Maurice and Claudine asked at the same time. Anna kept looking from Pax to her mothers, and vice versa. Rosie walked to Pax's side while everybody else was trying to make sense of the news.

Mauricio was crying and shaking his head.

"How could you?" The Priestess's rage was palpable, her hands two trembling fists by her sides.

Pax was seriously scared when she saw the intensity on the woman's face. What happened next was so unexpected it froze her on the spot.

The Priestess turned toward the closest soldier and yelled, "Give it to me."

"No!" In a blur Anna jumped in front of the Priestess, acting as a shield between Pax and the hand holding a gun.

"What—" Rosie looked up and the rest of the sentence died in her mouth.

"Your Holiness, please." Anna raised her hands and slowly pushed away the gun. Desperation was thick in her voice.

"Move out of the way or I'll shoot you, too." The Priestess moved the gun and pointed at Anna instead. Anna didn't budge, but her legs started trembling.

"Please, we'll do everything you ask." Claudine kneeled at the Priestess's feet, begging her.

"Please. I'll do anything, *anything*, to save my daughter's life." Maurice was crying by Rosie's side, trying to reach for Pax's hands.

"She's carrying an abomination. I can't let her live."

"Your Holiness, please reconsider," Anna said, moving carefully forward to get closer to the woman and the gun.

"Priestess?" The soldier whose gun had been taken was leaning with her hands outstretched. The Priestess didn't turn around to acknowledge her.

"How could you, a pure breed of your caliber, lay voluntarily with a slave?" The Priestess was looking beyond Pax and the room.

Pax didn't even think to answer the question. She lowered her head, hoping for a mercy that didn't come. The harsh sound of the projectile crashing against bones echoed in the air followed by Anna's screams. The Priestess pulled the trigger a second time. Pax felt her grandmother's hand pushing her forcefully out of the way, and other screams filled her ears while blackness fell over her.

CHAPTER 22

"You're lucky."

Pax looked the owner of the voice in the eyes without having the slightest idea of who she was.

"Two gunshot wounds, neither fatal, even though they were shot from a short distance." The woman was wearing white scrubs and had a stethoscope hanging around her neck. Pax felt the woman's professional hands slowly touching her right side, pausing on some places and hurrying past others. Pax looked up and read the name on the tag dangling with the stethoscope: Dr. Martin, followed in smaller print by the two letters indicating her affiliation to the Church of Ginecea: CG. "Your baby is alive. You aren't bleeding and that's a very good sign," the doctor answered Pax's unasked question.

Pax tried to move and raise her torso to see where she was. "Where am I?"

"Don't move; the bullets went in and out without touching any vital organ, but you were still shot. Twice," the doctor said, easing Pax down on the bed again. "You're in the men's hospital. Fortunately, the army managed to spare this building and its power sources; otherwise you'd be lying outside in the desert under an infirmary tent."

"Where is everybody?" Pax found the silence in the room oppressive.

"I have no idea. You were brought here by two of the Priestess's personal guards, and I found a piece of paper lying on you saying you were pregnant. Is there anything else I should know? Other than the fact that you had also hit your head earlier on?" The doctor went to brush her forehead with delicate fingers. "You've had a couple of eventful days, it seems."

"No, you've got the whole picture," Pax said, trying to economize on words. She had the feeling the doctor didn't know about the nature of her pregnancy. A knock on the door interrupted Pax's thoughts.

The doctor absentmindedly answered to come in.

"Is she awake?" The Priestess's voice preceded her.

"Your Holiness. What a pleasure." The doctor bowed, and then seeing the dark expression on the Priestess' face, she hastily added, "Yes, the patient is awake."

"Then leave me alone with her," the Priestess commanded.

The doctor curtsied again and obeyed. Pax started shaking.

"You are a pathetic monstrosity." The Priestess regarded Pax with a look loaded with such disgust she felt ill. "But here's the deal. You're still alive, and not for my lack of trying to rectify this mistake. However, I have to recognize I suffered a momentary lapse of judgment. It wasn't my fault though—" The Priestess steadied her hands, crossing them over her chest, then closed her eyes and sighed. "—thankfully, your mothers' secretary made me realize you are worth more to me this way, which is to say, breathing and pregnant. Thanks to you, I'll have absolute control of Ginecea through your mother, the next great president." The Priestess had resumed her usual sweet tone, as if they were exchanging family stories over a cup of tea.

"Where are the others?"

"Your grandmother fainted after I shot you. She's here. Your mothers, and the ever helpful Anna, are under my benevolent wing and they are being taken care of as we speak."

Pax understood the meaning of the Priestess's words. Both her mothers and she were hostages. She was blackmailing the Layans to do her bidding. They had all become puppets in the woman's hands. And it was her fault. Pax knew she had given the Priestess the ammunition she needed. "What do you want from us?" She was tired and in pain.

"Your Holiness…" The Priestess's eyes were sparkling again with mirth.

"What do you want from us, Your Holiness?" Pax amended. She had seen the woman lose her temper already.

"Not a lot, all considered." The Priestess, who had been standing the whole time, sat on the chair by the bed.

Pax didn't like it, but waited for the woman to speak her piece.

"Well, first, we are going to take care that your mother wins the election. To do so, of course, we must clean the Layans' slate and remove any spot from your family's pedigree. Your grandmother is ill; she won't be a problem in the long run. She'll spend her last days secluded somewhere, as she's done most of her life, anyway."

"But she'll need medical assistance and my mother's support," Pax couldn't help but interrupt.

"A doctor and an army of nurses are going to follow her. Regarding your precious mother's support, I'm afraid your grandmother will do without."

"But—" Pax closed her mouth when the Priestess put a finger on it. They both shuddered at the contact, but almost immediately the Priestess composed her face back to her usual mask of fake pleasantness.

"You're going to lose the baby." The woman worded the statement with such levity that, for a second, Pax thought she heard wrong. "Not here. I need my team of specialists at the Temple to keep it quiet and safe," she added with the same tone. Pax's trembling became evident. "Oh, don't worry, I promised your mothers you won't feel a thing."

"I won't let you kill my baby." Pax found her voice, but it came out unintelligible.

"Fine by me; I have a plan B anyway. Your mother Claudine will suffer a tragic car accident first, and then, soon after, Maurice will commit suicide."

"No!"

"And you *will* eventually lose the baby, one way or the other," the Priestess concluded.

"You can't do that." Pax stood up, ignoring the searing pain in her body.

"As a matter of fact, I can do whatever I want. But things don't have to be so—" The Priestess paused for a second, stood, and put some physical distance between them. "—stressful. You have the power to make it easy... easier—" she rectified "—for everybody."

"You can't do that," Pax repeated with less conviction and doubled over in pain. She fell on the bed with tears in her eyes.

"*You* can't keep talking to me like this." The Priestess snickered at Pax and shook her head sternly. "I've let it pass twice already. You may want to consider what's better for you and your mothers."

Pax watched the Priestess leave the room behind a curtain of falling water, and Doctor Martin came in with a big smile.

"I've just checked on your grandmother."

"How is she?"

"Well, given the advanced stage of her cancer, I'm surprised she's in such good physical condition. She's very upset, though."

"Could you help me into a wheelchair? I'd like to see her." Pax was already trying to sit back on the bed, but a sharp pain in her hip made her pause for breath.

"Slow down. I'll give you something mild for the pain. I can't give you anything stronger, I'm afraid. No good for your baby girl." The doctor raised her eyebrows apologetically and then gave her a shot. She went for the wheelchair Pax had asked for and came back immediately. "It's rusty, probably a model from twenty years ago, if not older, but still working." She helped Pax to sit on it. "Those men salvaged every relic they could put their hands on." She wheeled her out of the room. "Okay, if you feel tired, or in too much pain, I want you to call me and I'll bring you back to your room," she said before knocking on the door of Rosie's room.

Once left inside, Pax took a look at the sleeping figure on the bed and then slowly wheeled closer to touch her grandma. Rosie was attached to several IVs and seemed peacefully asleep, but a closer look revealed she merely had her eyes closed.

"I thought it was the doctor again," Rosie croaked with a tired voice.

"Just me." Pax wanted to leave the wheelchair to be closer to her grandmother, but even straightening up caused her to wince. She resigned herself to reaching out her hand to touch Rosie's arm.

"Thank Heavens you're alive. When I saw the Priestess shooting at you, I lost my mind. I woke up in this bed with Maurice screaming at the top of her lungs that you hadn't died and I almost fainted again." Rosie took Pax's hand in hers.

"I made a bigger mess than I thought," Pax said, looking away.

"I guess it started with me a long time ago, anyway. You can't be held accountable for something that goes beyond you. We are just pawns on a bigger board."

"I don't want to be a pawn. Not now that I know the truth about being one." Pax's eyes wandered from wall to wall of the small room. "Where are my mothers? Shouldn't they be with you?"

"The Priestess wants to finalize her deal and requested their presence. Anna went with them, of course."

"Of course," Pax repeated, and then she went on, asking the question she was terrified to ask, "Where are Mauricio and Prince?"

"I don't know. I asked Maurice and she wouldn't tell."

"What's going to happen to them?" Pax asked anyway, just to voice her thoughts.

"I don't know that, either, but I can't help being worried."

"I must get out of here."

"And lose the baby in the process? Be smart and wait to gain some strength, and then we'll think of something."

"I don't think they have enough time."

"And I don't think you can do anything about it." Rosie patted Pax's hand slowly. The door was timidly opened at that moment and Maurice's head appeared.

"Just checking you're still okay—" Then her eyes focused on the second person in the room and Maurice ran in to hug Pax. "You're awake! They wouldn't let me in your room. The Priestess was in with you, and I was told not to disturb her. I wanted to see with my own eyes that you were fine. The doctor told me, but I don't trust her," Maurice said all in one breath.

"I need to ask you something," Pax said when she emerged from her mother's embrace.

Maurice didn't say anything. Instead, she sat on Rosie's bed edge and gave Pax a wary look.

"Please, Mom, tell me where Prince and Mauricio are."

"It would be better for you to forget about them." Maurice slowly rested her hands on her knees and straightened her back. Her fingers went to play with the hem of her pencil skirt.

"Mother, by now you should know better than to ask me to forget Prince." Pax looked directly at Maurice's eyes without wavering.

"Please, don't say his name that way." Maurice winced uncomfortably, her fingers worrying the fabric of her skirt.

"Like what? You can tell from the way I say it that I care for him? Is that the problem?" Pax was being difficult on purpose, but when Maurice looked back at her in shock, she didn't back down and she didn't apologize. "This time we're not going to play games. You may not be asking, but I'm sure telling. I should've talked to you before, but there's no time now to apologize, cry, or try to make it all better." Pax paused for a second to breathe and Maurice immediately cut in.

"You don't know what you're talking about. Like Claudine, I still think you're experiencing some sort of trauma, due to being... abused. Now that I know you're expecting, it makes even more sense."

"By the Heavens, I wasn't abused!"

Maurice gasped at the blasphemy, but surprised Pax when she hugged her and said, "I promise we're going to make it better. This whole situation will be a bad memory, and in a few years, even that will disappear from your life."

"I'm not going to have an abortion." Pax slowly untangled herself from the smothering embrace.

"But it could be a boy... a *boy*... and what would you do then?" Maurice's expression showed much more than her words.

Pax was hurt by her mother's feelings. "I'd love him." She put some distance between her and Maurice, moving the wheelchair away from the bed.

"You're confused and don't know the facts of life." Maurice leaned toward Pax and put a hand on the wheelchair armrest to stop her.

"It's you, I'm afraid, who doesn't know the truth about life," Rosie intervened, shushing both mother and daughter.

"Mother?" Maurice turned as if finally noticing Rosie, when she had come to check on her in the first place.

"Do you remember the older man in the room? The one who looks so familiar?" Rosie spoke slowly, every word hanging between them like echoes.

Pax looked at the reaction on her mother's face while the meaning of Rosie's questions started to corrode Maurice's certainties.

"What are you trying to say, mother?"

"His name's Mauricio," Rosie said, and Pax saw her grandmother's body relax on the bed. Even the deepest wrinkle on Rosie's forehead, a constant frown that had always made her look angry with the world, slowly disappeared.

"I must tell you a long story." Rosie took her daughter's hand in hers and mouthed, "Please."

"I don't think you should tire yourself." Maurice looked alternately between her mother and her daughter.

Pax was surprised and not at all pleased to see Maurice, the strongest woman she had ever known, crumbling before a truth she didn't want to hear. But then she also remembered being enraged when Mauricio had first talked to her. And by the time he had given her the speech, she had been already in love with Prince.

"It doesn't matter anymore. I'm dying, and I don't want to die the same way I lived my life. You need to listen to what I have to tell you, and then you'll decide what to do with this knowledge. No matter what, I know you'll make me proud." Rosie gestured for Maurice to join her on the bed.

"Mother…" Maurice slowly walked toward Rosie, but she didn't sit.

"I should've talked to you long ago, but I was terrified of losing you. Now I'm leaving this life and I want to do it proudly." Rosie rearranged her body on the bed and caressed Maurice's arm.

Maurice didn't move. She kept sitting with her back ramrod straight, her knees closed, her legs slightly angled, her hands now one on top of the other on her lap. A pose she had perfected for the press.

"It's a long story, so I'll start from the most important part. Mauricio is your father, but you have already guessed this, right?"

Rosie smiled at her daughter, but Maurice's face was as paralyzed as the rest of her body and wasn't showing any feeling.

Pax saw how her mother's body had further stiffened at Rosie's words, if that were possible.

Rosie waited for Maurice to comment and then looked at Pax who smiled to show her support. She smiled back, closed her eyes, and then started talking. "Your pregnancy had a few bumps in the road, and I had to continue my stay for some time at the Temple, a guest of the former Priestess—" Rosie tried to engage Maurice in the conversation, but only Pax nodded at her words, although she had already heard the story. "I wasn't happy there. Every night, I went for a walk by the lake to release the tension I accumulated during the day, dealing with problems bigger than my age. Oh, I know it was all my fault." She gave another tentative look at her daughter, but it was Pax once more silently urging her to continue. "I blackmailed the Priestess to have a baby without a wife and without my mothers' consent—what could I expect?"

Pax studied her mother's expression at Rosie's last statement. Maurice's nostrils fluttered a moment, her eyes sparkled, but she was back to her calm self in no time. *Did you know you were born out of wedlock?*

"There was this beautiful, old tree along the path to the lake, just outside the Temple proper. It was a eucalyptus tree. I liked to sit underneath its foliage with my back against the wall and look at the placid waters of the lake. My life was in chaos, I'd almost lost you, and I knew an arranged marriage was in my near future. The landscape soothed me and I sang to you lullabies to let you know how much I cared for you. One night, I arrived late to my usual spot—the Priestess had ordered a whole battery of analysis and had taken the whole day. I hurried toward the eucalyptus, needing to put as much distance I could between myself and the rest of the world. The lake was dark and calm as usual, but the night wasn't silent. A voice, a male voice, filled the silence with the most heartbreaking melody I had ever heard. I followed it and saw the small opening on the wall I hadn't noticed before. The song stopped and my heart with it." Rosie's voice broke and she paused.

Pax squeezed her grandmother's hand to give her the strength to keep talking.

"I told him, 'You have a beautiful voice.'" Rosie let a tear fall, wiped it away, collected herself, and then resumed. "At first he didn't say anything back, then he talked and I felt something stirring inside me. That night I didn't sleep; I couldn't stop thinking of him. The next morning, I couldn't wait a whole day to talk to him again and I went outside his cell, only to discover he was at the infirmary. I ran back inside and waited until he was alone in the room. I wanted to see him."

Rosie's words evoked in Pax the memory of the first time she had seen Prince and she had to lower her eyes to the floor.

"I didn't care about the consequences. I opened the door and I went inside. He was lying on the bed, magnificent and frail at the same time. I'd never been so close to a man. He was bigger than I expected, but I wasn't scared by him. Instead, I longed to walk to the bed and see the exact shade of his eyes. I wanted to touch his skin. There was a beauty in him, a purity that called to me. He lay there beaten, starved, deprived of the most essential rights, and yet he retained a presence nobody could take from him. I felt at ease in his presence and I told him things I'd never said to anybody else. Then, while we were talking, my ring fell from my finger and we both went to pick it up. The moment my hand brushed his, my heart exploded and I stopped breathing. I think that was the moment I fell in love with him. Nobody had ever stolen my breath before, and nobody ever did after, but Mauricio."

Pax let go any pretense of hiding her reaction to her grandmother's tale and didn't remove her eyes from Rosie until she had finished speaking.

"The night he finally escaped the farm, my heart went with him. The pain I felt at being separated from your father almost consumed me. My love for you saved me, my sweet Maurice," she concluded several minutes later, after having recounted what had truly happened at Tarin.

"Grandma—" Pax could have listened to Rosie's and Mauricio's story hundred times and never grow tired of it.

"I've loved, and I was loved in return. It's more than I could've asked. Now that I finally saw him again, I can leave this life happy." Rosie smiled at her and then turned to confront her daughter.

Maurice hadn't moved a finger the whole time, resembling a handsome statue. Not even when Rosie had uncovered the truth behind the Tarin insurrection and its ramifications had she reacted. Pax had expected her mother to deny Rosie's words or to call them heresy, but she did neither.

"Mom? I'm sure you must have tons of questions for Grandma," Pax said, hoping to break her mother's stone mask. Pax wanted to see her screaming, or crying, or even cursing out loud, but the silence and the absence of human reactions were scaring her. Maurice was the more cool-headed of her mothers, but she was beyond calm at the moment. "Mom, say something, please." Pax went to lay a hand on her mother's arm and found it cold, like her demeanor. "Mom?"

"It's okay; she needs some time." Rosie attempted a smile. "It's okay," she repeated, but her voice had lost that calmness and was now on the verge of breaking.

Pax hoped for her mother to say something—anything at all— but Maurice's eyes had become blank and she looked even more withdrawn.

"I didn't expect you to understand me, but it was still important to me to tell you the truth—" Rosie said so softly that Pax had to strain her ears to hear her.

"No, you're right; I don't understand you, and I don't believe you. I don't think I ever will... I'm not sure I want to be here right now." Maurice talked over Rosie and caught Pax by surprise. "You should've told me. I had the right to know. *You* are my mother! And you decide to tell me now." Maurice was staring at an imaginary point in space, avoiding both her mother and her daughter.

"Grandma's in pain; can't you see that?" Pax said.

"I'm her daughter; of course I can feel her pain. I need time to even start thinking about what she told me. The only problem is I don't have time. And even if I wanted to, I can't change what's going to happen next," Maurice answered.

"What's going to happen next?" Pax shivered seeing her mother's face become darker.

"The price to save both your lives and my candidacy is to change my policy about fathered women and slaves."

"And? What else have you been asked to do? Apart from suggesting that I get rid of my baby." Pax was daring her mother to say it out loud.

"What? Maurice?" Rosie looked at her daughter with her piercing eyes, and Maurice capitulated.

"Once I'm elected president, I'll command the destruction of the City of Men, and I'll order the execution of their leader to make an example out of him." Pax and Rosie both screamed at the same time, but Maurice raised one hand and silenced them. "And since we're talking truth from now on, I've also been asked to execute your worker—" She gestured toward Pax. "—as the leader of the insurrection that almost destroyed Sundial and as the killer of a fathered servant girl."

"Prince never started any insurrection, and he is no murderer." Pax's voice was so loud that someone knocked from outside.

"I think my patients should rest now. I see they're getting overexcited." Doctor Martin appeared at the door with a worried face. She went for Pax's wheelchair and moved her aside without asking permission.

"We're discussing something important here; my mother can take me back to my room, but thank you, Doctor, for your concern," Pax said, putting a hand on the doctor's to halt her.

"The Priestess has given me new orders." Doctor Martin's face revealed how much she disliked the whole situation. "I apologize, but I must take you back to your room."

"This is outrageous; you can't treat patients as if they are criminals." Maurice had reverted to the Senator in a second.

"I apologize, again. I really hate it, but I could lose my job over this, and if you don't cooperate, I'll have to force you. And I don't want to reach that point, if it can be avoided." Doctor Martin seemed genuinely sorry about having to enforce the Priestess's orders.

It wasn't enough for Pax; she was quickly starting to resent the woman.

"Senator, I was also told to escort you outside the infirmary."
Again, the wretched look on the doctor's face.

"Let me talk to my family first, and I'll follow you without
causing any problems. Do you think it's possible to give us five
minutes?" Maurice used her public voice, and it worked.

Doctor Martin whispered an okay and left the room, but didn't
close the door all the way.

"Please, don't do anything reckless, and I'm talking to both of
you," Maurice whispered, keeping an eye on the door.

"You can't ask me to sit tight and wait for the carnage to happen.
You know it's not right," Pax said.

"I'm with her. I know I can't do much, but I'll help Pax with my
last breath." Rosie reached for her granddaughter's hand, and they
both stared at Maurice.

"Your act of defiance won't help you, or *them*." Maurice sighed.

"Probably not, but at least I won't have any regrets," Pax replied.

"And I have too many already," Rosie chimed in. A discreet
knock on the door silenced Maurice who was going to add
something.

"Please, wait for me. I'll try to think about what you said, but I
can't promise anything. And… never hide anything again, please?"
Maurice was looking at both her mother and her daughter, waiting
for them to pledge to her request. Doctor Martin knocked again and
entered to announce their five minutes were up.

Once inside her room, Pax was helped on the bed by a nurse who
had silently followed Doctor Martin like a shadow. Maurice
watched while the nurse connected her daughter to a machine
controlling her vitals and stood at the door until it closed in her face
when the woman left the room. Pax heard the lock click, her mother
complaining about it, and then steps and voices fading away. She
stared at the ceiling for a long time, trying to make sense of what
was happening. She was worried sick about Prince. Where did the
Priestess take him? What she was doing to him? Was she torturing
him? How long could he survive? Terrifying images populated
Pax's mind and she started feeling physically ill.

"Are you okay?" The same nurse came into the room and
checked her vitals; then she called the doctor from a two-way radio

she removed from a pocket on her scrubs. "The doctor's going to give you something to calm your nerves. Your state of agitation isn't good for the baby. Breathe slowly, in and out. Yes, like that. Good job. Keep doing it." The woman kept praising Pax's efforts at breathing.

Doctor Martin arrived a few minutes later, and she didn't look happy. "I'm sorry if this situation is causing you stress," she said while writing on a pad and then turned toward the nurse. "Give this to her and call me back if her vitals spike again." She left the room without a second glance at her patient, for which Pax was grateful. Her feelings toward the doctor had gone from annoyed to loathing in a very short amount of time. She knew she was looking for someone to hate, and she didn't care as long as the good doctor was there to take the heat.

"Walking relaxes me," Pax told the nurse conversationally.

"And in a day or two, walking is going to be very good for you, but right now, you have to stay put. Aren't you worried for your baby girl?" The nurse gave Pax a stern look.

"Of course I am. My baby is the most important thing to me."

"Well, then you have to rest." The nurse tucked Pax in.

"But I can't stay still for long," Pax tried again.

"I'll give you something to think about, then. I'll be right back." The nurse left with great purpose.

Pax stared at the closed door for a few minutes, wondering what the nurse had meant, when she came back dragging a cart behind her with a battered-looking machine on it.

"You'll see..." the nurse muttered more to the machine than to Pax.

"What's it for?" Pax watched the nurse plug the machine into the wall socket.

"Patience," the nurse said with a smile. She then went to set aside the linens covering Pax. "Now I'm going to put some gel on your stomach." She raised Pax's gown and lowered the sheet under her belly button. "I'm sorry it's cold," the nurse said when Pax grimaced. "It's worth it, though. Now look at the monitor."

Pax was going to ask what it was when the nurse started moving the transducer on her slimed belly. "Oh my Heavens." She was seeing her baby for the first time. She had seen many pictures of babies' ultrasounds in the pregnancy book she had read, but this was different. She could see little dots moving and her throat closed. "Is that the baby's arms moving? Or the legs?"

"I wouldn't know, I'm sorry. Your baby is too small and the image is low resolution and grainy; this is an old machine and I'm not an ultrasound technician, so I can't tell you anything specific, but isn't it incredible? But wait, there's more." She switched a lever on the machine and a whooshing sound came out of it. "Listen to your baby's heart. Can you hear how strong she is?"

"It's—" Pax could barely talk; mixed emotions were clouding her eyes.

"Yes, it's your baby girl's heart." The nurse nodded, her eyes misty, too.

The sound was more a cacophony, but for Pax's ears was the sweetest melody. "Thank you," she managed to say. She couldn't remove her eyes from the monitor.

"Judging from the quality of the sound, this machine will probably break any moment now—so much noise it's almost impossible to make out the heartbeat, but it will do. It's a miracle they had one. Who knows from where they stole it." The ultrasound monitor flickered for a moment and the moving dots disappeared for the briefest moment. The nurse turned it off. "The hospital is working at full capacity and the solar panels can't provide the energy we need to keep things going. We can't use it willy-nilly, but I wanted to give you a reason to endure this—" She indicated the room with a gesture of her hand. Even with the machine unplugged, the one light over Pax's bed went off and on. "Good thing the OR has a separate generator."

"Thank you." Pax wanted the woman to stop talking so she could be free to think about her baby.

"Now, please rest and be quiet." The nurse went to clean Pax's stomach with a warm, wet cloth. "You'll learn soon enough that you can do anything to protect your baby. Staying in bed for a day is nothing." A sharp click resonated soon after the nurse closed the door behind her.

Pax took it in stride that she was officially a prisoner and turned around to face the wall of her jail. Later, she thought about the nurse's words and realized she knew exactly what she was capable of doing for her baby. *I'll destroy Ginecea, if I have to.* She smiled at her resolution and finally fell asleep.

CHAPTER 23

"Good morning. You sure can sleep." The nurse was removing the sensor from her arm. "You don't need this anymore. You can have your walk later today. Probably not long after Doctor Martin comes to check on you."

"Can I go visit my grandma?" Pax shielded her eyes from the blade of bright light coming in from the window.

"She's not to be disturbed." The nurse was busy folding cables and hooking them up on the back of the machines previously attached to Pax.

"Is she okay?" Pax had read something between the lines.

"Doctor's running a few tests on her. My guess is that it will be fine to visit later."

Pax waited for the nurse to leave the room, dragging one of the machines on unsteady and noisy wheels and then slowly stood up and went to the door. The woman had left it open, which meant she was coming back right away. Pax didn't waste any time; she was at Rosie's door in two steps and put her ear to it. She tried to catch any sound inside the room, and when she couldn't detect any, she lowered the handle. The door didn't put up any resistance and she entered only to find an immaculate room. The bed was empty and ready for a new patient to be tucked in. After a moment of surprise, Pax left. When the nurse came back to wheel out the second machine, Pax was staring at the ceiling.

"I just passed Doctor Martin; she's preparing for a surgery, but as soon as she's done, she'll check on you. Until then, just relax and have something to eat." The nurse put a tray on the nightstand and then went to finish what she had started.

Pax watched the nurse holding the door ajar with one foot while trying to maneuver the cart without dropping the machine's electrodes on the floor. She had haphazardly put the pressure pump and a bag full of needles on top of the machine, and she was keeping everything together with her hands.

"There's never anyone around when you need help," the woman muttered to the deserted hallway and slowly managed to exit without smashing the cart between the door and the wall. Pax kept her eyes on the scene the whole time, waiting for the lock to click. The door closed in slow motion, but Pax didn't hear any locking sound. She didn't even think about it; she discarded the gown and donned the neatly folded clothes waiting for her on the chair, slipped into her shoes, grabbed a piece of bread from the tray, gulped a long drink from the cup of tea, and left the room.

As soon as she was outside, Pax made a mental note to slow down and breathe. She passed her fingers through her hair and smoothed down the knots that had formed during the night. Pax hoped it was enough to look confident and not out of place if anybody saw her walking by. She didn't know where to go and regretted almost immediately she hadn't taken a look outside the window to see what part of the city she was in.

"Looking for someone?"

Pax turned around and saw a nurse coming out of a room; the woman's face was hidden behind a pile of used towels and was in a hurry. "Yes, I'm looking for Doctor Martin. Do you know where she is?" She tried to slow down her words.

"She should still be in the OR. And with all the wounded out there, I guess she'll be busy for the next few days. Anyway, one floor up, three doors on the left." The woman bobbed her head, turned around, and moved away to her next destination without having looked at Pax once.

Pax waited until the pile of towels disappeared inside another room and then sprinted toward the end of the hallway, found the stairs and went down as far away as possible from the OR. She bumped into other women, but they were busy and didn't look at her. She found the exit of the building and she was out in the central plaza, only to find it was full of soldiers. The Priestess, standing on a makeshift stage, was talking to her army and she had the women completely enthralled. Nobody was looking anywhere but at the stage.

Pax looked at the sea of heads nodding in agreement to whatever the Priestess had been saying, and when the army applauded as a single organism, she went to hide behind one of the columns surrounding the plaza. She couldn't move ahead without being seen by someone standing in the lateral flank, and she couldn't stay still; at any moment, the nurse could come back to her room and, realizing she was gone, raise the alarm. The unified roar from the soldiers become louder and was accompanied by the rhythmic stomping of their feet.

"It is a great pleasure for me to present to you the woman who made all of this possible." The Priestess's voice echoed in the big space, and the soldiers greeted her words with another round of applause. Pax cautiously leaned out and took a peek at what was happening. The Priestess was shaking hands with Maurice. A few steps back from the stage were Claudine and Anna, both looking at Maurice with wary eyes.

"I'm sure your next president would like to say something." The Priestess pushed Maurice to the center of the stage.

"I—" Maurice looked ahead, and Pax saw that her mother's eyes were unfocused. "—I am overwhelmed by such warm reception." Maurice turned around for a second, looking for her wife. Claudine's reaction was to nod at Maurice while clutching Anna's arm.

Pax imagined what Anna whispered in Claudine's ear.

"I haven't done anything to deserve your affection." Before Maurice could add anything else, the Priestess took the stage again and led the crowd to another ovation.

"You're too humble. We've just driven out the most resilient enemy thanks to your fast thinking," the Priestess said, looking Maurice in the eyes.

Pax saw her mother Claudine getting more agitated and Anna stroking her arm.

"It is thanks to our future president that we caught the two slaves planning on overturning our world—" The Priestess made a come-hither gesture to a soldier standing on the other side of the stage from where Claudine and Anna were. "—and here they are, waiting for their rightful punishment." The Priestess's voice was triumphant and bordered on hysteria.

Pax watched as the soldier came forward, pulling two leashes. Prince and Mauricio slowly emerged from the darkness and were greeted by insults and threats. Someone threw a rock and hit Prince. Pax felt ill at seeing blood gushing out from a cut on his forehead, and unable to stop herself, she ran from column to column until she was closer to him. She remembered at the last second, just one column of being too close and out in the open, to duck again and hide. She didn't check if anyone had seen her, but had the sense to flatten against the stone once she stole another glance at him.

"Given the exceptional circumstances, and listening to your rightful requests, I've decided to give Senator Layan full authority to judge the criminals *in loco*, right here." This time the army's cries reached the sky. "Justice shall be served before we return to Ginecea."

She's just declared martial law. Pax saw Maurice's upset expression and how she looked for Claudine and shook her head in dismay. She steadied herself against the urge to run toward Prince and resigned herself to just peek at what was happening onstage. The Priestess took the chains from the soldier's hands and yanked the two men forward to make them kneel down. Mauricio stumbled against the podium and fell, hitting his head against one of the corners. Prince went to help him, but the Priestess tugged his chain and he went to the floor instead. Laughs and obscene comments punctuated Prince's efforts to right himself. The Priestess put one of her feet on his back and kept his face down on the ground.

"This is where you belong; you are worth less than the dirt you are on," the Priestess hissed loud enough to be heard, forgetting for a second she had a crowd's attention. A moment later, she was staring at the army with her usual artificial smile.

Pax couldn't stand to watch Prince's humiliation without doing anything. Another cheer from the soldiers and this time Pax heard Prince screaming. She didn't think and was outside of the safety of the column before her brain registered what her body was doing.

A shadow appeared before her and slim arms pushed her back. "Stay here. Don't let her see you." Anna was restraining her against the column. "Don't do anything stupid. You can't help them."

"Anna, I can't. The Priestess is crazy; she's going to torture him just for fun. And Mauricio is already dying; he isn't going to make it. Please, help me." Pax pushed against Anna's arms.

"I'm helping you, kid." Anna pushed her back in the shadow. "Run away and hide. You aren't safe here. Your mothers can't protect you anymore. The Priestess isn't going to let you have the baby."

"But I can't leave Prince—" Pax struggled against Anna's grip on her arms.

"If you want to have your baby, you have to run. Now. Don't turn around. Just go before it's too late."

"The Priestess is going to kill him." Pax was still trying to reason with Anna when both of them turned around at the sight of a woman in white scrubs moving through the crowd.

"Run. I'll create a diversion." Anna left Pax in the shadow and ran toward the podium, screaming as if her life depended on it.

Pax saw the nurse approaching the podium to talk to the Priestess, only to be thwarted by Anna, who was yelling that she had seen a man skulking around. Whatever the nurse had come to say was immediately dismissed by the Priestess's orders to find the worker and bring him to her. Part of the army charged ahead in the pursuit of the man, while another contingent of women closed around the Priestess to protect her. Anna, Claudine, and Maurice got swallowed inside the human wall. Pax gave a last look at the scene, hoping to see Prince, but he, too, had disappeared along with Mauricio.

She waited longer than it was safe and then ran away in the opposite direction of the crowd. She ran until her lungs exploded and her legs started aching. And when her eyes stopped seeing and only black stared back at her, Pax stopped and sat down and cried, holding the right side of her body. She slowly raised the hem of her shirt and took a look at the bandages covering the bullet holes. A red spot was blossoming on the white cotton. *It's nothing*, she repeated several times under her breath. *I'm so tired.* She closed her eyes for a moment.

"Come here," a voice called her from the darkness. Lucas's voice.

"Don't sit there. Come here." A second voice joined. Cordelia.

I must be dreaming. It can't be them. Her two wounds were throbbing and it was hard to think and breathe at the same time. "I'm too tired," she said, without knowing why she was bothering. She couldn't seem to open her eyes. Two strong arms lifted her from the ground and gently put her on her feet.

"Please, try and walk a few steps. We must get out of here and fast." Cordelia's voice was gentle, and Pax decided to oblige her request. She was dragged several steps. A door was opened and closed. "Let's put her here." A few more steps and she was lowered on a soft surface, a bed or a couch.

"Pax?"

"Is she going to faint?"

"I don't know. Maybe some water would help," Lucas said, and almost immediately a few drops of a cold liquid wet Pax's lips.

"Drink some of this," Cordelia pleaded, and again Pax listened to her.

The liquid was sweet and Pax felt better almost immediately. At first she couldn't see anything, but after a few seconds her sight came back, little by little. "Cordelia." She studied the woman's face and then finally said, "I'm so happy to see you." She slowly raised her head from what turned out to be a couch.

"As we're happy to see that you're still alive." Lucas came into view.

"What are you doing here?" Pax tried to look around to learn where she was. She had run through the city without a destination in mind, but she was inside someone's living room, that much was clear. They had probably taken shelter inside the first house they found on the way.

"We're trying to put together the few men and women who have escaped before the Priestess's Army took over," Lucas answered.

"We were scouting this level looking for fugitives." Cordelia offered Pax some more to drink. "It's just water, crushed aloe, and sugar. You need to hydrate your body, or you're going to collapse."

"I need to go back and save Prince and Mauricio. The Priestess wants to make an example out of them," Pax blurted out as soon as Cordelia took away the flask.

"Where are they?" Lucas asked.

"I don't know." Pax took another sip of the nectar and then made a succinct summary of what she knew.

"How long do we have before they are executed?" Cordelia sat by Pax.

"The Priestess has called martial law. My mother has been given full authority to act without Ginecea's consensus. And I'm sure the Priestess has taken my grandmother hostage. I'm guessing she's pressuring my mother to order Prince's and Mauricio's execution by tomorrow. She seems unstable."

"We don't have enough time to put together a plan, and we also don't have enough men we can count on at the moment," Lucas said after cursing.

"I don't think a man could do a lot anyway," Cordelia reasoned.

"She's right. I'll go back, and I'll find a way to free them," Pax said and slowly got back on her feet, steadied her body against the wall beside the couch when her head swayed, and then opened her eyes again to find Cordelia and Lucas looking at her as if she were insane. "I'm a woman—" She waved one hand in the air to dismiss their worries. "—and even if I'm caught, I still am Pax Layan. The soldiers won't kill me point-blank. I can get closer to Prince and Mauricio than anybody else here. I just need a uniform, and I'm good to go."

"Is that blood?" Cordelia asked, pointing at her stained shirt.

"It's nothing. A scratch." Pax brought both hands to the bloodstain.

"You're wounded," Lucas said.

"I just need a few minutes to rest, that's all."

Cordelia went to her side and examined the wounds under the bandages. "You can't go anywhere like this."

"Can you think of a better plan?" Pax asked, removing Cordelia's hands from her body. She put the bandages back. "See? I'm not bleeding anymore."

"Maybe it isn't that bad, but it still doesn't mean you should go ahead with this one," Cordelia said in a softer tone.

"I'll be fine. I only need help moving through the city without being caught before I get the uniform."

"Okay," Lucas said after a few seconds of uncomfortable silence.

"But—" Cordelia interjected.

"She's right; saving the Priest is the priority. The City of Men owes him everything," Lucas explained.

"And I'll take care of myself; I'm not going to recklessly risk my life," Pax concluded, involuntarily caressing her belly.

It was already afternoon when Lucas and Cordelia left Pax outside the new Priestess's Army headquarters. It had taken a lot to convince Cordelia she was able to undertake the rescue mission. Only when Pax had let her clean and dress the wounds with new bandages, and the cotton had stayed white, had Cordelia finally given her blessing and they had left the house.

"Are you sure?" Cordelia asked.

They were hiding behind the colonnade, just a few steps from the main entry to the building, but hidden by the large shadow. Ginecea was taking over what was left of the city one building at a time and with great speed and efficiency.

"See you later," Pax answered, attempting a smile. She had already answered the question several times and was worried about it herself. She didn't need the constant reminding. *Now or never*, she thought, and without looking back, she went for the door. *It worked once*, she repeated over and over in her mind, until she felt confident she could go in unnoticed.

Pax steadied her posture, straightened her back, and raised her chin. She steadied her hands by her side and strode through the entry as if she didn't have a worry in the world. She nodded at one woman who was going out and then headed for the closest room where she could find a uniform to wear. She didn't have to wait long.

Two soldiers were getting out of a room, and one of them was complaining about the heat.

"I need a shower like right now," the other said.

Pax made an effort not to lower her head and followed them to the end of the hallway. She waited a few seconds and then entered a communal shower room. The steam was hot and hit her lungs like a punch. The wounds under the bandages started throbbing, and it was a struggle not to press her hands over the gauze. She bit back a moan and kept her eyes on the women she was following. They were semi-hidden behind a corner, changing out of their clothes. Keeping her back to them, she got closer and started unfastening her pants to give the impression she was going to shower, too. She slowed down her movements and waited for the two women to leave, and then making sure nobody was watching, she grabbed the first pile of neatly folded clothes, donned them, and left.

In the hallway, Pax tied her hair with an elastic band she found inside one of the uniform pockets and strolled out without being stopped. She reached the column where Lucas and Cordelia had been hiding a few moments earlier and collapsed against it, her legs trembling. When she started breathing regularly again, she wondered where the two of them were. A pebble hit her foot and she looked ahead. They were motioning to her from under a low archway a few feet away from the column.

"A squad almost caught us," Cordelia said when Pax ducked under the crowded space to join them.

"Keep your head low." Lucas was already moving, advancing farther inside.

Pax gave a last look behind her and then followed them. "Where are we going?" A musty smell clung to the air.

"I found where the Priest and Prince are being held. I have been building this city since I was young, and I know every shortcut and hidden passage there is." Lucas was a few steps ahead and his voice was muffled by the closeness of the place. The corridor wound down almost immediately.

"Where are we, the dungeon?" Pax didn't like it when the passage got even smaller and her head bumped against the ceiling. The uniform she had worn over her shirt was sticking to her body.

"Hang in there; this is the safest way to reach the other side of the city without being seen." Lucas's voice guided her, although she could only see Cordelia's back.

"Where did they take them?"

"The army found our prison and is using it. The building is just outside the city's walls."

Pax endured the walking without complaining, but once outside, she almost cried in relief. Lucas didn't waste time waiting for her to get ahold of herself. He indicated what at first sight resembled a rock formation. "That's the prison. Let's move." They started traversing the desert, one dune at the time, being careful of not exposing themselves to the two guards standing on the building's roof.

"Take shelter behind the Great Wall," Lucas ordered as one of the two guards turned toward them, indicating one of the big dunes bordering at regular intervals the ridge towering over the prison.

Pax searched her memory for the familiar term, then Cordelia gave her a look, and she remembered when she had heard of it. "Okay."

From then on, every time the guards exchanged places, they ran and hid behind the artificial walls of sand. Up close, Pax could see the wooden scaffolds harnessing the man-made structures in place, to dam the sand as Cordelia had explained to her a lifetime ago. They waited for the moment both women had their backs to them and reached the next safe point, until they were a dune away from the building's entry. They finally stopped to have a breather, but it didn't last long.

"Time to put that uniform to good use." Cordelia tried to cheer up Pax, but the tension was impossible to ignore. Lucas patted her shoulders and said a few words of encouragement.

"If I don't come out in an hour, leave." Pax didn't stay to hear Lucas's and Cordelia's heartfelt protests. She went down carefully, following the natural slide carved by a recent wind and taking advantage of the slope wall to cover her. At the bottom, she briefly patted her clothes, shook her head to remove the sand, and came out of the hiding spot with her spine erect and the resolution to succeed. It was only when she faced the sentinel at the door that she realized her voice was shaking, her palms were sweating, and she must have looked a mess. She mumbled something about having been sent there to help.

"Have a sip of water first; this weather's killing all of us," the sentinel said without looking at Pax. The woman pointed at a door just inside the hallway. She didn't ask any of the questions Pax had expected. "Smoldering heat during the day and freezing cold at night. Hope we're leaving soon."

Pax nodded, murmured *thanks,* and followed the directions she'd been given. It was the cafeteria. Several soldiers were taking a break from the heat. She picked up a bottle of water and strained her ears, trying to catch any bit of useful conversation. She made a show of deciding what to eat from the buffet table, waiting for the right information. She was rewarded a few minutes later.

"Can't wait to go back to Ginecea," a soldier said over a sandwich plate.

"The execution has been scheduled for tonight; only a few more hours and we are out of here. Eat something now, because the rest of the day is going to be hectic," a second woman answered.

"The Priestess has just called. Captain Nori wants every guard upstairs. We're going to escort the prisoners to the main plaza. They're assembling the gallows as we speak," a third woman announced from the door, breaking the low murmur in the room.

Cheers exploded while everybody grabbed something from the table and left. Pax imitated what the other women had done and followed them. Nobody seemed to notice her presence and she went with the flow, carefully keeping her eyes on the floor. She went down two flights of stairs and entered the cold dungeon. The air was damp and the illumination scarce. The idea that Prince and Mauricio were kept there, in the dark, made her heart sink.

When Pax saw them, she had to put a hand on her mouth not to cry. The squad stopped before a low cell, and the guard on duty looked at them with obvious relief in her eyes.

"About time you showed up. It's disgusting down here. And they smell like men."

Some of the soldiers snickered at the guard's complaint, but someone else responded with sympathetic comments on the injustice of having to endure male company for more than a minute. Pax saw the cell's floor was flooded with water and two figures were huddled together in the far corner. Prince was holding Mauricio upright on a plank of wood, the only thing above the murky water. Another look revealed the plank was barely wide enough to contain both men and that Mauricio's body was limp.

"Lucky you. You can take your break now."

The soldiers in front of Pax moved to both sides of the oppressing passage, while the woman who had relieved the guard from duty opened the cell.

"Get out. Don't make me come inside that sewer, or I'll let you drown in it."

Pax heard a groan from the cell and then a few sloshy steps accompanied by the sound of something heavy being dragged. Prince came out a few moments later, carrying Mauricio with one arm under his shoulder, whispering to him to put one foot in front of the other. Mauricio didn't appear completely conscious, but obeyed Prince. Pax looked at the two men struggling to walk in a straight line, and she saw the fresh wounds crisscrossing the skin where the clothes had been torn. She had to forcefully flatten her back against the wall to avoid giving herself away. But Prince saw her, and their eyes met for the briefest moment before he was yanked away from Mauricio.

"I'm so glad we're almost done with all of *this*," one of the women commented.

The soldier who had opened the cell pulled Prince's chain, making walking difficult. Another soldier did the same to Mauricio, who collapsed on the floor as soon as Prince's strength wasn't there to support him.

"Let me help him," Prince asked and was immediately thrown on the floor.

"Don't you dare talk to a woman." The soldier pulled the chain until Prince made a choking sound.

"You, carry him." Pax used her best authoritative tone and hoped no one would question her presence, once she had talked.

"Man, do as you are told," the soldier who was holding Mauricio's chain commanded.

Prince immediately moved close to Mauricio and helped him up. Pax watched as he dragged the older man's body as if it were lifeless. The squad escorted the prisoners up the stairs and to the hallway and then out into the desert. Pax followed, feeling rather helpless. She had gone inside the prison to find a way to break Prince and Mauricio out, but she had never thought that one of them couldn't walk, or that they were going to be moved so soon. Not that she had a plan before, but she had hoped to pull the card of having to move them under the Priestess's orders. Now she was out in the desert, surrounded by women who were going to kill the three of them without thinking twice.

Pax moved closer to Prince, and he slowly shook his head.

"Stay away," he mouthed and turned his head in the opposite direction.

"What the—" one of the woman yelled when a low rumble broke the natural silence.

CHAPTER 24

Pax felt the ground trembling under her feet and looked at Prince. An enormous wave of sand crashed on them only a few seconds later. Pax stretched her arm to reach for Prince, but Lucas appeared from nowhere and was at his side first, pushing her out of the way before he was swallowed by the avalanche. Cordelia arrived soon after and grabbed a screaming Pax, dragging her away before the sand could entomb her.

Seconds passed in slow motion. "Prince?" Pax couldn't see him or Lucas. Cordelia kept her close until the last grain of sand dropped on the ground. "Where are they?" she asked Cordelia.

"It was the only thing we could think of." Cordelia looked at her with an apologetic expression on her face. "When we saw you coming out of the building... there wasn't anything else to do—"

Pax was barely listening to her. Her eyes swept around to take in the scene and she realized what Cordelia was talking about. The geography of the place had been rearranged; the artificial sand wall on the ridge was no more; a small hill stood now where the path had been only a few minutes before. Several pieces of the wood that had formed the scaffolding were scattered around. One of them, a big plank, had broken and its sharp edges lay at her feet. "You created an avalanche."

"There was no time. I unhinged the structure and Lucas ran down to help you."

"Where are they?" She got louder, and Cordelia put a hand on her mouth.

"Shhh, I can see something moving." Cordelia pointed at the base of the newly formed ridge. "Yes, it's a hand."

Pax broke Cordelia's hold and propelled herself ahead with the other woman in tow. She stood before the protruding hand trying to decide if it belonged to a woman. When she was positively sure it was too big, Pax reached for it and pulled with all her strength.

"Help me."

Cordelia immediately joined her, and they freed the hand until the whole arm, and then the shoulder, and finally Lucas's torso emerged from the sand.

"Where's Prince?" Pax cried in desperation and began digging next to Lucas.

"He's here." Lucas's strained voice made Pax pause. "Prince and Mauricio are behind me." Lucas tried to move, but his lower body was still trapped. Pax and Cordelia redoubled their efforts to unearth him completely, and when they finally reached his legs, another arm appeared and then a head.

"Help him, please." Pax recognized Prince's dark hair and her heart skipped several beats. She could only see the back of his head. She kneeled by Lucas's legs and dug until her nails broke. Thin strikes of red marred the golden sand, but she didn't slow down.

Lucas, now completely free, removed Pax forcefully and started digging Prince out. Cordelia joined him.

"Is he alive?" Pax couldn't tell from where she was. Her hands were stinging and she had to keep them by her side. Physical pain and fear for Prince's life were consuming her.

"He's breathing." Cordelia didn't turn around. "Come here and hold his shoulders."

Pax did as ordered and finally saw Prince's face. His skin had a sickly color, dusty yellow. His eyes were closed, and his lips were dark, but he was breathing. A slow wheeze escaped his mouth and she bent to kiss him.

"Move aside with him. Mauricio is still under." Cordelia gently helped her out of the way, while Prince's body collapsed on the ground.

"My love, please say something to me." Pax cradled Prince's body on her lap and rocked back and forth. She barely noticed Mauricio being pulled free. She caressed Prince's face, gently blowing the sand out of his eyelashes, and kissed his eyelids to wake him. "Please, say something." Her tears left a wet streak on his skin, and when one reached his lips, he finally opened his eyes. His mouth opened, but no intelligible sound came out of it. "It's okay. I'm here." Pax brought his head closer to her chest and then whispered in his ear, "I love you."

"I love you," Prince whispered back.

"Mauricio's unconscious," Lucas called.

Pax tried to hold Prince to her, but at Lucas's words, he stirred.

"He needs a doctor." Cordelia was checking Mauricio's body for fractures. "He has a broken leg."

"Let's go back to the tunnel. It's not safe here," Lucas said.

Pax helped Prince up, and then they both helped Lucas carry Mauricio's body toward the entry of the tunnel. Cordelia walked behind them, watching their steps.

Transporting Mauricio through the tunnel wasn't simple. The ceiling was too low, and the walls were too close. Lucas and Prince had to go down on their knees, put Lucas's shirt under Mauricio, and slowly haul him on the floor. They took turns pulling the makeshift stretcher, and even Cordelia and Pax helped when the two men had to pause for a moment.

Pax was so worried she didn't even mind the claustrophobic stroll through the dungeon the second time. When the pain in the right side of her body became difficult to ignore, she brushed the bandages and her fingers came back red. She didn't say anything. "What now?" she asked when they reached the city's entrance, just outside the women's newly appointed headquarters.

"You wait here while I go ask for help," Cordelia resolutely said. Pax gave her a puzzled look. "I don't have time to explain." She went out, leaving them in the uncomfortable safety of the passage.

Pax and Prince cuddled against the wall, conscious that two other men were sitting just a few inches away from them, but unable to stay away from each other.

"I went mad thinking the Priestess had killed you," he said, slowly caressing her arms.

"I'm hard to kill," she answered.

"Let me see."

"Here," Pax showed him where the bullets had gone in and out of her hip. She winced when he brushed the spot, but immediately said, "I'm fine."

"But the wounds are bleeding."

"You've survived worse than this."

"Yes, but I'm a worker, and you're a pure breed… and you're also pregnant," Prince said, and then his eyes clouded with worries. "Is the baby—?"

"The baby's okay," she said with the first genuine smile in days. She guided his hands on her belly. "A nurse gave me an ultrasound to let me see the baby."

Prince bent to kiss her belly and laid his head on it, taking care not to put any weight on it. "I wish I had seen the baby; it must've been the most beautiful thing in the world. Our baby."

They stayed silent for a while, and then he stood up. "We're going to the Caves," he said. "And we'll hide until the baby is born."

"I don't care where I am—" Pax couldn't finish the sentence because Prince stole her breath away. She hoped Cordelia would take longer to act on her plan, only to feel guilty when she saw Mauricio. But still, she felt happy in Prince's arms. She knew she should've been worried, but the only sentiment she could recognize was peace. She was at peace. In the midst of a nightmare, she had found serenity again. That was Prince to her. He gave her strength, whether in the middle of a raging fire or escaping from an army of angry women. "I'm only half without you," she whispered to him.

When the sound of steps approaching was too loud to ignore, Pax was forced back to reality. She had a glimpse of several soldiers walking toward the tunnel's entrance. Prince moved swiftly in the crowded space to put her behind him, while Lucas did the same with Mauricio. The soldiers didn't turn away at the last moment as Pax had hoped; they walked right in.

"Pax?" someone called.

Pax couldn't see anything; a wall of bodies obscured the already dim light in the tunnel.

"Is she okay?" another voice asked.

Pax squinted, trying to assign faces to the voices she was hearing. She was tired and probably severely dehydrated, but there was something familiar about them. Someone swore. "Sonia? Is that you?" Pax couldn't believe her eyes.

"Yes, it is. Who else swears that way?" Tai answered, following Sonia and Cara. Cordelia was just behind them, pushing them inside the tunnel and carrying a bundle.

They started greeting each other, but both Lucas and Cordelia cut short the pleasantries.

"The Priest is dying." Lucas's words had a sobering effect on everybody.

"Here, I brought a hammock we're going to use like a stretcher, and we'll use the chains to walk Lucas and Prince around," Cordelia said. She proceeded to open the bundle and laid it down to stretch the fabric, "The four of us are going to transport the Priest, and you—she looked at Pax—will be their guard."

"Can you walk?" Prince asked Pax.

"Sure," she answered and hoped she sounded convincing.

"I don't think it's a good idea to expose her. She's wounded, and she's—" Prince didn't finish the sentence because Pax shot him a warning look.

"And she's good to go now," Pax finished. "He doesn't have time," she murmured to him.

"We have to hurry; there're guards everywhere looking for them," Cordelia silenced everybody.

Prince looked at Pax with worried eyes, but she nodded slowly and said, "It's okay. I can do it. Trust me."

Without further comments, Lucas and Prince moved Mauricio over the hammock, carefully arranging his limbs inside the edges. Cordelia covered the still body with a white sheet, and before hiding his face under it, she caressed his cheeks.

Pax looked at the scene and realized the man being covered with a *sudario*—the cloth covering his still form resembled the ceremonial shroud the pure breed used to bury their dead—was her grandfather. She had finally come to think of him as her kin. Cordelia and the other three women were out of the tunnel and walking in the middle of the plaza before Pax could assign a sentiment to her thoughts. She was numb.

"Act the part," Prince urged her while they were leaving the safety of the tunnel.

Pax took a good look at him, silently apologized, and jerked the chains so both Prince and Lucas were forced to walk slightly bent. They reached the end of the plaza unnoticed. Dead or alive, men escorted by soldiers were nothing unusual.

"Our only hope is to reach the Caves," Lucas succinctly explained the rest of the plan once they were heading toward the main gate.

"I'm to escort these soldiers out," Pax said to the guard standing at the gate.

"Under whose orders?" the guard suspiciously eyed the other women.

"Captain Nori." Pax kept it short, hoping to sound convincing.

The guard went to raise the sheet covering Mauricio and made a disgusted face. Sonia, Tai, and Cara maintained their positions and didn't flinch, while Cordelia maintained her face down position.

"And what are your orders?" the guard asked Cordelia.

"We are to let him rot in the sand, after these two slaves dig a hole for him," Cordelia answered without hesitation.

"I see. Unpleasant task. You drew the short straw." The guard had a sympathetic tone. "I don't envy you; outside is so hot. Here, take some water." She moved to a cupboard and came back with four bottles. "I'm sorry I don't have more."

"It's okay, thank you." Pax, the only one with a free hand, reached for the bottles when she saw the guard looking at her fingers.

Something passed through the guard's mind. It was just a moment, but Pax reacted before the woman could say a word; she hit her in the head with the chain tightly coiled around her knuckles. The impact was hard on Pax's hand, but left the guard unconscious on the floor.

"Not that I'm complaining about how you handled the situation, but… what was that?" Cara asked.

"She recognized the Layan family crest on my ring." Pax raised her hand to show it.

"Nice," Cara commented, taking a better look at the double crown design on the ring.

"I should've put it in my pocket." Pax threw the chain on the floor and massaged her aching fingers.

"No arguing here." Tai poked the fallen guard with her foot.

"Make sure she stays down for a while." Cordelia gestured toward the closet.

Prince and Lucas dragged the guard into the closet, and before closing it, they used the chain to tie her to the hanger's rod.

"Let's hope she was at the beginning of her shift," Sonia said.

"We better move." Lucas relieved Cordelia from her duty of carrying Mauricio. Prince did the same for Sonia.

They reached the Caves without incident, and they took turns carrying the hammock, but it still was a long trip from the city, especially on foot and under the heat of a late afternoon sun still strong enough to make them sweat. Pax started feeling tired halfway through the hike, but she didn't say anything. When she could almost see the entry of the Caves, Pax's stomach painfully contracted.

"What is it?" Prince had been watching her the whole time.

"Nothing," Pax answered too fast.

"It doesn't seem like nothing." Prince made a sign for the others to stop.

"Pax, you're bleeding." Cordelia, a few steps behind, hurried to catch up with her.

"I'll change the bandages as soon as we reach the Caves." Pax felt another pang of pain.

"No, Pax, you are bleeding…" Cordelia repeated.

"What do you m—" Pax patted herself and looked at her body. She saw Prince's face go white and her eyes went to the spot where he was looking.

"No, not my baby." Pax sunk on her knees.

The other women turned at her words and stared at her. Nobody dared say anything. The pain on Prince's face was eloquent enough.

"The baby is fine." Prince scooped Pax up in his arms and walked in complete silence to the Caves' entrance.

Pax never lost consciousness and heard him pleading with someone hidden behind the entry. As soon as he explained she was having a miscarriage and the Priest needed medical attention, they were let in. Once inside, the group was separated. Pax and Prince were accompanied to the same room they had inhabited recently. Marie came right away.

"I've helped other pregnant women... I need to visit you," she carefully said and then tilted her head to indicate Prince.

"I want him with me." Pax leaned against Prince and he enclosed her in his arms.

"How long have you been bleeding?"

"She just started," Prince answered for Pax, who couldn't talk about it.

Marie delicately removed Pax's stained clothes and put them aside. Pax gasped at seeing the quantity of blood on her pants. Prince stroked her temples and shushed her gently.

"You would be surprised how much blood you can lose before it becomes a problem. Now relax for me," Marie said and opened Pax's legs with one soft push. "It's going to be over soon, I promise." She washed her hands with a wet cloth she had brought, along with a change of clothes for Pax.

It was brief, and Marie had feather-light fingers, but Pax felt the urge to cry while it lasted.

"Well, we must wait and see what happens." Marie cleaned her with another wet cloth, put several layers of soft cotton under her and then helped her into a loose tunic.

"Are we going to lose the baby?" Prince asked when the silence had become uncomfortable.

"I don't know." Marie shifted from one foot to the other.

"But?" Prince pressed for an answer.

"But, if she doesn't move and the bleeding stops completely in the next few hours, the baby could have a chance."

Marie left, and George came with some food. Prince played with the boy while Pax tried to eat something. "Still lightheaded?" Prince asked, when she put down the piece of bread. Pax nodded. He excused himself from the boy and went to her side. "Baby's fine. I promise."

"How can you say that?" Pax shook her head sadly.

"Because we have suffered enough already."

Later that night when Pax fell asleep, she dreamt of him playing with their baby —a boy. The next day was a blur, and she slept most of the time. She heard Prince and Marie talking, but only remembered bits and pieces of the conversations.

"She needs to rest some more. I'm surprised she didn't collapse earlier," Marie said at some point.

"*She's strong*," Prince commented later.

When she finally woke up, Prince was smiling at her.

"Good morning, love." He kissed her softly on her lips and whispered, "You haven't bled since yesterday."

"It's good."

"It's the definition of good." Prince lay down and placed one hand on her belly and slowly drifted to sleep.

Pax was adjusting her body on the bed, trying not to wake him up, when Marie came back with a man.

"Let me help you," Marie said and repositioned a pillow behind Pax's back. "This is Grant, George's father, my husband."

Pax didn't say anything, but wiggled against the pillow, still feeling sleepy. Marie looked at Grant and nodded at his unspoken question.

"Hi, Pax. I was outside for the night shift, and—" He turned toward Marie who whispered, "Tell her."

Pax yawned against her hand.

"I saw the city burning. It's still burning."

"How did it happen?" Pax's mind started working all of a sudden.

"I don't know." Grant hesitated for a moment. "I saw men fighting the women all night long, closing the gates and barricading every other entrance, and finally, they left." He spoke slowly, giving Pax time to take in the information.

Prince, now awake, asked, "What are you saying? The men let their own city burn? It can't be."

"Where's Lucas? I need to speak to him." Pax swung her legs to the side of the bed, but Prince and Marie both stopped her.

"Lucas isn't here and you can't leave this bed until it's safe for you and the baby," Marie said.

Prince hugged her. "Not now, love."

"My mothers are there. My grandmother's there. Anna is there. I can't sit and wait." Pax fought Prince's embrace, but he didn't budge.

"No, you stay here. I'll talk to Lucas when he gets back." Prince kissed her and made to leave the bed.

"*I* will talk to him. Bring Lucas here as soon as you see him." Pax held his arm until he nodded.

Almost the whole day passed without any news from Lucas; then George arrived saying he was back at the caves. Pax gave Prince a look. He nodded and left, only to come back half an hour later, accompanied by a somber-looking Lucas.

"What happened?" Pax asked.

Lucas looked at her and then lowered his eyes without answering.

"Are there any survivors?" Pax's voice was cold, but in control. Prince sat on the bed and took her hand, but she moved it away.

"We rescued most of the men—" Lucas stopped and raised his eyes for a moment. "We didn't look for the women."

It was to be expected, but the idea of her family out there was too painful to process. Prince took her hand again; this time she didn't reject him. Something in the way Lucas was standing warned her that more was coming and she leaned against Prince.

Lucas sighed and then went on saying, "I'm sorry for—"

"For what?" A sense of dread descended upon her.

"We didn't have a choice. The women took all the men outside the city. They built a high fence and corralled them inside, planning a mass execution. They shot anyone who came too close to the rail and left them without water or food. From the safety of higher ground, sheltered inside the apartments facing the desert, they watched the men suffer under the sun, while keeping them under their aim. I saw what those women ate and drank—they threw what they didn't want to rot on the sand just outside the fence."

"What happened next?"

"Before killing the prisoners, the Priestess wanted to make a speech and gathered her army to attend her folly. We couldn't pass the opportunity. We closed them inside and burned it."

"How did you neutralize the women guarding the men outside?" Prince asked.

"When the flames reached them, they panicked and went back inside to save the Priestess. My men opened the corral and everybody helped barricade the lower entrances to the city, closing the women inside and fighting the ones who tried to escape." Lucas gave her another look.

"Did my grandfather know of your plan?" Pax felt numb.

"No, I ran back to the city soon after I left you here. I had to make a decision... and I'm sure he would've come to the same conclusion." Lucas raised his hands.

"You can't possibly know that. The love of his life was in that city. She came here to be with him. You think he wanted her dead?" Pax's tone of voice had reached a colder shade.

"I'm sorry, but I couldn't have done anything differently. I don't regret my decision." Lucas stepped forward, getting closer to the bed, but Pax's demeanor prevented him from reaching out to her.

"I'm sure you're regretting the time wasted saving me." Pax's eyes were stinging, but she didn't cry.

"Of course not; I'm glad we could help you." Lucas tried another step forward, but this time Pax raised one hand to stop him where he was.

"You're glad I could help you save the Priest."

"Of course I'm glad of that." Lucas's tone was gentle and that irritated Pax even more. "And, you can believe me or not, but for what it's worth, I'm truly sorry for your loved ones."

"Maybe your mothers and grandmother aren't dead," Prince intervened. "We don't know for sure what happened. They could be alive."

Pax patted his hand and then turned away to face the wall. "Leave me alone, please. I'm tired."

CHAPTER 25

Pax was sitting in the same spot where she and Prince had watched the sunrise only a few days earlier, but now she was staring ahead at the City of Men, alone at sunset. Prince had gone with Lucas to find out what was left of the smoldering city. Pax was more concerned with *who* was left. Prince had committed to the excursion only when she had solemnly sworn she would stay put while he was away.

Now she regretted having walked outside. She could feel a few light contractions, but they were more than enough to make her worry. One hand massaging her belly and the other one trailing on the sand, Pax waited for the news. She hadn't forgiven Lucas yet. One full day had already passed, and she could hardly be in the same place with the man. It had come as a relief when he had announced his expedition to the city.

Given the circumstances, Pax knew deep inside he was right. The women were planning to kill them all. But when loved ones were involved, all reasoning was forgotten. For the same reasons, she hadn't felt comfortable visiting Mauricio. Her feelings were still too raw, and she didn't want to unload her suffering on the old man's shoulders.

"It could be hours before they come back." Cordelia's voice came from behind.

Pax turned and invited the other woman to sit with her. They silently stared at the dunes for a while—the sand slowly becoming colder, the sun setting lower. When the pain from the contractions became difficult to ignore, she finally asked Cordelia to walk her back inside the Caves. Once Marie checked her and gave her the okay, Pax lay down for a nap. She was still sleeping when the men came back in the middle of the night and Prince woke her up.

"Pax?"

"My love…?"

"Come, there's someone who wants to see you."

Pax followed him through the hallway and straight into the infirmary. There were lots of people inside, gathered around Mauricio's bed, their backs turned to her, busy talking to her grandfather. Then, when Prince announced their presence, the crowd opened and Pax saw someone else sitting alongside Mauricio. "Grandma!" She ran toward Rosie, who looked back at her with wide eyes. "You're alive!" She didn't care about being loud, and Mauricio, whiter than usual, looked at her and his eyes lit at her exuberance when she jumped on his bed and hugged Rosie.

"Oh, sweetie, you can't imagine how relieved I was when Prince and Lucas found me and told me you had left the city." Rosie kissed her granddaughter.

"The Priestess kept her in the prison. Just one floor above Prince's and Mauricio's cell." Lucas had just entered the room holding Cordelia's hand.

"How did you find her?" Pax asked Lucas, forgetting for a moment she wasn't talking to him.

Prince, standing by the wall, gave her a small smile, sadness etched on his face.

"When the fire started, one of my jailers set me free before fleeing herself. I stayed outside in the desert until the pyre consumed itself, and then I went looking for your mothers and you," Rosie answered instead.

Pax took a good look at her grandmother and saw the soot on her face where tears had left a clear path. "Did you find my moms? Or Anna?"

"I did."

"And? Where are they?" Pax accepted Prince's touch, but, for once, she couldn't draw any strength from it. Weariness took possession of her. She inhaled slowly, but the air felt too dry. Something was wrong.

"Pax—"

"What, Grandma?" A weight pressed on her chest. All of a sudden everybody's faces became a blur.

Rosie didn't answer. Instead, she looked at Prince for consent.

"Tell me already." Pax went to grab Rosie's hand and realized her own was shaking.

"Please, try to breathe," Prince said.

"Maybe you should have this conversation later." Cordelia walked toward the bed to join the chorus of people trying to calm Pax.

"Are they dead? Is that what you don't want to tell me? I have a right to know." Pax stood up and swayed.

"Your mom Claudine... she didn't make it," Lucas finally answered. "You must tell her at some point," he added when several shocked eyes focused on him.

"She's dead?" Pax felt the coldness of the floor when she couldn't control her legs and she went down. She never fully fainted, but she barely felt Prince's arms when he picked her up and laid her down on the first bed available next to Mauricio's. "How?" Her head was buzzing with sounds and images, but she wanted to know.

"A wall fell on her. Maurice and Anna freed her from the rubble, but she had lost too much blood." Rosie sat by Pax's side and gently stroked her arm. "Anna tried to make Maurice leave, but she wouldn't listen. They stayed there the whole night. I found them the morning after; my daughter mourning over Claudine and Anna guarding Maurice."

Pax felt the warmth of tears against her cold skin and shivered, but she didn't sob. She was looking at the whole scene as if she was standing in the corner and her grandmother was talking to someone else. When Rosie resumed with a broken voice, Pax could only see vague shapes looming around in the room.

"I felt so useless. Maurice didn't notice me at all at first. She was still, like a statue by her wife's side. When I reached her, I went down on my knees and I hugged her. I whispered her name over and over; then she finally broke and passed out in my arms. Once awake, she cried until there were no more tears to shed, and that is when she started screaming." Rosie paused, and a single sob escaped her lips. She took a few hard breaths and then finished her tale. "Soldiers heard her and called the Priestess. I couldn't stay. I left."

Rosie's last words resonated inside Pax's mind for several seconds until she fully understood them. "You left my mother?"

"The Priestess was coming, and Maurice didn't want to come with me. I had to look for you. I tried to reason with her. I tried to help her see that going back to the Priestess's side wouldn't bring Claudine back. But she wouldn't listen to me."

"You left her."

"I didn't know what had happened to you. I couldn't leave you to your fate. And… my daughter didn't give me a choice. "

Pax could see Prince slowly reaching out for her, and she knew this wasn't the first time he heard the story. "What happened?"

"Maurice told me I could leave if I wanted." Rosie's voice was so low Pax had to strain her ears to listen. "She told me I had five minutes to leave before the Priestess arrived. My daughter, my own daughter, said to me, 'I love you, but I can't stand the thought that my wife died because of your foolishness. You even brought down my daughter with you. How could you do this to me?' Her words cut into my heart deeply because she's right. My selfishness caused this tragedy."

"You couldn't know…" she said as low as Rosie. The pain cut deep through her. "It's not your fault the Priestess had her own plans about—" Finally Pax looked around and saw everybody else staring at the two of them. "—all of this. The City of Men, the workers…"

"She then said, 'If you are still thinking of living with that man you said is my father, you are free to go. Don't ever try to reach me again. You are dead to me.'"

"She was in pain. She didn't know what she was saying." Pax sought Prince's warmth. He sat closer and put his arm firmly around her shoulder. Pax let her mind drift for a few seconds, thinking it wasn't possible her mother was dead, and then she straightened up against Prince's body. "She wasn't thinking."

"Maurice's next words were, 'I'll help the Priestess in her plan to prevent the workers from obtaining any rights at all. I'll personally see that every man suffers for the pain they have caused me. What you told me is a lie. Nobody will ever believe you. I was born a pure breed because I had two mothers.'" Rosie lowered her eyes to the floor, her lower lip trembling, her hands clenching and unclenching. A heavy silence followed her last words. She went to sit back by Mauricio's side and he whispered something to her.

Pax watched as her grandmother shook her head and started sobbing. "She didn't have time to accept the truth. She'll come around. I'll talk to her." She didn't want to think about it. She wanted to go to sleep and wake up to find it had been a long, horrible nightmare. Prince leaned forward and silently rested his head on her shoulder.

"I'm afraid there's nothing to talk about with your mother," Lucas said.

"Why?" Pax felt drained of any strength.

"The women who survived our attack left, but they'll come back to destroy what's left of us. And your mother will be the one signing the papers."

"But I'm here. She won't do anything that could cause me harm."

"Pax, she left with the Priestess."

Pax cringed at Lucas's words, but she saw pity in his eyes. One of her mothers was dead, and the other had abandoned her. Prince started rocking her while she finally let out the tears she was trying to repress.

"I'm sorry, but we need to make a few decisions before it's too late," Lucas said.

Cordelia cleared her throat and added, "Pax, I know this doesn't seem the right moment to ask you to decide, but time's running out for us. We must know if you want to come with us—"

"Where are you going?" Pax interrupted Cordelia.

"We have decided to try our luck finding the system of caves near the farm from where Prince escaped."

"It's a long journey from here. I'm not sure it's safe for my baby—"

"If you want to go back to Ginecea, we would understand." Cordelia had moved from the wall and was now kneeling by Pax's bed.

"You would let me go?"

"We know you would never betray our trust." Cordelia took her hand.

Pax looked at the woman and saw how tired she looked and how thin she had become in the last few days. She felt Prince's body stiffen while he was still caressing her. She turned around and met her grandmother's eyes. Rosie was leaning over Mauricio, holding hands with him, and Pax was struck by the sight.

"I'll follow you to the end of world and back," she whispered in Prince's ear, and she felt him shudder in relief against her.

* * *

The exodus started the day after. The Caves weren't safe anymore. Not now that the future President of Ginecea and the Priestess had decided to wipe clean whatever was left of the men's insurrection. The Caves were too close to the City of Men, and once a full campaign against the men was launched, this secret place where the families had lived in peace for several years would be discovered.

Everybody helped, even the kids, who minded the babies during the night while the adults packed and organized for the long trip. Lucas and Prince went back to the city to gather the men and salvage what they could from the rubble. Cordelia, Tai, Sonia, and Cara followed Marie around.

Pax was left resting in the infirmary, where she had time to say good-bye to her grandparents. Mauricio's condition had worsened and he wouldn't survive the harshness of the desert.

"I can't leave him now. I've lived all my life without him. Now I can't bear the idea of spending a single moment separated." Rosie had explained her decision to stay with him until the end.

"Grandma, I can't stay behind with you."

"And you shouldn't even think about it. You're having a child. Think of building a future for your baby. Don't dwell on the past."

Little rest was achieved that night. Mauricio had so many things to say to his granddaughter, and Rosie looked at them the whole time as if they were the most beautiful sight. Pax saw her grandmother melting as she hugged him.

"I wish I'd had more time with you," Pax said to her grandfather.

"I'm happy I got to know you. As I told you before, I consider it an unexpected gift." Mauricio laid a soft kiss on her head.

When the moment came to leave, Pax had a final question for her grandmother. "You never told me why you gave me my name. What does it mean?"

Rosie smiled and then caressed her granddaughter's cheeks. "As I told you before, the first time I heard Mauricio's voice, he was singing. I was so taken by his voice and the beauty of the melody, but I couldn't understand the words. I asked him what language it was and he told me it was the men's. I loved the sound of one word in particular and I asked him about it—" She looked at Mauricio and he smiled.

"*Pax* is an ancient word, and it has the most beautiful meaning. Peace," he explained and then let Rosie finish.

"I wanted for you to find peace in the land of women. And you will. My sweet Pax, you will."

BACKSTORY AND ACKNOWLEDGMENTS

Pax in the Land of Women, chronologically the second in the Ginecean Chronicles series was written before *The* Priest. Pax is the character that started it all. I wanted to write a "coming out" story, and I wanted it to be out of the ordinary. A few years ago, I started playing with the idea of an alternate world where society had evolved in a different direction from ours. A reality where women were the absolute rulers and heterosexual love was considered unnatural. Ginecea was born and with it Pax, a young woman whose life of privilege is transformed by the realization she has fallen in love with a man. The rest is history, dystopian and alternate, but still a history that could happen somewhere.

***

My most heartfelt thanks go to the usual suspects. My mother and my father first and foremost, no need to explain why. Gaia and Giuseppe, for being my kids. Claudia, for having read and still reading all my works and giving me thoughtful feedback. Alessandro, his covers are out of this world and I'm thankful he agreed to work on my projects. Amy, the most patient editor this side of the universe. And finally, Roberto, because without him, I wouldn't have become the person I am.

***

Pax's cover deserves a special mention. While Alessandro was working on the Ginecean landscape, he found on Deviantart the image of a statue that perfectly matched the mood and the atmosphere of my stories. He had found the Ginecean Goddess: it was the Muse, a sculpture created by the Australian artist Julie Swan. Alessandro and I fell in love with the sinuous shape of the Muse, and Julie graciously gave us permission to use its image. Finally, as the cherry on top of an already great cover, Pax's face belongs to my sweet Gaia.

PERSONS OF INTEREST

A book is never a solitary endeavor, although the writer oftentimes thinks otherwise.

Amy Eye edited *Pax in the Land of Women*.

Cassie McCown proofread it.

Roberto Ruggeri formatted the novel.

Alessandro Fiorini created the cover.

You, who liked *The Priest* and came back for some more Ginecean's stories.

BIO

Monica La Porta is an Italian who landed in Seattle several years ago. Despite popular feelings about the Northwest weather, she finds the mist and the rain the perfect conditions to write. Being a strong advocate of universal acceptance and against violence in any form and shape, she is also glad to have landed precisely in Washington State. She is the author of The Ginecean Chronicles, a dystopian/science fiction series set on the planet Ginecea where women rule over a race of enslaved men and heterosexual love is considered a sin. She has published *The Priest, Pax in the Land of Women*, and *Prince at War*. She is currently editing the fourth in the Ginecean series. She also wrote and illustrated a children's book about the power of imagination, *The Prince's Day Out*. Her latest published short, *Linda of the Night*, is a fairytale love story celebrating inner beauty. Stop by her blog to read about her miniatures, sculptures, paintings, and her beloved beagle, Nero. Sometimes, she also posts about her writing.

Monica La Porta's blog:
http://www.monicalaporta.com

The Ginecean Chronicles on Facebook:
http://www.facebook.com/ginecea

The Prince's Day Out on Facebook:
http://www.facebook.com/ThePrincesDayOut

Monica's Author page on Goodreads:
http://www.goodreads.com/author/show/5757332.Monica_La_Porta

Monica on Twitter:
http://twitter.com/momilp